VAMPIRES of BUSTAMANTE

VAMPIRES of BUSTAMANTE

by

James Peyton

VAMPIRES of BUSTAMANTE
©2012 by James Peyton

Published by Franklin Scribes Publishers. Franklin Scribes is a registered trademark of Franklin Scribes Publishers.

Franklin Scribes books may be purchased in bulk for educational, business, fund-raising, or sales promotional use. For information, please email SpecialMarkets@ franklinscribes.com.

Publisher's Note: This novel is a work of fiction. References to events, establishments, organizations, locales, and real people living or deceased are intended merely to equip the fiction with a sense of authenticity and color. They are used factiously. All other names, characters, places, and all dialogue and incidents portrayed in this book are the product of the author's imagination.

Summary: On a college field trip to caverns near the remote Mexican village of Bustamante, the daughter of a U.S. senator is murdered and the blood drained from her body. Detective Artemas Salcido, a Harvard-educated, illegitimate son of a Mexican governor and a Yaqui Indian girl, is responsible for the investigation. Handsome and cosmopolitan, Artemas was banished to Bustamante because of his ill-advised propensity for solving politically sensitive crimes, and now he finds himself in the middle of yet another.

The international press, two FBI agents, and a brutal squad of federales with orders from the President of Mexico to make the problem go away, descend on the village. Among the reporters is Laffi Rendón, an old flame of Artemas' from Harvard. As more grisly killings occur, Artemas discovers a secret cabal, Grupo Vampiro, which leads him to a labyrinth of rituals and crimes stretching from mediaeval Eastern Europe to Mexico's most powerful people.

ISBN 978-0-9886433-6-9 (soft cover)

Printed in the United States of America

"Do you imagine that we see the hundredth thousandth part of what exists? Consider, for example, the wind, which is the greatest of the forces of nature. It knocks men down, it demolishes houses, it uproots trees, stirs up the sea into mountainous waves, it breaks away the cliffs and drives great ships on to the rocks. The wind whistles, groans, bellows, sometimes it even kills. Have you seen it? It exists nevertheless."

Guy de Maupassant, *The Horla*

Bustamante

Slowly, very slowly, Chaco Gonzalez raised his head from his straw pillow as his ears strained for a hint of what awakened him. He turned stiffly, trying to catch the sound, but the night was silent. He knew it was out there and if it came again he would not miss it, for in spite of his sixty-five years his hearing was still keen.

Time passed without a sound; Chaco knew he'd have to get up and check the goats. They were his life, the only living things he had left. For a moment he lamented the loss of his wife, who lay under a crudely carved stone on a rocky hill behind the house, and of his son, who, although alive in *el Norte*, seemed even more distant. With them he had never experienced loneliness, but now they were gone. Unlike the money his son sent him from Houston, the goats were something he understood and relied upon. He stretched his back and legs, trying to minimize the coming ordeal. Although his hearing was fine, he was riddled with arthritis and the effects of countless injuries.

Chaco rolled from the bed, a deep nest of straw covered with a thin blanket. He grasped a split-log shelf attached to the shack's adobe wall, and pulled himself to his feet. He stopped to listen again. Nothing.

He groped until his fingers found his glasses on a table under the building's lone window, then he grasped an old tin flashlight. He pushed aside the ragged curtain and stared into the night. It was as dark as it was silent—not one star or hint of moonlight, and dawn still hours away.

When he heard the sound again it was so faint that Chaco could not define it, but it made his spine tingle. He swept the flashlight's dim beam toward the nearest corner and reached for the rusty, single-shot 12-gauge that had stood there unused for years. Ever since he'd gotten the dog wild animals were no longer a threat. But last night the dog—another being that had shared his life—disappeared. And now a coyote, maybe a bobcat, or perhaps a mountain lion was after his goats.

Chaco broke open the shotgun to make sure it was loaded. He sighed in relief as his thumb traced the shell's brass outline; it was the only one he had.

Outside in the darkness Chaco crept toward the chicken-wire pen where he herded his favorite goats each night. As he neared, the noise stopped him in his tracks. This time he distinctly heard it: a moan followed by something like a slurp—a sound the dog used to make when it licked its paws with particular vigor. He held the flashlight in his left hand and pulled the shotgun to his shoulder with his right. As the beam swept along the ground into the pen, he saw that the dusty earth had became a dark, sticky pool seeping from beneath the bodies of two mutilated goats.

The dark-shadowed patch of ground suddenly came alive, moving in a swirling, undulating manner, almost reptilian. But not quite—it also seemed to rise from the earth with a flapping motion. Then the thing looked directly at Chaco through blood-red orbs.

The dim beam of light revealed a hideous half rodent, half bird-like face with long sharp teeth from which blood and viscera trailed down its chest. With a squeal of anger the beast flapped it wings, which to Chaco seemed immense, and began to fly toward him. A rank, sulfurous odor shocked the air from his lungs. Blood was rushing through Chaco's sluggish arteries and a shot of adrenalin to the heart gave him the strength to thrust the shotgun at the apparition and pull the trigger. The click of the misfire was drowned by his primal howl as Chaco felt the wind of huge wings upon his face. Overwhelmed, he gasped and staggered backward. His head spun round, and he sank into a weightless emptiness.

Minutes later Chaco slowly came to and his last vision of the winged devil flashed into his brain. His eyes darted about him. He was on his side, and from where he lay he could make out the grotesque bodies of the goats, now partially illuminated by a rising moon. His shotgun lay next to him. The soft, cool breeze carried nothing out of the ordinary. Painstakingly, using the shotgun for support, he got to his knees then shakily to his feet. Slowly, unsteadily, he limped to the house. He looked back only after securing the door.

At dawn Chaco pedaled into Bustamante on his 1957 Schwinn. On his ride through the village on his way to the police station he stopped and told his story to anyone up and about: the story of the great bat-like creature that had killed and sucked the blood from his two best goats, and how he had scared it off after it attacked him. And by the way, where was Apolonio Flores who ten years ago sold him that lousy dud shotgun shell?

The villagers speculated that Chaco had been the victim of a *chupacabra*. Although none of them had ever seen one, several spoke with authority, and Chaco nodded his head in agreement.

At the small police station just off the village's main plaza, Chaco related his horrific adventure to Captain Artemas Salcido. The young officer, who had recently arrived from Mexico City, listened intently to Chaco. After the old farmer left, Artemas listened even more carefully to his gut. He wasn't sure about the story, but, while he had often ignored his intuition to his detriment, it had rarely been wrong. And it was now telling him that something profoundly unpleasant was approaching.

Artemas knew that if he had paid better attention to it a year ago he would not have had to choose between losing his life and being stuck in this tiny village, six hundred miles from the seat of power. His green eyes stared at the cracked plaster ceiling and he thought of his long-dead Yaqui mother, his prospering Spanish-blooded father and the Jesuit priest who raised him. He wondered for the thousandth time whether he should have stayed in the United States after college.

By late morning Chaco's story came to the attention of Diego Ramirez, a senior editor of Monterrey's *El Norte* newspaper, who owned a small weekend house in the village. Stories of the *chupacabra* had recently appeared all over northern Mexico, but there was no evidence that the carnage was caused by anything but wild dogs. He found Chaco, placed him and his bicycle in his Dodge minivan, and drove out to the little farm. He stood next to the tearful old man and took in the horrifying sight of the goats. Their throats had been ripped to pieces and their blood reduced to sticky, dark stains on the dry soil. As he carefully examined the churned, sandy earth around the massacre, he could not be sure of what he saw, but of one thing he was certain: there were no dog tracks.

Bustamante

With the exception of Sundays, each dawn found Julio Martinez goading his team of oxen into the mountains. He invariably returned just before dark, his ancient wagon laden with firewood.

Julio's usual route took him past the village cemetery, along the road that led up to the *grutas*, Bustamante's famous caverns, then south, skirting the base of the mountain. On that Friday morning he had just left the unpaved main road for the southbound dirt track. He was anticipating his one evening a week in the town's only *cantina* as his eyes unconsciously followed the lazy circles of a pair of vultures. He topped a small rise, and his mind shifted focus to the soaring scavengers, wondering what they had found. Abruptly the oxen halted, stomped their hooves and snorted.

A hundred meters ahead in the road something lay crumpled. It reminded Julio of a bundle of trash he once found wrapped in an old carpet remnant. He smacked the heavy reins across the backs of the oxen, urging them on, but to no avail. It took the crack of the frayed bullwhip over their heads to convince the frightened beasts to continue. Once nearer the object, Julio realized it was a human body. When he was within a few feet, he pulled the oxen around into a U-turn so he could get a better look. He didn't dare dismount; the beasts were pulling wildly at the reins and would be halfway home before he caught them.

The naked corpse had once been a young man, but now there was a gaping wound in his uncommonly pale chest where his heart had been removed and the blood drained.

Julio gave the oxen their head. They needed no urging to return to Bustamante, where he quickly sought out the village policeman.

After Julio left the station, Artemas felt his anxiety level spike as he processed the grisly report and began making phone calls. Something evil was afoot, but he didn't know what to do. Surviving last year had been nothing short of miraculous, and he wondered if he'd get yet another chance to forestall whatever was coming his way.

Bustamante

Like many college freshmen, Julie Conners and Susan Anderson had fallen prey to their newly found freedom, and their grades reflected as much. The extra geology credits they'd earn by visiting the famous caverns of Bustamante would repair some of the damage. Just after 9:00 A.M. they left their Austin apartment, jumped into Julie's red Mustang, and headed two hundred thirty miles south to the Mexican border. By 3:00 P.M. they had traveled another hundred miles south and stopped at a crossroads to survey their surroundings. From dusty cafes and convenience stores on either side the girls caught the sweet scent of meat roasting over mesquite coals. Directly in front of them, and unexpectedly close, towered a jagged mountain range. The sign indicated that Monterrey was to the south and Bustamante to the north.

"Wow, not at all what I expected," said Julie. "These mountains are insane, like the ones near Cortina d'Ampezzo. You know…where I spent last summer at that ambassador's villa."

"Don't rub it in," Susan shot back. "My dad's not a senator, and the closest I've been to Italy is window shopping at Ferragamo."

Julie laughed at her friend's remark and floored the gas pedal, oblivious to the waves of mauve wild grass shimmering along the road. She eventually slowed down and motioned toward the mountains, now to their left. At the base of the lonely range lay a velvety field of green sweeping up to a rock ridge. Ahead, a ragged banner spanned the road, confirming that a left turn would take them to *Bustamante y Las Grutas*.

"Thank God, this must be it," said Julie.

As they drew near Bustamante, the girls entered a dense canopy of mature pecan trees camouflaging the village. Soon they passed stuccoed adobe and stone houses and shops, painted in various shades of blue, green and pumpkin. Although most of them were faded, a few blazed with bright coats. Julie swerved to avoid a flock of chickens chased by an old dog and then they emerged from the shaded, tree-lined lane, into a sunny village square.

It was late afternoon and the cobblestone plaza, with its church and municipal buildings on either end, was deserted. Shadows from the church steeple and central gazebo tiptoed across open space and iron benches. Just off the plaza, several cars and pickups were parked near a freshly painted building, *Hotel Ancira*.

Julie said to Susan, "Let's see if we can get a guide or some directions, check the caves, take some pictures, and split. We sure as hell don't want to spend the night here."

When they walked into the hotel restaurant the bustling room fell silent. Only the *thwak, thwak, thwak* of the cook chopping *cabrito* in the kitchen. Susan wondered if the villagers gathered for Sunday *comida* were unfriendly. Then she flushed as she saw that all the women in the restaurant were modestly dressed. *Two gringas in cutoff jeans and halter-tops, how much more disrespectful could we possibly be?* Susan thought with a frown.

A slender, elderly man with thinning dark hair came around the corner from the kitchen and greeted the bewildered girls, "*¿Buenas tardes, quieren comer?*"

Susan tried to explain that they did not want to eat, just visit the *grutas,* the famous caverns. But her Spanish deserted her, and at the word *grutas* several diners turned to stare. A tall bear-like, middle-aged man with round wire glasses and black beret came to the rescue. "Excuse me, I speak some English. How may I help?"

Susan explained and the man translated, quickly demonstrating that his English was not nearly as good as his initial phrase had implied. Other villagers joined the man. They spoke—or Susan thought argued—amongst themselves in rapid-fire Spanish. Finally, the man in the beret said to the girls. "It is dangerous to visit the caverns. There have been," he paused, searching for the right word—"accidents."

"No, no," said Julie. "We don't want to explore the caves, just check them out, take some pictures. A real quickie; we just need someone to guide us."

The man spoke again to the innkeeper. Then he said "Maybe someone can be found tomorrow."

Julie snapped, "Tomorrow — impossible!"

Susan sought a compromise. "We really appreciate your help, but we only have today. Could you please give us directions to the caves, perhaps draw a map?" She pulled a pen and small spiral notebook from her purse and offered them to the man.

He shrugged and did as bidden, then handed back the notebook. "Here, but please stay away from the caves after dark. It isn't safe."

Artemas Salcido entered the restaurant just as the two girls' conversation was unfolding. The sound of his name made him step back outside. Chaco Gonzalez was standing there with his son, who had left his job in Houston after hearing about his father's ordeal. They exchanged greetings and, reluctantly, Artemas led the men back to the police station to review the status of their case. He was later to regret the interruption and wonder, if it had not occurred, whether things might have turned out differently.

Julie revved her Mustang as they left the plaza, and said to Susan, "What was the big deal?"

"I'm not sure he understood us, or maybe nobody wanted to work on Sunday afternoon. Maybe we should take their advice and wait until tomorrow."

"Piss on that," said Julie. "It can't be far!" Susan looked away.

At the outskirts of the village they stopped at a tiny *bodega* to buy soda and snacks. They headed toward the mountain, now towering directly in their path, and noticed well above them a winding dirt road that worked its way up the steep incline and disappeared around a corner into a draw. "That must be the road," Julie said. "I thought I saw a car on it a moment ago."

"No-o, I don't think so," replied Susan. "The directions show us following the road we're on directly to the caves."

They passed a boy by the side of the road as he was putting something into a small cardboard box. He stared at them with a vacant expression.

Near the top of the incline at the very base of the mountains, they came to the intersection with the road they had just seen. A rusty gate with a *No Entrada* sign blocked their passage. Within a

hundred yards the road ended at a large parking area. Behind it sat the concrete skeleton of a partly complete, two-story building covered with graffiti. On the facing wall, in faded paint, was the word: *GRUTAS*. An arrow pointed up toward a pass in the mountains.

"Shit!" said Julie. "I thought we could drive all the way. Why the hell didn't he say something?"

"He did," replied Susan quietly. "He said, 'Don't go.'"

"The hell with that," said Julie. She slammed the car door and made for the building, angrily kicking an empty beer bottle out of her way. "Look," she cried over her shoulder, pointing at a rock beyond the structure at the edge of a well-worn path. On it in fresh white paint was the word *Grutas* and an arrow pointing up the mountainside.

Susan joined her, and the two girls looked up. The path twisted through rock, sagebrush, and cactus toward the draw where the higher road disappeared. Framing it was a line of palm-like trees that added a tropical ambiance to the otherwise desert landscape. "I've got your camera so let's go," said Julie.

"Julie," Susan implored, "we have no idea how far it is, and it's getting late." Her eyes darted up to the sun. It was sinking toward the jagged peaks above them. "Why go any farther? We can take a picture of the signs, and there must be plenty of photos of the cave on the Internet."

"I've already checked and there aren't many," said Julie. "This is Donaldson's favorite cave and he's bound to know every damn one of them. With my father's pull, he's got to pass us, but we have to prove we actually saw them. I get an F and my ass is in deep shit. I'm not taking a chance. Anyway, it can't be more than fifteen or twenty minutes. If it starts to get dark we can come back and try again tomorrow, but I'd rather not spend the night in this dump." Her hand swept to include the entire area.

"It won't be all that bad, and we can probably use the rest," Susan tried to cajole her friend.

"That's B.S. and you know it. This is really important. Why don't you just stay here? If I'm not back in, say, forty-five minutes, you can go for help."

"Julie, please, let's just go back!" Susan was on the verge of tears. "I've got a bad feeling."

"Come on Suz, I thought you West Texas ranch girls were tougher than that." Julie pointed at the arid landscape and added, "Isn't this just like where you come from?"

"Maybe a little, and maybe that's why I've got enough sense to be careful. I'm not going."

Camera in hand, Julie headed up the path alone, turning only to snap a picture of her friend. Then with a jaunty wave and a parting "Back in a jiff," she was gone.

Susan popped a Coke and sat down in the car to wait, eyes glued to the bend in the path where Julie had disappeared. It was still quite warm and, despite the sunscreen and hat, she noted in the rearview mirror that she had a sunburn. Catching a whiff of cloying perfume from a blooming cactus nearby, she suddenly wished she were back in her comfy Austin apartment. At one point she thought she heard the sound of a vehicle but it quickly dissipated. It seemed to have come from above.

As time passed, Susan became more and more distraught. *What if Julie doesn't come back? How long should I wait? Where do I go to make a report? Will my cell-phone work in Mexico? What will I tell Senator Conners? Will I be blamed?* Tearfully, she prayed for her friend's safe return.

A half hour later she looked upward for the umpteenth time and was horrified to watch the sun turn into a crimson ball, give one blinding flash, and disappear behind the mountains. The temperature dropped and shadows began to race down the *arroyos* toward her.

Susan got out of the car and walked to the foot of the path. "Ju-lee," she called out to the gorge-riven mountain. Her voice echoed in the stillness. "Ju-lee, ple-ease," she called again, an edge of panic in her voice. She began to walk up the path and after fifty yards rounded the bend where Julie had disappeared. The empty trail in front of her wound steeply up into the deepening gloom, giving no hint of its final destination. She called again and again, until she was screaming. When she stopped there was nothing but eerie emptiness and the call of some distant bird of prey. She looked behind her and panicked as she realized that darkness was obliterating the path back to the car. She wiped away her tears and ran, falling once and badly skinning her knee.

At the edge of the car park she stopped and looked back up the path, willing Julie to appear. Then, as she stood very still, she thought she heard the crunch of a footstep and the spattering of stones. "Julie!" she yelled. But no answer came, and the sound did not repeat.

She ran for the car. For a moment she struggled with herself, refusing to abandon her friend because of her own fear. Then she peered through the windshield into the darkness, concluded she had no choice, and turned the ignition key.

A few minutes later Susan was parked in front of the hotel. Except for the innkeeper going about his closing chores, the restaurant was empty. "*Señor, por favor ayudame, mi amiga no regresó,*" she said, her Spanish now instinctive. His face blanched as he put an arm comfortingly around her shoulder. He guided her quickly out of the hotel, across the nearly dark plaza, down a side street and into the small concrete-block police station.

The strong smell of coffee and tobacco overwhelmed her. Past the counter, across the room behind a cluttered desk, sat a tall, slender man with ink-black hair. Smoke curled from a half-finished cigar resting in a crystal ashtray. His skin was the color of light copper, and his features indicated Indian heritage: not the rounded lines of the Navajos Susan had seen around Santa Fe, but the sharply chiseled planes of the Apache. Most striking were his piercing, green eyes.

The innkeeper quickly explained the situation. As Artemas listened, only a supreme exercise of will allowed him to conceal his dark premonition.

Desperately hoping her Spanish would be up to the occasion, Susan was astonished when the policeman, who appeared to be in his late twenties or early thirties, spoke to her in nearly flawless English. "I am Captain Artemas Salcido, at your service. Would you be kind enough to tell me exactly what happened in your own words?" Noticing her surprise he added with a flash of perfect white teeth, "I spent four years in the United States in college, but I don't get much opportunity to speak English. Please forgive any mistakes."

Susan tearfully described the last two hours, blurting out that she feared something terrible had happened to Julie. Artemas's stomach churned and he must have winced, because Susan, who'd been following his every expression, grew distraught and began to sob. Artemas came around the counter and took her hands in his.

"Don't worry, we'll find her," he said, trying to fill his eyes with reassurance he didn't feel. "Now go with Eduardo. He'll get you some dinner and a room."

He spoke softly to the innkeeper, trying to mask his concern. "I'll find Rodriguez and his dogs. Get this young woman a room. I have a feeling it's going to be a long night."

Susan ate nothing and slept poorly. She continued to question what she might have done differently, all the time praying that somehow Julie would be all right. Several times she got up, pulled aside the curtains and stared at the moonlit mountains. Before they had seemed so beautiful. Now they were frightening. She wondered if she should try to call home — call Julie's parents. Wondered if the Senate was in session, if they were in Dallas or Washington. She didn't know what to do and grasped at the hope that Julie would somehow be found unhurt.

A little after nine the next morning, Susan answered a knock to find the policeman and innkeeper standing outside her door. By the men's grim expressions she immediately knew the news was bad. "I'm terribly sorry," said the policeman, lowering his head slightly but maintaining eye contact. "We found your friend. There is no nice way to say it; she was murdered, and under very unpleasant circumstances."

Dulled by lack of sleep and distracted by the formal policeman-speak, Susan stared dumbly at the men for a moment. Then she began to wail.

WASHINGTON, D.C.

The National Security Council meeting was breaking up when a White House aide approached the president and handed him a note. He scanned it, read it again and his jaw muscles began to clench and twitch.

Those remaining in the room noticed the telltale signs of fury and quit their banter and paper shuffling. The president's eyes left the slip of paper and focused on Jonathan Sharp, Director of the FBI. "I'm glad you're still here Jonathan," he said. "I just learned that Senator Conners' daughter has been murdered in Mexico — someplace called Bustamante — and quite gruesomely. It seems all the blood was drained from her body," he added, handing over the note.

"See what you can find out, then get some agents down there. Instruct the attorney general to coordinate with the Mexicans. Tell him I said not to take 'No' for an answer." He focused his gaze on the Secretary of State who instantly decided this was neither the time nor the place to voice his objections.

MEXICO CITY

The President of Mexico was sitting in a drawing room at Los Pinos—the Mexican White House—wearing a white shirt, maroon tie and pinstriped gray pants. His attorney general was more formally dressed in a dark blue, double-breasted suit and intricately patterned Hermes tie. Between them on a low, highly polished, mahogany table rested a china tea set. The ornate, gold-rimmed cups were unused, and none of the pastries on the silver tray had been touched. The men had finished their greetings and were deep into the business at hand.

"So, to sum up," began the president, "we have a request from the U.S. attorney general, which actually comes directly from the White House. We are being asked to allow FBI agents to assist in the investigation in Bustamante. Under the circumstances, a pretty difficult appeal to deny."

"*Claro que sí, señor*. That's about it."

"Don't you have anything to add, perhaps a suggestion or two?" snapped the president.

"Actually," replied the attorney general, ignoring the rebuke, "we already have what may be the best detective in the country in Bustamante—" The president leaned forward in his chair and narrowed his eyes.

"Artemas Salcido," continued the attorney general. "You may not know the story. He's the illegitimate son of Alvarado Salcido, the former Governor of Sonora, born to a Yaqui servant girl."

"I do remember something of it," said the president, arching his eyebrows. "Didn't the mother eventually meet with an accident sometime after Don Alvarado married his present wife."

"*Sí, señor*, exactly. The boy was then sent to a Jesuit priest to be raised. The man did a fine job because Artemas was accepted on a full scholarship to Harvard University, where he majored in criminal justice. Following graduation he returned to Mexico and went to work for the Federal Police. Because of those rather unusual circumstances there was a bit of a stir in the press at the time."

"Wasn't there ultimately some trouble?"

"There was," replied the attorney general. "Young Artemas was at first quiet and diligent in his work and circumspect in his dealings with his colleagues—the perfect recruit. Unfortunately, he was merely studying the real world of Mexican law enforcement—in order to change it. He began solving crimes with no thought of the consequences. He had no idea when to stop, when to pull back and reassess a situation, to find out who was involved and how it should be handled. He soon began to make such fools of his superiors that he either had to be sent away or he would have been killed. Even his father's intercessions couldn't change the outcome. A few months ago he agreed to be sent to Bustamante. To my knowledge he's been working quietly there ever since." The AG hesitated, looked his boss in the eye and added, "I just wanted you to be informed. Salcido could affect our current situation for better or worse."

"He sounds like a first rate detective, and an honest one at that," said the president, finally leaning back in his chair. "But... it seems to me that perhaps we need someone with a little more experience in actually getting the job done. Someone who can go up there and make the problem go away."

The president cleared his throat, leaned over and spat into an empty teacup. Then he dabbed his mouth with a napkin and continued. "It was before my time, but do you remember when those guys took pot shots at *gringos* floating down the Rio Bravo in West Texas and killed one of them? I recall that a small but very efficient group was dispatched and quickly made arrests. One of the fugitives was killed while resisting arrest. Do we still have such a unit?"

"Yes we do. The men have different assignments, but I can have them brought together and dispatched to Bustamante. I'll also warn Salcido that his career depends on his cooperation with them."

The president rose to his feet, signifying the meeting was over.

Bustamante

Clutching the wheel of her rented car, Laffi Rendón blew a wisp of hair out of her eye and squinted into the setting sun at a small sign that read, Bustamante 80 Kilometers. She sighed in relief at confirmation that she was finally on the right road.

That morning her boss, the senior editor of a venerable Washington D.C. newspaper, had assigned her to cover Julie Conners' murder. She barely caught the flight from Washington, and arrived in Monterrey an hour and a half ago.

She knew why she had been selected for the assignment. She had grown up in Mexico City where her father, a Cuban-American, was a high official at the embassy. It was her knowledge of the culture, language, and connections to the diplomatic community that had gotten her the sought-after job with the paper in the first place.

But nothing had worked out the way she had hoped. While she had found some of the things she had anticipated—cultural events and the excitement of being near history in the making— she was disappointed with the people she met in Washington. She found both men and women narrowly centered on themselves and their jobs. She had nearly given up dating after discovering that the opening gambit was inevitably to determine who was closest to power. She knew she should have been elated at the opportunity to finally use her talents, but she was ambivalent.

An hour later she saw the Hotel Ancira on the other side of the village plaza. Through a carefully guarded White House source, her paper was the first to receive news of the tragedy. She should be the first representative of any major U.S. news organization in town, other than someone stationed in Mexico City or Monterrey. Nevertheless, there seemed to Laffi to be a lot of cars parked along the street near the hotel. She hoped her reservation was in order.

She walked through a tall entryway painted with the hotel's name in crisp, sky-blue letters. To her left was a small gift shop. To the right was a screen door through which she could see a crowded dining room with a high ceiling and white plaster walls. Metal tables with plastic tablecloths were loaded with food and drink, and around them sat what Laffi assumed were villagers. She was met with the same hush that Julie and Susan experienced the day before. All of them stared at the striking, although somewhat frazzled, blond.

She had forgotten just what a sensation blond hair could cause in Mexico. The prominent cheekbones and full figure she had inherited from her mother's Polish-Jewish side of the family enhanced the effect. Remembering their manners, the diners quickly resumed their conversations. As Laffi stood, undecided and disoriented from the day's travel, a tall, slightly stooped figure appeared from around the corner. The dark-haired man wore black pants and a white, long-sleeved white shirt.

"*Buenas noches, señora,*" he said and took a couple of steps closer to her. "*¿Quiere comer?*" he added, as if wondering if she understood him.

"*Buenas noches, señor. Sí, tal vez, pero primero creo que tenga una reservación para una habitación. Me llamo Laffi Rendón*" she rattled off in formal Spanish.

Obviously relieved he did not have to deal with a foreign language, he said, "Of course, *señora*. I am Eduardo, owner of the hotel. Please follow me and I'll show you to your room."

He led Laffi back the way he had come and they entered a second dining room, decorated with mounted deer heads and lit by a fixture fashioned from an old wagon wheel. Just before the small kitchen's gaily-tiled counter, the innkeeper turned left, passed through a scullery and out a screen door. He held it open for Laffi.

In the middle of the patio was a magnificent pecan tree. Around it sat terracotta pots filled with roses and bougainvillea. As they walked her host said, "You have come a long way, *señora*?"

"Yes, from Washington D.C., *la capital*," she added, without thinking.

"Then you must be very tired," he said.

They reached the end of the patio, and beyond a narrow gateway another tiled area opened up to a row of rooms plastered in white stucco, the doors and windows bordered in blue. Opposite the rooms, the dark silhouette of jagged mountains loomed over a six-foot wall.

Eduardo took her to a room toward the back. He opened the door and motioned with his head. "You may park your car there," he said. "*Pasele,*" he added, stepping aside and beckoning her to enter.

The room was small, but scrupulously clean. There was a single bed, dresser, table and chair, and a tiny bathroom. On the smooth concrete floor was a brightly woven Indian rug.

Laffi thanked the innkeeper then added, "It's been a very long day for both of us, but I would be grateful if you could tell me what you know about the murder?"

His voice became guarded as he gave Laffi a description of the girls and what he knew of the crime. He included the incidents involving Chaco Gonzalez's goats and the body found by Julio Martinez and his oxen. He ended by giving her directions to the police station.

"I hope that's helpful," he said. "Now I must get back to the restaurant, so let me again welcome you to Bustamante."

"Thank you, *señor*. May I call you Eduardo?" Receiving a nod in return, she continued, "You've been more than generous. I look forward to my stay, and perhaps to returning under more pleasant circumstances. Eduardo, forgive me, but one more quick item. Who was the man in your restaurant who translated for the girls?"

Warily, he said, "Humberto Alcazar, he is a writer, quite well known in the area."

"Thank you again, *señor*."

Wearily unpacking several changes of clothes, shoes and toiletries Laffi flashed on three things she must do before finally going to bed. First, she turned on her satellite phone and called her neighbor to make sure she still had a key to Laffi's house and would feed her tomcat.

Second, she fetched her car and stopped at the police station. Posted on the locked door she found a note directing her to a nearby cardboard box. Inside were copies of a one-sheet entitled, *Statement of Facts*. It provided essentially the same information she got from the innkeeper.

Last of all, she hooked up her computer to her satellite phone and emailed her editor an account of everything she'd learned so far.

Bustamante

Jet lagged and anxious to land a scoop, Laffi arose with the sun and decided to walk the three or four blocks to the police station. She figured the police chief would be working early, getting a jump on his day before all hell broke loose with the arrival of the FBI and journalists following her trail.

Dressed in brand new jeans and a white cotton blouse, she left through the hotel's back entry and followed the narrow dirt road she had traveled the night before. She observed a typical rural village: small homes of adobe and stone flanked the road; some were coated with plaster, while others were exposed, along with the mortar that held them together. Most of the roofs were corrugated tin, although a few were thatched and some were a collection of mismatched, salvaged shingles.

The houses opened directly onto the street and therefore lacked front yards, but they all had back patios surrounded by ancient stone walls. She caught glimpses of bougainvillea, palms, and fruit trees just beginning to bud. Above everything towered the ubiquitous pecan trees, many of them seventy-five feet tall. Down the road, toward the far end of the village, she had a clear view to the base of the jagged escarpment. The mountains beyond were peacefully shrouded in early morning mist.

Energized by her surroundings, she felt a wave of the old enthusiasm. Catching the pungent scent of bacon, *chorizo*, and eggs sizzling over wood fires, she realized she was hungry, which reminded her she hadn't eaten anything since the airport, except a couple of energy bars.

After walking three blocks Laffi reached the plaza and saw some shops: a tiny grocer, a candy and pastry store, and a small restaurant called *Fito's Burgers*. A narrow, one-way road circled the plaza, separating it from the stores and other buildings. In the middle stood an iron bandstand, and at the perimeter of the otherwise open space were cast-iron benches.

On the opposite side of the plaza were several substantial homes, and a picture-perfect village church with a rose garden. At the other end sat the municipal building, or Municipio, with wide, arched entryways. Its windows were covered with intricate wrought iron in geometric, sunburst patterns. And like virtually all the buildings in the village, six-inch borders of contrasting color — reddish brown in this case — accented the entry and windows.

Laffi crossed the road and cut across the square toward the police station, located on a side street just past the Municipio. She noticed what appeared to be a radio tower on top of the building and recalled that until recently Mexico's telephone system had been unreliable, especially in the back country.

The note was still posted on the police station door, along with the box of handouts set outside. Through the small window at the top of the door she could see a light shining inside. Local protocol was the last thing on her mind, so Laffi quickly grasped the latch and swung open the door. She was immediately struck by the odor of stale cigars and fresh coffee, and was startled by a male voice, saying, in English, "Good morning…..Laffi?"

She spun around. The man who had spoken stood quietly, holding a cup of coffee.

"Oh my God, Artemas!" she exclaimed. "What are you doing here?"

Artemas gave a formal bow. "*Para servirle*. From time to time I see your pieces on the Internet. I thought you might show up."

"Thanks, but you didn't answer my question. What are you doing in Bustamante?"

"That *would* be telling. Especially considering your profession and reason for being here. Let's just say that all those years ago in Harvard you were more right than I was in our discussions about the feasibility of bringing change to Mexico."

"What exactly does that mean? I remember you were anxious to reform the justice system. I simply pointed out that it would be both dangerous and difficult, probably impossible."

"Let's just say that I should have paid more attention to your advice."

As Artemas spoke, Laffi noticed he still had the whip-like build of a cowboy. His khaki uniform fit him perfectly, though his straight, jet-black hair seemed longer than she would have thought appropriate for his position. He was as handsome as ever, actually more so. No longer the boy she had known, his sharply sculpted, lightly bronzed features had matured to a perfect blend of northern Indian and European.

"How long ago was it?" asked Laffi.

"Seven years. You were only at Harvard for a semester — a graduate course in Latin American economics, wasn't it? It was the beginning of my sophomore year..."

"Artemas, why the hell are you in Bustamante?"

Artemas frowned. "Laffi, this is difficult for me. I've tried to be subtle, now I'll be direct. You already know a lot about me, and I'm afraid to give you any more. There won't be much news released today, and you'd undoubtedly be tempted to use it. If you did, it could cause me *serious* problems."

Stunned, Laffi reached out and touched his hand, then drew back and looked him in the eye. "Artemas, I promise I'm not going to reveal any confidences from an old friend just to better my career. Besides, even then you were pretty tight-lipped. You never would tell me about your childhood or even explain the unusual spelling of your name.

"You're quizzing *me* about unusual names? laughed Artemas. "You never told me about yours."

"If you'd bothered to ask, I would have."

"Well?"

Laffi's eyes creased into a smile. "Knowing that my mother was fond of horses and having read about a sensational jockey from Panama who was riding that afternoon, my father took her to the races for their first date. On a whim, he wagered the money he had set aside for dinner on the jockey, whose name was Laffit

Pineda. He won at long odds, and my father proudly announced that instead of the Cuban sandwich he had planned, he would take her to the best restaurant in town. Later, after she allowed him to kiss her goodnight, he looked into her eyes and said, 'You know, we're going to name our first child Laffit!' My mother shot back, 'What if it's a girl?' To which my father replied, "Then we'll call her Laffi!'"

"Now," added Laffi, "it's your turn!"

Artemas relaxed visibly. "Maybe later. Oh, and by the way, I just read your article on the Internet."

"Then you noticed I have very little information, snapped Laffi. And does that ancient computer actually work?" She motioned to the Apple IIe on a small table in the corner.

"I have clear instructions as to what I can and cannot say. This thing is being handled from Mexico City." He paused. "I hope you're happy. I've already said too much." Then he smiled. Nodding toward the computer, he added. "As you can see Mexican law enforcement is not exactly current. I use my laptop at home."

She raised her eyebrows. "Perhaps some background that doesn't pertain directly to the case?"

Artemas caught himself staring at her. *She's as beautiful as I remember, I wonder if...* He shrugged and said, "Forgive my manners. Please come in and sit down. How about a cup of coffee?"

"That would be wonderful. Black."

Laffi followed him around a long counter, past peeling, military-green metal file cabinets set against unpainted concrete block walls. Between the dusty cabinets was a cubicle with some sort of radio set, confirming her earlier guess. They stopped at a heavy wooden desk with an old wooden swivel chair and two captain's chairs in front. Artemas set his cup on the desk, pulled back the nearest chair for her and went to a small table with a French press and several mugs. In a moment he handed her a brimming cup and seated himself behind the desk. Methodically, he pulled out a yellow legal pad and a pen and looked up at her.

Taking this as an invitation to begin, Laffi said, "Can you say where Julie Conners' body is now?"

"It's at the morgue in Monterrey undergoing further tests, and the results will be available. I can't say when, but it'll be soon; we're under a lot of pressure to release it to U.S. authorities. "

"I've heard there have been similar incidents, at least one where a man had his heart removed. Can you tell me about that and if you think it's related to this case?"

"That's something I can't get into. See what I mean?"

"Under whose jurisdiction will this case come?" she asked. Do you think you'll be in charge? I understand a request has been made to allow the FBI to participate. Do you know how and to what extent?"

"Some colleagues from Mexico City will be arriving later today. Those things will be determined in due course."

Laffi thought she detected more in his brilliant green eyes, but decided that she had been pushy enough, at least until she had an opportunity to analyze the situation. As she stood up, Artemas extended his hand. She brushed it aside, put her arms around his neck and gave him a hug. As they separated, she said, "I know, I know, but that's for old times sake, and nobody's looking. Artemas, I know this is going to be difficult. Very soon Bustamante will be filled with the most aggressive journalists in the world, the FBI, and whomever you said is coming from Mexico City. But somehow I hope we'll have time to catch up, and at least I'll be able to convince you I can be trusted. All I can do is demonstrate it with what you won't read on the Internet."

Artemas put a hand on her shoulder, gave it a quick squeeze. "Maybe we can get together. I hope so."

"I'd like that," said Laffi and turned to go. She stopped after two steps and looked back. "Artemas, how *did* you get your name?"

"It was given to me by my mother. Now, if there's nothing else..."

After closing the door, Artemas's eyes followed Laffi through the small window as she walked from the station. He had been attracted to her at Harvard and now felt the same stirrings. Then he considered the problems he'd face associating with a journalist and shook his head in frustration. In Mexico City he had focused on his police work and only allotted time for dalliances with the many women who found him attractive—though most were not exactly marriage material. After the harrowing chain of events that sent him to Bustamante, he became consumed with establishing himself, and led the abstinent life of his Jesuit mentor. The shortage of eligible women made it easy. But now that Laffi had rentered his life…

His thoughts migrated from the buxom blond to images of himself, first as a little boy, happily watching his mother creating her art in the vast hacienda in Sonora, then again the day he learned he would never see her again. He saw himself in the car with his silent father on the way to the village and later in the tiny room behind the church learning his lessons. Then he was with his mother's family at their remote *ranchería* during summers, and later arriving at Harvard. Then came his return to Mexico and induction into the Federal Judicial Police, followed by his *real* education, culminating in his disastrous transfer to Bustamante. Last night the attorney general had punctuated the precariousness of his current situation, ending his phone call with the warning, "A mistake this time, Salcido, and Bustamante will turn out be the least of your troubles." Artemas's face hardened as he returned to his desk.

Bustamante

The dining room was open by the time Laffi returned to the hotel, and she ordered breakfast. When Eduardo brought the coffee she said, "I just discovered that Captain Salcido is an old friend."

"Bustamante is lucky to have him. Where did you know him?"

"We were at Harvard University together. We didn't have much time to catch up, but he said he had been transferred to Bustamante from Mexico City. Do you know why?"

"You will have to ask him," replied Eduardo, looking over his shoulder, obviously anxious to end the conversation.

"I'm afraid he'll be busy and don't want to bother him with trifling details."

Eduardo relented, and bent close to her. "Perhaps he was too honest," he whispered. He straightened up and looked over his shoulder into the kitchen. "I think your breakfast is ready."

After the meal, which was served with fresh baked *bolillos* and homemade jam of some exotic fruit, Laffi returned to her room. She typed a summary of her findings into her laptop, omitting any mention of her previous acquaintance with Artemas—something she knew was a serious violation of her employer's policy—added a few requests, and emailed it to her office.

She left the hotel and set out to get a better feel for the village. As she walked along the road toward the looming mountains, she thought about her previous relationship with Artemas. They had met at a Harvard reception for the Mexican Foreign Minister and had immediately discovered a shared background in Mexico. She found Artemas bright and extremely attractive. But he was several years younger, and despite his fine education he was still finding his way, both in life and a strange country. Although she had a strong sexual attraction to him, she had just gone through a messy breakup. In spite of Artemas's attempts to make their relationship more physical, she concluded that hooking up without a serious future was not worth it. But now he was even more striking and sure of himself. And might not heating up the relationship enhance her access to information that could furthur her career? She was immediately ashamed of the thought and turned her attention to work.

Laffi stopped at every shop along the way and soaked up stray gossip. About four blocks down the road the shops ended and homes were set further apart. So far she had learned that while many of the villagers were farmers, others owned small businesses, yet others were retired, and more than a few received their income from close relatives in the U.S., confirmed by several cars with U.S. plates parked beside modest dwellings. The village also had sporadic infusions of income, mostly from the sale of liquor and *cabrito* to weatlthy hunters visiting nearby private hunting ranches — some stocked with exotic game.

After half a mile of walking, Laffi found that the road ended at a cross street near the village cemetery. The masonry walls of the *campo santo* — halllowed field — gleamed with the most lustrous white paint she had ever seen. Directly behind the cemetery, rising so steeply she had to crane her neck, were the saw-toothed mountains.

Without thinking, Laffi walked up to the cemetery gate. A light breeze stirred the petals on wilted flower arrangements, and small birds flitted about. Since the wrought-iron gate was not padlocked, Laffi shoved against it, and the old hinges creaked open in classic horror movie style. She wasn't sure why, since graveyards normally didn't spook her, but she felt a bit unsettled.

Laffi looked around. The headstones were mostly cast concrete or carved marble; the plots well manicured, though a few had overgrown weeds. Looking farther into the cemetery she saw the grandest monument of all, a marble mausoleum with an arched entry. She walked toward it, careful to stay on the narrow gravel paths. Along the way she paused to read inscriptions with dates ranging from the mid-1600s to the present. She was surprised to find that while some of the earlier residents of this isolated village had died young, many more had lived into their seventies, eighties and nineties.

At the entrance to the marble edifice was carved the legend, *Familia Zamarripa*. The surface looked so silky smooth Laffi was tempted to trace the lettering with her fingertips. She entered the passage, sliding sideways to avoid rubbing against the polished walls. Inside, she examined the names etched above ornate, locked iron gates. The earliest was Arlín Zamarripa, 1655-1714. The most recent was Rudolfo Zamarripa, 1918-1989.

Laffi suddenly felt a creepy sensation. A chill stole through her body, raising the hair on the nape of her neck. She quickly left the mausoleum and the feeling subsided. *That was weird*, she thought, as she stood in the warm morning air. *Time to go.*

While heading back to the entry she noticed another crypt at the far side of the cemetery, just below the base of the mountain. It was a mirror image of the first, but slightly smaller. *Why hadn't she noticed this one before?* Laffi forced herself to walk over and check the inscription on the exterior marble wall, it said: *Familia Alcazar.*

The signficance of these grand family tombs could prove useful as Laffi gathered background information about the village, but she'd had enough freakiness for one morning, and swung herself around to retrace her steps to the gate. She sucked in a quick breath. Now, standing not ten feet in front of her was a priest. Dressed in black, the tall stooping man could have stepped out of a painting by Goya. He had a long, narrow face with thinning jet-black hair peppered with grey. Large, almond-shaped eyes, both soulful and hard, regarded her calmly.

"May I help you?" he said in a lisping accent that was pure Castilian.

"No," stammered Laffi, trying to recover from her second fright of the day. "Thank you but I..." For once she had no words.

"I come here often," he said. "To be here among those who have already fulfilled His destiny can be beneficial." He kept his eyes on her.

"Yes," she agreed.

The man remained silent, continued to regard her with little or no expression, except for an odd glitter in his eyes. She observed that his black shirt, pants, and collar, though lovingly maintained, were threadbare. Laffi said she must be going, and wished him good day.

The priest hesitated, closed his eyes momentarily, then stepped aside, allowing her to pass. Without altering his expression, he bent in a small, formal bow. "*Que vaya usted con Dios,*" he intoned as Laffi walked away. As she latched the gate behind her, the priest vanished.

She walked along the wide dirt road that fronted the cemetery for several blocks, carrying a strange, uneasy feeling with her. She finally shook it off as she turned onto another paved road that led back toward the village. On the way she noticed a small canal with running water and guessed that at least a portion of the village's supply came via this ancient *acequia* system.

As she passed one particularly dilapidated adobe dwelling, a very old woman in a straw-seated rocking chair caught her eye. "*Buenos días,*" the woman said.

The tone of the greeting and the expression in the ancient woman's eyes were so vibrant that Laffi stopped dead in her tracks. "*Buenos días,*" she responded. " I hope you are well today?"

"Yes, but I suspect not as well as a beautiful young girl such as yourself."

"You are very kind," replied Laffi, trying to match the old woman's sparkle. "Have you lived in Bustamante all your life?"

"Yes, which probably makes three of yours." Laffi could not believe that so much energy could come from the wrinkled, little face rocking back and forth in the crumbling doorway.

"This is my first time in Bustamante. I'm a journalist. Unfortunately I'm here because of the murder of the North American girl. Have you heard of it?"

"Oh yes." The woman shook her head sadly, and the vigorous glint in her eyes faded into something far away. She coughed into a bony hand with transparent skin.

Trusting her instinct, Laffi stepped even closer and lowered her voice. "I heard there was a similar murder, not long ago. Has anything like this ever happened in Bustamante before?"

The old lady ceased rocking and locked her eyes on Laffi's. "Many, many years ago, when I was even younger than you are now such things were common." Her eyes left Laffi's, and she said, "That is all I will say."

"I'm sorry, I didn't mean to offend you." The woman seemed weary now.

"No, no, dear. It is nothing to do with you." The woman's dry lips pursed, and she coughed again. "It's just that some things should be left alone."

Puzzled, Laffi said goodbye and walked away.

Although it was still early, the humidity had her sweating by the time she returned to the hotel. She decided to take a shower and short rest before lunch.

ZAMARRIPA ESTATE

A few miles south of Bustamante, down a narrow, unpaved road that winds from the main highway back to the very base of the saw-toothed mountain, lies a sprawling hacienda. It is the ancestral home of the Zamarripa family. Begun in the late 1600s, it was still a work in progress until the early 1980s when Zarco Zamarripa, the family's current patriarch, moved to Monterrey to be closer to his extensive business interests. Since that time, and until about six months before Chaco Gonzalez fainted near his dead goats, the hacienda had been used only once or twice a year for family getaways.

A few months earlier, Zarco's two sons, Ignacio and Armando, expressed an interest in moving back to the hacienda. The elder Zamarripa could not fathom his sons' motives—not that he spent much time in the process. Their mother had died soon after Armando was born, and the boys were raised mostly by servants and each other. Their father was always somewhere else attending to "important affairs." Zarco's sole affection was lavishing on them whatever "things" they wanted. The results had been predictable.

"Spoiled, urban, white trash" was how he referred to the fruit of his loins in a recent family meeting. He had had to bribe policemen assigned to investigate two brutal rape cases and drug use in the local club scene. A charge of forcible rape of a seventeen year old honor student, whose plaid, school-uniform skirt the boys had apparently found irresistible, was the latest and, Zarco vowed, the last incident. It was only through bestowing an enormous lifetime endowment on the girl and her family that Zarco was able to keep his progeny out of prison. He immediately cut off all but a subsistence allowance to the boys—something he knew he should have done long ago—and told them he would never again lift a finger to get them out of trouble.

Not long thereafter the pair told Zarco they wanted to move to the hacienda, away from the city's pressures and temptations. Although suspicious, he immediately assented, glad to have them out of sight and out of mind. Zarco had no desire to be reminded of his failure to raise sons to whom he could convey the teachings that had been passed on to him by his father and to his father before him. And so on back into the mists of ancient Europe where his clan had learned the ways that made them a powerful force. It was certainly not that the boys were squeamish about the tradition of intimidation and torture that was his tribe's most successful tactic. It was that they had no understanding of the centuries old code dictating its proper exercise. Zarco was intimately aware that its continued violation would bring about the family's destruction. It had done so before—centuries ago in both Eastern Europe and Spain—and could easily do so again.

The afternoon of the day that Laffi Rendón arrived in Bustamante, Ignacio and Armando Zamarripa sat at a table in the hacienda's vast patio. Amidst a cloud of acrid smoke that curled skyward from rough, hastily made joints, the two twenty-something scions faced each other beneath an umbrella in the courtyard of the stately hacienda.

Although only a year apart in age, the boys were physically distinct, except for their light-skinned features and brown hair. Ignacio, the elder, had the high energy, almost pathologically thin, snake-hipped, self-indulgent look of a rock star. His narrow face sported a wispy mustache and goatee. He affected sleeveless, Italian shirts that displayed fanciful, cartoon demons tattooed on his skinny arms. His pants were alternately too tight or too baggy, and his neck and right wrist invariably sported substantial gold ornamentation.

Armando had the sleek, prosperous look that was the natural result of too much good food and plenty of leisure. He leaned toward designer jeans, silk western shirts, expensive snakeskin boots, and huge Rolex watches. He was never without a heavy silver bracelet on his right wrist. His moon-shaped, smooth-shaven face wore a kindly, bemused expression that belied his sadistic personality, which made it both easy and natural for him to carry out some of the less pleasant activities conceived by his cleverer but slightly more squeamish brother.

It was early afternoon and the sun slanted across hand-hewn cobblestones, fountains, and perfectly manicured plots of grass. "*Jesús Cristo, hermano*, did you see what's going on in the village? It'll soon be full of reporters and all kinds of fucking cops — PGR, American FBI and God knows what else? We've got to do something!" said Ignacio, taking another drag, drawing the smoke so deeply that he choked then coughed, spewing spittle over the table.

"No shit, man!" Armando replied, somehow thinking this was an appropriate response to any great deliberation. As if those might have been the very words uttered by Isabela upon being informed by Columbus that he had discovered the New World.

Ignacio wiped his chin and said, "The first one, the guy, was a good idea. It scared the shit out of everyone and kept them away from the cave. Besides we had to do it. But then the fucking girl...I wonder who the hell...? Sooner or later the cave's going to attract attention. Foreigners and the federal police will pay no attention to these *rustico's* superstitions. *¡Que pinchón!* I think the only chance we've got is to clean out the cave, tonight. We can hide the stuff somewhere here. *¿De Acuerdo, hermano?*"

"*Sí, hermano. Tienes razon, como siempre.* You are always right," grunted Armando, showing he had not been paying attention for the last 25 years.

Bustamante

Eduardo seated Laffi in the dining room around two-thirty. It was overflowing with new arrivals and a crew from the *Los Angeles Times* had finally vacated her table.

She waved at Diego Ramirez, who sat with colleagues nearby. He had introduced himself earlier that afternoon, and invited her for supper at his weekend home in the village. She politely declined, but listened to his description of the *chupacabra* attack on Chaco Gonzalez's goats.

A pair of ancient ceiling fans did little to cool the hot muggy air, and a cloud of tobacco smoke wafted to the ceiling. Accustomed to US restrictions, Laffi found it odd to see people enjoying a cigarette with their meal. Leaving her purse on the table, she went to the icebox just off the scullery, extracted a Coke and and popped off the cap.

Back at her table she sipped thoughtfully from the ice-cold bottle. *What the hell's wrong with me?* she wondered. *Normally I'd be happy as a hound on a scent.* While she had no more facts about Julie Connor's murder than were already known, she did have information about the earlier killing, some interesting gossip, and news that the Federal Police were coming from Mexico City to handle the case. She had also filed a good background piece on the village. Most important, of course, was her connection to Artemas. Despite her promise, she could justify disclosing personal information about him since it would be dug up by competitors anyway. No, she wouldn't do that. She cared for Artemas and although she couldn't put her finger on why, intuition told her he was in a difficult and possibly dangerous situation.

Laffi looked up from her menu. Coming around the corner was a tall Anglo man with wavy, blond hair. Like the others, he wore a khaki shirt and blue jeans, but she knew immediately he was no journalist. His jeans were beat-up Levis and the shirt looked army surplus. His wire-framed glasses were unlike the designer frames favored by her peers. He was tan and relaxed, and she noted a resemblance to the young Robert Redford. But he also seemed a little confused as he moved uncertainly through the room toward Laffi's table.

One of the young waitresses greeted him. *"Buenas tardes, señor. Todas las mesas estan ocupadas. ¿Puede esperar unos minutos?"*

"Perdóneme," he replied, *"no hablo español. ¿Habla ingles?"*

"No, señor, no speak English," replied the harried girl and looked around for help.

On impulse, Laffi gestured to the seat across from her and said in a voice loud enough to attract his attention, "The place is packed. I've been here twenty minutes and haven't ordered yet. You're welcome to join me."

The man looked at her gratefully and brushed a blond lock from his forehead. "That's the best offer I've had all day. Thank you!"

He extended a large, tanned hand down to Laffi. "I'm Jason Peterson, college professor — at least for another month and a half — and proprieter of Bat Watch, Inc." He pulled back the empty chair and stiffly lowered himself.

She gripped his hand firmly. "Laffi Rendón, reporter for at least another few days." She waved toward the scullery."There's beer and soft drinks over there. You better help yourself."

He got up, walked to the cooler and returned with a bottle of *Peñafiel* mineral water. When he was seated, he said, "I assume you're here to cover the murder of Senator Conners' daughter?"

"Yes. I got here last night from D.C."

"I just heard about it last night, on the Internet. You must have taken the express."

"Pretty much. I feel like I was shot through one of those pneumatic tubes banks use at the drive-through…. So why are you here?"

Jason explained that while teaching biology at the University of Texas at Austin he had founded Bat Watch to promote the conservation of at-risk bat populations. It had quickly grown from a part time operation staffed entirely by volunteers to an all-consuming organization with a budget over a million dollars.

"I finally realized," he said, "that I couldn't handle both teaching and running Bat Watch, so last month I gave notice to the University. I was just beginning a one-man field trip in Durango when I heard the terrible news."

Laffi found Jason's conversation a refreshing change from the urbanized males she knew in Washington. He was passionate about something besides status and power, and bats were far more interesting than she could have imagined. It didn't hurt that he was boyishly handsome, with an earthy, unaffected manner. But, for now, what caught her attention most was him mentioning the Bat Watch fundraising events sponsored by Senator Connors, and how he met Julie Connors. She tamped down her growing excitement at this tantalizing piece of information. She'd need to reel in this fish carefully, lest he get away.

Jason went on to relate how he had come to Bustamante to hear the facts first-hand and to inject as much accuracy as possible into the inevitable speculation about vampires, *chupacabras,* and anything else that might affect bats, in order to prevent the needless cruelty that often followed such gruesome events.

When he finished, Laffi was almost speechless. Besides knowing the Connors, his unique perspective could provide her an incredible advantage in covering this story. She mentally crossed herself, and in a voice so low only God could hear, she promised to go to church as soon as she got home.

"That's fascinating," she finally said, and then added, "you and the police are probably the only ones with a legitimate reason to be here. But Jason, I'm puzzled. You told the waitress you didn't speak Spanish, and yet you did so rather fluently."

"Actually, I can read it O.K., especially with the help of a dictionary," he replied. "But I'm a little deaf, so I've never learned to speak well. Because I spend so much time in Mexico I've learned that one phrase."

"Perhaps," Laffi said, drawing the word out, and flashing her warmest smile, "we can collaborate to mutual advantage. What if I help you with fact finding in Spanish and with media coverage that gets your points across, and you fill me in on bats, vampires and *chupacabras*. Maybe some background on the Conners family." She paused and studied his face, "I understand your fascination with bats, but vampires and *chupacabras*...?"

"Vampires are all the rage—I want to give factual presentations. In cases like this, it's vital to communicate scientific facts, especially in a place where people are likely to act on superstition."

"Ah, that makes sense. By the way, do you have a reservation? The hotel is full."

"No. I've been here before to explore the caves. There's a nice park on the outskirts of town, just below the mountain. My Suburban's pretty well set up for camping, and the place has a swimming pool and showers with plenty of parking spaces. All the comforts of home!"

"I think I saw it this morning," said Laffi, not mentioning that her idea of camping was a hotel that *did not* put chocolates on the pillows. The waitress arrived to take their order. Laffi deferred to Jason.

"I heartily recommend the *biftec a la mexicana*," he responded. "It's called *cortadillo* in other parts of the north. Sliced, grass-fed beef, sautéed with tomato, onion, garlic, and chiles, served in its own gravy with refried beans and tortillas. Maybe a little hot, unless you're used to it."

"Don't worry, I was raised in Mexico City," she said. She gave the waitress their order and requested more drinks. "So," she asked, "What do you tell people about vampires?"

"We...ll," he said, "I tell them that vampires exist, that they're a fact of life. That they've probably been around since not long after the Garden of Eden. But I also tell them that vampires of the human kind bear no resemblance whatsoever to any bat, including *Desmodus rotundus*—the vampire bat. I also tell them that real vampires have only a superficial resemblance to the fictional, immortal variety."

Laffi wondered if she should get out her notebook, but decided not to. "Real, human vampires?" she prompted.

"Those stories and legends come from a combination of superstition, human nature, and bad science. Like so many other myths, they have just enough truth to make them believable.

"My version of real vampires don't need wooden stakes to kill them and aren't the least bothered by a cross or holy water. But they do gain both strength and pleasure through taking the blood of others—sometimes metaphorically, but not always."

"Where did the notion of the Dracula-types come from?"

"The concept began in the Middle Ages and was actually fostered by the church. Early ecclesiastical teaching instructed that the devil possessed certain people and gave them unholy powers of evil."

"Salem...Faust," she muttered.

He nodded. "With regard to vampires, the bad science I mentioned entered the mix. Diseases—like catalepsy, cataplexy and sleep paralysis—that make the sufferer appear to be dead, sometimes led to premature burials. Occasionally, with just the right timing and circumstances, the unfortunate subjects would be exhumed or otherwise discovered and appear to return to life, creating the legend of the undead."

Laffi leaned forward, placed her elbows on the table, and rested her chin in her joined palms, fascinated and calculating how she could use the information.

"Not long ago," Jason continued, "a professor in California concluded that there's a relationship between vampire legends and a blood disease called porphyria. It drastically lowers the body's ability to resist the sun's ultraviolet rays and converts hemoglobin, the component of blood that carries oxygen to the brain, into a toxin. Symptoms include burning of the skin, especially the lips. In extreme cases, they curl back, emphasizing the size of the teeth. In the Dark Ages those afflicted hid from the sun and were often discovered cowering in dark places. The writer postulated that some of them might even have drunk blood, which was a common folk remedy. Any of that sound familiar?"

Laffi nodded.

"Another trait that encouraged the myth was that people affected by porphyria were also repelled by garlic, which increases the disease's toxicity and makes them violently ill. Of course, they were persecuted by the clergy, who thought they were possessed by the devil. It's not hard to believe that the victims shrank from garlic, and exhibited fright at the sight of a cross, the symbol of those they knew would eventually drag them from their hiding places and burn them to death."

"People are easily motivated by fear," Laffi said.

Jason shook his head in disgust. "Then along came more bad science: What passed for logic at the time told people that since losing blood could take life, drinking the stuff might extend it."

"Ugh," said Laffi, wrinkling her nose. The room was stifling and there was no sign of the waitress. "I think I'll get the drinks myself." She returned with two ice-cold bottles and seated herself. "Anything else I should know about vampires?"

"Human nature. Unscrupulous people realized that by cleverly playing on the superstitions of ignorant villagers, they could both frighten and control them. All these things, coupled with the natural feeling of domination that some people derive from taking the blood of an enemy, caused a few powerful families to adopt the practice, keeping the legends alive through the centuries."

Bustamante

The waitress finally came with their food. Jason took a bite and said, "It's as good as I remember. Of course with the subject at hand, perhaps we should have ordered the *fritada*, kid cooked in its own blood."

Laffi burst out laughing and clapped her hands, pleased to discover that Jason was not just some humorless academic.

For a while they ate in silence, and Laffi thought about the angle for her article. "Any modern day vampire stories you would like to share?"

Jason looked her in the eye. "You're obviously very good at what you do, because I've been doing all the talking. So, tell me what you've found out. All I know is what my assistant sent me by email."

"Not a lot. What you've been saying is much more interesting. By the way, what *is* your view of the *chupacabra* legend?" she asked.

"Alright," Jason laughed, holding his hands up in submission. "But your turn's coming." He cleared his throat and continued. "As far back as the nineteenth century there've been reports of animals, usually sheep and goats, being found with the blood drained from them, often through throat wounds. Actually, the reports seem to come in spurts."

Laffi groaned.

"The stories come from all over: England, Ireland, the Balkans, and more recently the United States, Mexico, and Puerto Rico. In some places the stories are woven into UFO lore, and in Latin America the legend of the chupacabra, or "goat-sucker," was born.

"People claim to have seen them. But no such animal has ever been spotted by a reputable scientist, nor have any remains ever been produced, making it highly unlikely that anything but mangy dogs, and maybe satanic cults, are involved. That reminds me—I found something on the Internet last night that fits right in with what we're talking about." He went on to describe a bizarre piece he had found on the cult of Huitzilopochtli, the Aztec god of the sun and war. "It's pretty weird."

"Do you have a copy, or the web address?" asked Laffi.

"I've got a hard copy in the car, would you like to see it?"

"If it isn't too much trouble."

"Certainly. But first to finish the *chupacabra* question. To be perfectly honest, while it's highly unlikely any such creature exists, that doesn't mean it isn't amusing to discuss it or even look for it. But for god's sake, don't quote me on that!"

They finished their meal and left the restaurant to fetch the printout.

Bustamante

Outside the air was still hot, but less stifling than the smoke-filled dining room. Laffi leaned against Jason's Suburban and began to read the document.

The piece started innocently enough, recounting the fact that Huitzilopochtli was the Aztec's principal god, to whom the people believed large quantities of blood must be offered if the sun was to rise, their crops to ripen, and their battles won. It noted that entire wars had been fought for no other purpose than to obtain victims to sacrifice to the bloodthirsty deity.

Her attention riveted as the piece veered from gruesome but accepted history into a strange, superficially logical dream world with present-day parallels. It contended that rather than a god, *Huitzilopochtli* had at first been a living being—a vampire. That he was the first of a new clan of blood-feasting, power seeking leaders who received their strength and superiority from the essential fluid of friend and foe alike. It went on to praise them for their strength, explain their downfall, and chronicle their rebirth.

"Now the *Huitzilopochtlis* have begun to awaken, to arise and assert their assent to their rightful ancient rank and station. Throughout the new nation of Mexico, using Old Ways in the New Times, they feed on the blood and souls of the people. They use chemistry rather than obsidian to rip out the hearts that provide the Huitzilopochtlis with the power, the strength, and the means to regain their lost dominion."

The piece concluded with a concise message that chilled Laffi: "Those who are of the blood of the *México* are invited to join the ascendancy, to put their lives in the service of *Huitzilopochtli*, to bear witness by the taking of blood in both the Old and New Ways, with a willingness to sacrifice everything to their own covetousness and hunger."

What she had just read seemed like a twisted, allegorist's history of Mexico, from the Conquest to the brutal drug trade, with a less than subtle invitation to join the latter.

"Could this be connected to the girl's murder?" she mused.

Jason shrugged. "I suppose it could."

"Do you mind if I hold on to this?" she asked

"No, I can find it again."

Laffi watched a man come out of the hotel and said to Jason, "That's Diego Ramirez, from *El Norte*. He interviewed the farmer right after the *chupacabra* attack. He seems pretty interested in the subject and might be a good contact for you. I'm sure he speaks English. If you like, I'll introduce you."

Jason had plenty of questions of his own for Laffi, but his work trumped his personal interests. "Thanks, I'd appreciate that. My objective is to get the facts about what happened so that Bat Watch can issue press releases, particularly in Mexico. We need to forestall knee-jerk efforts to eradicate bat populations. It's bad enough in Southern Mexico already. I just read an article claiming that about 3000 cattle in Chiapas have been killed by rabies, supposedly spread by vampire bats. You simply can't imagine the horrible things that can happen."

"Actually I can," replied Laffi. "My first priority is to get the same facts and then weave background from your information into the stories. Let's work as a team. We can begin by checking at the police station to see if a news conference has been scheduled, then we ought to take a look at the crime scene. How does that sound?"

"Sounds good. Your car or mine?"

Monterrey

That evening, Zarco Zamarripa was in his home in Monterrey's exclusive Garza Garcia district, sixty miles south of Bustamante. He was not looking forward to his upcoming meeting with Jugo Gandara. He thought the drug lord was a perfect example of all that was wrong with Mexico. Although the man had recently acquired some polish, Zarco knew that Jugo was a man of little education and even fewer manners. But he was cunning, brutal, and rich, and therefore important.

After the peso crashed, Gandara and his fellow *narcotraficantes* were the only people with money. All the businesses that Zarco and his group were involved in: banks, hotel chains, brokerage houses, factories, and real estate went bust. He and others were not just eager, but desperate to bargain with the devil himself to escape disaster, and that is what they did. The fact that Gandara lacked a conscience and was not only willing to earn his daily bread on the misery of others, but actually enjoyed the process, did not bother Zarco at all.

Zarco struggled for years to free himself from dependence on drug money and had recently achieved that goal. But he was well aware that severing the drug dealer's connections to Grupo Vampiro, the secret camarilla of ostensibly legitimate businesses that Zarco controlled, would not be easy.

Because Gandara was fairly well known in Monterrey, because of the nature of the business to be discussed, and for his own personal safety, Zarco had decided to hold the meeting at his home.

Zarco scanned his huge mahogany paneled office, assured himself that all was in place, and walked out into the courtyard. The neighborhood was comprised of high stone walls offering glimpses of outrageously expensive *nouveau riche* architecture. The house was situated partly up the hill at the base of Chipinque Mountain. Zarco had always thought the craggy peak looked as if it had been uprooted from Bustamante and dropped on the otherwise flat desert south of Monterrey.

Zarco stood in the darkness, listening to the tiers of fountains that cascaded into his swimming pool. He considered his angst over the approaching confrontation and wondered if he was getting soft. Was this just another manifestation of lack of attention to his heritage and traditions that had caused the mess his sons were in? He decided that if the meeting went as planned, fine. If not, he would revert to the old ways, use his instincts, and wouldn't Jugo be in for a surprise. A sudden chill sent him back inside.

Zarco heard the doorbell just after 8:00 P.M. Gandara, carrying a briefcase, was shown into the office by a manservant who was actually an off-duty policeman. Zarco rose from behind his ornate desk, strode to his visitor, and enveloped him in an *abrazo*.

"*Buenas noches, y bienvenido*," Zarco said as he separated from his guest. He motioned to a low chair of highly polished leather next to a glass coffee table. A bottle of brandy, two snifters, and a sealed envelope sat on the table. The differences between the two men were striking. Gandara was medium height, powerfully built with a surprisingly large head. He had a rough, dark complexion, and his rounded features and large nose were unmistakably Indian in origin. Zarco exemplified the European ancestry associated with Mexico's upper class. He was tall and slender with sharp features. His skin was very pale, almost transparent, with an unnatural luminescence.

After seating themselves, the two men sloshed brandy into the crystal snifters and locked eyes.

"*Don* Zarco," began Jugo, with just a trace of sarcasm in the honorific, "Thank you for seeing me."

"*Al contrario*, it is I who need to thank you," broke in Zarco. "In fact, the main reason I asked for this meeting was to thank you for your help during the past...difficult years. Without it, things would have been very different for me and my group. However, it's also a fact that we've weathered the storm and are now able to proceed using much more conventional and, of course, less expensive sources of financing."

He raised his hand as Gandara was about to interject, then continued. "I understand that you would prefer to continue the relationship, but for what should be obvious reasons we believe it's time to move forward as we did before the unpredictable problems — on our own. However," he paused and forced his smile to reach his eyes, "the last thing we want is to be perceived as ungrateful, so we wish to present this."

Zarco picked up the envelope and offered it to the impassive drug dealer, "Payment of our final obligation to you, with the addition of a substantial amount in evidence of our sincere appreciation for your help."

Gandara looked at the envelope, turned it over, and looked at it again. Then he held it up to the light, angled it slowly from side to side, examined it once more, like a philatelist inspecting a rare stamp. Then with his powerful fingers, effortlessly he tore it into small pieces and allowed them to flutter to the floor.

Mimicking Zarco's earlier gesture, he raised his hand in a forestalling motion. "My dear Zarco, your thoughtfulness is touching. But you see, I'm now having my own problems. It's increasingly difficult to hide the money I bring into the country, and it's time for you to repay my favors to you. Tell me, what is the occupancy of your hotels? Maybe 65 percent at most? Are your restaurants and clubs completely full?

"Those enterprises," he continued, "much of whose business is conducted with cash, would be far more valuable if they were operating nearer capacity, or at least *appeared* to be. Combined with the capabilities of your banks they could go a long way toward solving *my* problem."

Your problem, thought Zarco, is that within a short period of time you'll be nothing more than a bloody stain on some concrete floor. Aloud, and successfully ignoring the torn up envelope that had contained a check for $105 million, he said, "I understand your situation. However, your surfeit of riches doesn't qualify for the type of sacrifice that we would offer under more urgent circumstances."

Gandara looked at his host, eyes deadhard, his face flushed with anger. Managing to keep his voice under control, he replied, "Whatever *I* want *is* urgent. Now I'm going to show you something that will change your mind."

As the man reached into his briefcase Zarco stiffened, wondering if he should summon his guard. Jugo extracted a DVD and examined the disc in much the same manner as he had the now destroyed envelope. "It's a shame the father cannot be as easy to deal with as the sons," he muttered almost to himself, then locked his eyes on Zarco, who remained motionless and silent.

"As you know," Gandara continued, now speaking directly to Zarco, his face twisted into a sneer. "Your sons recently fell on hard times. I offered them an opportunity and they were wise enough to take advantage of it." He paused to study Zarco, whose anger was betrayed only by an infinitesimal narrowing of his eyes. "I presume you have a DVD player, so let's view this before we waste each other's time."

Without expression, Zarco picked up the DVD and carried it to the other end of the room. He pushed a button on the side of a mahogany credenza. Soundlessly, a door slid sideways to reveal a large-screen television and DVD player.

Gandara raised his voice. "I require an initiation of everyone who works for me. What you are about to see is the one your sons participated in. As you'll see, it was enthusiastically carried out."

Zarco finished loading the DVD, then stepped back to one side as light flickered on the screen. "You don't need to sit down unless you want to," said Gandara, sounding cheerful for the first time. "This won't take long."

Projected before them was what appeared to be the interior of a large cave lit by torches. The camera focused on a bare ledge about counter-height along one wall, then panned to the right to show two men walking slowly, carrying something heavy in between. Zarco caught his breath as he recognized his sons, stripped bare to the waist. Ignacio and Armando held in their arms an unconscious, naked man, and laid him on the ledge, face up, securing his arms and legs with chains attached to metal stakes. The image began to skip, then went to black.

The video cut to a close-up of the bound man's face. Appearing to be in his early thirties, he had wide cheekbones and a broad nose with a small mustache. His eyelids fluttered as he regained consciousness, his pupils dark and dilated. The camera pulled back, Ignacio and Armando stood on either side of the prone man, moving their lips as if in a trance or solemn ceremony. The sound was poor, and Zarco could not make out what they were saying, but their words seemed intoned, rather than spoken.

The brothers looked into each other's eyes, lifted their gaze to the nearest torch, and recited words that Zarco could now hear. "Ancient gods of the México, we pray that you will accept this offering of sustenance and return its power to us, the chosen ones, who have dedicated our lives to your service."

With that, Ignacio pressed down the shoulders of the naked man with all his might and Armando withdrew a six-inch blade from his belt, carved from black polished stone. The man's face contorted with horror and the cave echoed with his screams as Armando plunged the razor-sharp knife into his chest. His body jerked and spasmed as Armando violently hacked into his flesh. Armando tossed the blade aside, plunged his hands into the cavity and wrenched out the still beating heart. He raised it in triumph over his head, and passed it to Ignacio, who did the same. Shrieking and yelling, the brothers painted their bare chests, taking turns using the bloody organ as a crude brush. The video ended abruptly.

"It's a good thing the effects of the drug hadn't completely worn off. Ignacio could never have held him still," said Jugo, matter-of-factly from his chair.

Zamarripa's fists clenched by his side. His eyes darted to the drawer where he kept a loaded pistol.

"Don't even think about it," sniggered the drug dealer. "I've got a van full of *pistoleros* outside that your people couldn't handle for fifteen seconds." He stood up and moved menacingly toward Zarco, jabbing his right forefinger at him, "I want papers drawn up and ready one week from today giving me the controlling vote in the management of Grupo Vampiro. From now on," he hissed, stabbing his index finger into his own chest, "any 'blood' you and those other pricks get will be dispensed by me." Then bowing in mock courtesy, he said, "*Hasta luego*...Don Zarco," this time emphasizing the honorific "*Don*" with unconcealed scorn. He spun around and stalked out the door.

Zarco stood still, lost in thought. Suddenly, as if the weight of the world had been lifted from his shoulders, he let out his breath in a prolonged hiss. He went to the table, picked up his glass of brandy, swirled it in the snifter, took a small sip, and smiled.

Bustamante

Before walking across the plaza to the police station, Laffi stopped to introduce Jason to the Mexican newspaperman, Diego Ramirez. The two seemed to hit it off and they agreed to meet that evening.

From a short distance Laffi observed three men shaking hands outside the station entry. Laffi recognized Artemas before he turned back to his office, and assumed the other men wearing dark suits were FBI agents. One was a tall, strikingly handsome black man in his early thirties with close-cropped hair. The other was white, in his early fifties, with the hard square body and determined jaw of a career marine. The afternoon temperature was in the humid eighties, and they looked uncomfortable in their suits and ties.

Laffi stepped in front of the pair and held up an I.D. card she'd pulled from her purse. "Laffi Rendón," she announced. Her tone was both brusque and courteous. "May I ask if you are the promised agents from the FBI?"

The one with the crew cut responded. "Yes ma'am, but we have nothing to say to the press at this time."

"That's fine. But how about your names for the record and a quick discussion off the record? I've been here since last night. I've talked to Captain Salcido and may actually know something that could be of help to you."

"Really?" the black agent replied with obvious sarcasm.

Jason stepped in and introduced himself.

"Homer Robinson," said the agent, extending is hand. "Lester Grunwald," said the ex-marine, following suit.

"You've spoken with Captain Salcido?" asked Laffi.

"Yes, he was helpful," said Robinson.

"Perfect English," said Grunwald.

"Wouldn't expect less of an educated man like him," Robinson added.

Laffi realized she was being subjected to a well-practiced routine.

"Ms. Rendón. You will keep us apprised of any pertinent information?" added the black man, more a statement of fact than question.

"Call me Laffi, please."

"Yes, of course."

The agents turned away, heading toward their car, but after a few steps Grunwald stopped and looked back. "Just one thing, where can we get a decent meal?"

"The Hotel Ancira, across the square," said Jason. "I can heartily recommend the *fritada*. It's a local delicacy."

When the agents were out of earshot, Laffi elbowed Jason lightly in the ribs. "You've got real potential," she said. "Now let's stop in and see if *Capitán* Salcido has heard anything from the Mexico City delegation."

Two reporters who'd been in the dining room earlier that day were just leaving the police station. One of the men said to Laffi as she entered, "Nothing yet. Wait, wait, wait. *Mañana, mañana, mañana.*" Undeterred, Laffi pushed past them. A young man in uniform stood behind the counter separating the office from the waiting area where she had first encountered Artemas. The officer frowned at them.

"*Señor*, we are not here to pester you with idiotic questions," she spat out in rapid Spanish. "I spoke with Captain Salcido this morning and would like to see him for just a moment on another matter." She pitched her voice just high enough so that Artemas could hear it.

He looked up before his assistant could reply, his eyes narrowing briefly as he took in Jason. "Yes, *Señorita* Rendón. How may I help you?"

"I just wanted to take a moment of your time to introduce you to a friend of mine, one I'm sure you'll be thankful to learn is not a reporter."

Artemas rose, placed a half-finished cigar in an already full ashtray and walked over to the counter. "Dr. Jason Peterson, meet Captain Salcido," said Laffi. "Dr. Peterson is a professor at the University of Texas," she said. "He specializes in—"

"I know who he is," interrupted Artemas.

"Well, I doubt you are aware of this," Laffi said, a little miffed, and handed Artemas the document Jason had given her.

Artemas spent a full two minutes reading it. Then, without comment, he placed it on the counter. "I had several interesting experiences with bats when I was growing up in Sonora," he said.

"I'd like to hear about them some time," said Jason.

Artemas said, "I know you're acquainted with the Senator and hope you'll convey my sincere condolences and assure him that everything possible will be done to apprehend and punish those responsible, and…"

As Laffi caught herself evaluating the two men, Artemas stopped in midsentence and looked past her toward the door.

Jason and Laffi turned to see three men entering the station.

"I believe my colleagues from Mexico City are here," said Artemas.

Although of different sizes and shapes, the men shared the same feral eyes. None were in uniform. Instead they wore blue jeans and cowboy boots that Laffi suspected were made from the skins of endangered species. Two of them had Western shirts, the third wore a black t-shirt with PGR—the initials representing *Procuradoria general de la Republica*, "the office of the attorney general"—on the back in large white letters. On their hips gleamed pearl-handled, semiautomatic pistols in black leather and sterling silver holsters.

Laffi immediately held out her hand to Artemas. "Thank you *señor*. We look forward to hearing from you."

Artemas shook her hand then Jason's. "It was good to meet you."

Jason and Laffi walked past the men without so much as a nod.

A battered Humvee, painted military green with PGR stenciled on the hood was parked at the curb. Through the narrow windows Jason saw what looked like a stack of automatic weapons in one corner. Lounging against the vehicle were two more tough looking men in fatigues and mirrored sunglasses, smoking cigarettes.

"I'm glad those Clint Eastwood wannabes aren't after me," Jason said in a low voice.

"I'm afraid they're the real thing," said Laffi. "Mexicans may seem inefficient and backward to *gringos*, but when they decide to go after somebody they don't screw around. That's why their excuses about not catching major drug kingpins don't wash. Now let's see if we can take a look at the crime scene and maybe have a peek at the cave before anybody else gets there."

ZAMARRIPA ESTATE

The sun had not yet risen when Ignacio and Armando Zamaripa's red Ford Explorer drove into the family estate. After they parked and got out, Ignacio slammed his door, and gave it a vicious kick. "Damn it, Armando," he said. "I told you to make sure we had plenty of batteries. By the time we get these lights charged it'll be too late to go back."

His brother closed his door softly and walked to the rear of the vehicle. "I told you they wouldn't hold a charge. It was you who decided to go ahead. Don't worry, I think we got most of the stuff."

"Fuck that! We both know we didn't get it all. We'll just have to hope no one goes there today. Then we can go back tonight and finish."

"I've been thinking," said Armando. He paused, not wanting to endure his brother's wrath, then continued, "We've done a lot of shit in that cave. There's got to be blood, marijuana, cocaine, speed. We can never be sure we've gotten everything. Who knows what the cops might find? Let's just blow it up! We've got dynamite in the old paint shed. It shouldn't take much to bring down the ceiling and seal the whole thing off."

Ignacio stared at his brother in astonishment. It was unlike his sibling to think of something that didn't have to do with hurting an animal or human being.

"Not a bad idea, but the potential problem," he said aloud, "is that the blast could draw attention to the cave. But so what? The only real risk will be if it doesn't work, and we've got enough dynamite to make sure that doesn't happen. O.K. *Está bien*. Let's get some sleep. Later we can go into town and see what's happening then back to the cave and close it—*para siempre*—forever. Now let's get this shit stashed."

Bustamante

"Do you know where the crime scene is?" asked Jason. "I've been through the caverns several times, but I don't know where the body was found. And I'm not sure if the gate to the road is unlocked. Without it you've got more than an hour's hike, nearly straight up."

Laffi brushed perspiration from her forehead. "Let's check back at the hotel. I could use something to drink."

"Sounds good to me," agreed Jason. As they approached the hotel he noticed a red Ford Explorer parked directly behind his tan Suburban.

It was a little after three, and the dining room was still half full. Jason and Laffi were seated next to a table with two young men. One was skinny with fantasy tattoos on his pipe-stem arms, an unhealthy pallor, and a defiant, swaggering expression. He wore tight black clothes. The other was in jeans and a western-style shirt and sported a garish, obviously expensive watch on one wrist and a large silver bracelet on the other. Jason sensed they both were bad news.

As Jason went to the cooler for their drinks, Laffi motioned for Eduardo to join them. He came over, wiping his hands on a towel. He shook hands with Laffi and said, "I hope you are enjoying Bustamante," then looked at Jason.

"I am indeed. This is Dr. Jason Peterson. I believe he's been here before."

"Yes," said Eduardo, reaching for Jason's hand. "About two years ago, with a group of students to explore the *grutas*, wasn't it?" Jason looked at Laffi for assistance. She translated and Jason said "Yes."

"Eduardo," she said. "We want to visit the crime scene and take a look at the *grutas*. Is there anyone around who could guide us?"

"I don't think so. Several groups of journalists have already been to the area, but not to the *grutas*. It's not difficult to find. You take the road from the plaza to the parking area then follow the footpath up the mountain to the murder site. I believe it's been roped off and there may be a guard stationed there.

"But," and he looked at Jason, "the professor probably remembers the road that goes directly to the *grutas*. I don't think the gate is locked. That would be much quicker and easier. But be careful, the road's in poor condition. From the entrance to the cave, take the pathway down the mountain a short way to the site."

Laffi translated, and Jason confirmed he remembered the road to the caves and the gate to the shortcut.

Then Laffi said to Eduardo, "*Muchas gracias*, we'll take your advice. Do you know if the police or anyone else has examined the *grutas* since the murder?"

Eduardo pondered the question. "I don't know, but I doubt it. Not many people from the village would go into the caves, much less near them after what's been happening. I've heard nothing to that effect from the men who were with Captain Salcido when he found the girl."

"We can take my car," said Jason.

Jason and Laffi walked out the door, and the Zamarripa brothers looked at each other, clearly freaked out by what they'd heard. They waited a few minutes in silence, Ignacio tossed fifty pesos on the table, and they quickly left the restaurant.

The wide dirt road to the mountain dropped into a gully then headed sharply upward. "This is the way to the parking area. It's a long hike to the cave's entrance," said Jason. "But the alternative, if it's open, is that little road that takes you nearly to the entrance." He pointed just above the base of the mountain where Laffi could see a narrow winding track. "The road's passable, but not well maintained. The locals usually leave the gate unlocked."

At the top of the incline Jason stopped in front of the gate that Laffi quickly opened and closed behind them. They drove on for a short distance until they reached a fork. One branch continued ahead along the base of the mountain. The other veered to the right, almost straight up. "That's probably where the guy in the ox cart found the first victim," said Jason, motioning straight ahead. He turned to the right, up the mountain.

The road had deteriorated since his last visit. Potholes and deep crevices slowed them to a crawl. In one section the edge of the road had collapsed, forcing them to hug the mountainside to keep from plunging into the deep valley below. Above, the looming mountain was dotted with palm-like trees amidst the otherwise arid brush. "That's why," said Jason, pointing at one of the trees during a rare respite from the disintegrating road, "the caverns are called *Las Grutas del Palmito*, as well as *Las Grutas de Bustamante.*"

After a succession of hairpin turns Jason calculated they were nearing the top when, around a blind corner, they surprised a small herd of wild horses. Nostrils flaring, a stallion snorted at their approach. Afraid he might spook them over the edge, Jason waited until the stallion and his mares trotted up the road ahead. Around the next turn they came to a cleared area suitable for parking. It provided just enough space for the horses to get around them from a safe distance, and head back down the mountain.

"I suggest we go to the cave first," said Jason.

"Sounds good to me."

"We park here, walk about 10 minutes. I hope you've been getting your exercise," he added. "It's damn near straight up." Then he grabbed two flashlights from the Suburban and strapped on a webbed belt with several leather pockets attached to it, including what looked like a holstered pistol.

"What's that for?" asked Laffi. "I thought guns were illegal in Mexico."

"They are, at least the kind with gunpowder. This is an air-powered pellet gun. I travel alone in back country Mexico quite a bit, and more than just a few travelers off the beaten path have been killed these last few years. It's not a lot of protection, and I've never used it on anything more than an aggressive snake, but it's better than nothing. Remember, two people were recently murdered not far from here."

She quickly realized that Jason had not exaggerated. The path wound up over sharp boulders interspersed with spiny cactus. They had to stop twice, once while she caught her breath, and again for her to extract thorns from her ankle. It was well over ninety and getting more humid by the minute.

She thought Jason seemed preoccupied as he gazed up at the sky. "Looks like a thunderhead coming over the mountain," he said. "During this time of the year they can pop up quickly and it rains like hell. We don't want to be in the cave if that happens. Most of the interior was carved by flood waters, and it could be dangerous."

Laffi followed his gaze and saw that a few clouds had indeed appeared directly above. "I'm assuming we aren't going so far in we couldn't get out in a hurry?"

"Let's go," was all he said.

Nearly at the top of the mountain they finally saw an indentation in a cliff covered by an iron door about six feet high.

"The opening was once completely hidden by a rock slide," explained Jason. "In the early nineteen-hundreds, some citizen happened by and felt cool air blowing on him. A little digging revealed the entrance to the world's third largest caverns." He walked up to the door. "Fortunately it looks like it isn't locked. I'd forgotten about that."

"Fortunately for you," said Laffi, wiping her forehead and hoping her heart rate would return to normal.

With surprisingly little effort Jason slid the door's iron bolt and pushed it open. "I remember there was a light switch just inside. The village used to run tours and strung an electric wire to light the first section of the caverns."

He turned on his flashlight, stepped inside the door, and Laffi moved to see what was happening. She heard a click, then what seemed like the entire inside of the mountain was illuminated.

Artemas Salcido glanced at a set of computer printouts on his desk to reassure himself they were in order then focused on the men sent by the attorney general. Each of them, in turn, wondered how cooperative the former, and possibly current, troublemaker would be.

Artemas handed the papers to Raymundo Valenzuela, the group's leader. "Here's a summary of the investigation to date. I've already faxed a copy to the attorney general."

As Valenzuela carefully read the report, Artemas observed his likely adversary. He was a medium height, powerfully built man with a military haircut and unfashionably long sideburns. A long-healed scar extended from the right side of his cheek down to his mouth.

Raymundo had carefully studied Artemas's dossier and knew he was intelligent and sometimes devious. From what he'd heard about Artemas's father, the young man was also not without connections. He finished the report and looked up. "This seems complete. Since you've been here from the beginning and must have formed some conclusions, why don't you give us an unofficial conclusion?

Artemas was amused that the man thought he would buy into the notion that anything said in the meeting would remain off the record. He placed his hands palms down on the table and leaned forward. "The death of the American girl was preceded by that of a drifter and the killing of several goats in an equally bloody manner, which may or may not be related."

Artemas looked at each man. "In the first murder, the victim was killed by having his heart cut out. There were marks on his wrists and ankles and other parts of his body, indicating that he was bound and struggled violently. There is also evidence, both on the body and in samples of his blood, that he was injected with a sedative. It's probable that more than one person was involved in the crime. The only other physical evidence is the butt of a marijuana cigarette discovered near the body.

"It seems reasonable to conclude that this first murder was part of some satanic ritual and was well planned, perhaps by a cult of some sort, although nothing like it has happened before." Then, remembering that he had been told that mysterious deaths and disappearances were once fairly common in Bustamante, he added, "At least during the time I've been here.

"On the other hand, the killing of the girl shows no evidence of planning. There's also nothing to indicate that more than one person was involved. It seems probable that her killer met her on the trail and got close enough to grab her in a strangle hold with both hands. He must have been strong enough to nearly lift her off the ground—and to hold her there, possibly even shaking her when she struggled, until she lost consciousness. Her throat was then slashed and the blood drained. It's difficult to know exactly which was the cause of death; both occurred at roughly the same time. Although her clothes were removed, there's no indication she was sexually molested.

"As with the first murder, a marijuana butt was found near the body, as was this." Artemas extracted a heavy sterling silver bracelet from the envelope on the desk and handed it to Raymundo. "There were no prints. Odd, don't you think? Very few materials are more susceptible to fingerprints than polished silver."

The men remained silent.

Artemas continued, "There's also something we did not find, which could be just as important. The victim's friend said that the girl had a camera with her when she left for the *grutas*, that the whole purpose of their trip was to get pictures to prove to their professor that they'd been there and to illustrate their report. We searched the crime scene and all the way to the bottom of the canyon but couldn't find it.

Artemas leaned back. "That's about it, except for the possible witness."

"What witness?" interjected Raymundo.

"There's a boy, an *alacranero*, who gathers scorpions to be imbedded in souvenir glass ashtrays. He claims he saw a car ascending the road to the *grutas* late in the afternoon then returning sometime later. Problem is, the boy is retarded."

"So, what do you think?"

"I've questioned him at length. His description is vague. The one thing he seems certain of is that there was only one person in the vehicle. Interestingly, his description of the girls' car was accurate, and he remembered that it arrived just after the other car passed up the mountain. The other interesting point is that his parents collected him well before dark. So, if he actually saw the car return as he said he did, it probably did so *before* the girl was murdered. Incidentally, I checked with the girl's companion. She said she thought she heard a car at one point but saw nothing."

"Just what 'vague' description did he give of the first car?"

"That it was large and white, but no further details."

"And what do you conclude from all this, *Capitán* Salcido?" asked Raymundo, slouching in his chair.

Artemas chose to ignore the sarcasm. "The witness will be useless in court, but perhaps helpful to the investigation. What I conclude in general is that the first victim was killed by more than one person, probably as part of some sort of sacrificial rite. The American was murdered either by one or more of the same killers — or by someone else entirely."

"What makes you even consider someone else?" interrupted Raymundo. "Killings are few and far between in a place like this. To have two sets of killers with similar methods of killing, particularly such bizarre ones, and in such close proximity to each other...? Makes no sense to me."

Artemas understood what was happening. The men from the attorney general's office had one assignment: to arrest someone for Julie Connors' murder. Preferably they would select the person or persons who actually committed the crime. At the very least it had to be someone who could be plausibly linked to it and whose innocence would be difficult to prove, a critical factor in Mexico, whose Napoleonic legal code at the time stipulated that the accused is considered guilty until proven innocent. And because the other crime was so similar and so near in both time and location, even considering the possibility of different killers would only complicate their job. Their sole definition of justice in this case was removing the problem from the desk of the attorney general, and by extension from that of the president.

"It would have been nice," he said to Raymundo, "if there had been matching fingerprints on the marijuana butts or some other similarity. Actually they seemed to be made with different papers. Perhaps we could ask our new friends in the American FBI to test them for DNA?Raymundo scrutinized Artemas as he considered his response. He said, "My understanding is that DNA testing takes a long time. The case might be closed by the time we learn the results, at which point it might cause more problems than it solves. Of course, depending on circumstances, the testing could still be done at a later date, but I would not advocate it at this point."

Artemas realized he was being tested. "Now that you are familiar with the evidence and with some of my thoughts," he said, "let me relate my specific suspicions as to the person or persons who may have been responsible for at least one of the killings."

That got the group's attention and they leaned forward in their chairs.

"What I have to say is not the result of great police work. Nearly every citizen of Bustamante has undoubtedly come to the same conclusion. There is a family by the name of Zamarripa that has lived in Bustamante almost since it was founded. It now consists of a father and two sons. The father is a wealthy businessman who lives in Monterrey. The sons also lived there until their most recent scrape with the law, just a few months ago. Shortly after that, for some unknown reason they moved back here.

"The family has never been popular in the village, and the arrogant young Zamarripas have rekindled those feelings. One of the boys wears a bracelet exactly like this one." He tapped the envelope on his desk, "And both boys are said to be heavy users of marijuana. Also, although they have never been officially involved with drugs, I would not be surprised if they have some association with traffickers and possibly an involvement in a related satanic cult."

Raymundo actually beamed. Two other *federales* winked at each other. "Well," said Raymundo, "that does sound interesting. You said the brothers have not been 'officially' involved with drugs. What *have* they been 'officially' involved with?"

"Very little, thanks to their father, who I have been told has spent huge sums of money cleaning up their messes. However, as you know, policemen have long memories. My understanding is that their crimes range from drunk driving to assault, usually involving women — and rape — always involving women," Artemas added.

The PGR leader's first smile convinced Artemas that he was now being viewed in a more favorable light. "From what you said, I assume you haven't questioned them?" said Raymundo.

"No."

"Well, it seems to me that should be the first item on our agenda. Where do they live?"

"The family owns a hacienda a few kilometers south of town."

Raymundo looked at Artemas, his brow momentarily furrowed in thought. "Tell me more about the father."

"I don't know much more than I've already told you. His name is Zarco Zamarripa. He lives in the Garza Garcia district of Monterrey. He is the principal in a little known camarilla called Grupo Vampiro that's into just about everything, including banks, hotels, and a bunch of distributorships."

"Grupo Vampiro," muttered Valenzuela. "Sounds appropriate. I'd better call the attorney general before we do anything else, just to make sure."

"Just to make sure," repeated Artemas. Raymundo shot him a quick glance, but the young policeman's expression seemed guileless.

Raymundo went out to use the satellite phone in the Humvee and returned in less than ten minutes. "Alright he said, rubbing his hands together. Let's go talk to those rich kids."

"Sounds good to me," said Artemas. "I'll come with you. Just wait a moment while I make a call."

Raymundo clapped him on the back. "*Por cierto, amigo.* It'll be a tight squeeze, but we can do it. We'll be outside. *¡Vamonos!*"

Artemas admonished himself as he reached for his address book. Why hadn't he thought of this earlier? Turning to the C's he found what he needed: the number of Domingo Casteñeda. The man had been the one honest banker he'd dealt with in Mexico City. Because of that trait, he had been set up by powerful forces to take the blame in a money-laundering scheme. Artemas had cleared him, much to the consternation of his superiors, putting the banker in his debt.

The call went through immediately. After the obligatory pleasantries Artemas said, "Domingo, I need your help. I need to know everything you know about a camarilla called Grupo Vampiro and the man that runs it, Zarco Zamarripa."

The silence on the other end lasted so long that Artemas wondered if the connection had been broken. Finally, the man cleared his throat and said, "Can you tell me what this is about?"

"Sorry, not at this point except to say it's important and that your assistance will remain anonymous. Can you put the information in writing and e-mail it to me?" He gave the address.

After another silence, Domingo said, "I'll get you what I can." The reluctance in his voice was obvious to Artemas.

Caverns of Bustamante

The cave's cool climate was a welcome relief from soaring temperatures outside. Laffi marveled at the spectacle before her; she had never seen a cavern so grand. The low entry swept up into a cathedral-like gallery extending the length of a football field, then disappeared into a twilight zone of shadows and darkness.

Giant stalactites hung from the ceiling in a profusion of abstract shapes, as if formed by many artists with different visions working in the same medium. Below them a path with a rope handrail snaked down to the floor of an amphitheater thirty feet below. Light bulbs strung along the ceiling illuminated the cavern's interior. To Laffi it looked like a set from an Indiana Jones movie.

"Is this most of it?" Laffi asked Jason, who stood in front of her on the threshold above the descent. "Where are the bats?"

"This is all most people ever see. The majority of this cave hasn't been explored yet," replied Jason. "On my last trip we went down some side passages. Some of them open into grottos almost as impressive as this one. As for bats, there's no opening to the outside, and even if there were, there's too many visitors—at least there used to be. Bats like their privacy."

"I'll say this," said Laffi, blowing a wisp of hair out of her eye, "it's sure as hell a lot cooler in here, but there's something odd about the smell, something I'm not sure I like. Let's have a quick look around then get out of here."

"It's the humidity combined with very little fresh air," Jason explained.

He began the careful descent down the narrow twisting path. At the bottom he raised a hand in warning. "Careful," he said, pointing at the ground, which looked to her like slick, grayish-brown clay. "From here on it's damn slippery, so watch your step.

"You can see from the erosion making those ravines how much water gets in here, even with a light rain. A gully-washer would cause a flash flood that could put us in deep trouble. That thunderhead coming over the mountains is another reason not to waste any time."

Slipping and sliding on the slick surface they made a circuit of the gallery and were about to leave when something caught Jason's eye. "You can tell very few people have been here recently, except there." He pointed ahead with the beam of his flashlight. "See that? Compared to the rest of the place it looks like a herd of elephants came through."

In front of Laffi the cavern floor was scuffed and cut in numerous places, clearly by something other than water. The markings formed a crude pathway that led toward a narrow opening in the nearby wall, but there was not enough light to see properly.

The beams of their flashlights converged on the area.

"We explored in there on my last visit," said Jason. "That narrow passageway leads into a very small cavern and from there into another one. I think we've got just enough time to see where those tracks, or whatever they are, go."

He moved slowly into the narrow passageway, his light skimming the floor and walls in front of him. After twenty feet he stopped with a jerk and urgently beckoned Laffi to join him. When she reached his side she saw his light playing over a small cavern that was about twenty by thirty feet. Along one wall ran a bench-like shelf about three feet off the ground. At both ends, about six feet apart, a pair of metal spikes had been driven into the shelf. Their flashlights illuminated dark splotches that trailed down the sides and onto the cavern floor.

"Oh shit," said Laffi, catching her breath, "could that be what I think it is?"

"Looks like blood to me." He sniffed the air. "Smells like blood too."

"*Hijos de la puta,*" whispered Armando to his brother. They had quietly entered the cave not long after Jason and Laffi and hidden themselves where they could watch and listen. After the couple entered the passageway, the brothers crept silently down the pathway and crouched behind a huge formation not twenty yards from where Jason and Laffi had disappeared. Although neither of the boys understood much English, there was no mistaking what the pair had found.

"Let's kill them and seal the entrance, put a stop to all this bullshit right now," said Armando.

"*De acuerdo, hermano.* For once we are in total agreement. You've got your pistol?"

"Right, let's go." Armando carefully placed a sack of explosives on the cave's floor, pulled a revolver from his belt and began edging his way toward the small passage.

"See that," Jason said, motioning with the beam of his light toward the wall above the shelf. A long piece of metal wrapped with a burnt rag had been inserted into a chiseled-out hole. The wall and ceiling were stained with black soot. "It looks like a torch," he said.

Shifting his flashlight to his left hand, Jason reached for the makeshift torch, and thinking it might be evidence, pulled a handkerchief from his pocket to grab the iron pipe. He turned it over in his hand, but couldn't find any identifying markings. Jason aimed his beam back at the sandstone shelf. Laffi was staring at the dark bloodstains, imagining the horrors that caused them, hearing the cries. Jason looked at her curiously and broke the silence. "I think this is now a police matter."

"You're right, so let's get the hell out of here!" Laffi couldn't wait to be back in fresh air and sunlight, away from the dread of this evil place that conjured the devil himself. *Could those villager's crazy stories be true?* she wondered. She aimed her flashlight down the passageway they had entered and began to lead the way.

Laffi jumped back and let out a shriek when she caught sight of two approaching men. There was an explosion of gunfire, and Laffi screamed in pain after a second blast echoed through the cavern. Jason flung his arm around Laffi's shoulder and pulled her to the side. A third shot shattered the air, raking his cheek. He managed to flick off his flashlight with his thumb and pull Laffi to the ground.

Sensing movement nearby, Jason rose from his crouch, and with all his strength flung the iron pipe he'd been holding. A yelp of pain was followed by a wild shot. Quickly, Jason whispered to Laffi, "Are you O.K.? Can you move?"

"I think so; it's my arm, but...."

" Hold onto me with your good arm and follow as best you can. Keep low." His urgency sounded harsh in her ear.

Laffi hooked the fingers of her right hand around the back of his belt. "O.K., let's go."

Moving as fast as possible and with just a spurt from his flashlight, Jason made for a small opening in the rocks that he remembered from his previous visits. They almost made it when a beam of light caught them from behind. Jason flung himself to the ground, reaching behind with his right hand to drag Laffi with him. She cried out in pain as another gunshot exploded. The bullet richocheted above their heads. Immediately Jason was up, pulling Laffi with him, and they quickly entered the narrow passageway, following short bursts from Jason's flashlight.

"Down this way," he whispered. "That pipe may have slowed up whoever it is, or possibly they're reloading. In any case, we better hurry."

Moving like a clumsy couple in a three-legged race, they emerged from the passage into a larger cavern. Jason aimed for what appeared to be a crevasse, about four feet wide, and ten feet long. When they reached it he looked into the opening.

"Just as I remembered," he whispered. "A couple of the kids got stuck down there and we had to haul them up. There's a little tunnel at the bottom that goes for about nine feet where it ends at a water hole. It's about ten feet to the bottom, so give me your good arm and lower yourself down as far as you can. I'll ease you the rest of the way. At most you'll have only a two foot drop."

"O.K.," said Laffi, grimacing with pain in the darkness. "Even if you don't know what you're doing that's better than anything I can think of," she whispered as she gave Jason her right hand then gingerly lowered herself over the edge. She dropped onto the squishy surface. Jason slid the flashlight into his belt and quickly lowered himself after her.

"That's the opening that goes back about ten feet and drops into the pool," whispered Jason. "When I was here it was too full of water to tell much about it. Anyway it's as good a hiding place as we're likely to find, so let's go. You don't have claustrophobia do you?" he asked.

"If I did this would be the cure, wouldn't it," she murmured.

Jason led the way on hands and knees into the tunnel, sliding along the damp clay. He heard Laffi scrambling behind him and marveled at her composure. After about eight feet, the tunnel widened and Jason's flashlight revealed the small, crystal clear pool he remembered. He noticed the water level was much lower than on his previous trip.

"Let's take a quick look at that arm," he said. "Let me know when to turn on the light."

Laffi said, "O.K.," and Jason focused the beam on her upper arm. Her shirtsleeve was torn and soaked in blood, but Jason was pretty sure it was only a flesh wound. The bullet seemed to have skimmed her arm and missed the bone.

"Your face!" exclaimed Laffi. "You were hit, too."

Jason gingerly touched his cheek and saw fresh blood on his fingers. He rotated his jaw and felt around his face, and satisfied himself that his wound was superficial. Laffi's injury, however, was far more serious; she was losing a lot of blood.

He pulled a knife from his pocket, sliced off a piece of Laffi's shirtsleeve, and carefully lowered himself down near the pool of water to wet the cloth. Propping up the flashlight, he quickly cleaned her wound then cut off a chunk of his own shirt, made a crude bandage, and wrapped it around her arm. "The best I can do for the moment," he said, flicking off the light.

"Beats most HMOs," she quipped. Jason once again applauded her nerve.

"O.K.," he said, whispering through the blackness and patting the holstered pellet gun. "Here's the bad news. This is the best hiding place we could find, but if whoever is here looks long enough they'll eventually find us. It seems to me that it would be better to fight than to be killed like rats trapped in a hole. I'm going to see if I can't do something about that."

Laffi shivered, "Just be careful." He reached out in the darkness and gave her face an affectionate tap then crawled back down the tunnel, hoping she could handle absolute darkness and a confined space.

"Only you would forget to bring extra ammunition," said Ignacio.

"Well where's *your* gun and *your* bullets?" replied Armando. "Anyway, who would have thought we'd even need a gun, and if we did, that six bullets wouldn't be enough? Anyway, I've got one shot left, and I intend to make it count."

The brothers, both carrying flashlights, crossed the small cavern past the bloodstained bench. Ignacio smirked at the memory of what they'd done. Then they carefully entered the small passageway they'd seen Jason and Laffi leave through.

Jason emerged beneath an overhanging ledge and silently felt his way to where he knew some students had despoiled the cave by cutting foot and handholds into the wall. Afraid to use his flashlight, he moved along by feel until he found the small slots and slowly scaled the wall. He was able to pull himself up and peek over the ledge.

The cavern was totally dark, but in the distance he saw a glimmer of light. He found a foothold high enough to stand in a reasonably stable position and carefully pulled his pellet gun from its holster and rested it on the ledge. Though it wasn't a real gun, it was capable of inflicting serious damage.

The light became brighter. He heared whispered voices—how many he couldn't tell—and cursed his poor hearing. Beams of light streaked across the ceiling, and Jason was able to make out two indistinct figures standing hesitantly at the entrance to the small cavern. Deciding this was his best and only chance, he aimed the pellet gun and squeezed the trigger. The spat of air from the pellet exiting the barrel was immediately followed by a cry and the thunder of a large caliber revolver. Jason screamed.

ZAMARRIPA ESTATE

The late afternoon sun accentuated the sharp edge of the mountain range as the PGR Humvee left Bustamante. Artemas had squeezed into the back, nearly on top of one of the *federales*, and several automatic weapons poked his side. Raymundo rode shotgun. Wedged in one corner were two oversized black briefcases. Artemas had learned about these infamous devices in Mexico City. Made by a secretive U.S. company, they were filled with wires, coils, alligator clips, and electrodes and were laughingly called "lie" detectors. "After a few jolts of this in the right place," his captain had said with a sneer, "any lie is easily detected."

A few kilometers down the two-lane highway to Monterrey, Artemas directed the driver to turn right onto a narrow blacktopped road. They passed through a grand entry, spanned by a stone arch carved with the name *Hacienda Zamarripa*. He was surprised to find the gate wide open. The road wound gradually through desert landscape, and after cresting a rise, the hacienda came into view, nestled at the base of the mountain. The white plaster walls of the sprawling compound and its extensive grounds were cast in shadow by a menacing cloudbank hanging over the mountain.

The Humvee pulled up to a gate set within a low wall surrounding the front patio. A flagstone pathway led to a massive oak door. The *federales* got out and immediately checked their automatic rifles. Raymundo pointed out positions and rushed toward the front door.

"Federal judicial police!" Raymundo shouted. He saw a window curtain move slightly and shouted again, "Come out with your hands up or we'll come in, shooting!"

The door opened slowly and a thin man, bent with age but sporting a full head of gray hair appeared. His trembling hands were stretched high above his head. His voice quavered, "Please do not shoot, *señor*. We will do as you say."

"*¡Andale, ven aca!*" ordered Raymundo, motioning impatiently with his weapon for the man to come out.

He did so, obviously terrified, as was the plump old woman who followed behind. When they were well clear of the house, Raymundo demanded, "Who are you?"

"I am Ramón and this is Celia. We have worked for the Zamarripas for many years."

"Where are the Zamarripa brothers?"

"Ignacio and Armando left a few hours ago and did not say where they were going. Please don't hurt us. We've done nothing wrong."

"Nothing will happen if you cooperate."

"*Sí, señor,*" replied the old man, a bit less stressed. The woman stood close, her gaze averted. As if to avoid some evil spirit, thought Artemas.

Raymundo said, "We intend to search this property. Where should we begin?"

"*Señor,* last night the boys put many little packages in the old hay barn, over there." Ramón pointed toward the back of the property. "We no longer have horses here," he added, feeling compelled to offer an explanation.

"*Muy bien,*" said Raymundo, placing his weapon against the wall and rubbing his hands together. "Take us to this hay barn." Then he paused and said to his driver, "Hide the truck somewhere. We don't want the brothers to see it."

"*Señor,*" interjected Artemas, sensing an opportunity. "There's no telling when they'll be back or how long this will take. Maybe I should return to Bustamante. The FBI expects a briefing." Before Raymundo could object, he added, "I don't think we want them to claim we're being uncooperative."

"*Tienes razón,*" agreed Raymundo. "Tell them we're working on a lead that may result in an arrest." Then to the driver: "Take him back and return as quickly as possible."

On the way to the Humvee, Artemas turned around and called out to Raymundo, pointing to the darkening sky. "Looks like we're in for some rain. I think I'll have a quick look around the outside before it gets too wet."

Raymundo again agreed, and Artemas walked the perimeter of the hacienda. He stooped once, as if tying his shoelaces and within five minutes was back at the Humvee, signaling that he was ready to go.

Caverns of Bustamante

"Hijo de la chingada! I'm hit," shrieked Armando. "He must have a silencer." He felt his left shoulder with the heel of his hand. "It sounded like I got him, but we better get the fuck out of here, just in case." He saw Ignacio already scrambling back down the passageway in front of him.

When they reached an antechamber near the bloodstained bench, Armando pulled off his shirt. "Thank God, he must only have a .22. I'm glad those assholes are going to starve in the dark. It's a good thing I already wired the dynamite," he added, reaching for the sack of explosives.

"*Momentito,*" said Ignacio, reasserting his position as brains of the outfit. "Let's think this through." He kicked the iron pipe that had once been a torch. "You should have gotten rid of this last night," he said venomously. "Now," he raised his hand forestalling Armando's retort. "It sounded like you hit him and the girl, but we don't know for sure, or how seriously. One of them may be alive, possibly with the gun. It doesn't make sense to risk going back, especially since we don't have any more bullets and we're going to blow the place up anyway.

"*Sí, hermano*. It's the only way. Let's do it."

"Of course," said Ignacio, patting his brother's arm. "It's a pity though. If you'd brought enough ammunition we might have had some fun with the woman first."

ZAMARRIPA ESTATE

Raymundo slit open a plastic bag. He wet his finger on his tongue, touched the powder in the bag and tasted it. Talking more to himself than his men he said, "So far so good."

While searching the barn, the predicted thunderstorm had unleashed a torrential downpour, so they were now gathered in the hacienda's formal dining room. Below the vaulted wood ceiling flame-shaped lightbulbs flickered weakly in the crystal chandelier, and Raymundo anticipated that the lightening crashing down from the mountain might knock out the power.

He didn't care much for art, or more precisely, it wasn't something he noticed, but his eyes rested on several oil paintings hanging on the wall. One in particular caught his attention: a man in top hat and tails stepping down from a horse-drawn carriage on a darkly lit street. A dozen women's faces were crowded in the coach window behind him, eyes wide open yet dead. Their heads, at least to Raymundo, looked to be severed from their bodies. Next to the paintings, art niches were carved into the thick adobe walls. They displayed Pre-Columbian clay objects — snarling jaguars, serpent-headed devils and a priest ripping the heart from a sacrificial victim. Why would rich people want this this freakin' shit? Raymundo wondered.

Evidence collected by his squad was strewn over the massive oak table that sat twenty. Raymundo mentally inventoried the items: two sharp knives chiseled from obsidian; a leather loin cloth stained with what looked like blood; a nine-millimeter, semiautomatic pistol; two boxes of ammunition, one for the nine-millimeter, and the other in .38 caliber; a kilo bag of marijuana; a package of cigarette paper; and twenty kilos of cocaine. Also: a pornographic videotape, *The Younger the Better*, featuring a five-year old girl; two silver bracelets identical to the one Artemas found at the murder site; and a film camera of the same make the murdered girl brought to the cave.

Caverns of Bustamante

Laffi sat crouched in the tunnel, straining all her mental and physical resources, hoping to figure out what happened. She heard nothing, felt nothing, smelled nothing, and her eyes were useless in the absolute darkness.

She breathed shallowly through her mouth and, in spite of the cave's coolness, sweat trickled down her forehead and between her breasts. She had first heard a muffled cry of pain after Jason launched some sort of surprise attack. Then came the distinct blast from a gun and Jason's scream. After that, nothing.

Hunkered down in her hiding place she had never felt more helpless and alone, and she began to panic. What happened to Jason? Did the scream mean he was wounded? Surely if he were still alive he would be calling for help or trying to return to her. But if he were dead or wounded why didn't she hear the attackers? Wouldn't they be moving in to finish Jason off and then look for her?

Jason had screamed as soon as he heard the gunshot, which as far as he could tell came nowhere near him. It had been an involuntary impulse, perhaps an instinctual reflex. Whatever the case, he hoped his assailant's guard was down. Jason was pretty sure this was their sixth, and final shot, though that only applied to standard revolvers. Semiautomatic pistols could hold up to seventeen rounds.

He lowered himself into the gully, careful to keep his head below the cavern floor to avoid being detected. He reloaded his pellet gun and listened intently for footsteps. He couldn't be certain how much time had passed and could only imagine Laffi's anguish after hearing his scream. Silently counting out three minutes, and hearing nothing, he decided to return to her.

In pitch darkness he retraced his way to the tunnel where he had left Laffi, pausing every few seconds to listen. When he reached the tunnel entrance he whispered her name.

"Jason, are you alright?" she whispered back.

"Stay still," he said, "I'll be right there." He chanced a quick flash of light and saw Laffi hunched miserably at the end of the passageway. She was on her knees near the small pool, damp hair plastered to her face.

"What happened? I was afraid that..." she whispered in a husky voice as he crawled closer.

Without replying Jason hugged her. She held her cheek against his then gently pushed him away.

"I'm sorry I gave you a scare," he said. "There were two of them, and I'm pretty sure I hit one with the pellet gun. I screamed after the return shot. Hoped they would think I was down and take off. It may have worked, but I better go check. Anything could be happening, including them getting more ammunition, in which case we'll have to come up with plan B."

"I thought this *was* plan B," she replied.

Jason reached out and touched her cheek. "I'm going to try and find out what's happening. Climb up after me as best you can, but stay where you can duck back down. It'll be difficult with your bad arm, but there are decent hand and footholds." Still on his hands and knees, he began crawling back toward the tunnel entrance.

Pausing again to listen, Jason stood upright and tiptoed his way to the other end of the gully. After Laffi caught up with him he guided her to the hand and footholds in the wall and whispered, "Follow me to just near the top. I'll be back as soon as I can."

He moved silently toward the passageway leading back to the main cavern. Suddenly, Jason was hit by a violent explosion and thrown to the ground. A searing wave of heat passed over him, and chunks of the ceiling and wall pummelled his body. Instinctively he buried his face in the damp clay floor. He thought the entire cavern was collapsing, but after a few seconds the shaking stopped. Now, just dead silence and the sharp smell of explosives.

Still lying on the floor, Jason aimed his flashlight—which survived the blast—at their exit passageway. Through dirt particles sifting in the air he saw a mound of rubble. Immense stalagmites, smashed to pieces, were among the debris.

"Jason, Jason!" Laffi cried out.

He directed his flashlight toward the sound of her voice. "I'm O.K. You might as well come on up," he called, then added bitterly, "I don't think the sons of bitches are coming back."

She struggled over the ledge, trying to get a grip on the slick clay. She finally scrambled to her feet and reached Jason when another explosion erupted, this one muffled like distant thunder but still powerful enough to shake their shrinking world. Laffi clutched Jason's arm with her good hand. He pulled her close then released her once the tremors subsided.

Laffi scanned her flashlight around the cavern, saw the pile of rubble near the cavern entrance. Jason said, "They've sealed us in."

His tone was matter-of-fact, maybe a little somber but Laffi noticed he was not alarmed. "The first explosion," he added, "must have collapsed that little cavern where we found blood—and with it the passageway between the main cavern and this one. They've obliterated all the evidence. My guess is that last explosion sealed the main entrance to the cave.

Just then they felt another blast, though farther away and less severe. "The bastards certainly are thorough," said Jason. "I guess we're lucky the whole cave didn't come down."

"Thanks for counting our blessings. Any suggestions?"

"The first thing we need to do is conserve our batteries. Let's keep the lights off unless we absolutely need them." Switching his off, he continued, "Eduardo knows we're here and I imagine someone in the village heard the explosions. Surely they'll put two and two together. The search should begin soon, but who knows how long it'll take them to clear the cave. We've got water back where we hid, but no food, and your wound could easily get infected. It could be close."

"Dare I ask about the possibility of another way out?"

Jason thought for a moment. "We explored this cavern pretty thoroughly on the last trip and couldn't find any way out except the way you and I came in. But there is one possibility..."

"Wait. What's that?" interrupted Laffi, grabbing his arm in the darkness.

They were silent for a few seconds, straining their ears. "There it is, did you hear it?" she whispered.

"I'm afraid not, my hearing's not so good."

"It sounds like trickling water."

Jason put his hand against the wall and felt water. "The thunderstorm..."

Bustamante

The approaching thunderstorm darkened the late afternoon sky and promised to be a gully-washer. The PGR Humvee rumbled past the plaza, close enough for Artemas to see the village *presidente*, or mayor, speaking earnestly with an overweight man in an expensive suit outside the *Municipo*. Undoubtedly negotiating election year goodies with one of the national parties.

He was glad to leave Hacienda Zamarripa; he had no stomach for observing harsh techniques applied to the brothers. He hoped that Raymundo had clear instructions about limiting their "lie detection" to a few jolts and jabs. But he wasn't so sure. "Dead men tell no tales," was still a tenet of Mexican law enforcement.

Artemas spotted the FBI agents sitting on a bench below a large pecan tree. They had loosened their ties, finally succumbing to the heat and humidity of the looming storm. Several journalists circled their bench, eager for any scrap of news. When the Humvee stopped in front of the police station, the agents jumped up and cinched their ties.

Artemas waved cheerfully, inviting the small group to join him. They hustled to his side while the Humvee roared up the street on its way back to Hacienda Zamarripa. He said. "I apologize for keeping you waiting a little longer. By tomorrow I believe we will be in a position to make an important announcement regarding the case. I'm sorry, but that's all I can say at the moment. He turned to the FBI agents and lowered his voice. "Please join me inside?"

A deep booming sound came from the direction of the mountain—now covered by a massive thunderhead—drowning out frantic questions from the reporters. Big drops of rain splattered onto the sidewalk.

"I'm sorry but I'm not at liberty to say more at this time," said Artemas. Then he opened the door for the agents as the journalists sprinted for shelter. "It looks like we're just in time."

Artemas seated himself behind the desk and rested his chin in his hands. "I'm sorry for what must have seemed like a lack of cooperation, but I'm now able to brief you. Earlier a lead was developed that my colleagues wanted to check out before we met. They are now at a ranch just outside of town, possibly to make an arrest."

Artemas filled them in on the events of the last two hours. As he finished, lightening flashed and thunder shook the building.

Lester Grunwald was unfazed by the storm. "Are you pretty sure you've got the right people?" he asked. "Finding the bracelet without prints does seem a bit much. Sounds like someone could have planted it."

Artemas locked eyes with each agent, in turn. "Nevertheless," he said, "the evidence seems overwhelming. Certainly, regarding the first murder."

"But you're not sure of the second, the senator's daughter, the reason we're here?" said Grunwald.

"I didn't say that. I don't know what was found at the hacienda. But I want you to see the evidence when they return. I would also appreciate the opportunity to speak with you before you leave the village."

He continued before either could reply. "You must be tired, hot, and hungry, and I have a few things to do. If you can make it through the rain to the hotel you might want to refresh yourselves. I'll get word to you as soon as anything happens." He waved toward the counter. "You'll find an umbrella under there. You're welcome to borrow it."

They thanked him, shook hands and headed for the door, grabbing the umbrella on their way out.

Artemas quickly exited the police station through the back door. Although his house was only two blocks and he ran the whole way, he was still soaked to the skin before pushing through the rusty iron-gate to the front yard.

The little house lay nestled under a canopy of pecan trees. Like many others in the village it was constructed of a combination of stone and adobe. Under Artemas's occupancy the front yard had returned to its natural landscaping. Even with mostly dry weather, vines and grass grew unkempt everywhere. A narrow veranda with a tile roof supported by cedar posts ran across the front of the small building. The original stucco on the exterior walls had long since deteriorated, leaving a patchwork of stone and baked mud. When Artemas moved in he had dug out an old bullet near the doorway, from the Revolution he guessed. The walls were a heat-mitigating meter thick, which more than made up for its cosmetic blemishes.

Inside the front door, which Artemas never locked, he stripped off his khaki uniform and dropped the shirt and pants on the worn tile floor. He headed into the bedroom, changed into another uniform, and looked out the front window. The storm was abating, though rain still lashed down and thunder still rumbled in the distance.

He reflected on the irony that he had been banished to Bustamante just in time to be involved in a crime that could be as important as any in recent Mexican history, one that could affect relations with Mexico's powerful neighbor. He realized that his years in school in the United States, a place where success was often directly related to one's aggressiveness, had only accentuated the part of him that came from his Spanish father. He knew he had tried to do too much before both he and Mexico were ready. In accepting the transfer to Bustamante he had consciously reverted to the patient, fatalistic approach of his mother's people. Could this be a sign that for once his judgment had been correct?

He went into the spare bedroom he used as an office, where he kept research material he'd collected on Bustamante. Like the rest of the house, it was furnished with odd bits of used furniture. In a roughly finished bookcase he found what he was looking for, an old hardback volume he had borrowed from Gerardo Manzano, the village schoolmaster. Entitled *Recuerdos de un pueblo antiguo*, or "Memories of an Ancient Village," it was written by Humberto Alcazar, the villager who had given the girls directions to the caverns.

Alcazar's family had been in Bustamante nearly from the village's inception. Even though the man spent most of his time in town, gave generously to various charitable endeavors, and lived in one of the stately old homes along the north side of the plaza, Artemas had never met him. And only once or twice had he caught sight of the imposingly large man. Although he was not current on literary matters, his impression was that Alcazar was a writer of minor fame, one of those Mexican intellectuals with enough money to live and publish their own work. They often flitted, like nectar-seeking butterflies, through the prestigious salons and cafés of Mexico.

What piqued Artemas's interest was a passage he remembered from the afternoon he skimmed the book. The volume itself was a collection of stories about Bustamante and other small villages in Mexico, presumably where the author had also lived or spent time.

At last he found the passage. "Because of their vile use and treatment of the people, the worst of it hidden by the dark of night, and virtually all of it unnecessary to maintaining their place in the world, the Zamarripas are certainly among the worst vampires in all of Mexico."

Artemas marked the page and set the book aside. Next he withdrew a large binder from the bookcase. It overflowed with newspaper clippings. Since Bustamante had no newspaper, daily or otherwise, he had spent a long day searching the files of Monterrey papers, making copies of items relating to Bustamante. And there it was, just as he remembered, an article about an exhibition of regional artists at the Marco, Monterrey's Museum of Modern Art. It was dated September 2003, three years before. The accompanying color photograph was a painting by an artist named Ricardo Chavana, "resident of the village of Bustamante." Artemas had seen the tall, elegant man, reportedly a constant companion of Humberto Alcazar, riding a motorbike around town, but had never been introduced.

The painting depicted a man in the clothing of a *hacendado*, a wealthy hacienda owner, sitting calmly at a table, sipping a dark red liquid from an ornate crystal glass. The table was set upon an immense pile of gruesomely mutilated, brown-faced bodies in colorful Indian costumes. The painting was titled, *Hacienda Zamarripa.*

Artemas checked the wall clock. He'd already been gone forty-five minutes so he needed to wrap this up. He removed the clipping from the binder and placed it on top of the book by Humberto Alcazar.

He was about to leave for the station when he thought of the earlier call he'd made to the Mexico City banker. He connected to his e-mail and found one message. Scanning the first few lines, he saw the information he'd hoped for. He whistled softly at the name of the sender, *wieghorst.com.* He was certain it was a clandestine router, possibly somewhere in the Middle East, a setup used by everyone from pornographers to drug dealers — and now obviously bankers — to hide the sender's identity. "Interesting," he said out loud. He printed the message, which ran three pages. Because time was short he placed it in a file folder behind some books.

By this time the rain had ended, but dark clouds still blanketed the mountain, and he quickened his pace as he considered the situation. His first decision was to cooperate with Raymundo, while still maintaining his options. As he had inferred to the FBI agents, while he believed the evidence pointed toward the Zamarripa brothers committing the first murder in some sort of satanic ritual, he had not made up his mind about their guilt in the American girl's death. He would be better able to judge when he reviewed the evidence the *federales* brought back with them — if they came back. And if the brothers were still in one piece. Nevertheless, he knew Raymundo was right about one thing: it was difficult to believe that the two murders were not connected.

Caverns of Bustamante

"How bad do you think it'll get? asked Laffi. "The water's coming in fast."

Jason traced the beam of his flashlight over a vast expanse of smooth, unblemished clay. "You can see how this cave was carved by water. Just look at these walls. It could be a couple days before they find us, so we better prepare for the worst."

They made a circuit of the cavern, assessing their options, and stopped at a formation that rose, stair-step fashion, eight feet high. "We could climb to the top of that ridge. That should be plenty of elevation to keep us safe, even if there's a flash-flood," said Jason.

A drop of water splashed on his forehead. Trickles from the ceiling became rivulets working their way down streambeds carved into the floor of the cave over thousands of years. The water flowed toward the small gully where they had hidden.

"Wait a minute!" exclaimed Laffi. "Aren't we assuming someone in the village heard the explosions and would start looking for us?" Not waiting for an answer, she continued. "All this water is from the thunderstorm we saw forming on our way in. They probably thought the dynamite blasts were thunder… if they heard them at all."

Jason nodded, his expression grim in the ghostly light. He motioned toward the gully, "We've got to get back down there. It could be our only chance. Quick, we don't have much time. I'll explain later."

Jason ran to the gully and disappeared over the edge. Laffi followed several steps behind and found him near the small pool at the end of the tunnel. With his flashlight wedged into a crevice she could see Jason shrugging out of his shirt, his equipment belt already lying on the ground. "What are you doing?" Laffi demanded.

"Sorry, but we've got to hurry. On my last visit one of the other professors, an experienced diver, checked out this water hole. She said she was almost sure it wasn't a dead end, that it looked like there was a passageway a few feet below the surface, heading off at an angle. Without diving equipment it was impossible to tell how far and the only probe we had was a shovel. Now that the water level's three feet lower, I want to see if there's even the slightest possibility it could lead to a way out of the cave — before the damn thing fills up again."

"You better get going," urged Laffi, spotting an eddy of water rolling toward them.

Jason lowered himself into the pool and kicked his feet into the water. "Here goes." He landed upright with his head several feet below the cave floor.

"Give me the flashlight," he said, reaching his hand up toward Laffi. She leaned over the lip of the pool to pass it down. He focused the beam on what appeared to be the top of a passageway, about eight inches above water level.

"Quick, hand me the butane lighter. It's in the pocket on my belt, on the other side of the pistol." Jason's voice echoed in the confined space.

Laffi found the lighter and placed it in Jason's hand. With a flick of his thumb the flame burst into a bright orange swirl, then the flame bent toward the passageway. He looked up at Laffi, whose face danced in the shadows above him. "There's enough air coming through this passageway to create a strong draft," he said. "So there might be enough airspace to breathe."

"But not for long," replied Laffi, pointing to a stream of rainwater trickling into the hole.

"Look," he said, his voice again urgent. "We don't have the luxury of discussing this properly. Our options are, one: go back up to the cavern, climb onto that ledge and hope it keeps us above water and we'll be found before we die. Someone will eventually find my SUV and see the blocked cave entrance and put two and two together. But will they get to us in time? I'd say the odds are fifty-fifty. Two: I can take an exploratory run down this tunnel. If I'm careful, I should be O.K. I just might be able to find a way out. The odds are bad, but you won't be in any more danger than before."

"You're going to try it," challenged Laffi.

"Right now, this hole will fill up with water again, and we won't get another chance. What I'm going to do is take a breath, go only until I'm sure I have enough air left to get back. It either works or it doesn't.

"While I'm gone, you need to go back into the gully and detour the rainwater with some type of dam, use those chunks that fell in the blast. It won't last long because this is probably the lowest point, but we need any help we can get. Oh, and quick, there's a penlight in the same pocket you found the lighter. I'll try to keep it dry enough to work."

Confused and in pain, Laffi had no idea if Jason's plan made sense, but it sounded better than anything she could devise. Jason exchanged his flashlight for the small penlight and held it in the airspace at the top of the tunnel.

He looked up at Laffi as she knelt above him, and gently said, "The best thing you can do is try and divert the water." He motioned to where it had begun to cascade into the hole. She held his eyes for a moment. "Just be careful," she said.

Jason's gaze followed her for a moment then he faced the watery passage. He took several deep breaths, held the last, submerged and began moving into the tunnel. He led with his left hand, holding the tiny flashlight above water.

Bustamante

A crowd of journalists had camped outside the police station waiting for Artemas's return. He politely declined providing further information other than to promise an announcement first thing in the morning. Once inside he peered out the window into the darkening night and watched several reporters making their way to a small park down the street. They hunched unhappily beneath umbrellas like vultures waiting out a storm.

He went back to his desk to wait for Raymundo and news of what happened at Hacienda Zamarripa. With a sigh he attacked the paperwork built up the past few days.

He finished what he could and propped his feet on the desk. At first he thought of Laffi, about how good she had looked. Then, as he often did when he was anxious, he let his mind drift back to Sonora, to the hacienda where he was born, where his mother had died and where his father still lived. His thoughts wandered to the village, to the priest who had raised him, and to the *ranchería* where his mother's family lived, and where he had spent so many summers learning to track and hunt in the old Yaqui ways.

He raised his head upon hearing Agents Grunwald and Robinson step inside his office. A quick glance at his watch indicated it was just after 8:30 P.M.

"Sorry to disturb you," said Grunwald, matter-of-factly. "We thought we'd check in to see if you'd heard anything."

"Not a word. I have no idea how long it will be. It really depends on when the suspects return to their hacienda and if they resist. In the meantime, you're welcome to pull up a couple of chairs. I'll put on some coffee."

He meticulously ground glossy black beans stored on a side table and poured bottled water into the French press, then extracted a medium-sized cigar from his desk and waved it at the agents. "Anybody object, or care to join me? They're Cuban," he added, knowing full well that any American smoking one would technically be breaking U.S. law.

The men glanced at each other, and Grunwald responded, "Thanks, but no thanks." While Artemas contentedly puffed on his cigar, the agent continued. "Could I ask you some questions about the process?"

"Certainly."

"We understand you operate under the Napoleonic code, which means that the accused is guilty until proven innocent. But what rights does the accused have? Can they be questioned without an attorney being present? Do you expect the Zamarripa brothers will be questioned before being brought here?"

Artemas blew out a stream of smoke, looked at the ceiling and rolled his eyes in mock pain. "Under the assumption that what I say will not be repeated—to anybody," he looked each man in the eye until they nodded, "the answer to your first two questions is that it usually depends on how much money the accused has. But in this case the need to find the guilty party transcends the usual. So, to answer your real question, I would be surprised if the suspects have not been interrogated and probably confessed before we see them. If we see them."

"What does that mean?" said Grunwald.

"Well," said Artemas, "we have no guarantee that the suspects will be brought back here. Circumstances—and don't ask me what they might be—may dictate they be taken directly to Monterrey or even Mexico City. Of course there are other hypothetical reasons we might not be graced with the Zamarripa brothers' presence."

The agents swiveled in their chairs to the sound of the door opening behind them.

It was Eduardo, the innkeeper. The man looked tired and nervous.

"Please forgive me gentlemen. Artemas, may I speak with you a minute?"

"Certainly, Eduardo." Artemas got to his feet to approach the front counter where Eduardo stood. "The coffee's ready. Won't you join us?"

"Thank you, but I better get back to the hotel."

"What can I do for you, my friend?"

"It may be nothing, *señor*, but early this afternoon one of the American journalists, one I believe you know, *Señorita* Rendón, left with the American professor to visit the scene of the crime and the *grutas*."

"Yes, I spoke with them," said Artemas, suddenly becoming uneasy. "What's the problem?"

"It's probably nothing, but I thought you should know they haven't returned, and there've been a lot of calls for her from her office. Of course the professor is not staying at the hotel, and she may be with him. I thought you ought to know."

"Thank you Eduardo. You were right to come. Under the circumstances, we should wait at least until tomorrow morning before doing anything. Would you let me know what happens?"

"*Sí, señor*." They shook hands and Eduardo left.

Apparently not having understood the conversation, the FBI agents looked questioningly at Artemas. "Nothing serious," he said, as he set down three coffee cups with matching saucers.

The black agent looked at him suspiciously, so he added, "Just a temporarily missing journalist." Artemas desperately hoped he was right, in spite of his intuition which told him the opposite.

Caverns of Bustamante

Jason moved awkwardly through the subterranean channel, submerged but with both hands above water. His left one trying to keep the penlight dry, his right pushing against the top of the smooth passageway, working against his body's natural buoyancy so he could shuffle along underwater, like a weightless astronaut. After a few steps he cautiously rose in the water until he could take a tentative breath. When that worked he breathed more deeply. He repeated that cycle—submerging, propelling forward, breathing—heading farther into the unknown. After about ten feet his air space was nearly gone and he began to shuffle backwards. He immediately realized how easy it would be to get disoriented, go the wrong direction. The tunnel could have widened, he could be heading sideways where there might be no air at all instead of returning the way he'd come.

He was near the end of his lung capacity, and getting dizzy from the carbon dioxide he needed to expel. He knew he should take a small breath, but instead Jason gasped violently, half expecting to drown. He was elated to find air and concentrated on taking several short breaths.

When his breathing returned to normal, Jason knew he had to make a choice. He could return immediately and help Laffi to the safety of the rock ledge, where they would stay until they were rescued or died. Or he could give his current effort one more try. That meant going much farther down the passageway and hope that the tunnel opened to more air. Knowing how slim their chances of being rescued, he decided to take the gamble.

He forced himself to relax, breathed deeply several times and took one more long breath before submerging. This time he made great progress, traveling several feet beyond where he'd been before. Then he noticed the water level rising, pressing him up against the passageway. Jason took two more steps, prepared to make a desperate return if he could not find air soon.

His head struck something hard and he flailed his arms and legs and and plunged himself forward in a panic, thinking this must be the end. He dropped his penlight and was cast into darkness. Then, as his body rushed upward, forms around him began to take shape, like a Polaroid photo developing. There was light, and he saw that he was in a small pool much like the one he'd left. Through a lens of water above he could see the shape of a cavern roof. He burst from the water and caught his breath.

After he recovered, Jason grasped the edge of the pool to look around. He was in a huge cavern and light was filtering in through fissures high up the walls. Rainwater was seeping inside, but from what he could tell, draining toward another part of the cave. When he spotted a large opening near the cavern floor, Jason yelled out "Yes!" This could be their way out.

Jason quickly considered what he should do next. It was still raining, which meant the water level in the tunnel would continue to rise. He guessed he had traveled about twenty-five feet, maybe more. Too far to go without taking at least one or two breaths, especially for Laffi, with her wounded arm.

He decided the best thing would be for him to get out of the cave and go for help, bring back people and equipment for Laffi's rescue. He could probably even find diving equipment and guide her out through the tunnel. But then he thought out the logistics and realized it could take hours if not days to gather what he needed. He could not leave Laffi alone, back there in the damp and darkness. If he were gone too long she would assume he had drowned or suffered some mishap. She was tough, but just how tough he didn't know, or to what end despair might bring her. He was asking more of Laffi than any human could bear. Jason took a deep breath and began the reverse trip through the underwater tunnel.

Like most journeys, returning was far easier and faster, and he was able to feel his way in the absolute darkness. With little discomfort he reached a section of the tunnel where air was readily available. This would still present a danger for Laffi, but he was certain he could get her through, dragging her along if necessary. When he felt his hand slip past the top of the tunnel and into open airspace, he pushed himself out of the water, took a deep breath and called out to Laffi. Immediately her flashlight switched on and he could see her looking down at him from the edge of the water hole, crying and repeating his name. Her face was red and swollen.

Laffi shook off the fear that had gripped her and regained composure as Jason explained their situation. He suggested that she could either wait in the cave for him to bring help, or she could risk the underwater passage and come with him. "I'm not spending another minute in this god-forsaken place" Laffi blurted. "I'm coming with you. And don't worry, I'm a good swimmer, with or without a bad arm."

"O.K. then kick off your shoes and come on down," began Jason. "Wait," he continued, "we'll need our shoes. Hurry, the water's rising faster. Hand me my boots and the belt, then take yours off and tie the laces together." Then he instructed her "When I squeeze your hand, allow your body to rise then carefully take a breath in the airspace. Keep your nose and mouth close to the roof of the tunnel. When you're ready to go on, squeeze my hand. The only thing that can go wrong is if you get a mouth full of water." After she lowered herself into the water he gave her a hug; then it was time to go.

Now confident of the route, Jason hurried them through the passage without incident and they burst into the pool at the other end of the tunnel well before they'd exhausted their oxygen.

"I can't believe it," Laffi managed to gasp, treading water. "We made it. How deep is it? I can't touch bottom."

"I barely can, so it must be around six feet to the bottom, but we're only about two feet below the edge of the pool."

"And there's light here," she added, gratefully.

"Let's get out and see where we are," said Jason. "I think I can boost you high enough so you can get a grip on the edge. If you can with your arm, try and hold on, and I'll get out and help you the rest of the way. Now stretch your arms up as far as they'll go."

Bending his knees, Jason lowered himself under water, and wrapped his arms around her knees and ankles. With all his strength he vaulted upward, raising Laffi high enough so that she could grasp the rim of the pool. Immediately, he crouched again and blasted through the surface, gripping the edge of the pool and pulling himself out in one fluid motion. Seeing that Laffi was barely holding on, he seized her belt and hauled her safely over the edge. Then he pulled her onto her feet.

Her long hair stuck in tendrils over her head and shoulders, and her shirt was ripped, revealing her bra and what it supported. Realizing he was staring, Jason managed a grin. "It's a good thing your center of gravity is higher than most."

Trying to hide a smile, Laffi bent her head and rearranged her shirt as best she could, and then looked back at Jason. He was naked to the waist, wet pants wrapped tightly around his legs and both pairs of shoes still attached to his utility belt.

"You've certainly earned some slack," she said. "So I'll assume that's a compliment."

"Indeed it was!"

Laffi looked up to where light was coming through fissures in the cavern walls. "And what a gift to be able to see, even a little."

"It's getting dark," he said, "let's see what we've got. At least it looks like the storm's over," he added.

Jason pointed out the large opening, about three feet above the carvern floor, and they picked their way towards it, stumbling around broad stalagmites, and jumping over several small gullys. "Try not to touch anything," Jason cautioned. "The oils from your hands will damage the limestone, the formations in this cavern are still growing." Laffi stared in disbelieve, "Really? You're going to play scientist right now?" Jason shrugged and kept moving until they were a few steps from the opening.

They felt a gentle breeze of warm, fresh air and were able to catch a glimpse of twilight sky. Gingerly, Jason pulled himself up and put his knees on the ledge of the opening. It felt solid, so he crawled out toward the outside edge. Jason's heart fell when he looked down. Below him was a vertical drop at least five hundred feet down, which then transitioned into a gentle slope. "It's a long way down," he finally said to Laffi. Not willing to give up just yet, he inched out further and noticed a long, narrow slab of rock supporting the top of the opening. He grasped the rock and pulled himself outward and upward, hoping to see the terrain above. It appeared to be a rocky slope rising up the mountain. Straining to see more, he lost his balance, and with his body tipped dangerously toward the vertical drop, his feet scrambled beneath him.

Laffi yelled, "Jason!" and flung her arms around his legs. With all her strength, she threw herself backward. They crashed together onto the cavern floor. Disentangling himself from her, Jason got up slowly, reached out a hand and pulled her to her feet. "Thanks," he said. "That was close."

Laffi threw her arms around his neck, held him close for a moment then slowly pushed away. "No more, O.K? It's too dark, and we're too tired. Dare I ask what it looks like?"

"About a five hundred foot sheer drop, but maybe we'll be able to get out by climbing up. It looks steep, but possibly doable if we take it slowly, and start after sunrise." Then he noticed she was shivering, and put his arms around her. "We'd better figure out how we're going to stay warm and get some rest. With the temperature and humidity in here that's not going to be easy."

"Good start though," Laffi said, snuggling closer for a moment. Then she reached up and kissed him on the cheek. "It's a lot warmer near the entrance; we probably ought to stay here. By the way, where are the bats? I don't see any here either, and that opening seems plenty big. How come?"

"Good question." Jason said. "We would have seen or smelled the bat guano if they were around."

" I don't suppose there's anything around that we could use to make a fire, is there?" asked Laffi.

"Hardly, unless you want to sacrifice the rest of your clothes." They scanned the darkening cavern. "What's that over there?" Laffi saw something nearby on the cavern floor that seemed out of place. Once they got closer it turned out to be a mound of sticks and mud about three feet in diameter.

"Looks like a giant nest," said Laffi. "But you tell me, you're the scientist!"

"I'm not sure, it's too dark. Let's see if this still works." He pulled the flashlight from his belt and flicked the switch. Nothing happened. He shook it and tried again. Nothing. He then got his lighter from its compartment and flicked it on. In the dancing glow of burning butane he saw it was indeed some sort of nest, held together with mud.

"Do you think it'll burn?" asked Laffi.

"I don't know, probably too wet from the runoff," he said slowly. Then spacing his words out, he added, "And I think we better leave it alone until daylight."

"Why?" she asked.

"I don't know, let's just wait and see. Perhaps," he paused, then continued in a lower voice, "it has something to do with the absence of bats... Now, which side of the bed do you prefer?" he added, gesturing to the smooth clay floor near the opening.

Ignoring his question, she said, "All of a sudden I'm thirsty. Do we have anything that'll hold water?"

"Just my boots."

"That's not even close! If you'll be kind enough to hold onto my ankles I'll drink directly from the source, thank you very much."

Twenty minutes later, after drinking water and after Jason checking her wound, they were stretched out together on the floor, fighting off hunger. Jason kissed her on the check and rolled over.

"Tell me something, Jason?" she asked, propping her head on her hand. "It just occurred to me that you handled this whole thing with a lot more composure than one would expect of the average biologist. Am I missing something in your background?"

The only response was even, slow breathing.

Bustamante

Just after 1:00 A.M., light blazed through the police station window, and the sound of tires skidding to a stop brought Artemas and the FBI agents to attention.

The Zamarripa brothers, hands cuffed behind them, were pushed roughly inside. Behind them came the entire PGR contingent led by Raymundo Valenzuela carrying a leather briefcase.

"I hope your finest suite is ready; we have some distinguished guests who're used to nothing but the best." Raymundo's expression reminded Artemas of a jaguar he had seen in a zoo after a dove flew into its enclosure.

"It's ready."

Artemas carefully noted the prisoners' condition. They were obviously frightened and a little disheveled but with no obvious injuries. Must have cleaned them up before leaving the hacienda, he surmised. As the little parade passed into the back of the station, he asked, "We have two cells. Do you want them together or alone?"

Raymundo pursed his lips as he surveyed the accommodations. "Let's keep them apart for tonight or what's left of it. And if you don't mind, I'd like to leave Raul in here to watch them."

"Certainly," said Artemas, guessing what Raymundo really wanted—making sure no one else questioned the prisoners. "Glad for the help."

"I almost forgot," Raymundo remarked. "The fat one has a wound in his shoulder, a small puncture. He said it was an accident."

"O.K.," said Artemas. "I'll call the hospital in Sabinas and ask them to send someone up in the morning."

After Ignacio and Armando were locked up everyone returned to the office, except for Raul, the wiry, hatchet-faced *federale*. Artemas watched him flop into a chair just outside the cells and thump a black nightstick against his knee.

Artemas introduced Raymundo to Grunwald and Robinson then made a show of shaking the *federale's* hand. "Congratulations are in order! Tell us what happened? I'm sure Washington is pressuring our guests for information. I'll be happy to translate."

"*Claro que si.*"

Raymundo spoke, a sentence or two at a time, so that Artemas could translate. "After you left the hacienda we searched it thoroughly. We found a great deal of evidence. When confronted with it the brothers readily admitted committing both the murder of the man and the girl. Of course they still deny slaughtering the goats, he added, deadpan. "I have signed confessions." He picked up his briefcase. "May I leave them and the evidence in your safe until we're ready to leave?"

"Of course," said Artemas.

Agent Grunwald had been listening carefully and raised his hand. "Could you describe the evidence and tell us the procedure from now on? What I mean is, where will they be taken and when, and will we have an opportunity to question them?"

Raymundo thought carefully before replying. "We found some very sharp knives made of stone, the type used for ceremonial purposes by the Aztecs. We found clothing that appears to be soaked in blood, one pistol at the ranch and another in their car that was recently fired. There were also several silver bracelets exactly like the one found at the crime scene—same as the fat boy was wearing. We also found what is probably the murdered girl's camera, some marijuana and cocaine, and a child-porn videotape. It's all carefully packed in plastic bags, and you're welcome to see it.

"We'll have the clothing checked to confirm that the stain is blood and that it matches at least one of the victims. We'll also check the camera for prints. But I'm sure of the results. The ease with which we obtained the confessions....Your other questions? It's been a long day."

"Where and when will they be taken, and will we have an opportunity to question them?" Artemas asked again. "I would like to confer with you briefly about the latter."

Raymundo nodded assent and followed Artemas to the other end of the room. Grunwald and Robinson looked on warily as he began speaking quickly in Spanish.

"You've done a fine job," Artemas told Raymundo. "The evidence seems overwhelming, even without the confessions. The only negative I see is that those guys feel they've been shut out of the investigation. I don't think either one of us wants their president complaining. It can't hurt to let them question the prisoners, particularly if I translate the answers. By the way, do either of the brothers speak English?"

"I don't know."

"If they do, I'll speak quickly using words they won't understand. Then we'll fix the tape to conform. Same with the final transcript. The agents will undoubtedly want a copy of the tape. We'll promise to send it to them, by which time it will say exactly what we want it to say."

"I'm impressed; you aren't what I expected."

"Thanks." Artemas patted the *federale* on the shoulder as they returned to the seated FBI agents. "We all make mistakes," he added, fighting hard to keep a straight face.

Turning toward Raymundo, Artemas began, "The next question was where and when will the prisoners be taken."

"I don't have final orders, but I believe they'll go to the prison in Monterrey, probably sometime late tomorrow morning or early afternoon. The sooner we get this wrapped up the better."

Artemas translated the answer for Grunwald and Robinson then added, "And you'll have an opportunity to question them. Let me check on the time. To Raymundo he said, "How about doing the questioning about 9:00 A.M. tomorrow?"

"*Está bien.*"

"Is nine tomorrow morning O.K.?"

"That's fine," replied Grunwald, gratefully. "I want to

thank you both for your cooperation. I'm sure it will be equally appreciated in Washington. Now, perhaps we can take a quick look at the evidence, and could you make us a copy of the confessions, or would you rather wait until tomorrow?"

After a brief discussion with Raymundo, Artemas replied, "Now would be as good a time as any." Anything to take his mind off his concern for Laffi.

Caverns of Bustamante

Laffi slept for nearly ten hours and upon waking felt as if she'd been physically knocked out. Her forearm was throbbing with pain and her back and neck were sore and stiff. Sunlight was streaming into the cave and Jason was no longer sprawled beside her. She cautiously stretched her body, sighing in relief as vertebrae popped and cracked, and saw Jason approaching from the direction of the small pool. "Is breakfast ready?" she called out.

Jason hurried his pace. "Would madam prefer the English breakfast with kippers or banger sausage?" he asked.

"Right about now I'd eat one of your beloved bats. What time is it?"

"I'm not sure. My watch stopped, but I think it's probably 8:00 A.M. If all goes well we'll be back in Bustamante in a couple of hours."

Jason led her to the small pool, helped her take a drink and wash the wound. When they returned to the opening, he said, "See this side," he waved toward the left of the ledge. "The outside slope rises gradually. There are also rough foot and handholds, maybe made by Indians. They make climbing up easy. I've already done it as a matter of fact."

"Oh, that's great. What if you'd fallen? Would your screams have woken me up?"

Ignoring her irate remark Jason said, "It'll still be tricky with your arm, so I've come up with a hedge against disaster." He reached into the cave opening and pulled out what looked to Laffi to be a thin rope. "Double thickness parachute cord. I keep it in my utility belt. It's tied to a boulder above. I hope you're not afraid of heights."

"Honestly, a six foot ladder scares the hell out of me. I just won't look down."

"Good, I'll be right behind you—and then there's the rope." He carefully secured it around her waist and under her arms.

After showing her the hand and footholds and climbing once to demonstrate, Jason got behind her. He put his hand on her waist and urged her up, steadying her as she climbed. She made it look easy, with no more than a muffled "Ow" and "Shit" although he knew using her left arm was painful. When she made it safely to a more gradual incline, he followed her up. They sat down to rest and looked westward. "My God it's beautiful," Laffi whispered.

Jason took in the panorama, washed clean and sparkling in the morning sun. The sheer cliff below them dropped into a semi-arid valley with no sign of human occupancy. Beyond it, as far as the eye could see, stretched one mountain range after another. It was a forbidding landscape, but particularly inviting to Jason because of its inaccessibility. "You're right," he said. "Maybe someday we'll explore...but now let's get you and your arm back to civilization." Laffi gave him a quick glance, but said nothing as she stood up.

They were close to the peak, but it still took a good ten minutes of steady climbing around rocks and cacti before they reached the summit. Jason was wary of rattlesnakes and asked Laffi to be on the alert for their characteristic warning, a sound like dry rustling leaves. Once they made it to the other side of the mountain they saw the village of Bustamante, nestled under a green blanket of trees at the base of the mountain. And just below them was Jason's Suburban, still parked where they had left it.

After a quick descent they reached the SUV. Jason fished around his pant pockets and pulled out his keys with a satisfied cry. "Hah! I also have a hide-a-key under the wheel well. Just in case you wondered." Before climbing into the passenger side Laffi paused and placed her hand on his arm "Thank you for everything you did to get us out alive. And especially for being so calm and cool headed. I'm going to bet you didn't learn your survival skills in Boy Scouts or graduate school."

Jason gave her a sideways glance. "My folks didn't have a lot of money so I enlisted in the army and signed up for Special

Forces. I spent several years in the unit and applied a lot of my training last night."

"Why did you leave?"

"A lot of things happened, including damage to my hearing, which ended that career."

"I'd like to hear more, about you, about your experiences."

"I think I'll enjoy telling you, but right now we better get back to town and get your arm treated."

Several minutes later they entered the outskirts of Bustamante, Laffi's arm freshly bandaged from the first aid kit in Jason's SUV, their hunger pains sated by a handful of energy bars. "I hope," she said, "that you plan on stopping first at the hotel."

"Laffi, I may not be a doctor but I know something about wounds. Your arm needs professional attention right away, including a tetanus shot. I want to get you to the nearest doctor or hospital, which is probably in Sabinas Hidalgo, about thirty miles away."

"I appreciate your concern, but I look like a bum that was rolled in an alley. If you take me to the hospital looking like this they'll think it's something worse than my arm and may insist on keeping me there. I need to get back to work."

Jason considered the mud on her pants, shredded blouse, and overall disheveled appearance and thought that she still looked beautiful. But he understood why she didn't want to be seen in that condition, especially by other journalists. He turned toward the hotel. After parking in back he told her she had ten minutes before he started telling people what happened, which was the last thing she wanted. She reported the news; she never wanted to *be* the news.

In nine minutes flat Laffi emerged from her room. Other than the bandage around her arm and silk scarf covering her stringy hair, she looked like she'd spent all morning getting dressed.

Bustamante

Dr. Raul Ramirez had recently joined the Sabinas hospital staff after completing his residency. Well after 8:00 A.M. he emerged from Armando's jail cell and handed a small Ziploc bag to Artemas. "Here's what caused the wound. It looks like a pellet from an air gun." His thin mustache twitched nervously.

Artemas held the bag up to the light. "That it does. Did he say where it came from?"

"No. Just that it was an accident, then the guard told him to be quiet."

"Is he alright...any sign of infection?"

"No. Your people did a good job on the first aid. I've given him a tetanus shot and some penicillin as a precaution. The wound needs to be checked in a few hours. This is my day off, but I'll be happy to stay."

"Thanks. Just for a little while," Artemis replied. "Until I find out when and where they're going. The prisoners will be questioned in a little while. Why don't you go over to the hotel, have breakfast on the government. But please don't talk to any of the reporters. And that won't be easy; they're like zoo animals at feeding time. I had to put Moreno at the door to keep them out."

The young doctor said, "I understand. I'll be back in an hour."

Not long after Dr. Ramirez left for breakfast, the FBI agents strode through the station door carrying briefcases. Artemas waved them to his desk, removed a folded piece of paper from his pocket and handed it quickly to Grunwald. "I would respectfully offer a few suggestions." His green eyes narrowed as they met Grunwald's.

The agent looked at him thoughtfully, unfolded the paper and carefully read the typewritten sentences. His eyes again met Artemas's. "You won't be participating in the questioning?"

"Yes, I will." Artemas's expression gave nothing away.

"You're still not sure they killed the girl?"

Artemas's silence seemed to be all the answer the American needed. "O.K., I understand." Refolding the paper, he slipped it into the inside pocket of his suit-coat.

With a calculated flip of the wrist, Raymundo slammed the station door behind him and joined the men standing around Artemas's desk.

"Ready for the questioning?" asked Artemas.

"Yes, but I expect a telephone call from the attorney general any moment."

"Well let's get them answering some questions," said Artemas.

"Let me make sure everything is ready," said Raymundo. He headed toward the cells.

Artemas thought he knew what Raymundo meant by "ready." To Grunwald and Robinson, he said, "You guys about set?"

Grunwald rolled his eyes. "It's about time," he blurted, then quickly added, "but it's not your fault—and thanks."

Raymundo motioned them inside the cellblock. "Please," he said to Artemas, "no briefcases or recorders other than the official one. They can take notes, but that's all."

Artemas asked Moreno to lock the station door and wait just inside to listen for a phone call, then he translated Raymundo's instructions to the FBI agents.

"Because of the limited space I thought they could stay in their cells, and we can question them from here," began Raymundo. To the prisoners he said, "Both of you come up to the bars and stay there."

The brothers said nothing but quickly obeyed as the Americans and Raymundo seated themselves in chairs placed in the cellblock hallway. Artemas remained standing.

Raymundo pushed the start button on the tape recorder sitting on a metal table and gestured for Artemas to begin. "You know who I am," Artemas said, after giving the date, time, and those present. Then he introduced Grunwald and Robinson and explained that he would be translating. "First I have a few questions." The brothers remained sullen and silent.

Artemas looked carefully at each of them in turn. "You have signed a statement admitting to murdering the North American girl, Julie Conners. Is that correct? Did you, in fact, kill her?"

Armando tapped his foot, as if sending his brother a signal. Ignacio said, "*Sí, señor*, that is correct."

Artemas looked at Armando. "And you, why did you kill her?"

"To scare people away from the cave." Armando's eyes darted toward Raymundo then back to Artemas.

"And how did you kill her?" Artemas kept his gaze on Armando.

Armando inhaled loudly and stared at his feet. "We strangled her then cut her throat to make it look like it was a *chupacabra* or something," he said, "To scare people away from the cave."

"Why did you want to scare them away?"

"Because that's where we were storing drugs," Armando replied, without hesitation.

"Wouldn't it have been easier to put the drugs somewhere else?"

Armando shrugged and kept his eyes on the floor. Artemas continued, "I understand that you also confessed to the murder before the girl's, and that it was a requirement of the dealer who supplied the drugs. Some sort of initiation. Is that correct?"

"Yes," answered Ignacio.

Artemas noticed that Raymundo never took his eyes off the boys. "I could not find the name of the dealer in your confession; what is it?"

"That," Ignacio said, refusing to meet Artemas's gaze, "I cannot tell you."

"You're facing charges on two brutal murders that could put you in jail for the rest of your lives, and you won't give us one name, even if it would help your situation?"

"*Señor*, one choice means jail for sure, but we don't know for how long. The other..."

Artemas went quickly to the next question. "So the first murder was one you had to commit — is it fair to say — to join the club. The second was to keep people away from the cave?"

"The first one was to scare people, too," Ignacio said, now more sure of himself.

Artemas said, "That's all I have. Now for our colleagues from the United States." Grunwald cleared his throat and looked at both brothers, then at Artemas, who nodded, ready to continue translating. "Where exactly did the killing take place?"

"On the path up to the cave," replied Ignacio.

"I understand that but where exactly? Halfway up, fifty meters from the entrance — where?"

Ignacio thought for a moment before answering. "Not too far from the entrance or we wouldn't have seen her."

"Did you sexually molest the girl, either before or after you killed her?"

It was evident from their expressions that neither Raymundo nor the Zamarripas had a clue as to what was being said before Artemas translated, which he quickly did. Raymundo shifted uneasily and glared at the brothers. Each looked back at Raymundo. Artemas saw the PGR man give an almost imperceptible shake of his head.

"N...no," stammered Ignacio.

"Please address this one to Armando," Grunwald continued. "I understand both of you have a history of assaulting young girls. You were completely alone with her. She was beautiful, scantily dressed, totally in your power, and you were going to kill her anyway. Why did you *not* molest her sexually?"

As Artemas translated, Raymundo flashed him an angry look but said nothing. Armando looked up, as if seeking divine inspiration, then back at Artemas. He said, "We just didn't. That's all."

"Her body was naked. Why did you remove her clothes?"

"To see what she looked like," stammered Ignacio.

Grunwald paused then continued. "The silver bracelet that was found at the scene of the crime belonged to you?" he again directed the question to Armando.

"Yes."

"Can you think of any reason why there were no fingerprints on it—not even a smudge?"

Armando, considered a moment, then shook his head. "Answer the question," said Raymundo.

"No. I can think of no reason."

"The girl had a camera with her when she was killed. It also had no fingerprints on it. Can you think of any reason why?"

"No."

"It was an older camera—film, not digital. It was loaded with film when the girl left her friend to climb to the caves, but there was no film in it when we found it at your home. What happened to it?"

"I don't remember," said Ignacio. Raymundo shifted uneasily in his chair.

"Well, which one of you brought the camera from the murder scene back to your home?"

The brothers looked at each other, at Raymundo then back at Artemas. Finally Ignacio said, "I don't know. By that time we were stoned and things were pretty confused."

"Are you trying to tell us that neither of you remember figuring out how to open the camera, removing the film, and doing whatever you did with it?" asked Grunwald, incredulously.

The brothers looked at each other and shrugged. "We don't remember," said Ignacio.

"You," Grunwald said to Armando, "were wounded with what looked like a pellet from an air gun. How did that happen?"

"It was an accident."

"I asked you how it happened."

Armando's face flushed and his jaw clenched. "You've got our confession for two murders. That's enough," he blurted out, belligerently.

"One last question," said Grunwald, ignoring the outburst. "Has anyone in this room, or anyone else connected with this investigation threatened you with any sort of violence, or abused you physically?"

Ignacio and Armando stared straight ahead. "No," said Ignacio, "not at all."

A tap on the steel door leading to the station's office interrupted the questioning. It opened slowly and Artemas's assistant peeked in. "*Capitán*," he was looking at Raymundo and speaking in a voice filled with awe. "There is a telephone call for you, from the attorney general of the Republic."

"*Muy bien*," said Raymundo to Artemas. "That's what we've been waiting for. I assume we're finished here?"

Artemas stood aside to let Raymundo pass. Instead, the *federale* stood back and motioned for the others to precede him out of the cellblock. He's taking no chances, thought Artemas, even with the notoriously impatient attorney general waiting. He noted that Grunwald and Robinson also picked up on the situation.

After a brief conversation Raymundo hung up the phone and said to Artemas, "We are to leave immediately for the airport in Monterrey, then fly to Mexico City. The prisoners are going to La Palma at Almoloya, not Monterrey, probably to minimize the possibility of their father using his local influence to help them. We need to clear the area while we get them to the Humvee. Also, two of my men will have to take the bus into Monterrey, pick up the vehicle at the airport and return it to the garrison. When does the next bus leave?"

Artemas made a snap decision. It had been gelling in his mind all day and had taken hold during the questioning. "The next bus leaves in about two hours, but they can come with me. Since this affair is wrapped up I'm going to fly to Sonora for a quick visit with my father. In the meantime, what should I tell the journalists?"

"Tell them where we are taking the suspects and that we have strong evidence, including written confessions, that they're guilty. Say that Mexico sincerely regrets what happened, but justice will be served."

The station door opened and Officer Moreno entered quickly, locked the door behind him and addressed Artemas directly. "*Señor Capitan*, there are two *norte americanos* that say they were attacked in the cave. It is *la rubia,* the blond, and her friend who were here before."

"Bring them in," ordered Artemas. Trying to hide his relief, he looked sideways at Raymundo and raised his eyebrows.

Bustamante

While Laffi had made enough repairs to her appearance to pass cursory inspection, she received a more critical assessment from the policemen inside the station. The bandage, scratches, and bruises on her arms indicated something significant was amiss. But it was Jason, whose clothes were torn and muddy and whose skin was badly scraped — including a gash on his cheek — who received the most scrutiny. He began to explain what had happened to Artemas in English.

"You must translate immediately," urged Raymundo, sensing something was about to destroy his carefully constructed success.

"Perhaps, in deference to my colleague from Mexico City," said Artemas softly, "*Señorita* Rendón could give the account in Spanish and then in English for our North American colleagues?"

Laffi quickly recounted the events in the cave. When she got to the part about Jason shooting at the attackers with his pellet gun, Artemas held up his hand for her to stop. From his desk he picked up a small plastic bag. "You probably didn't hear, but last night two suspects in the girl's murder were arrested. One of them had been recently wounded by this." He handed the bag to Jason. "He said it was an accident."

"That looks like one of mine," said Jason. "It was no accident."

Laffi finished the Spanish version of her story and began speaking in English to the FBI agents. A beaming Raymundo pulled Artemas aside. "It looks even better than we thought. I didn't tell you because I didn't think it was important, but we also found some dynamite at the hacienda."

Artemas said, "It's too bad the Americans didn't see them well enough for a positive identification, but the pellet and the dynamite you found should clinch it. Do you want to get their formal statements before you leave and re-question the prisoners?"

"No," said Raymundo. "Time's short and there are better ways to add what we've just learned. Just get the *gringos'* statements and send them to me in Mexico City. Oh, and thanks for everything. Except, maybe...well, some of the questions of our colleagues."

Artemas held out his hands palms up, shrugged and rolled his eyes in the traditional Mexican expression meaning, "*Gringos, quien sabe,* who knows why they do anything."

Raymundo regarded him speculatively then clapped him on the shoulder. "Anyway, well done. I will tell the attorney general."

"*Muchísimas gracias.*" The uncharacteristic softness in Raymundo's eyes did not fool Artemas.

Jason approached Artemas.

"I'm sorry about your ordeal," said Artemas. "Thank God you're both safe."

"Thanks, but Laffi's wound needs immediate attention. Where's the nearest doctor?"

On cue, Dr. Ramirez re-entered the station having finished his breakfast.

"There," said Artemas, pointing at the young man. "He needs to check the prisoner, then he's all yours."

Artemas motioned for the doctor to join them and began to introduce him to "Dr. Jason Peterson" in Spanish, but Ramirez interrupted, telling them he had studied English and would be delighted to use it. As Jason described Laffi's gunshot wound they glanced her way and noticed she had finished her narrative and was now answering questions from the FBI agents. Meanwhile Raymundo had disappeared into the cellblock.

Artemas walked over to Laffi and the two agents stepped aside. Carefully, he took Laffi's left hand and examined the bandage on her forearm, though what he really wanted to do was throw his arms around her. Instead, he said, "Dr. Peterson just explained the circumstances of your wound, and fortunately we have a medical doctor here who will examine you. Things are a little crowded, but since it's nothing more intimate than your arm," his eyes twinkled at the shared secret of their past relationship, "perhaps over there would be O.K.?" He motioned toward the far corner of the station lined with battered file cabinets.

"Thanks," said Laffi. "It'll probably be all right but it does hurt quite a bit. Perhaps, Dr. Ramirez, you could come to my room at the hotel, number sixteen. I've got a story to file, and this arm can wait a few more minutes."

"That will be fine. It'll take only a moment to check the prisoner, and then I'll be with you," said the doctor as he made his way to the cellblock.

Artemas gently escorted Laffi toward the door. "I guess some prayers do get answered," he whispered. Then louder, he added, "Now please come back as soon as possible so that we can take an official statement." Turning toward Jason, he said, "Dr. Peterson, could you stay here for just a few moments? There's something I want to ask you."

"O.K." said Jason. "I'll hang around outside and watch the fun."

The cellblock door swung open and Raymundo and one of his men led the Zamarripa brothers through the room, hands cuffed and attached to leg shackles. Dr. Ramirez trailed behind. Artemas knew the villagers who had endured Armando and Ignacio's arrogance around town would be very satisfied to witness their sorry predicament. Word had spread quickly that the Zamarripa brothers had been arrested for the murders.

"I'll clear the way." Artemas motioned to Officer Moreno to follow him as he left the office to address the gathering crowd outside. Most were residents of Bustamante, but among them were at least forty reporters and photographers. From the station doorway Artemas estimated a crowd of 200 and spotted Chaco Gonzalez and a couple of his cronies frowning at him from under beat-up straw hats. He gave them a cheery wave.

The reporters, under the watchful eye of Officer Moreno, more or less backed off the fifty feet he had requested. Artemas saluted Raymundo and his men, and gestured toward the door, *"Vayan con Dios."* Then he followed the small procession out of the station. Among a volley of angry jeers the prisoners were led to the Humvee and placed in back with one of the *federales*. Raymundo seated himself next to the driver. A few American reporters shouted questions at him in English but were ignored.

Once the Humvee disappeared down the street Artemas said to the crowd, "Thank you for your cooperation. I will be back in about two minutes to answer your questions." He returned to the station to find agents Grunwald and Robinson sitting by his desk. "I promised our friends in the press that I would answer some questions. Would you like to participate in the news conference?"

The agents looked at each other and shook their heads in unison.

"I didn't think so. I'll be as quick as I can, and I'd like to meet with you briefly. Can you stick around?" This time they nodded.

It took Artemas two minutes to share the information he was permitted to disclose and another ten minutes for the journalists to conclude that "no comment" meant just that. He waved to Jason, mouthing that he would be just a little longer, and then returned to his office where Grunwald and Robinson were waiting.

"Have fun?" asked Robinson.

"Oh yes. One guy wanted to know if we had determined whether the suspects were vampires."

"Well, have you?"

"What I said is that aspect of the investigation will be handled by the FBI, whose experience with cults is much greater than ours."

"Ouch," said Grunwald. "I was just beginning to like you. What I mean is that if those punks killed the girl, I'm J. Edgar Hoover come back from the dead. What, if anything, do you intend to do?"

"I see you grasp the situation," said Artemas. "I intend to ask you to do me two favors, aand then we'll see what happens." The agents looked at him expectantly as he went to a file cabinet, unlocked it and withdrew a manila envelope. He handed the envelope to Grunwald. "In here are three plastic bags with marijuana butts. One contains a single butt and is from the site of the first murder. The butt in the second bag is from the site of Miss Conners' murder. The third contains several butts I found at the Zamarripa hacienda. I would be most grateful if you could have them analyzed to see if any of them match."

Robinson looked questioningly at Grunwald. "We can do that," he said. "A legitimate request for corroborative evidence. And the other favor?"

"This one is a bit more delicate," said Artemas. "If I decide to pursue the investigation I may need to monitor certain private conversations. I have some crude equipment that requires wires, but was hoping you might be able to supply something more sophisticated?"

Grunwald gave him a hard look. "'A bit more delicate' is an understatement. What would we get in return?"

"Whatever I can give you," came the prompt reply.

"I'll see what I can do. Give me a card with your address on it."

"Thank you, but the sooner the better. I will probably be out of town until day after tomorrow."

"I said I'd see what I can do. But no guarantees," grumbled Grunwald.

Artemas pulled out his wallet, extracted a stack of pesos and offered them to Grunwald. "DHL delivers to Bustamante."

"You are a persistent bastard," said Grunwald, waving away the money. "By the way," he added. "I think I'll take one of those cigars you offered. One of the ones with no label that you told me are made in Veracruz, if you know what I mean."

Artemas rummaged in his desk, found two cigars, removed their labels, and handed them over.

"Thanks," said Grunwald, and stood up. "Homer, I guess we better get out of here. If we hurry, we can be back in Washington by tonight." Then he extended a hand to Artemas. "We appreciate it," he said.

Robinson held out his hand. When Artemas took it, the black agent broke into a grin. *"Capitan Salcido, fué un placer conocerle. Gracias por todo y espero que nos veamos otra vez,"* he said with a perfect accent. The three men looked at each other and burst out laughing.

Bustamante

Finally alone in the office, Artemas made several phone calls: one to his home town in Sonora, one to Mexicana airlines, the third to Gerardo Manzano, the village school teacher, and the last to the new *taquería* down the street. Finished, he stuck his head out of the office and motioned for Jason to join him.

"Thanks for waiting. Things have been hectic, but nothing to what you've been through. That's why I hesitate to ask you a favor and want you to be honest if it's a problem. After a meeting that should take no more than an hour, I have to leave immediately for the airport in Monterrey. Before I go, I need to get a detailed statement of your experience in the caverns. I was hoping to presume on your good nature and ask you to drive me to the airport. We could tape your statement on the way. The round trip should take about two and a half hours. If you're too tired or just don't want to, please say so."

Jason thought for a moment. "I guess I can, depending on whether Laffi needs any help. I'll check with her and be right back."

"Thank you," said Artemas, somehow annoyed by Jason's response. "I'll be here for another fifteen minutes."

When Jason left, Artemas peered through the window and saw no one outside. He went to a file cabinet against the back wall that separated the office from the cellblock. Quickly, he unlocked the bottom drawer and removed a cassette from a voice-activated, tape recorder. Returning to his desk he popped the cassette into a portable tape recorder, donned the headset and turned it on.

The first thing he heard was his own voice asking Raymundo whether he wanted the brothers to be locked in the same or different cells. After a minute of skimming through the tape he found what he had been expecting: Raymundo's voice. "Do you two remember what happened yesterday and what I said?" The *federale's* voice was pure menace.

"I'm going to remind you very quickly before the *gringos* question you. We've got you for sure on the first murder and are pretty close on the second. For the first time in your miserable lives you're in a situation you can't get out of, no matter what your father does. But you can make it better or worse—much better or much worse. And it's me, not your father or anyone else who'll decide how good or bad it will be. If you cooperate I'll personally help you get the lightest possible sentence. Our prisons are not too bad if you have enough money to pay for conveniences—and you do. If you don't cooperate you'll discover that what happened yesterday was just a *botana*, an appetizer. In every jail in the country there are men that will do anything to anybody in return for better treatment. One fuckup and your life expectancy will be measured in hours."

Artemas was now certain that Raymundo was aware of the weaknesses in the case. Also, since the increased scrutiny brought on by the NAFTA agreement, Mexican judges had become sensitive to police brutality and the manipulation of witnesses. One never knew when extreme circumstances might present themselves, and the tape could prove valuable.

Jason returned to the station. Artemas pulled off the earphones and went to meet him.

"The doctor wants to make sure Laffi's bone wasn't injured. He's taking her to the hospital in Sabinas. She'll stay there overnight, not altogether willingly I might add, so it looks like I'm free to drive you to the airport."

"That's great," said Artemas. "I'm sure she'll be fine. And please consider me in your debt. I'll be back in an hour. Is that convenient?"

"Fine."

"Oh, and one other detail," added Artemas. "We could take the police Jeep, but if anything happened on your way back there could be a problem—for both of us. If we can take your car I'll reimburse you?"

"O.K.," said Jason. "See you in an hour."

After carefully hiding his tape, Artemas emerged from the police station. He left the office in the care of Officer Moreno, asking him to alert the two stranded *federales* that he would be leaving for the airport in an hour.

Artemas squinted at the brightness of the day and wished he had brought his sunglasses. The morning air was clean and refreshing. Tired as he was, the tonic of a beautiful day worked on him and put a spring in his step. He passed the bus station and continued two more blocks along the street. He stopped at the new *taquería* on the corner to pick up a brown bag of tacos and two Cokes from a cooler of slushy ice. A left turn brought him to the village school, occupying an entire block. Half of it was a play area enclosed by a chain link fence. There, among dozens of yelling children, Artemas found Gerardo Manzano.

At thirty-one, Gerardo was the village's senior *maestro*. Except for Elfrida Vasquez, a retired nun of ninety who still worked an hour or two each day. He was whipcord thin and his tortoiseshell glasses, precisely trimmed mustache, and delicately chiseled features tagged him as a compulsive neat freak.

Raised in a poor Monterrey family with eight siblings, Gerardo—like Artemas—had a priest for a mentor. The man took a keen interest in the bright little boy who actually enjoyed school. The result had been not only the first college diploma in his family, but one from the United States: the University of Mississippi. Much to everyone's surprise, and much to the joy of the people of Bustamante, Gerardo returned to Mexico and married his childhood sweetheart. After that he accepted the teaching job.

Although the position paid next to nothing, somehow the couple, with the help of his wife who started a small dressmaking business, made ends meet. They'd lived in Bustamante nearly four years, seemed to be completely happy, and even the most cynical villagers were starting to believe they might stay.

Gerardo waved Artemas toward a gate in the chainlink fence. As he entered, a soccer ball grazed his cheek, hit the fence, and ricocheted to the ground in front of him. Balancing Cokes and tacos in both hands, Artemas pivoted on his left foot, trapped the ball with his right and precisely kicked it back to the group of little boys, who stood silent, fearing they'd be in trouble. With the ball back in play they resumed their frenetic activity.

"Hey that's pretty good," said Gerardo, extending his hand. "I was wondering where I was going to find a soccer coach."

"It's been a long time, but it actually might be fun." Artemas set the sack of tacos and frosty Cokes on the table. "I hope you don't mind. I picked up an early lunch for us. I'm leaving to visit my father right after we meet."

"Sounds good to me. And, by the way, congratulations on both catching the killers and ridding the town of those disgusting pests. But since your time is short and I have to be back in the classroom in 20 minutes, how can I help you?"

"First, the credit for the arrest goes mostly to my colleagues from Mexico City," said Artemas, seating himself at the table. "You were very helpful in giving me some village history when I first arrived. Now I'd like to go deeper."

Gerrardo sat across from Artemas and selected a foil-wrapped *taco de barbacoa*. "I'll do my best, but remember I've only been here a few years."

"You talk to everyone and soak up history like a sponge. This whole incident has made me curious about the history of the Zamarripa family. What can you tell me?"

"I'll tell you what I know, but you really need to talk to someone else, maybe old Father Buendía."

"I've seen him around, but I've never spoken to him. Doesn't he spend a lot of time wandering the mountains?"

"That's right. He preceded Alfredo Mares as the village priest."

The teacher took a dainty bite from the taco, washed it down with Coke then dabbed grease from his lips with a flimsy paper napkin.

"But, getting back to your main question, the Zamarripa family came to Bustamante very early, I think sometime in the late sixteen hundreds. Almost immediately they acquired a position of power and authority. I'm not sure exactly how, but they ended up controlling most of the land in the area. To say they've never been popular is an understatement. However, what is really interesting is that a branch of the family split off not too long after they arrived. While they never had quite the power of the main Zamarripa clan, they've been a lot more popular. Have you met Humberto Alcazar?"

"No, but I've read most of his book you loaned me. I believe he refers to the Zamarripas as Vampires?" said Artemas, who had yet to take a bite of his lunch. He also remembered that Alcazar was the one who translated for Julie and Susan before they left for the *grutas*.

"He's the last surviving member of the family that split from the Zamarripas, at least in this area."

"I appreciate the information. Where should I go for more? A moment ago you suggested Father Buendía. What about Father Mares?"

The young teacher finished his taco and reached for another. "Father Buendía would certainly be very close to the source, in spite of the fact that he's a bit odd. After he retired he went to live with relatives in Michoacán, but something must have happened because about two years later he came back. Father Mares found an abandoned house for him behind the church, and a group of parishioners refurbished it, but Father Buendía spends a good bit of time wandering. Sometimes he's gone for days at a time. He's also often spotted in the cemetery. He's very odd, maybe eccentric would be a better word. He tells people he has seen vampires, werewolves, and other half-animal, half-human beings as well as the ghosts of their relatives. He even brings messages from the departed that I'm told sometimes make sense. But there are other times when he appears perfectly normal. It might be best to speak to both him and Father Mares."

"Thanks," said Artemas, draining his Coke. "Just one more thing. The artist, Ricardo Chavana—doesn't he have some connection to Alcazar? I understand he's not a fan of the Zamarripas either."

"He's another one you'll need to talk to an old-timer about. What I know is that Alcazar's father took Chavana into the family after his father was killed in an accident. I think he'd been working for Zarco Zamarripa's father. Anyway, Chavana and Humberto

Alcazar lived under the same roof for most of their teenage years and treat each other like brothers."

Gerardo paused and stared at Artemas. "I think I see where you're going. Does this have anything to do with the recent murders?"

"I don't know," shrugged Artemas, picking up the sack of uneaten tacos. "Probably not."

Gerardo rose to his feet. "I'll do some more checking, but now I need to get to class."Artemas stood and they shook hands. "Thanks for lunch," added Gerardo. "Please think seriously about coaching. It would be great for community-police relations."

Artemas waved goodbye.

A little ahead of schedule, he strolled back to the police station, purposely straying several blocks out of his way to absorb strength from the near perfect day. He pondered how such evil things could happen in a sleepy town like Bustamante. Life here was so simple and serene, or so he thought. As he nodded in greeting at the villagers he passed, it occurred to him that he was *noticing* them for the very first time.

He crossed into the plaza near the village church and caught a glimpse of Father Buendía slipping into the sanctuary. Artemas wished he had time to talk to him before he left.

HIGHWAY 1

Artemas found Jason and the two *federales* waiting for him by Jason's Suburban near the police station. Artemas had changed into pleated khaki pants and a blue polo shirt and hoisted an oversized gym bag into the trunk.

As they turned onto the narrow two-lane highway to Monterrey, Artemas tugged a small tape recorder from his pocket and asked Jason, "Can you tell me what happened while you're driving, or would you rather have me drive?"

"I'm O.K., you can turn on the recorder if you want."

Artemas held up a cigar. "Do you mind, or care for one?"

"That's fine but no thanks for me." Clouds of cigarette smoke were already billowing from the PGR agents sitting in back.

Jason's statement took twenty minutes. When they'd finished, Artemas rewound the tape, put it in an envelope, and handed it to one of Raymundo's men. Then he looked thoughtfully at Jason. "There are not many professors or journalists that could have done what you and *Señorita* Rendón did."

"I'm sure the outcome saved you considerable paperwork, not to mention intensive shoveling of rubble in the *grutas*."

"That and more," said Artemas. "Tell me, Dr. Peterson, how did you find your way to your present position?"

"Call me Jason," said the scientist. "It seems that policemen and journalists share a spirit of inquisitiveness. Laffi asked nearly the same question on our way back from the cave."

"So, what did you tell her?" snapped Artemas, and immediately regretted his reaction.

Jason gave his passenger a sharp glance then returned his eyes to the road. They were now winding down a steep hill flanked by farms with rows of low-slung poultry barns.

"I told her that in my youth I enlisted in the army, but had an accident that affected my hearing." He tapped his right ear.

"In the process of deciding what to do next, someone advised me to consider what I would like to do every day if I won the lottery, then figure out how to get just a little money for doing it. I grew up on a farm in Indiana and always loved animals. I was fascinated with the bats I discovered in an abandoned barn, joined every conservation group I could find, and won a regional science award. I even designed and built special houses for bats, sort of like birdhouses, and sometimes made them pets. Needless to say I was considered eccentric. Spending a lifetime doing those kinds of things appealed to me. It was that simple."

Jason shifted in his seat. The two *federales* were dozing in back, and Artemas took a puff on his cigar. "Please continue," he said.

"After being accepted by the University of Texas, I majored in biology and it worked out beautifully. Except recently. I've been spending too much time on fund raising and administrative details and less time in the field."

He paused and looked briefly at Artemas. "You're good! I only told Laffi the first part."

Ignoring the comment, Artemas said,"I guess a lot of people ask you about vampires?"

Jason explained the same history to Artemas that he had given Laffi the day before.

"So you're saying that the use of blood symbolized the life force and that vampires actually exist, but not in the usual supernatural, immortal sense?"

"Pretty much. The way of the world is that people are born, live their lives, then die. But there have always been individuals who refuse to accept science, the laws of nature or conventional wisdom. They believe they can overcome whatever stands between them and what they want. Their egos compel them to do whatever they think will enable them to prevail. Centuries ago it was only natural to believe that blood held the key to extending life, and it was used in bizarre ways.

"Many of these individuals were—and are—consumed by ambition and lust for power. They believe they have a divine right to carry out their twisted ambitions. Here's the key: whenever someone brings that kind of passion, combined with total ruthlessness, to any endeavor, the results are often amazing, far beyond the norm. In earlier times they took on the aura of the supernatural. Although I haven't researched it, my perception tells me these people often outlast their adversaries, giving the appearance of immortality. Of course that would have been particularly true earlier in history when life expectancies were shorter. On the current world scene, Fidel Castro might be an example. Of course there are countless more on a smaller scale, even, it seems, in a place like Bustamante." Jason paused then said, "Sorry, I'm lecturing."

"Actually, I find anything to do with human nature fascinating," said Artemas, flicking dead ash from his unfinished cigar into the ashtray. "But, it does sound a little too neat and tidy. Haven't you ever found anything that doesn't fit the theory?"

"Absolutely. But scientists rarely bring up anything that doesn't conform to their theories. The *chupacabra*—that's the most obvious one I can think of. There's nothing in the legends that claim it's a human exercising supernatural powers in an effort to conquer or rule, only that it destroys animals and drinks their blood. Interestingly, that newspaper guy I just met with, Ramirez, is convinced they exist after examining the recent incident."

"Do you believe in them, or do you subscribe to the theory that the killings come from wild dogs and satanic cults?" asked Artemas.

"Nothing's ever been confirmed. What do you think? Didn't you investigate the incident in Bustamante?"

"I did, and although I'm a pretty fair tracker I found no evidence of dogs. On the other hand, the Zamarripa brothers claimed they knew nothing about that incident. But I don't believe they were questioned about it, at least not in any *depth*."

"So," Jason said, "How did you end up in Bustamante?"

For several moments Artemas stared straight ahead. The

landscape was now dotted with small farms and the occasional roadside business as they approached the outskirts of Mexico's financial capital. He calculated they were about fifteen minutes from the airport. "There isn't time to explain it all," he finally said. "But if I can talk you into picking me up tomorrow at 4:30 P.M. I can finish it then."

"That sounds reasonable, but I want to make sure I'm available to help Laffi, if she needs it."

"I think she can take care of herself," grunted Artemas. Then more upbeat, he added, "But think about this: if she has to return to Washington, it would allow you to see her off!"

"You're a clever guy," said Jason. "O.K., it's a deal. Now get on with your story."

Wondering briefly why he was about to give Jason, someone he now recognized as a rival for Laffi's affections, information he normally guarded closely, Artemas began. "I was born on a huge hacienda owned by my father in the State of Sonora—where I'm going this afternoon. My mother was a full-blooded Yaqui Indian and died when I was very young. I was sent to live with the priest of the nearest town. Sort of the equivalent of being sent to boarding school, except I didn't go home during the summers, at least not to my father's home. I went to the *ranchería* of my mother's family. Are you familiar with the term?"

"Yeah, it's the traditional, pre-Hispanic, Yaqui living arrangement, a series of decentralized rural homesteads," replied Jason.

"In any case, my mother's relatives did their best to teach me to be an Indian, but weren't completely successful. I learned the language, traditional ceremonies, to track, to hunt, to fish, to farm, to survive in the wilderness—basically to live off the land in the old ways. But I didn't *want* to live off the land. And I only partially learned their most important lesson: patience. I understand what it is, but have difficulty practicing it."

"We all do," admitted Jason.

"You know," continued Artemas, "in intellectual Mexican circles, the phrase 'yin and yang' is more often used to refer to the relationship between the Indian and Spanish aspects of one's personality than to the usual male and female qualities. The Spanish side of me has a natural impatience, maybe even a touch of arrogance," he added ruefully. "And the education I got made it impossible for me to be comfortable with anything too simple.

"For better or worse, I owe that to Father Luis Laverdiere, the Jesuit priest of Bácum, the village nearest my father's hacienda. He taught me English and as many of the ways of the world as I was willing to absorb. Mostly he taught me that I could accomplish anything I wanted as long as I worked hard and made the right choices—even in Mexico. He not only told me, he showed me by arranging a full scholarship to Harvard for a kid with little academic record."

Artemas stopped his story short when he saw the airport entry, and roused the sleeping *federales*. "Pull over at Mexicana/ Aero Litoral; both our gates are there."

SONORA

The flight to Ciudad Obregón in the western state of Sonora was uneventful, and Artemas read and reread the e-mail he had printed from the Mexico City banker. Among other things, it contained a partial list of the members of Grupo Vampiro. He was not surprised to find his father's name among them.

Stepping out of the airport, Artemas was immediately rejuvenated. In spite of close proximity to the Sea of Cortez the region enjoyed a desert climate. The dry heat was especially welcome after the relentless humidity of Bustamante.

Although it would have been cheaper to hire a taxi to Bácum, for the sake of convenience Artemas had arranged for a rental. He spotted the green VW Passat waiting in the lot, loaded his few things and began threading his way along roads he knew well. The city's evening rush hour was in full swing.

Just before 8 P.M. he pulled into the sleepy village, one of the eight original Yaqui Indian communities consolidated by the Jesuits around mission churches during the seventeenth century. He quickly made his way to the old church, the only place he thought of as home, and parked near the apartment in back. To one side of the main plaza, the rambling adobe structure had been rebuilt and added to over the centuries but still maintained the character of a typical Spanish mission church. It was in the tiny room off the main living area, formerly used by the priest as a den and library, where Artemas had slept, studied, wept and raged through his formative years.

By now the village and plaza was dark, with few streetlights to cast away shadows. When Father Luis Laverdiere emerged from the softly lit apartment his sillhoutte seemed to shimmer. Artemas rushed over to embrace his mentor.

"Your call was a nice surprise. I hope the trip went well?"

Artemas's answer was to hold the shorter man affectionately by the shoulders, then stand back to look him over. The wiry frame, the light-skinned face with its aquiline nose and prominent cheekbones, the high forehead crowned with an unruly thatch of dark hair—yes, everything was as he remembered, and for that he was grateful.

"Yes, I'm still here," said the priest, his voice a deep baritone. "Grab whatever you need from the car and come in."

"It's good to be here...to see you. I'll get my bag."

They gathered in the living room below heavy beams surrounded by white plaster walls lined with handmade, mesquite wood bookcases.

"Would you care for a drink, or are you hungry?" asked the priest. "There's a new restaurant that I thought you might like."

"Truthfully, I'm starving. A new restaurant?"

"Yes. It's just beyond the plaza, *El Steakhouse*. I guess they're hoping for a boost from the cachet of *el Norte*. But they don't need it. They do a fine job with our local beef."

"Sounds great, let's go."

Soon the two men were seated at a heavy wooden table. Surveying the interior, Artemas observed a well-stocked bar along one entire side of the large, high-ceilinged space. At the far end was an open kitchen covered in traditional Talavera tile, its centerpiece a brick and tile grill overhung by a huge, beaten copper vent. On racks beside it were stacks of mesquite logs.

Artemas again scrutinized his mentor. Although it was now legal for clergy to wear religious garb outside of church property and functions, Father Laverdiere still wore his customary brown slacks, white dress shirt and a light brown leather jacket.

After they ordered drinks, the priest said, "I assume congratulations are in order. From what I read you just did just a fine job in Bustamante?"

Artemas caught the questioning lilt. "You're right on one level. The attorney general and president should be pleased with the outcome, which will not hurt my situation at all."

"There's another level?" Luis raised his eyebrows.

"I don't think those two punks killed the girl. It's virtually certain they committed the first murder, but not the second. Notwithstanding the fact that there's enough circumstantial evidence to convict them and make the whole thing go away."

"Sometimes you have to settle for what works rather than what's technically right, as long as no one is hurt. You should have learned from your last experience that you can't do anything positive to change things—other than become a minor, largely unknown martyr—from outside the system."

"Live and learn. Those words go together, although I'm not certain which should come first. And at the risk of sounding pedantic, I'm more convinced than ever that Mexico can't progress without a fair legal system. But I do realize I can't do anything to help bring it about from outside the system—or from six feet under."

"Progress!" said the priest, silently clapping his hands. "As we've discussed before, without at least some legal protection no one except the elite will believe they'll be allowed to keep the results of their sacrifice and work. And without that they won't do those things in the first place. And without those personal investments by millions of people, Mexico simply can't progress."

He leaned forward and looked straight at Artemas. "But if they didn't kill the American girl, who did, and does it have anything to do with why you're here?"

"I don't know. There are several possibilities. Why am I here? Truthfully, I'm not sure. Perhaps I'm just fishing, following my intuition. I guess I figured my father must know Zarco Zamarripa, and I wanted to see you. I discovered a financial connection between the two. I don't have any reason to believe Zamarripa senior had anything to do with the killings, but there's also no question he's involved in criminal activities, probably on a huge scale. Inevitably that means involvement with drugs. And village gossip aside, I'm just beginning to pick up some suspicious vibrations related to the family's history. If nothing else, learning more about the man could be useful in the future."

Father Laverdiere again raised his eyebrows. "As might the possibility of revenge on your father and his wife?"

Artemas lowered his eyes. "You're probably right." Then raising his gaze, eyes resentful, he added, "And why not, if it's justified and legal?" He sat back, his body language challenging and defensive at the same time.

For a moment Father Laverdiere saw before him not the mature man, but the angry adolescent. "Artemas. I understand your emotions, but you cannot give into them; they will destroy you...I—"

"What's wrong with my emotions?" Artemas burst in. "Pretty natural to have toward someone who took away my mother, maybe by murdering her."

The waiter bringing their drinks approached the table cautiously and cleared his throat, ending their heated conversation.

"*Sí, señores,*" he said. "*Una cerveza.*" He set down an ice-cold bottle of *Dos Equis lager* along with a frost-covered mug in front of Artemas. "*Y un tequila.*" For the priest, a tall shot glass of light amber liquid, another filled with a chaser of reddish-orange *sangrita*, and a dish of quartered limes. "Are you ready to order or would you like a little more time?"

"A little more time, thank you," said Luis. He faced Artemas and raised his glass. "*Salud*, good to see you."

His gaze was steady, a faint smile on his lips as he took a long sip from his tequila, followed by the *sangrita*. "In all fairness, there's something you should know," he said, carefully choosing his words.

Artemas knew this tone of voice meant, "Shut up and listen."

"When I was in the process of applying for your financial aid to Harvard, your father, who had just become Governor, heard what I was doing. He came to me and said that although you were illegitimate, he was proud that you carried his name. He went on to say that he considered it improper for the son of the governor of Sonora, *his* son, to accept financial aid, even though the circumstances made it legally acceptable. He arranged to pay all your fees, living expenses, allowance and travel. The total came to nearly $180,000 U.S. dollars over four years. He never complained or questioned the amounts, and he made me promise not to tell you. But I think that vow has expired."

Stunned, Artemas finally asked in a low voice, trying not to sound sarcastcic, "Is it not possible that he was afraid of the scandal if it came out that the wealthy Governor of Sonora had a son receiving huge amounts of financial aid, and that his son was illegitimate, not to mention the circumstances of his mother's death and how he had been banished from the family?"

"That too, I suppose," said Luis. "All I'm trying to say is that you still allow your attitude to interfere with your more useful qualities of patience and self-discipline. He paused and added, "I know what I told you will eventually sink in. Now, I thought you were starving?" He picked up the heavy, cowhide-covered menu. "I can heartily recommend the T-bone, especially with the *rajas de chile verde, hongos silvestres, papas fritas, y frijoles maneados.*"

"Sounds perfect." Artemas had not even glanced at the menu.

They gave their dinner orders, plus another tequila for Luis, who gestured at Artemas's barely touched beer. "Relax," he said.

"I shall, but first tell me what arrangements you made with my father for a meeting."

"You said your flight leaves at 11:30 A.M., and Don Alvarado agreed to meet you at Alejandro's café at 9:00 A.M."

"Perfect. And how is Alejandro? He was always fair."

"He put up with you didn't he?" Luis chuckled. "He's doing fine. Like the rest of us, not any younger, but fine. Now," the priest shifted his position as his conversation changed focus, "do you have anything but intuition to tell you who actually killed the American girl, and what do you intend to do about it?"

Artemas thought carefully for a moment. "Nothing even faintly concrete, but I've had zero time to work on the problem. And that's what I intend to do. I've got a couple of vague leads. As there's normally not a lot to do in Bustamante, I should have time to follow them. But don't worry, I intend to be *very* low key. In any case, after what's just happened, I wouldn't be surprised if the attorney general concludes that my 'rehabilitation' is complete, and brings me back into things, sooner than later."

"Just be sure you don't say anything to your father that might incline him to make a phone call to Mexico City that could give you more opportunity than you want to follow up vague leads in Bustamante, or maybe someplace even less propitious. Remember he still has considerable influence."

When they returned to the church apartment, Father Laverdiere put his hand on the young man's shoulder. "Just one last piece of advice, *bien*?"

"Of course," said Artemas.

"Make a conscious effort to clear your mind of anger and resentment. They're truly poisonous. Your mother died many years ago, and nearly everyone with first hand knowledge is either dead or long gone."

Artemas gave the man who had truly been a father to him an affectionate *abrazo*. "Everyone, that is, except my father and his wife," he said, and headed for his tiny room.

SONORA

It had been a long time since Artemas had been in the café, so long that no one recognized him besides the owner. Alejandro gave him a joyful *abrazo*, slapping his back as if he were a long lost friend rather than a former employee. "What brings you back to Sonora, *amigo*? Not enough girls in the capital?" Seeing Artemas's embarrassment he quickly added, "I know they're enough crooks there even for a policeman of your talents."

"Just a quick trip," Artemas replied. Anticipating the meeting with Don Alvarado, his insides were churning. "Anyway, I haven't been in Mexico City for over a year. I'm in Bustamante, Nuevo León now."

"You mean, where that *gringa* was murdered? That was you who caught them?" Almost breathless, Alejandro looked around, wondering how quickly he could take advantage of this prime morsel of gossip.

"Partly me."

"Well, congratulations. Why did they do it...for sex?"

"I can't really say."

"Sure, sure. Well anyway, how's your father?"

Artemas's face darkened. "I wouldn't know. That's part of why I'm here — to find out. How do you think he is?"

"Still the uptight Yaqui, eh?" Alejandro said, beginning to lose interest as the spell of camaraderie dispersed.

"I guess so, it must be in the blood." Artemas smiled, making an effort to repair the damage. "How about a cup of the best coffee in Mexico?"

Artemas stared into his coffee trying to decide why he really had come back. Then painfully he conjured up his first memories as a child. He was by his mother's side as she painted murals on the wall of the vast hacienda. So entranced was he at the bright colors that flowed from her brushes into whimsical forms that he had only wanted to watch her, never to play with the other children. After every few strokes she would reach down and pat his head. He had hoped that time would never end.

But it did, and the first sign that things would be different came a month or two after Don Alvarado's return from Spain with his new wife, who was said to come from one of Europe's wealthiest families. One day Artemas's mother told him that she was no longer allowed to decorate the hacienda with her art. She would be working in the kitchen, and he would have to play with the children of the other servants. He remembered with clarity the hurt in her eyes as she uttered the word: *criadas*. He knew that Don Alvarado was his father and that his relationship with him was different from that of other children and their fathers. At the time he didn't understand why, nor did he understand his mother's feelings. He just knew something was very, very wrong.

Then a week later he remembered, with equal clarity, the day Don Alvarado came into his room, picked him up and held him so tightly he had wanted to cry out. As far as he knew it was the first time his father had touched him in such a manner, and he was frightened. He remembered calling out for his mother all the way into the village, and Don Alvarado staring ahead at the road and saying nothing.

He remembered being taken to the little adobe apartment behind the church, still crying for his mother, and that father Laverdiere had held him tenderly and explained how, because she was such a wonderful person, God, our Lord, had selected his mother from among all those on earth to go to heaven, to be with him and his son Jesus.

Of course, Artemas later heard that Don Alvarado had one day seen a serving plate his mother—one of many Yaqui servants at the hacienda—had painted. He was so impressed that he had promoted her from cook's helper and commissioned her to decorate the entire hacienda. Don Alvarado had also seen other things — the girl's ample breasts, her slender, strong legs, her perfect brown skin, and perhaps most of all, the creative sparkle in her eyes. Years later Artemas learned that his mother had died in a riding accident. Something he considered highly improbable as she had no access to horses.

Father Laverdier, Father Luis, as Artemas came to call him, liberally endowed on the sly by Don Alvarado, had raised the boy as if he were his own. This was a rare and unexpected joy for the priest, and he made the most of it, giving the boy an education the likes of which had never been seen in backcountry Sonora. In addition to the basics, he assiduously tutored Artemas in philosophy, trying but never wholly succeeding in being objective where religion was concerned. Perhaps most importantly, he incorporated in the process the innate pragmatism of the Jesuits, a perfect complement to that of the Yaqui. In that regard he made sure that Artemas spent summers at the remote *ranchería* where his mother's family lived. There, Artemas had been schooled in the ancient ways and skills.

The hair on the back of Artemas's neck began to tingle and he glanced up from his reverie. Looking down at him was his father.

SONORA

Don Alvarado looked at Artemas over his half-raised cup, his eyes mere slits under an expensive black felt Stetson. "Well?" he said.

Artemas matched his father's gaze. Two pairs of identical green eyes sized each other up with the same mannerisms. "I'm tying up some loose ends," he replied.

His voice was level and his eyes bored into his father's. After a lengthy pause he continued, "The murder of the American senator's daughter. You heard of the case, and that I'm in Bustamante now?"

Don Alvarado's lips, below a perfect pencil mustache flecked with gray, curled into a mocking smile. "Oh, that's right, you had to leave Mexico City. Still can't get along eh?"

When he spoke, Artemas's voice held a trace of his father's mockery. "I'm sorry if it caused problems for you, not to mention a lot of money." Artemas detected a flash of surprise in the man's eyes. "You know, during the time I spent working in the capital I always wondered how a kid right out of school got to be a detective so quickly—and somebody finally told me." Then softening his voice, he added, "But thanks for trying." He reached over and touched his father's hand.

Don Alvarado's eyes were as silent as his tongue.

Artemas examined his father for a moment longer. "Those guys I blew the whistle on were into every racket there is—drugs, kidnapping, murder, extortion—you name it. And don't forget," he added, caustically, "after my mother was killed you sent me to be raised by an honest man. Didn't you think it would stick?"

The color drained from Don Alvarado's face, but he kept his silence.

"Anyway," Artemas continued, as if nothing more than pleasantries had passed between them, "in case you haven't heard, some PGR agents the attorney general sent up to help with the case think that two brothers, Ignacio and Armando Zamarripa, killed the girl. Their father is Zarco Zamarripa, the industrialist. I thought you might know the family?"

"I believe I've met him," replied Don Alvarado, suddenly wary. "Of course when I was governor I met just about everybody."

Artemas looked his father squarely in the eye. "Zamarripa is head of a secret camarilla made up of some of the richest, most powerful men in the country. I believe it's called *Grupo Vampiro*."

"Where...?" blurted out Don Alvarado. Then regaining his composure, he lowered his voice nearly to a whisper. "That's very interesting, but as you know I've been out of the loop for a long time." He pulled the Stetson lower over his face.

"Don Alvarado," Artemas spoke in a low voice, devoid of rancor, curbing his impulse to try and further embarrass the man. "I don't want to cause you any trouble. Although officially the investigation is closed, I'm not convinced that the Zamarripa brothers killed the girl. The previous murder? Without a doubt. But this one... I just want to make sure we have the real killers. Not so much for the sake of the brothers, who are an unpleasant pair, but to ensure there's not another vicious criminal on the loose rubbing elbows with the people of Bustamante."

"I understand what you're saying, but I don't see how I can help you."

Artemas, looked at his coffee, took a sip, then raised his eyes to meet his father's. "Before I asked for this meeting, I did some research. Not only did I find out a great deal about the activities of Grupo Vampiro, I was also provided a partial list of its members."

Artemas paused, his gaze steady. "There are some vague rumors around Bustamante that revolve around the Zamarripa family. They include others who might be involved. The more I can learn about the family, and particularly the father, the better."

Don Alvarado looked at his son, as if for the first time in his life. To mask the emotion he felt, he made a show of finishing his coffee. He reached over, covered his son's hand on the table with his own, and rose to his feet. "I'll see what I can do." He tipped his hat, turned and walked out.

SONORA

After meeting his father Artemas had plenty of time to pack and get to the airport. Disliking long goodbyes, he purposely took an old road meandering back to the church. He wondered what the outcome of his meeting with his father would be. He knew that "nothing" was not an option with Don Alvarado Salcido.

The church apartment was empty when he returned. Father Luis found him shoving dirty clothes and toiletries into his kit bag.

"I just received a message for you." The priest, dressed in his brown pants and white shirt, held a small sheet of paper.

Artemas looked at him expectantly but detected no hint of what was to come. Luis cleared his throat. "A *Señor* Zarco Zamarippa would like the pleasure of meeting you. He hopes that you can come to his home in the Garza Garcia district of Monterrey between 6:00 and 6:30 P.M. today, but no later." Luis handed Artemas the note.

Artemas looked at the paper then back at Luis. "Very interesting, don't you think?"

"Very."

Monterrey

Refrigerated air chilled Artemas as he stepped from the plane's ramp into the Monterrey terminal. The flight was late, but he still had over an hour to get to Zamarripa's house, assuming that Jason would be amenable to the change in plans. He scanned the crowd and easily spotted the tall, blond biologist.

"Thanks for meeting me. How is Miss Rendón?"

"She's fine," beamed Jason, shaking his hand. "I picked her up at the hospital earlier today, and she's recovering nicely. Took her computer with her to the hospital and never stopped working. Our little adventure gave her more than enough material to blow away the competition. And she's decided to stay in Bustamante a few more days to recover. She suggested I bring you back for dinner at the hotel, if you're available."

The invitation and the thought that Laffi still had not mentioned their previous acquaintance pleased Artemas. Seeing Jason so upbeat, he seized the opportunity and explained his need to interview the father of the boys in custody.

"Okay," Jason agreed. "As long as we're back in time for dinner with Laffi."

Artemas patted Jason on the shoulder. "Let's get going," he said, almost certain he could not keep the promise.

Artemas had hatched a plan, knowing that what he was about to do could have serious consequences. He'd been down this road before. He was well aware of the potential appearance of impropriety by meeting privately with the accused's father, especially at this stage of the proceedings. However, Zamarripa was the one who asked for the meeting, undoubtedly taking the bait offered by Artemas when he told his father of his doubts of Ignacio and Armando's guilt in Julie Connor's murder.

Artemas was wired. A small, digital tape recorder in his pants pocket; a tiny mic clipped inside his shirt. Still, he knew he must be extremely careful. Assuming that Zamarripa might also record the conversation, Artemas could not give him anything to use as blackmail or to discredit the case against his sons. Returning from his thoughts, Artemas said,"If you can, get over and take Gonzalitos, that'll bring us to Garza Garcia."

Once they settled into the new stream of southbound traffic, Jason asked, "Tell me, Artemas, what's your motivation in all of this?"

"That's easy. I came home from Harvard with the firm belief that Mexico will never make real progress until we have a fair justice system. Because so much is resolved with bribes and intimidation, people just don't have enough confidence they'll be able to keep what they've earned for them to make the sacrifices necessary to earn it in the first place. For police, it's not enough to solve a mystery and catch a criminal. If the perpatrator's rich and powerful, he'll probably be set free by a crooked judge. Whoever arrested him is likely to be punished—or worse. So most of us decide it's easier and safer to just take a bribe. That's got to stop or we'll never make it to the first world."

Jason gestured toward a series of signs and exits coming up, and Artemas said, "Keep going straight. This takes us over Constitución and the river then into Garza Garcia where some of the world's richest people live."

Jason nodded, well aware that although Mexico City was the official government and cultural capital of Mexico, Monterrey was the financial center and had more than its fair share of billionaires. Many of them were old Jewish families who found their way here after being expelled from Spain.

The city rolled up a hillside and extended as far as the eye could see under a yellowish pall of smog. Billboards were scattered everywhere, on buildings, streets and vacant lots, with a preponderance of pretty blond women promoting beer, cars and cake mix.

There were few cars on the road as they approached the exclusive enclave of Garza Garcia. The jagged Chipinque Mountain towered before them.

"When I first got here," said Artemas, "I spent a lot of time getting to know the area, and I think I can find Zamarripa's house."

Following Artemas's directions, they eventually turned into a neighborhood of tall masonry walls interrupted by heavy gates and guardhouses. They pulled up to a massive, yet delicately ornate, stainless steel gate that Artemas judged cost well over $100,000 U.S. It opened to a large circular drive leading to a pink stucco mansion of sleek modernist design.

"Back up and park here. I'll walk in," said Artemas. "I'll be as quick as I can. Shouldn't be more than half an hour to forty-five minutes." He paused to turn on the concealed recorder.

"O.K.," said Jason, who was fishing around in the Suburban for his cell phone to call Laffi.

Monterrey

Artemas walked briskly across the street, humming an old Yaqui spirit song, intent on ignoring potential damage to his career. Beyond the gleaming entry gate and circular drive paved with black-grouted flagstone, stood a grand, double entry door, also made of brushed stainless steel. His finger had just touched the bell when the ten-foot high doors swung open.

Although Artemas had no description of Zarco Zamarripa, he instinctively knew the man before him was not the head of Grupo Vampiro. He was stocky and powerful, but with the loose-jointed limberness of a gymnast. Above the craggy, handsome features was a full head of black hair, flecked with grey. However, the man's demeanor and expensive, casual clothes were not those of a servant.

"*Capitán* Salcido." It was more statement than question.

"*Sí, señor.*"

"Please follow me," he said, turning on his heel. Artemas trailed him across a large foyer of polished black and white marble tile then down a wide hall of the same material. The man stopped at a pair of tall mahogany doors, pushed them open and stood aside. "*Pasele,*" he said, motioning for Artemas to precede him.

Entering a large paneled study, Artemas looked back at his guide. "*Señor* Zamarippa will be with you momentarily," the man said, then silently closed the doors.

Artemas quickly assessed his surroundings, a stark glass and steel coffee table flanked by leather chairs, and a disturbing painting on the opposite wall. This time there was no doubt that the man coming toward him through a paneled rear door was Zarco

Zamarripa. He was tall and thin with unnaturally wide shoulders. His perfectly postured body, clad in a dark, double-breasted suit and maroon tie, seemed to glide across the room.

"I'm so glad you were able to accept my invitation," said Zamarripa, extending his hand. His voice was low and deep. Now that he could clearly see his host's face, Artemas was both taken aback and repelled. The skin, stretched drum-tight over aristocratic features, was an unnatural, milky white, except for prominent blue veins and mauve lips. What gave the face life were the eyes that gleamed with unnatural brightness. Artemas noticed the man's hand was surprisingly long and bony. It was also very cold.

"Please sit down." Zamarripa motioned toward a chair by the glass coffee table. "Would you care for something to drink?"

"*No, gracias.*" Artemas seated himself.

Zamarripa sat down in the other chair and focused his glittering eyes on Artemas. "Thank you for seeing me on such short notice. I know you're probably tired and would like to return to Bustamante, so I will not detain you unnecessarily." He paused then leaned toward his guest. "As you must know, I spoke with Don Alvarado this morning, and he mentioned there was some doubt in your mind regarding my sons' guilt?" His mouth curled in distaste.

Artemas composed himself then raised his eyes to meet his host's. "I appreciate your directness and will try to reciprocate. I don't know what my father told you. Although the test results are not complete, the evidence is overwhelming that Ignacio and Armando killed the drifter. The office of the attorney general has also decided that the evidence in the case of the American girl is conclusive. I am sorry but I cannot discuss the details. I probably should not even be here, but have come as a courtesy to my father."

The moment the words left his mouth he knew he'd made a mistake. Zamarripa leaned even closer and his eyes became even brighter. "But didn't you tell your father you wished to see me? And do you agree with the attorney general's conclusion?"

"I told my father that as background to the case I would like to know more about your family's history with the village. That's all."

"But do you agree that they killed the girl?"

Artemas noticed that Zamarripa's voice had become testy. "I have no evidence that would contradict that conclusion."

"But perhaps you have unsubstantiated doubts? Why don't you ask me whatever you would like and perhaps..."

"I can assure you again that I have no evidence that would cause me to doubt your sons' guilt in both murders. I am in charge of enforcing the law in Bustmanate, so the more I know about it, including its history, the better I can do my job." The feeble justification was the best he could offer.

Zamarripa leaned back and folded his arms. But he said nothing and his gaze never left Artemas.

"Could you tell me about your relationship with Humberto Alcazar and Ricardo Chavana?"

A glimmer of surprise passed through Zamarripa's eyes. "*Señor* Alcazar is a distant relative. We know each other, but have never been close."

"Is there any reason for that?"

"His branch of the family and mine split generations ago. I don't think anyone remembers the reason."

"And Ricardo Chavana?"

Zamarripa cleared his throat. "His father worked for my father and they lived on our property. Unfortunately, his father was killed in an accident. I don't remember the details. He then went to live with the Alcazars. I'm sure they convinced him that my family was somehow responsible for the accident. We had played together as children, but after he left we never spoke again. That's unfortunately the way it's always been between our families. I think that's all I can tell you about those two. Why do you ask?"

Inwardly quaking, Artemas decided it was time to finish baiting the trap he'd conceived on the plane. "Can you think of any reason, beyond a long-forgotten family dispute and bitterness over the accident you referred to, why either of them would wish you ill?" He spoke slowly, choosing his words with extreme caution.

Again surprise flashed in Zamarripa's eyes, then he looked pointedly at his watch. "I appreciate your coming and have enjoyed meeting you, but unfortunately I have another appointment. Before you go let me ask you one other thing. I have not yet spoken to my attorneys but it seems to me that if doubts were raised that Ignacio and Armando are guilty in the girl's murder, the penalty would be less severe. Does that not make sense?"

"That, *Señor* Zamarripa, is not for me to say." Artemas stood and extended his hand. "I too have enjoyed meeting you, I just regret the circumstances."

Zamarripa stood and shook his hand. "Joaquin will show you out." The man who had first met Artemas at the door materialized close behind him.

As he was escorted through the marble entry, he reflected that the painting he'd seen was the very same *Hacienda Zamarripa* featured in the newspaper article about Ricardo Chavana. Though striking in color and composition, it was grisly in detail: a hacienda owner drinking wine, but more likely blood, from an ornate goblet atop a pile of mutilated Indian bodies.

Monterrey

When he returned to the Suburban, Artemas told Jason that his meeting merely reinforced his opinion that the Zamarripa brothers didn't kill Julie Conners. In fact, it was highly probable that the crime had been committed for reasons unknown, related to Bustamante's history. He'd given Zarco a hint, hoping that if his guess were correct it would precipitate action.

"If the seed I've planted is going to germinate it'll happen fast. Mind if we stay and watch the house for a couple of hours?" What he didn't tell Jason was that he feared he had done the equivalent of turning a hornets' nest into a *piñata*.

Jason looked at his watch. "Damn it, we'd barely get back in time for dinner if we left now. I tried to call Laffi to tell her we'll be late, but her cell wasn't working. They don't have phones in the rooms, and I couldn't make the clerk at the hotel understand."

"I'll be happy to make the call," said Artemas, "Explain to the charming Ms. Rendón that I've imposed upon your good nature to help in a bit of police business."

"I'd appreciate that."

Having already thrown caution to the wind, Artemas said casually, "Did you know that she and I are old friends? We were at Harvard at the same time."

"N-no," Jason stammered, surprised.

Once the hotel staff tracked her down Artemas spoke eloquently and apologetically to Laffi then handed the phone to Jason who finished the conversation with, "If it's not too late, is it alright if stop by your room? Maybe we could take a walk."

"Let's drive around for a few minutes," suggested Artemas, purposefully ignoring the evident relationship developing between Jason and Laffi. After all, Laffi would soon be gone, once again out of his life. "In case anyone checks, it'll look like we've left for good."

When they returned to Zarco's house Artemas asked Jason to park across the street at an angle where they could see into the driveway but could not be seen from the front door.

Soon thereafter a late model black Lincoln Town Car cruised down the street. It was followed closely by a white Ford van with dark tinted windows. Artemas slumped down in his seat and advised Jason to do the same. The Lincoln and white van slowed to a crawl upon entering Zamarripa's driveway, and parked in front of the mansion. A short, powerful man in a tan leather jacket emerged from the Lincoln, looking around cautiously before walking through the front door. Artemas noticed his head was abnormally large.

"That man looks familiar, but I can't quite place him," whispered Artemas. "He must be the appointment Zamarripa mentioned."

Meanwhile, another van, this one dark blue, swung down the street and hesitated near the entry gate. Suddenly it accelerated, squealed around the corner into the driveway and slid behind the parked van. Before even stopping, men poured out. They were dressed in black, wearing baseball caps and flak jackets, carrying automatic weapons. They swarmed around the white van and yanked open the doors. Five tough looking men were hauled outside, searched, handcuffed and shoved back into the van. One of the men in black jumped into the driver's seat and another stayed with the prisoners. After securing the Lincoln, a procession of town car and two vans sped out the driveway and headed toward the main road back to Monterrey. The entire operation took under a minute.

"That looked like a SWAT team, and a damn good one," said Jason, as the vehicles disappeared around the corner. "What's going on?"

Artemas shook his head.

Jugo Gandara sat opposite Zarco Zamarripa. "So," the drug dealer began with a sneer, "your brilliant children killed an important *gringa* and got caught. But don't think this changes our deal. If the attorney general gets a copy of the tape I showed you things will go a lot worse for them." He leaned forward and glared at his host. "Now, where's the paperwork giving me control of Grupo Vampiro?"

Zamarripa's gaze was steady. "My dear Jugo, did you sincerely believe that would happen? Did you really think you could intimidate me like some frightened official terrified for the safety of his family?"

Gandara's dark face flushed to purple. "*Tu hijo de puta.*" He pointed his finger at Zamarripa. "You'll live just long enough to see your sons in jail, their throats slit, and their balls cut off." He stood up, still pointing at his host.

Zamarripa remained very still. "Now, now, Jugo," he said. "You're not going anywhere, at least not yet. You see," he looked over Gandara's shoulder, "Joaquin and I have plans for you."

The drug dealer spun around to find Zamarripa's sidekick aiming a short-barreled shotgun at his chest.

"Put these on. Catch." said Joaquin, tossing Gandara a pair of handcuffs attached to a foot-long chain. Gandara let them drop to the polished wood floor with a heavy clank, then spat loudly and looked at his watch, "My men have instructions to break in within ten minutes if I don't call them off."

Zamarripa's lips curled with a satisfied sneer. "Jugo, I'm afraid your men are now occupied with the process of dying. Now pick up those handcuffs and put them on, with the chain behind you, or Joaquin will be forced to make a mess here. Now do it!"

Joaquin jabbed at the cuffs with his shotgun to emphasize the point.

Bustamante

By now it was twilight and Artemas and Jason were anticipating a second act to the black-ops drama. They didn't have long to wait. Soon they saw a black Lincoln Navigator exit a narrow driveway next to the mansion and park near the front door. Artemas recognized Joaquin leaving the vehicle to enter the building. Shortly thereafter Zamarripa and Joaquin returned through the massive doors, closely flanking the short man with the large head. He and Joaquin climbed into the back, Zamarripa took the driver's seat.

"Pull forward," Artemas whispered urgently. "Get around the corner before they see us, then go around the block and stop. We should be able to see them, whichever way they go, then follow."

Jason threw his Suburban into gear, and accelerated. He sped around the block and parked halfway down the street with the engine running. He kept the lights off.

The black Lincoln came into view heading toward the main road. "O.K.," said Jason. "Here we go."

"Don't use the headlights until we hit traffic," cautioned Artemas.

The Navigator led them to the main thoroughfare and turned north toward Monterrey. Rush hour traffic was traveling in the opposite direction so Jason was able to keep up with Zamarripa's SUV from a safe distance. As they continued north, Artemas said, "I'm going to bet they're heading exactly where we want to go: back to Bustamante."

"What's happening, any idea?"

"Several, and none of them particularly pleasant. We'll just have to see." Inside, his gut was churning.

Cruising along the freeway just west of Monterrey's center, the traffic thickened and twilight became night. Jason compensated by decreasing the gap. Once they passed through the northernmost suburbs the cars thinned out. Again Jason increased his distance.

Soon the Navigator turned onto Highway 1, confirming Artemas's guess. It was almost certain they were headed to Bustamante. Artemas speculated they would turn off before the village, onto the road to Zamarripa's hacienda.

The Lincoln settled into a steady sixty miles per hour on the narrow two-lane highway. They were now the only vehicles on the road, and Jason dropped back further. He was afraid their quarry would slow down or stop, forcing them to pass, providing a good look at his Suburban and its Texas plates.

Jason turned to Artemas and said, "You said you knew Laffi at Harvard?"

"Indeed, unfortunately we were only together for the one semester that she was there." Artemas purposely did not elaborate, did not explain that what he really thought was unfortunate was the mostly platonic nature of the relationship.

The moonlit desert streamed by as they wound gradually up into the foothills, straining for a glimpse of distant taillights. Nearing Bustamante, Artemas said, "Pull up a little. We don't want to miss them if they turn off at Zamarripa's hacienda. It's about a mile ahead."

They closed the gap while cruising past run-down convenience stores and garages at the intersection where Julie and Susan had first glimpsed the mountains.

"They're not turning, pull way back!" Artemis shouted. "They've got to be going to the village."

The *Bustamante y Las Grutas* banner ahead signaled the turnoff into town. Jason switched off his headlights. "No worries, they won't see a thing."

They crossed over railroad tracks that paralleled the main highway and went another quarter of a mile past the village's first house before Jason restored the lights. They watched as two red dots took the road toward the plaza. They followed as the Lincoln climbed the slight hill.

"Turn right, then left at the next block" said Artemas, "and stop just before you get to the plaza on the other side. I think I know where they're going."

Jason accelerated and quickly parked on the left side of the road. Above them stood the church, moonlight reflecting off white washed adobe. Beside them a vine-covered stone wall enclosed a property of mature trees. Opposite were ancient two-story houses, their sheer curtained windows glowing from incandescent light. No one was visible inside.

Artemas jumped out, trotted to the corner and peered around. The plaza was empty. To his left, a hundred yards away, the Lincoln was parked in front of the substantial old home belonging to Humberto Alcazar. He made out shadowy shapes within the SUV's dark interior.

Artemas leaned against the stone wall, glad no one was about. After just a day in Sonora he was more conscious of the damp breeze. As he waited, puffy gusts stirred the leaves in the canopy above and in the trees ringing the plaza. Rather than cooling off, the humidity seemed to build. A shadow passed over the moon, and distant lightning foretold an approaching thunderhead.

The door to Alcazar's house opened, and a tall figure he recognized as Zamarripa exited and quickly made his way to the driver's side of the Lincoln.

Frantically, Artemas motioned for Jason to crouch down. He sprinted toward the Suburban and was barely inside and on the floor before the Lincoln's headlights swept through the interior and passed by.

"It's a good thing they didn't get a good look at us earlier," said Artemas. "But now we've got to be extra careful."

"I'll pull around the square and make a left on the main road, back the way we came in," said Jason as they resituated themselves from their crouched positions. "What happened?" he added.

"Zamarripa spent about fifteen minutes in that house, which belongs to a writer named Humberto Alcazar, a relative of Zamarripa."

Jason had noted the intricate wrought iron and antique

double doors. The house had been completely in shadow, light coming only from somewhere deep within. "What do you think it means?"

"I don't know. I'm guessing they'll go to the hacienda now. I'm sorry about wrecking your evening, but if I could impose on you just a little longer, I'd like to see if I'm correct."

"No problem. Actually, this is kind of fun."

He made the left turn onto the main road and drove back to Highway 1. In the distance ahead was the Lincoln. As Artemas anticipated, it soon turned right and passed under the arch elaborately lettered *Hacienda Zamarripa*.

"Now what?" asked Jason, carefully finding a parking spot to await further instructions.

"May I use your phone?" asked Artemas.

After several bursts of Spanish, Artemas handed back the cellphone. "Thanks. Moreno will be here soon to take up the watch, and we can go back to the village."

Artemas's assistant arrived in a battered Toyota. Following directions he parked down the road toward the village and raised his hood, to signal engine trouble.

"Call me if you see anyone coming or going," Artemas told Moreno, then got back into the Suburban.

"*Muy Bien*, my friend," he said to Jason. "I can't thank you enough for the help. Just drop me at the office. I want to get caught up before tomorrow." Once they neared the police station, he added, "I know it'll be difficult, but please tell Laffi as little about what just happened as possible, and stress the need for confidentially."

"I understand," said Jason, anxious to get to the hotel.

Bustamante

Back in his office, Artemas unlocked the drawer where he kept his eavesdropping paraphernalia. He placed a tape recorder and several other items in a small canvas bag and pulled the drawstrings. Then he turned off the desk light and leaned back in his chair to take a nap. He was awakened several times by thunder and lighting and the battering of a downpour. Around midnight he grabbed the canvas bag and slipped out the door.

The storm had passed. Artemas sloshed to the corner of the plaza and leaned casually against the Municipio wall. The last bus had long gone and no one was in the plaza. He walked across its length toward the church, keeping to the shadows of dripping trees. He saw no lights in Alcazar's house, or anywhere else. He continued nearly all the way around the block, stopping by a telephone pole about halfway back to the plaza.

He waited a minute or so to survey his surroundings and tied the canvass bag to his belt. A banner was strung across the street, directly over a fresh pile of bricks, proclaiming that the president's political party was improving the village. As usual, this flury of activity was a couple months before the election.

Once he felt secure in his mission, he examined the telephone pole more closely. About two feet above his head were the first set of spikes used as a ladder by utility linemen, set high enough to discourage children and mischief. Artemas jumped and reached the first spike and pulled himself up. He quickly scrambled up the pole and did what he had come to do. From his perch near the top he could look down through trees at the back of Alcazar's house and its heavily wooded yard, extending the entire length of the block. He slipped down the pole and walked quickly back to the station.

Bustamante

On his way to the Hotel Ancira Jason realized he was badly in need of a shower. The past few hours of stress, heat and humidity had left an unpleasant residue. Although he doubted the evening would hold much by way of intimacy, he wasn't taking any chances.

He pulled into the little oasis park at the outskirts of the village. There was a green cement-block shower and restroom building and a large stone swimming pool, its shimmering surface restless in the gusty breeze. His was the only vehicle in the lot, faintly illuminated by a stormy moon. Taking his camp light, soap, razor, and towel into the shower area, he made the necessary repairs in a few minutes.

He needed to stretch his legs, so he walked back to the hotel, cutting across the village to save time. He noticed that the wind was gaining in strength and that the moon was almost obscured by a heavy black cloud. When he reached the hotel entrance it was already locked and dark. He walked around back and tapped on Laffi's door.

"Just a minute," came her voice. "Come on in," she said once she opened the door, though she made no move to step aside.

Jason leaned down and gave her a tentative hug, wary of her bandaged forearm. She gently pushed him away.

Jason took in her new jeans, pink cotton shirt with two buttons undone, and kitten-heel pink sandals that revealed ruby toenails. She spun around with a flourish, her luxurious blond hair catching the light.

"Courtesy of Soriana and Gigante, Mexico's versions of Walmart and Target," she said. "And where have you been, Batman—out pollinating cactus plants?"

"Nothing quite that fun," replied Jason, not yet ready to elaborate.

Laffi was displeased by his noncommital response and let the conversation drop. The ensuing silence between them became increasingly uncomfortable. After a heavy sigh she finally spoke. "Now you better explain why I got stood up. You and Artemas were supposed to be here for dinner! Where is he?" Her eyes and tone conveyed she was not kidding.

Hoping to salvage the evening, Jason summarized what had happened that day, mindful of Artemas's injunction to confidentiality. "So..." she said, perked up by all this tantalizing information. "Did he say specifically what makes him doubt those fine young men killed Julie Connors?"

"No, and I didn't ask."

Laffi shook her head in mock disgust. "Never send a man to do a woman's job.

"But he did say that you and he were at Harvard together. That was a surprise."

Still irritated with the change in plans, Laffi chose to ignore his implied question regarding the nature of their relationship. "We decided to keep that a secret so that neither of our bosses could accuse us of being unobjective." Then she added, "I'll bet you're starved; I had Eduardo send up some sandwiches and beer." She pointed to a Styrofoam cooler on the floor next to the bed and sat herself in a vinyl chair next to a chest of drawers.

Jason decided to bide his time and accept a sandwich. He was hungrier than he thought and inhaled the sliced beef on Bimbo, Mexico's Wonder Bread. There was more mayonnaise than meat so he decided to forego the second sandwich. Between sips of beer, Laffi mentioned that her arm was better, she'd caught up on her work, and she'd eaten in the dining room right after his call. And, by the way, she was bored.

"How about that walk you suggested?" she pouted. "While you've been out playing policeman I've been cooped up here."

"You have an umbrella?" he asked. "It looks like we could be in for another storm."

"No, but after what I've been through the last few days a little rain should be no problem."

Jason arched his eyebrows. "Well, there's always lightning."

She threw him a don't-screw-with-me glance, and headed toward the door.

Outside, the wind gusts came in violent bursts, and the humidity weighed heavy on their skin.

"Hmm," said Laffi, scanning the dancing tree limbs far above. "The hell with it. Let's go up the street toward the cemetery and cut right. There are a lot of trees and old buildings in case we need cover."

This was the direction from which Jason had just come, and all the houses fronting the street had flat, parapet roofs with no sheltering overhang. But he kept silent and followed Laffi as she headed toward the hotel's back entry, enjoying the sexy effect her sandals had on her stride.

Making their way up the street, they saw a distant sheet of lighting illuminate the mountain against dark sky. "You do remember what happened the last time we went somewhere right before a thunderstorm?" said Jason, now walking beside her.

Dare I say that lightning never strikes twice? Now let's go right here; there are some beautiful old houses," said Laffi. As they headed down the dark, unpaved road the first heavy drops hit them. A crash of thunder shook the ground and lighting struck to their side. Jason was reminded of artillery fire followed by the crack of a high-powered rifle.

The few homes with lights went dark. The wind seemed to be attacking them from all directions and tree limbs shook frantically above their heads. Any moment Jason expected to hear branches snap and fall. Instead, the wind subsided and rain poured in earnest.

Jason and Laffi dashed to the shelter of a massive pecan tree, hugging the trunk as rain pelted the ground. "See that," said Laffi, brushing water from her forehead and pointing down the road. "I didn't notice it before."

The neighborhood was one of the oldest in the village. It consisted mostly of larger homes, many with side yards screened by crumbling stone walls and thick vegetation. Most of the houses were badly deteriorated and appeared vacant, but it was difficult to be sure as the lightning had knocked out the village power supply. Across the street, following Laffi's pointed finger, Jason saw bright flickers of light through an opening in the wall of a house.

"Let's give it a try," said Jason. They dashed across the road and through the vine-choked entry and found themselves inside a large room paved with worn, cracked tile. Torches set in iron wall holders provided the illumination they'd seen, and rain poured through a gaping ten-foot hole in the center of an unusually high ceiling. But it did not seem to bother the people crowded at the sheltered edges of bare stone and adobe walls. Most of them held plates of food and were laughing and talking. At the far end of the room coals burned brightly in a colonial-style hearth made of adobe and ceramic tile. On its ancient surface, immense clay *cazuelas* bubbled and steamed. Near Jason and Laffi, flames blazed in a stone fireplace.

A man in his thirties with thick, black hair, long sideburns, and a flowing mustache approached them. Laffi quickly explained their predicament.

"Welcome," said the man, his voice deep and gravelly. "We are celebrating my father's birthday. Please join us. Allow me to serve you, while you dry out by the fire."

He returned with an earthenware platter piled high with rice, a stew of some sort, and freshly warmed tortillas in one hand, two steaming mugs in the other. He placed the food and drink on the hearth beside them. As they thanked him he excused himself, saying, "Please stay as long as you like, *nuestra casa es su casa.*"

"What a nice guy!" said Jason, hungrily devouring a tortilla filled with a selection from the platter. "I can't figure out what it is, vegetables mostly. Anyway it beats hell out of that sandwich."

"Mexico!" said Laffi, sipping her drink, enjoying the warmth of fire and food as the wetness and chill began to dissipate. "Where else would someone invite strangers to a birthday party?" She had already eaten one filled tortilla and was considering another. "But," she added, looking around the room. "Don't you think it's a bit strange? A party in a room with a huge hole in the roof? And no one seems to notice us. It's as if we weren't here."

At the far end of the room she thought she caught sight of the priest who had surprised her at the cemetery on her first day. He looked away as their eyes met.

"You expect them to stare at you, like an animal in a zoo?" Jason laughed, feeling giddy. "Or worse—like I do? They're definitely too polite for that." He took a long pull from his mug. "What is this? It's good."

"Some kind of fruit *ponche*." She giggled. "And I'm beginning to think it may have a bit of a kick to it."

"Please allow me." Their host had suddenly appeared beside them and refilled their mugs, then just as quickly he was gone.

Jason looked at the center of the room where rain still spattered the floor, focusing with difficulty. It must be the firelight, he thought.

"Look's like the rain's slowing down," he said. His voice sounded far away to him. He took another drink. "Maybe we shouldn't wear out our welcome."

"I can see you're no party animal." Laffi put her cup down by the half empty platter, stood unsteadily on her toes and nibbled his earlobe. "But that's O.K. with me," she whispered. She saw and heard herself as if watching a stranger. It struck her that she should be shocked at her boldness, but she wasn't. Just a little dizzy, she thought.

Jason looked down at her in surprise, as if he was having trouble focusing. Then the music started. It was a melancholy instrumental with a hauntingly slow beat, and the people around them began to dance. Jason took Laffi in his arms and they melted together, spinning endless, slow circles around the room. A female voice began to sing, with the pure tones of opera. The voice grew huskier, throatier, until there was nothing but raw emotion. Jason could not understand the words, but he felt them deeply within and knew that the song told of life, love, and death in a way that went beyond his experience.

That haunting voice was the last thing either of them remembered.

Bustamante

Laffi's eyes fluttered then sprang open. Her first waking impression was of two wide-eyed young boys with black tousled hair. The boys chortled and ran away.

At first she thought she was in a glass cage, then as her senses returned she realized she was on her back, looking out the rear window of Jason's SUV. And she was naked, except for panties hooked over her left ankle. A sideways glance revealed that Jason lay next to her. Also naked.

She tensed her body in an isometric stretch, and detected nothing amiss. She looked down at her full, lightly freckled breasts, over her pleasantly rounded stomach and the mound of golden curls, to the smooth skin of her legs and brightly painted toenails. Everything seemed to be in place.

She moved her head gingerly to the right. The expected hangover was curiously absent. Just Jason on his back, breathing deeply, obviously still asleep — with an erection! Laffi turned away, trying to suppress a snort of laughter.

Jason shifted his body, and sat up, startled.

"Wh — what the — Laffi, are you O.K.?"

"Jason, what the fuck was in the punch?" she croaked.

He was silent for quite awhile. "My vote is for the stew, probably some sort of magic mushrooms."

"Do you remember anything?" she asked.

"Just dancing, then nothing. How about you?"

"The same, then *nada*. We better put on something. Whatever story the two little boys looking through the window are telling may draw a crowd."

She saw him staring at her. "Oh my God," she giggled at his hard-on and reached down to pull on her panties. Then she hunted for her clothing, which was tossed around like a tornado. Everything was sopping wet.

"You don't have a dryer do you?" she asked.

"Only the radio antenna."

Jason looked carefully at Laffi. "Puts me in mind of an old saying..."

"If you are about to say I look like I was rode hard and put away wet, don't, and save your worthless life."

They moved to the front of the Suburban in soggy clothes, and decided to skip comfort, and instead investigate their peculiar situation.

"Let's first revisit the scene of the crime," said Laffi.

"Whatever crime was committed was back there." His head bobbed toward the back. "The fact is," retorted Laffi, "we don't even know what happened. But I can guess. And the only problem could be if..."

"If you're pregnant," Jason finished her sentence.

Laffi changed the subject. "Let's go back around to the road that goes from the hotel to the graveyard and approach it from the same direction we did last night."

"Sounds like a plan."

Jason parked in front of the gap in the wall they had entered the night before. It was now covered with chicken wire and dense foliage. "Doesn't look like anybody's home," he said. The house looked as abandoned as the rest of the neighborhood.

"Let's take a look," said Laffi, hopping out of the SUV. "But let's hurry, I look like hell." She ran her fingers through tangled hair.

Jason pulled back vines and undid pieces of bailing wire securing the ersatz gate. He wedged himself through the opening and Laffi followed. It was definitely the same place. There was the huge opening in the roof, water ponding in the worn tile floor below. But other than a few empty beer cans and soiled toilet paper, there was no evidence of habitation in years.

Jason picked up a rotted pecan branch and poked around the dead leaves and decaying debris in the fireplace. He did the same at the hearth. "Damn," he whispered. "This is weird. What do you think it means?"

She considered for a moment. "It means that all over this country there are places like Bustamante. We come down here and think, 'Gee, what a charming little spot.' But under the surface all sorts of things going are on we're not aware of. The people don't understand them either—they just accept them. Various kinds of witchcraft, magic, and just plain inexplicable events have been occurring for as long as anyone can remember—since long before the Conquest. A lot of Mexicans live in a world somewhere between superstition and magic. It's their reality.

"I once did a feature on Mexican witchcraft. Did you know that the Bishop of Mexico City keeps eight priests as exorcists, and that there are thousands more, unsanctioned? People die every year in the ceremonies; seven alone recently suffocated from breathing incense. There's also a market near Mexico City's main plaza where for about ten dollars you can hire a witch to do pretty much whatever you want. The stuff goes deep, believe me. People just shrug and ignore it as best they can, mostly by minding their own business. There's really no other choice. By accident we've been touched by it. I know that sounds like bullshit, but what else is there to say? How else can we deal with it?"

She hugged herself and shivered. "It's cold. Let's go."

Jason touched her on the shoulder, and then she was in his arms kissing him deeply. After a moment, she broke the embrace, turned and walked back to the car without saying a word.

Guessing that she was frustrated about what had happened, Jason followed her silently. Trying to get things back on track, when they were in the car he said, "What you said about Mexico... I'm a lot more tolerant of the unprovable than the average scientist, but some things, like what happened last night, I just can't accept. There must be an explanation."

"Undoubtedly there is," Laffi replied, as if nothing had happened. "We just don't know what it is, and probably never will. At least not until it's too late to matter. It's like religion. The proof is all around you—you just can't prove it—if you see what I mean."

Jason pulled onto the road back toward the hotel.

They parked by Laffi's VW. She waited a few moments to be sure Eduardo and the staff weren't around to see her, then made a dash to her room. Jason followed and stood at the door, unsure of what to do.

Standing just inside the room and holding the door partially closed, Laffi said, "Forgive me Jason, but I need some time to think."

"I understand. Maybe later this afternoon you and I could…? There's something we saw a couple days ago that's been bothering me. I thought that maybe we…?"

"That nest of sticks or whatever it is in the cave," she shot back. "I've been wondering about that myself. You want to go back and have a look, don't you?"

"Yup."

"O.K., come by later, I'll be here."

Laffi closed the door quietly, though her real impulse was to slam it. But the message that would send Jason would be unfair—and possibly not in her best interest. He had done nothing wrong—at least nothing she knew about. Mostly she was angry at herself. For the first time in her life she felt conflicted and indecisive, a feeling that had been building ever since she arrived in Bustamante and laid eyes on Artemas.

She admitted she was drawn to both men. Jason was an appealing, mature man, whose actions in the cave proved he was capable, trustworthy and dependable, with considerable inner strength. On the other hand, Artemas was more exciting and, for her, more sexually attractive. Was part of that because he had a vulnerability about him that triggered her maternal instincts? She knew that in the end that didn't really matter. He was wedded to his dangerous work and unlikely to put any woman before his idealistic ambitions. *What the hell! Am I looking for a husband or some fun and adventure?*

After being fed up with D.C. where it was raining men, the last place she expected to meet anyone interesting was on assignment in a tiny Mexican village. *Maybe I just wasn't paying attention?*

By 11:00 A.M. Artemas had already been in his office several hours, and Moreno had twice reported from outside Zamarripa's gate that no vehicles had entered or left the hacienda. One piece of good news was the return of Marta, Artemas's secretary. She had been away caring for her sick father. He noticed she had lost weight she could ill afford, making her narrow features even sharper.

He was about to leave to see Humberto Alcazar when the station door flew open. Twisting a battered straw hat in his hands was Julio Martinez, the wood hauler. "I found another one," he stammered. "In the same place."

"Another body?" asked Artemas, his stomach sinking as he pictured the large headed man he'd seen with Zamarripa.

"*Sí, señor*. A man. There were vultures like last time."

"Did you stop and look around, notice anything or anybody?"

"*No, señor*. I...the oxen...*Pero sí!*" he reconsidered. "There was a hat near him."

"What kind of hat?"

"A little round one, black. Like the one *Señor* Alcazar wears. But it was not him."

"I understand," said Artemas. "Where is your wagon?"

"Outside, *señor*, tied to the lamp post. But I cannot trust the oxen for long."

"*Está bien*. I know the spot where you found the body. Please come by later so I can take down your statement."

"*Sí señor*. I will come." He backed up, bumped into the door, turned and was gone.

Heart in his mouth, Artemas raced up the backroad and parked twenty yards from his destination. Just as Julio had said, the body lay naked on the rocky track at the base of the mountain, in almost exactly the same location as the drifter. Even from a distance he could see the abnormally large head and a black beret flung to the side. He looked carefully around. It was still cool with a slight breeze, the only sign of life the disgruntled vultures, chased off into a nearby mesquite tree.

Artemas swung out of his Jeep Cherokee and slowly approached the corpse, checking the coarse gravel surface along the way. All evidence of last night's rain had vanished, only traces of Julio's cart and oxen remained.

He made a wide circle around the body. On the far side he thought he detected tire tracks, but the recent storm had pretty well destroyed any distinguishable tread. Gazing toward where the rutted track disappeared around the mountain, he remembered Zamarripa's property was about a quarter mile away. *I'll bet there's a gate.*

To no great surprise, Artemas observed the heart had been torn out of the corpse's gaping chest. Like a leftover giblet, it was tossed into the dirt nearby. There was also an ugly gash to the neck. Based on the wide, jagged edges, vultures had clearly torn chunks of flesh from both wounds. Deep purple marks around both wrists indicated he'd been bound before death. Yet, despite all the gory details, there was very little blood.

Is this the result of my clever little game? Did Zamarripa kill the man to create doubt that his son's arrest had solved the crime?

He was pretty confident he could ID the victim, based on the photo he'd been faxed first thing that morning. He had called a colleague in Monterrey and described the man with the big head he'd seen with Zamarripa. He was most likely Juan "Jugo" Gandara, one of the most vicious drug dealers in Mexico. Comparing the body's face with its rough, dark skin and blunt features to Jugo's photo made him almost certain.

Before long, the medical examiner arrived on the scene, accompanied by two policemen on loan from Sabina Hidalgo. Artemas had requested their presence prior to leaving the station, knowing the examiner, who'd processed the first murder, would easily find his way.

After meeting with the examiner, Artemas asked the two cops to take up watch near the Zamarripa hacienda entry, so Moreno could catch a nap in his car. He instructed them to arrest anyone trying to enter or leave the property. Although he suspected there was another route to and from the ranch, he decided this was the best he could do at the moment.

Artemas considered arresting Zamarripa and his accomplice on the spot, since they were the last people seen with the victim, but the beret gave him pause, and he wanted to question Alcazar first. Something deep in his gut, however, warned him to confer with the attorney general before he took action. Back at the station he left an urgent message with the A.G. that he needed to discuss the Conners murder, and instructed Marta to reach him at Alcazar's house as soon as the A.G.'s call came in. He then set off on a short walk across the plaza to Alcazar's. He was soon startled by Jason's Suburban, which pulled up beside him.

"What's up?" asked Jason and Laffi in unison.

"Together again I see," Artemas snapped. Suprised and ashamed of his rudeness, he inhaled deeply and gave them a wide grin, as if he'd spoken in jest. Then, he quickly launched into a summary of what had happened. "Now," he concluded, fixing his gaze on Laffi, "I know you have what I believe is called a scoop. I would appreciate your waiting an hour or two before using it. Give me time to speak to the attorney general."

Artemas had his reasons for breaking protocol. The A.G. would be so worried his case against the Zamarripa brothers could unravel he would try to cover up any connection with the earlier killings. That would now be impossible. To deflect any blame, Artemas would say Laffi had been in the office when Julio blurted out his story. *Shit,* he thought, *why do I do these things?*

Artemas could see that in spite of his effort to diguise his rudeness, Laffi was steaming. Eyes narrowd to slits, she briskly asked, "So, the cause of death was like a combination of the first and second murders, torn throat, missing heart — and blood?"

"According to the medical examiner's preliminary investigation."

"Doesn't that screw up your case, make it seem like either the wrong guys, or at least not all of them, were arrested?" Her tone indicated she was not unhappy at that prospect.

"I think that was the intent," said Artemas. "But please leave out any such speculation."

Still looking furious, Laffi retorted, "The problem with that is my editor will inevitably add something like, 'This new development will undoubtedly reopen an investigation that was thought to have been finalized.' And that will be nothing compared to the Mexican tabloids."

Artemas shrugged. *"Así es,"* he said quietly, "and where are you off to? And how is your arm?"

"We were on our way back up to the *grutas* to check on something," chimed in Jason, hoping to difuse the tension.

"But that's going to have to wait for my 'scoop,' interrupted Laffi. "And the arm is much better. Probably due more to some folk medicine I inadvertently tried last night than the antibiotics."

Concerned at the notion of Laffi and Jason returning to the caverns, Artemas looked at them carefully and thought he detected in Jason the rosy glow of infatuation. But anxious to get to Alcazar's, he decided not to interfere and said, "Be careful, we've had enough excitement to last the year and it's getting late."

"Don't worry," said Jason. "Eduardo packed us a snack, and we'll take it easy. How about dinner tonight, say at seven-thirty?"

"I'd enjoy that." And Artemas walked off toward the stately old home fronting the plaza.

Bustamante

Tall colonial doors in the old house swung open as the echo of antique chimes faded away. Among his countrymen Artemas was considered tall, but he had to look up at the man in the doorway. Given his schooling, he usually applied the American rather than metric system for informal situations. He figured Alcazar must be at least six four, and a good two hundred and fifty pounds.

Tent-like corduroy pants and a green plaid shirt covered the writer's substantial girth. The warm, humid day notwithstanding, he also wore a brown, cashmere cardigan. Dark eyes with almost invisible pupils under bushy black eyebrows looked down at the policeman. "*Capitán* Salcido, isn't it?" His voice was deeply resonant, with almost a rumble.

"*Sí, señor*," replied Artemas, extending his hand. "I am sorry I have not taken the time to introduce myself to you sooner. Of course," he added as his hand was smothered in Alcazar's bear-like paw, "after reading *Recuerdos de un Pueblo Antiguo*, I already feel acquainted."

"Oh, you found a copy, I'm flattered." said Alcazar, obviously pleased.

Artemas could barely see the man's teeth through his voluminous, salt-and-pepper beard and mustache. What he did see plainly was a painful looking bruise on his right forehead, below his black beret.

"I'm glad you're here. I wanted to speak with you," Alcazar said. "*Entonces, pasele.*" He stepped aside for Artemas to enter.

The spacious room was floored with smooth, gray tiles and occupied nearly the whole front of the property. Hallways on each side led back to other rooms, creating the traditional U-shaped, Spanish-style home with a private, interior patio. In this case the patio was the entire backyard. Through French doors Artemas could see a half-acre of densely wooded, brambly land, flanked by a ten-foot stonewall—same as what he had observed from the telephone pole.

Alcazar led Artemas to a sofa and purple chairs facing the French doors.

"Please," said Alcazar, gesturing toward the dark leather couch. "May I bring you some refreshment, perhaps some coffee?"

"No thank you," replied Artemas, seating himself in a chair. "You said you wanted to see me?" He cocked an eyebrow.

"Yes," replied the writer, lowering his bulk slowly onto the couch, "Last night a noise woke me. When I got up to investigate I found one of those doors open," He waved toward the French doors. "I stepped out onto the veranda and was looking around when something struck me from behind. I must have fallen and hit my head on the stone floor. See for yourself." He removed his beret and Artemas saw that the bruise extended well into the man's receding hairline. Further back was a gauze bandage, speckled with blood.

"I don't know how long I was down," Alcazar continued, "but when I got up I felt sick and dizzy and barely made it back to my bedroom. It has a heavy door, so I locked it and lay down. That's all I remember until this morning when I woke up feeling much better, although quite sore. There was blood all over my pillow, so I took a shower and dressed the cut. Then I searched the house to see if anything was missing."

"And?" asked Artemas.

"I could find nothing gone but one of these." He held the beret out to Artemas and turned it over before replacing it gingerly on his head.

Artemas noticed the label was the same as the one found next to the dead body. "Do you remember what time this happened?"

"No. It was sometime after I went to bed at about eleven. The thunderstorm was over. I never even turned on a light."

"And you're certain nothing else is missing?" asked Artemas, remembering that Zamarripa had entered the house a little after eight-fifteen.

"I haven't gone through everything. There's too much, the clutter of a lifetime. But nothing obvious, and I keep little of real value here, at least of value to a thief. Anything like that's at my ranch."

"I see."

"Now, if you'll excuse me a moment, I think I'll get some coffee. Sure you won't join me?"

"No thanks."

Artemas appraised his odd, swinging gait, more a lumber than a walk, as he left the room. Once alone, Artemas sprang to his feet and moved quickly to a sideboard where he'd seen a blood-soaked bandage on his way in. Using the thumb and forefinger of his left hand, he stuffed it into his pocket and returned to his seat.

Bustamante was a small community, and while it had its share of petty theft, breaking and entering was nearly unheard of, much less accompanied by violence. But the evidence clearly indicated that Alcazar had been hurt. That part at least was true, thought Artemas.

The writer returned with a steaming mug of coffee so large it looked like a German beer stein.

Artemas waited for his host to be seated, then asked him, "Can you think of anyone who might have done this, or why someone would want your beret?"

Alcazar held out his hands, palms up, perplexed. "I can think of no one, and certainly nobody would wear it around here. I may be the only person between Monterrey and the border who owns one."

"Did you have any visitors last night?"

"Uh...yes, I did. But...that was much earlier."

With Alcazar's last response, his demeanor radically shifted. His deep voice jumped an octave, his body stiffened, and his eyes darted around the room.

"Who was it?" Artemas kept his tone calm and casual.

Alcazar hesitated, obviously considering his response.

"Zarco Zamarripa, a distant relative and father of the young men arrested for the murder of the American girl." His eyes were glued to Artemas.

"May I ask the purpose of his visit? I've heard that your branch of the family and his are not exactly friendly."

"That's true, although the reasons for the enmity are cloudy, there's no question it exists. The reason that..."

Artemas raised his hand to interrupt. "Before you go on I just want to make sure I understand. You are hazy as to the actual points of contention between your family and Zamarripa's?" His voice projected idle curiosity.

"For the most part, yes."

"I mentioned that I was familiar with your book. But I didn't tell you that I had actually memorized portions of it. For example, one passage I found particularly intriguing goes: *Because of their vile use and treatment of the people, the worst of it hidden by the dark of night, the Zamarripas are certainly among the worst vampires in all of Mexico.*

Artemas paused, then asked, "Did you have anything specific in mind when you wrote that, or was it based solely on hazy perceptions?"

Alcazar's lips tightened, but he kept his temper. "Children in both our families were raised to hate those in the other," he said evenly. "Each side was told that the other is evil, but rarely was anything specific mentioned. The result was often petty acts of vandalism that served only to perpetuate the problem."

Artemas was indifferent to the explanation. "I believe you were going to tell me the purpose of *Señor* Zamarripa's visit."

"He wanted to know if I had any information that might help in the defense of his sons." Alcazar stopped. Just as the silence became uncomfortable, he continued, "I told him I did not."

"And that was it?" For the first time Artemas's voice cracked like a whip.

"That's what I said. He was here only a few minutes. When he didn't get what he wanted, he left." Alcazar's tone verged on belligerence.

"Did he say specifically what information he thought you might have, or why he thought you might have it?"

"No."

"You mean he came in here and said something like, 'Gee, even though we were brought up to hate each other and haven't spoken in decades, I drove up from Monterrey on the off chance you might have some information that could assist in the defense of my sons who are detested by everyone in the village. I don't know what it could be, but I'm sure hoping for something helpful?'"

"I know it sounds a bit odd, but that's what happened," said Alcazar. He was obviously trying hard to appear reasonable, but like most independently wealthy people he was not used to anyone questioning his authority, much less his word.

"Are you certain he didn't get what he wanted?" Artemas's voice was so low the writer cupped his coffee mug in both hands and leaned forward to better hear him. "The reason I ask," he added, raising the volume a notch, "is the reason *I* came to see *you*.

"The body of a man was found early today. The last time that man was seen alive, he was with Zarco Zamarripa. The body was naked. The only article of clothing found near him was a black beret, the same make and size as the one you're wearing. And although I haven't measured it, the man's head appears to be larger than yours. You did mention that you might be the only man between Monterrey and the border who has such a hat, didn't you?"

The writer sagged in shock. Artemas thought it was not from surprise, but rather due to obvious consequences coming to pass, like an alcoholic being told his liver is shot.

"I...I... don't know what to say," he finally stammered.

"That," said Artemas, "is probably the most truthful thing you've said since I got here. Now, do you know, or have you ever heard of a man named Juan Gandara? He goes by the nickname Jugo."

Alcazar made an obvious effort to compose himself. "*Capitán* Salcido, I have never heard that name. And furthermore I resent your attitude and intend to lodge a complaint with your superiors."

"My superiors are much more likely to admonish me for not arresting you than for injuring your feelings."

Artemas stood up and looked down at his host. "By the way, the reason I'm not going to arrest you is because I don't believe you killed that man. One reason is the beret by the body — your most distinctive possession. It's too obvious. But I'm just as certain that you're somehow involved in this matter, and your role is something I intend to discover."

He nodded politely to the writer and walked out of his house.

Artemas hurried back to the station and cringed when Marta told him the attorney general's office had called to say the AG would call him at exactly 5:00 P.M. He knew what would probably happen.

"Oh," Marta added. "Jesús Vargas came in. Said he wanted to report that a *chupacabra* attacked and killed three of his goats. He doesn't have a phone, so I told him to come back later."

"Also, Chaco Gonzalez was in again, wondering if you'd made any progress on the investigation into the death of *his* goats."

"Very interesting." Artemas grunted as he removed the soiled bandage from his pocket, sealed it in a plastic bag and gave Marta instructions where to send it.

Humberto Alcazar picked up his phone and dialed from memory. "It's me," he said, when Ricardo Chavana answered. "I was right, our dear friend took the beret to leave it with a body. The policeman came by, and he's damned suspicious."

"Is our friend still at home?"

"I don't know. Why would he be?"

"Maybe he hopes to lure us, and then...Well, if that's what he's up to perhaps I'll give him his wish, but not like he expects. The time has come. I'll call you, probably late tonight."

"Wait," interjected Alcazar, "you won't be attending to any business before dark, will you?"

"No, why?"

"I don't know if it'll work. It's a long shot, but we might be able to take out some insurance. I'd rather discuss it in person. Can you meet me at the hotel in half an hour?"

"Certainly, if you think it's important. I'll see you there at... about 4 P.M."

The writer hung up, slowly shaking his sore head.

Bustamante

Artemas walked across the plaza for the second time that day, this time to the Hotel Ancira where he found Eduardo in the kitchen butchering *cabrito*.

When he saw Artemas, the innkeeper said, "I just heard there was another *chupacabra* attack at Vargas's place and another murder. What's the world coming to, and what can I do for you?"

"I want you to think back to when the American girls first came in. Try to remember who was in the dining room."

"Let's see," Edwardo began, wrinkling his brow. "It was pretty much the usual Sunday crowd. Certainly there was Alcazar who helped translate. He was with Chavana, as usual — The Council of Arts and Letters I call them. Then there was..." He rattled off a list of names that did not concern Artemas, but to which he listened patiently.

"Do you remember if anyone in the dining room left directly after the girls?" Artemas knew he risked sparking a flood of rumors with that question, but saw no other way.

Eduardo put down his cleaver and scratched his chin. "Yes," he said, "Chavana and Alcazar left. I remember at the time being grateful Humberto was here long enough to translate." He looked at Artemas, and his eyes held a question.

Artemas stepped closer and lowered his voice. "Eduardo, I don't want you to repeat any of this; it probably means nothing. Do you remember if they had finished their meals?"

The innkeeper shot him a sharp look. "I don't know. It was busy and one of the girls would have cleaned the table."

"Thank you," said the policeman.

"You know," said Eduardo, "there is talk that maybe the Zamarripas were innocent, or involved with someone else who wasn't caught."

"I know," said Artemas, waving goodbye. "Please don't forget what I said."

Bustamante

Jesús Vargas lived on a tiny farm on the outskirts of the village. The chunky little white-haired man in his sixties pointed to the remains of his goats. "I heard nothing — not a sound! What do you think…?"

Artemas observed the goats lying in pools of dried blood, their bloated bodies covered with flies. It was remarkably similiar to what happened to Chaco Gonzalez's goats. And there, just outside Vargas's little adobe house, was Chaco himself with a couple of friends, talking to Diego Ramirez, the newspaperman.

During summers with his mother's family, Artemas had developed considerable tracking skills, but he could find nothing to explain the mutilated goats in the muddy soil. The small group of men drew closer as Artemas surveyed the ground. "*Señor Capitán*," said Chaco respectfully, his straw hat in his hands, "It's almost the same as at my place. What can we do?"

Artemas had no answer.

While Artemas was occupied with Vargas's goats, Humberto Alcazar stood in the Hotel Ancira kitchen, watching Eduardo dismember the last of his own goats. "Eduardo," said the writer, "I'm looking for the American scientist you told me about. Is he still in town?"

"He and *Señorita* Rendón went up to the *grutas* about an hour ago. I expect them back — certainly before dark. I don't think they want to get stuck up there again."

"*Gracias.*"

Eduardo watched the writer as he left. After Artemas's questioning, Alcazar looking for the Americans seemed an interesting coincidence.

Outside, Alcazar found Ricardo Chavana parking his motorbike on the sidewalk by the writer's Ford Explorer. "Put that thing in the back, and come with me. We may be in luck."

Jason and Laffi were flush with excitement as they picked their way down the treacherous mountain slope, keeping a sharp eye for loose rocks, cactus and rattlesnakes. Jason had finished carefully photographing the nest-like pile of sticks on the cavern floor and taken samples of what he thought might be reptilian scales. With so much inexplicable evidence, he was finding it impossible to suppress some wild ideas, and Laffi, having talked herself out of her previous bad temper, wasn't helping with all her *whoops* and *hollers* as he methodically examined the site. He left behind his camera, set on a tripod with a battery-operated motion detector. Whatever belonged to that nest would trigger the flash and shutter. Emerging from the cave's opening on the other side of the mountain, they saw a mass of thunderheads approaching from the west. Though the system was still some distance off, they could see flickers of lightning.

When they reached the parking area they noticed two men approaching. One was a veritable giant with a bushy, graying beard. The other was slender with wavy black hair. Extremely good looking, in an almost feminine way, thought Laffi.

Bustamante

Finding he still had time before the A.G.'s call, Artemas stopped by his house on his way back to the office. He wondered if news of Jugo's murder had already been leaked. He knew Laffi and Jason were headed for the caverns and doubted if she'd respected his request for even an hour's delay. Connecting to the Internet confirmed his suspicion. There, on the home page of the online edition of Laffi's newpaper was the headline "Solution of Julie Conners' Murder In Doubt."

He was furious at himself. It would have been far better for his career if he'd left well enough alone. His cooperation with the PGR men during the investigation, if not impeccable, had at least appeared to be, and would probably have led to a transfer back to Mexico City. Now if he wasn't very lucky he could lose his job altogether. Better that, he rationalized, than being stuck in Bustamante with no chance of accomplishing anything important.

Although elections were just a couple of months away, even the possibility of a new national administration wouldn't help him. The current attorney general was from the rival party, chosen by the president to demonstrate there would be no more cover-ups. Artemas snorted in contempt. Oh, well, he mused, I suppose I'm still young enough to become a lawyer, maybe get into politics. But deep down he knew he lacked passion for anything but police work, at least when it was conducted properly, as he'd tried to do before he'd been banished.

On his way back to the police station he detected a sudden stillness in the atmosphere, accompanied by a rise in humidity. Another storm for sure.

The phone rang at five sharp. Without preamble the A.G. loudly demanded, "Salcido, what the fuck is going on up there?" News of the recent murder had clearly reached the seat of power.

Artemas quickly related specific events, beginning with his sighting of Zamarripa coming out of Alcazar's house, through the discovery of the body and his interview with Alcazar.

"So, you're convinced Zamarripa committed the murder to make it look as if his sons were arrested by mistake?"

"*Sí, señor*. Another bizarre murder that combined the methods of the other two and in exactly the same place as the first. It can't help but lead to speculation that we've arrested the wrong people."

"And did we?"

Artemas hesitated. "No, at least not in the case of the first killing, but the girl may be another matter."

"Another matter, you say!" yelled the A.G. Artemas held the receiver away from his ear.

"It's nothing more than a hunch," said Artemas. "You asked my opinion. Without additional evidence and particularly if Zamarripa is caught in his little scheme no more will ever come of it."

"And how the hell do you think we're going to convict Zamarripa? On the basis he had a motive? We're talking about one of the wealthiest men in the country," the A.G. shouted.

"I understand sir. But remember, I told you that by chance I saw Zamarripa leave Alcazar's house. I also saw the victim in his car. There was also another witness, an American scientist who was with me at the time."

The line was silent for so long that Artemas thought he'd lost the connection. Finally the A.G.'s voice came back, now under control.

"*Jesús Cristo*, Salcido. Why didn't you say that in the first place? Do you know where Zamarripa is?"

"He was seen entering his hacienda, just south of the village last night. I posted men at the entry with instructions to arrest him if he tries to leave."

"And why haven't you already arrested him?

"I wanted to discuss it with you first, and I wanted to interview Alcazar to make sure he wasn't involved."

"Well...I. And how do you know Alcazar wasn't involved, that he didn't leave later and participate in the killing?"

"It's extremely unlikely; the two men and their families hate each other. I think Zamarripa went to see him last night, clubbed him from behind and stole the beret so he could plant it."

"If that's the case, and if they hate each other so much, then why didn't Alcazar call you and report what happened immediately? Why be so reluctant to name Zamarripa?"

"That, sir, is one of the things I intend to find out. I suspect he either had no faith that the law would act against Zamarripa on his word alone, or perhaps this is something he wishes to settle personally, maybe a little of both."

"O.K., Salcido. Get out there and arrest Zamarripa, then call me. But listen to me very carefully. This is so sensitive I want to personally handle the interrogation — all of it — from this end. When you arrest Zamarripa be *absolutely* sure to tell him those are *my* instructions. And for God's sake, whatever you do, be extremely careful he isn't harmed. That's a direct order! Someone is always here and knows where to find me."

The A.G. paused, and raised his voice even higher. "And no screw ups, not a peep from you or your people to anyone. Is that clear? Don't forget that you now have the unusual opportunity to work directly with me. If the outcome's favorable, it'll go well for both of us. If not, we'll both suffer, but I promise that you'll get the worst of the deal, by far. Also, make sure that the *gringo* will testify. As you well know, the word of a policeman isn't worth shit." The A.G. hung up.

And that's what damned well has to change, thought Artemas angrily as he stared at the phone.

Artemas sat down to think. He concluded that he lacked the necessary background to properly understand the relationship between Zamarripa and Alcazar, and therefore to reach an informed conclusion. He decided to take the teacher Gerardo Manzano's advice and confer with the strange old priest, Father Buendía. He dialed the church and Father Mares, the current priest, answered.

"I would like to speak to your predecessor," said Artemas. "Is he around?"

"He's right here, just a moment."

Artemas spoke briefly to the old priest, telling him he would like to talk to him, but that he would be tied up for the rest of the afternoon and early evening. Father Buendía seemed nervous and guarded, but after a little negotiation he suggested that Artemas come by his house at 9:30 P.M. Artemas agreed and thanked him.

ZAMARRIPA ESTATE

Rain was falling steadily as Artemas pulled onto Highway 1 for the drive to Zamarripa's hacienda. The storm brought with it an early twilight, and darkness was quickly approaching. He had called ahead, so when he pulled up under the *Hacienda Zamarripa* sign Moreno and the two policemen from Sabinas were waiting. The Sabinas men carried AK 47 automatic rifles and .45 caliber side arms. Moreno had a .45 and a short-barreled, pump action shotgun. Although it was a serious rule violation, Artemas rarely wore his own .45, but he had donned it for this occasion and also carried a twelve gauge.

After emphasizing the importance of not harming Zamarripa, Artemas instructed one officer to remain by the entry gate with his radio. Then he climbed into the passenger seat of his Jeep. Moreno drove, while the second cop rode in back.

Lightening crashed, thunder boomed, and rain hammered the windshield as they topped the rise overlooking the hacienda.

"At least they probably won't see us coming," grunted Moreno.

Artemas remained silent as he scanned the approaching cluster of buildings through the sheeting rain and twilight. A black Lincoln Navigator was parked in front of the main house, undoubtedly the one he and Jason had followed.

Pulling up to the Lincoln, he hoped the storm would cover their arrival. He was not particularly worried about Zamarripa; he would assume he could buy his way out of anything. But there was something about Joaquin that made Artemas nervous.

After delaying long enough for Moreno to report on his position at the back of the rambling house, Artemas and the other policeman rushed to the front entry, sheltered by a tiled overhang. Several bangs on the iron knocker produced no response, so Artemas gently pushed at the carved door. It was unlocked, so he kicked it open and sprang inside, shotgun leading the way.

The vast wood-beamed living room, heavy in shadow, was silent and still. Artemas flicked a light switch by the door, and tried a few more. The power was dead. He silently cursed himself for forgetting his flashlight, but realized the foolishness of fetching it and losing the element of surprise. Instead, he waved the policeman to follow him inside.

"Police," he yelled. "Is anybody home?" There was no answer.

Doing their best to avoid heavy furnishings obscured by the descending gloom, they quickly surveyed the room. Satisfying himself that it was unoccupied, Artemas focused his attention on the two large doors leading toward the rest of the hacienda. He guessed the closed door to his right led to the bedrooms, and the other, probably to the dining room. He ordered the cop to take the right door and waited until he disappeared before entering the left.

Artemas was stunned by what he saw. His memory flashed on the crime photos he'd seen of the immense dining room table where Raymundo's men had strewn evidence against the Zamarripas brothers. Now on display in the middle of the very same table was a human body, spread eagled on its back with something protruding from its chest. In the faint light it appeared to be Zarco Zamarripa. Slumped in a chair to the right of the table was the body of another man.

Artemas stood frozen at the doorway, trying to make sense of the scene before him. His mind raced through the possible scenarios. The sons were in custody, and besides, their father was their meal ticket. Alcazar certainly had motive, but this seemed too sordid to be his handiwork.

The heavy door suddenly slammed into Artemas, followed by a blur of movement and an offensive tackle that sent him crashing to the floor. His head hit the wall on the way down, and the shotgun fell from his grip, clattering loudly on the tiles.

By the time Artemas regained his feet and retrieved his weapon, his attacker was long gone, probably through the front door. Artemas ran outside. The Lincoln Navigotor was still parked in front. Otherwise, he saw nothing. Although the storm had abated, it was now the full darkness of night with no hint of moon. He radioed Moreno and the two other officers to be on high alert for a possible murder suspect fleeing the scene on foot. On his way back to the hacienda, he grabbed his flashlight from the Jeep.

The other policeman met him in the living room and reported finding nothing in any of the bedrooms nor seeing the intruder. Moreno soon joined them and declared he had also seen nothing. A quick conversation with the officer at the gate yielded the same answer.

The two policemen followed Artemas into the dining room. He aimed his flashlight upon the grisly centerpiece. The two men gasped in horror. It was indeed Zamarripa. His head lolled to one side, nearly unhinged by a huge gash in his neck, blood still oozing and spreading slowly across the table like thick gravy. Protruding nearly a foot above his chest was a wooden stake through the heart. It had been driven with such force it pierced all the way through his body and into the table. Obviously, the murderer had been in a rage.

The body in the chair was Joaquin. He was shot in the chest, but was otherwise unmarked. The only other evidence was a pool of blood on the floor near the table. Probably where Zamarripa had actually been killed, thought Artemas.

Artemas instructed Moreno to go to the car, call Sabinas, and request the medical examiner and crime scene analyst.

"They'll say they should just move up here," Moreno said. "We'll never hear the end of it."

When Moreno returned, Artemas searched the bodies and placed the contents in Ziploc bags his deputy brought from the car. Among Zamarripa's effects was a set of keys that gave Artemas an idea. What he planned was risky. He knew it was exactly this sort of choice that had caused most of his serious problems, but such gambles had also led to his greatest successes. He desperately needed the latter.

"Moreno," he said, "take over here. I have a suspect in mind and need to follow up right away." Then, picking up the plastic bags, he added, "I'll stick these in the safe on my way in."

As an afterthought, he slipped on a pair of latex gloves and searched the Lincoln. He found nothing of interest except a pair of handcuffs connected by a chain on the back seat and, in the center console, just as he had hoped, a garage door opener. Certain he wasn't being observed, he slipped the transmitter into his pocket.

Artemas drove quickly back to Bustamante. Rainwater still pooled dangerously along the highway, and he had to stay alert. He dreaded the report he'd have to make to the attorney general, and decided he would wait until morning. The crime scene investigation and preliminary medical examination would be finished by then, and he concluded it was important to have as many facts as possible. In his heart he knew he was kidding himself, but decided to follow through with his plan anyway.

At the station he carefully removed Zamarripa's keys from the plastic bag and popped them into his pocket, along with the garage door opener. The rest he locked up with other evidence in the safe. He left the office and headed across the plaza to Alcazar's house. There were no lights on and no answer to his repeated doorbell pushing — nothing but the distant echo of chimes.

Good!

Monterrey

The Jeep Cherokee's heater blasted and the defroster struggled valiantly against the fogging windshield. Although soaked to the skin by the evening's downpour, Artemas had decided not to waste precious time changing clothes—time that could be the difference between success and disaster. But still, it was uncomfortable driving inside a sauna.

He judged he could make it to Zamarripa's house in an hour and fifteen minutes. The recent flooding would slow him down, but there would be less traffic, assuming he wasn't ensnarled by another motorist's misfortune. With any luck he could be back in time for his meeting with Father Buendía, or at least not unacceptably late. As his mind relaxed to the rhythm of driving, he suddenly remembered his dinner date with Jason and Laffi and called the hotel to cancel. Eduardo answered on the second ring.

"I'm sorry," he said, "I haven't seen either of them since they left for the *grutas*. I hope nothing's wrong? Because of our conversation, I should tell you that soon after you left Humberto Alcazar came to see me. He was looking for Professor Peterson, and I told him where they'd gone."

Artemas said he was sure there was no problem, but his instincts told him otherwise.

Exactly an hour and thirteen minutes later he cruised into Garza Garcia then drove along the street in front of Zamarripa's mansion. Since no windows faced the street, he couldn't tell if any lights were on inside. Come to think of it, he didn't recall seeing any windows at all when he'd been invited into the house. There were no cars in the drive, a good sign, and the entry gate was curiously ajar. He'd have to take his chances whether there were any live-in servants.

After circling the block he pulled throught the gate into the drive and headed for the driveway he'd spotted between the house and perimeter wall. A garage the size of a house loomed ahead. He pressed the transmitter from Zamarripa's Lincoln and the door slowly opened, like the yawn of a hippo. He drove his Jeep into an empty stall, hoping he wouldn't be swallowed up forever.

He shut the garage door, grabbed his flashlight, and felt for Zamarripa's keys in his pocket. He recognized the lock on the plain door leading into the house, and it took him but a moment to find the right key.

No one works his way up the PGR in Mexico City without learning a fair amount about locks, and the keys that open them. It was the stainless steel keys on the chain, with identical round heads, which initially attracted his attention. To Artemas the resembled safe keys. He was betting that Zamarripa kept his most important documents in his home rather than some less secure office. More importantly, he was also betting that Zamarripa and Joaquin had left with their prisoner in such a rush they'd forgotten to set the alarm. He knew he didn't have the technical expertise to disarm the type of device the industrialist could afford. If he was wrong he'd just have to get the hell out before security arrived.

Slipping on latex gloves, he slid carefully into the house, ears tuned for any signs of habitation. He heard no voices, no television or radio, and most gratifying, no warning signal from the alarm panel blinking near the door jam. Only the soft hum of A/C. Once he shut the door, the alarm returned to a steady green glow. He breathed deeply in relief and made his way to the large den where he'd met with Zamarripa.

He adjusted the dimmer switch so that the room he'd remembered was bathed in the radiance of pure halogen. A quick look around left him puzzled. He couldn't find any file cabinets, closets or drawers. Even the desk in the far corner was nothing but a slab of marble resting on steel legs. Not possible, he thought; there must be a secret compartment built into the paneling. It was made of mahogany veneer, with a beveled, two inch molding every four feet to cover the joints. He ran his fingers along the molding, but couldn't detect any displacement.

Sitting at Zamarripa's desk and desperate for inspiration, he pulled out the key ring and examined the keys one by one. Nothing came to mind. Then he inspected the key ring itself. It was attached to a flat piece of decorative silver, about an inch in diameter, with a raised rendering of the world globe. He put it between his forefinger and thumb and pressed. From behind he heard a muffled click. He spun around to discover a section of molding askew. A quick tug swung it open to reveal a floor to ceiling recess about 2 ½-inches wide. Inside were two buttons.

Gingerly, Artemas pushed the top button and at the far end of the room a panel slid open exposing a large television and video setup. He pushed the second button, heard a click to his left and saw that another molding had popped open, along with the entire wood panel. Behind it was a steel door with a key slot. Artemas selected the largest of the safe keys. It turned in the slot but nothing happened. When he released pressure it snapped back. He tried again, this time pulling back while the key was turned. The steel door slid open on silent, smooth hinges to reveal a steel-clad room about five feet square. Within each wall was a large, flush-mounted door with its own keyhole. He quickly opened them with the smaller keys.

Checking his watch, Artemas realized he'd been in the house nearly twenty minutes and would have to hurry. He couldn't explain being absent from Bustamante for too long, and he hoped to keep his appointment with the priest.

Within the secret room walls were file drawers, and he quickly skimmed through them. Most of the files contained computer printouts with columns of numbers, obviously financial statements, none of which meant anything to him. But behind the third and final door he found a ledger stuck in the drawer in front of a series of files. On its cover, in red magic marker, were the initials, "G.V." Surely Grupo Vampiro.

He was right. Each page listed a name, and below it a summary of what appeared to be debits and credits. Flipping through the pages he recognized several names, including that of his father and three notorious drug lords. While he didn't see the president's name, he knew that didn't mean the man wasn't part of the camarilla; Mexico's chief executives usually used a *prestanombre*, someone without formal links to the president—either a trusted friend or a frightened one—to front their graft. On the last page was a final name that caused his heart to jackhammer: the attorney general.

Artemas felt lightheaded, but forced himself to continue his search. Behind the ledger were files, one for each of the ten men summarized. One file in a blue folder was different. Artemas pulled it out and unfolded a large, single sheet of paper and whistled softly with surprise. It was a hand-drawn organization chart that he was certain showed Grupo Vampiro's holdings and their relationship to each other. Quickly he gathered the ledger and all the files.

Artemas relocked the steel doors and closed the wood panel. Quickly but methodically he retraced his steps, making sure he had left behind no evidence of his presence. He knew his life depended on it.

Bustamante

Still hoping to make his meeting with the priest, Artemas pushed the Jeep to its limits, nearly losing control in some standing water. As he fought to stay on the road he flashed on the seriousness of what he had just done. He was now in possession of information that could potentially destroy some of Mexico's most powerful men.

While it was not illegal to belong to a camarilla, Mexico did have a law against "inexplicable enrichment." It provided severe penalties to anyone unable to plausibly explain the source of their wealth. Although it was rarely prosecuted, the law had ended both the career and freedom of one of Mexico City's most powerful police chiefs. The fact that the attorney general came from humble roots and had been a government employee for his entire career meant that his ledger balance would be automatically incriminating.

Artemas knew he was playing with something worse than fire. Even though the files might theoretically give him enormous power, he had no illusions. Men far more important than he were frequently murdered, often in faked suicides, simply because they knew too much. If it were even suspected he had this information he would be squashed like a bug.

Although anxious to see the old priest, he turned in at Zamarripa's gate, passed the Sabinas policeman on guard, drove to the Hacienda, and parked beside the black Navigator. He returned the garage door opener to the center console and quickly left.

He pulled into the village just before 10:15 P.M., forty-five minutes late for his appointment with Father Buendía, but well within acceptable punctuality. He drove directly to the priest's cottage in the block behind the church.

Tacked to the rough, wooden door was a note over a scrawled signature. "*Capitán* Salcido: Forgive me but something has come up. If possible, please meet me at the end of the road by the *Ojo de Agua* at 7:30 tomorrow morning."

Artemas was disappointed and puzzled, but still had plenty to do and shrugged it off. On his way home he stopped by the police station to return Zamarripa's car keys with the man's other effects stored in the office safe. He kept the globe key ring with its keys to Zamarripa's secret vault.

On his desk he found a note from Eduardo. "*Señorita* Rendón and the professor have not yet returned." The uneasiness he'd felt before returned in spades. Although Jason had shown he was capable of taking care of himself and Laffi, that did little to to ease Artemas's fears and frustration as he realized that he could do nothing until he checked with Eduardo first thing in the morning.

When he got home, he stripped off his damp uniform and took a quick shower. Then he pulled on a pair of jeans and a dark shirt, lit a cigar and sat down to read the files.

An hour later he closed the last folder, leaned back and stared at nothing in particular. If he was reading the numbers correctly, and he believed he was, the attorney general had an investment of well over $3 million at the current exchange rate. During the last few years the man had withdrawn a total of just over $1 million. Not bad for a civil servant! Artemas was surprised that his father's investment was only $1 million dollars.

The three drug Lords whose names he recognized, including the recently departed Jugo Gandara, had far more, averaging nearly $100 million each. The total investment of the thirty-two listed participants was over half a billion dollars and read like a *Who's Who* of Mexico's political elite. Adding the $600 million under Zamarripa's name, the total was well over $1 billion. He knew that was just the equity. When the amount of loans and mortgages was added, the camarilla could easily control more than five billion dollars in assets.

Artemas went over the numbers and organization chart again and again, until his brain spun. Then gradually, as if he were looking into a kaleidoscope, patterns that were vaguely familiar began to form, and finally something appeared that was concrete enough to be labeled a hypothesis.

It seemed clear that Zamarripa brought in most of the money from drug dealers. He ran it through the group's banks then invested it in legal businesses: hotels, apartments and shopping centers, laundering it in the process. But the *narcotraficantes* were allotted only a minimal participation in profits. The lion's share, including the appreciation of the assets, went to the politicians and law enforcement officers whose main investment must be the "help" they provided to the drug cartels and Grupo Vampiro itself.

So what did the drug lords who seemed to have been providing most of the money get? It seemed to Artemas that they got their money laundered and a small percentage of the camarilla's profits, not an insignificant reward. The only anomaly was what seemed to be a loan to the camarilla from Jugo Gandara for seventy-five million dollars. More than enough motive for murder, thought Artemas.

He wasn't positive of any of it, but it fit: bribery of politicians by criminals on a large scale and at little or no out-of-pocket cost to them. Plus, they got their money laundered and a return on their investment. It was obvious why the attorney general wanted Zamarripa kept safe, the interrogation handled entirely by himself.

Artemas was now even more leery of breaking the news of the industrialist's death to his boss. The man would surely panic at the possibility he could lose his illicit nest egg. He would be equally distressed that its existence might become public.

Then it struck him. He, Artemas Salcido, illegitimate son of a former governor, Harvard graduate, and member of the federal police force, might have the only copy of the list containing both the group's membership *and* its members' individual holdings! If so, he possessed a weapon more powerful than he had imagined. And he was in even more danger than he'd imagined. The trick would be to figure out how best to use the information and stay alive in the process.

By the time Artemas finished the files it was well after 11:00 P.M. Since Bustamante went to bed early, especially on weeknights, he thought it was late enough for what he had in mind. But first he had to decide where he was going to keep the Grupo Vampiro documents, something perhaps more valuable than the Hope Diamond, and as dangerous as radioactive plutonium. He was certain no one would look for the files until the news of Zamarripa's death became known. He figured he had less than a day. Artemas decided to lock everything in his file cabinet for the night, after he went to the station to make copies. He knew this might be his last opportunity. Tomorrow morning he would have to find someplace much more secure, someplace with no links to himself.

It was nearly 1:00 A.M. before Artemas had copied the ledger, files, and organization chart and returned home to lock them up. He then slipped out of his house one last time to retrieve the recording device he'd placed on Alcazar's phone line. Back home, he slid the cartridge into the recorder and immediately heard a dial tone followed by ringing. The first voice he heard was Alcazar's.

"It's me. I was right, our dear friend took the hat to leave it by a body. The policeman came by, and he's damned suspicious."

"Is our friend still at home?"

"I don't know. Why would he be?"

"Maybe he hopes to lure us, and then…Well if that's what he's up to perhaps I'll give him his wish, but not like he expects. The time has come. I'll call you, probably late tonight."

"Wait," interjected Alcazar, "you won't be attending to any business before dark, will you?"

"No, why?"

"I don't know if it'll work. It's a long shot, but we might be able to take out some insurance. I'd rather discuss it in person. Can you meet me at the hotel in half an hour?"

"Certainly, if you think it's important. I'll see you there at… about 4 P.M."

Artemas stopped the playback. "I guess I know who murdered Zamarripa," he said out loud. Then he asked himself what Alcazar meant by "insurance." Could that somehow have something to do with the disappearance of Laffi and Jason? He listened to the conversation again and discovered it was the only one on the tape. Exhausted, he went to bed.

Ojo de Agua

Artemas awoke at six-thirty the next morning, feeling like he'd barely slept. He massaged his eyes, stumbled into the bathroom and turned on the shower. While he waited for some meager hotwater—guiltily he'd decided against pestering his landlord about fixing the plumbing, since so many villagers did without— he phoned the Hotel Ancira. Eduardo told him that neither he nor his wife heard anyone arrive during the night. He had no reason to believe Laffi had returned. Artemas swore loudly to himself, "*Híjole, cabrones como friegan*" pacing to and fro, and finally took his shower.

Half an hour later he drove west up the narrow valley that sliced into the mountains north of the village. The original and a copy of the Grupo Vampiro documents were stuffed in a canvas bag under the front seat. He hadn't yet devised a secure hiding place, but didn't expect a *situación de la chingada* or shitstorm, until he reported Zamarripa's death to the attorney general. The Medical Examiner and other officials from Sabinas Hidalgo had promised not to release any information until that afternoon, and all the reporters except Laffi had left. Still, his empty stomach churned at the thought of her and Jason missing again and his inability to think of anything he could do about it.

The morning sky was clear and Artemas was alone on the road. Lower portions of the mountains were covered with sage, yucca and seasonal grasses. As his Jeep wound it's way up the steep elevation, vegetation gradually disappeared, leaving only rocks and cactus. To his right ran the stream whose source was farther up, at the *Ojo de Agua* spring—literally "Eye of Water." Why the old man wanted to meet him there he could only guess. Probably he'd decided on the spur of the moment to set out on one of his rambles.

The Jeep crested a rise where the paved road ended. Artemas cursed under his breath and pulled to a stop. A dozen vultures soared a few hundred yards ahead, beyond a low hill, riding air currents in lazy circles. Occasionally one would drift down toward whatever lay below. Were it not for their quantity Artemas could have deluded himself, imagining nature's bounty of rabbits, lizards or other once living creatures.

Artemas searched the ground around his Jeep, but nothing seemed disturbed or out of place since yesterday's rain. He paused and inhaled deeply. It was an otherwise glorious spring morning, crisp fresh air with hints of pollen, birds chirping and singing. Artemas suddenly understood the priest's attraction to this soulful place. Nevertheless, he was now on a different and dark mission.

At his grandparent's *ranchería* he had often played Cowboys and Indians with the other children, except they called it Spaniards and Yaquis. During those rough games he discovered he had an uncanny ability to sense, even from great distances, being watched. That familiar uneasiness came over him now. Artemas chided himself for poor judgment, realizing he'd left his gun in his desk at home. Spite, pride, naivete, he wasn't sure why he broke police protocol, but until now he'd safely protected the fine citizens of Bustamante from their miscreants, unarmed.

He scanned the tall cottonwoods in the distance, which he knew flanked the mouth of the spring. Beyond them, mountains rose from the side of the narrow valley. To their left, mostly flat ground until the valley reached the base of the mountain bordering the village. Seeing nothing amiss, he could not pinpoint the source of his unease. Finally, he returned his attention to the small hillock between him and what he strongly suspected was the body of Father Buendía.

Artemas continued his search on foot. From the top of the hill, he saw a cluster of vultures hunched over a body lying in a sandy depression. His heart sank, it was worse than he could have ever imagined. Artemas tamped down his emotions and began his formal investigation.

He found tracks at the three o'clock position of his circuit of the crime scene. There were two sets of footprints undisturbed in the sandy soil, one set coming toward the body, and the other returning. They were fresh tracks, certainly made after the storm. Artemas continued his circle. At the nine o'clock position he found another set of tracks leading toward the body. Finding nothing else, he steeled himself and approached the corpse. The vultures, loudly expressing their agitation, flapped angrily away.

It was indeed the old priest, dressed in his frayed black shirt and trousers. He was on his back, features frozen in death, facing the cloudless sky. As with Gandara, vultures had plucked out his eyes, and the gash in his neck torn open so viciously only the flesh behind vertebrae remained. But unlke the other victims his heart seemed to be untouched, a fact Artemas filed away for later consideration. Dead bodies usually didn't bother Artemas. He'd seen plenty in Mexico City, and the drug cartels had a fondness for beheadings and other medieval terroristic methods of which the police had become all too familiar. Moreover, Bustamante was quickly amassing its own heap of gore. But this time he was bent over, stomach empty and heaving. Beyond the visceral reaction to this particular murder, was the sickening realization of what it meant.

After Artemas regained his composure, he continued to look around. His eyes lingered toward the right of the priest's body, where he was certain the killer had come and gone. He couldn't shake off the feeling of being watched, and his imagination pictured crosshairs on his heart and the killer's slow expulsion of breath as the trigger finger pressed down.

He returned to his Jeep to phone Moreno and head downhill to the station.

Bustamante

Once Artemas had cell phone reception he told Moreno to contact investigators in Sabinas Hidalgo, get out to the body, and both track and make a cast of the killer's footprints. He would have prefered to track them himself, but he'd put off calling the attorney general long enough. This new death would only make it worse if he delayed any further. He lit a cigar to calm his nerves.

Marta had made coffee and brought in some *pan dulce*, but his stomach was still queasy from the sight of the old priest's mulilated body. As he braced himself for the call he must make, his desk phone rang and he quickly picked up. "*Bueno, Capitán Salcido.*"

"*Capitán* Salcido, I'm glad I caught you. This is Humberto Alcazar speaking. Because of my injury I was not thinking clearly, and I fear there may have been some misunderstandings. I would like to get together with you to correct the problem, this morning if possible. Oh, and if by chance you have been looking for *Profesor* Peterson and *Señorita* Rendón, they're here. The ranch is just outside of town to the north. Turn right off the road to the *Ojo de Agua.*"

"O.K.," said Artemas, both baffled and relieved. "I noticed the gate this morning. I've got a call to make then I'll be out." Artemas had feared the worst and was relieved Jason and Laffi were safe, but what were they doing with Alcazar? First though, the phonecall.

This time the A.G. picked up on the first ring. He was silent during Artemas's description of finding the bodies of Zamarripa and his companion. Never asked if there was a suspect. Artemas volunteered he had evidence that Humberto Alcazar and another villager might be involved and he was on his way to see him. No reaction. Upon learning of the death of Father Buendía, the A.G. seemed even more distant. Finally, he said, "Report back as soon as you've finished. You've made a real mess," and hung up.

Artemas pushed back from his desk, stood up and let out a long breath. To Marta he said, "Tell Moreno I should be back before noon."

"*Está bien*. Oh, this just came for you from the United States."

She handed him a DHL delivery package the size of a shoebox. He looked at it carefully and tucked it under his arm as he headed out. On his way home Artemas thought about the A.G. The man, as one of his classmates at Harvard used to say, must be shitting spinach. For all the A.G. knew, the worst-case scenario — his money lost and its existence made public — was about to unfold. He was undoubtedly on the phone with other Grupo Vampiro members.

The first thing they would do is search Zamarripa's office and home for the camarilla's records. But who would break in? And even if they found the files, whom could they trust and how could they establish claims and apportion assets without risking exposure? These men were not used to doing this sort of operation themselves. For that matter, how much did the members know about each other? Did they even have documents attesting to their ownership positions? They were about to discover the downside of clandestine dealings without a legitimate corporate organization.

Artemas parked in front of his house and quickly phoned Father Laverdiere in Sonora, asking him to relay news of Zamarripa's death to his father. He figured the least he could do was give the appearance of trying to forewarn him. Then Artemas went inside, strapped on his pistol and opened the DHL package. It was, in fact, an actual shoebox containing a typed, unsigned note and a black plastic bag. "Thanks for your help. Hope this is of assistance and will lead to something you can share." Here was the sophisticated eavesdropping equipment he'd asked for — the Americans had come through.

Even without diagrams or instructions Artemas knew exactly what to do. His skill with electronic surveillance was technically what got him in trouble in Mexico City. Not only did his unsanctioned activities expose damaging information on important people, but he'd committed the unforgiveable "crime" of acting upon it. He hated that his father's influence had been nexessary to protect him from a worse fate than Bustamante, which was, truth be told, starting to grow on him.

Artemas grabbed a thumbtack and some super glue and made a quick modification to one of the devices.

Alcazar Ranch

A quarter mile outside the village on the road to the *Ojo de Agua*, Artemas drove under a tall entry portal. Made of welded re-bar, it spelled out *Alcazar* and was badly in need of paint. The dirt track winding over the low hills before him was also in poor repair.

Artemas came to a wide depression filled with water. He tossed a rock into the middle and judged his Jeep could make it through without getting stuck. First, though, he scanned the ground and saw faint marks of several tire tracks, including the distinctive pattern made by Jason's Suburban. He compared them with his own furrows and concluded no other vehicle had passed since last night's storm. He got back into the Jeep, shifted into 4WD, powered through the water and continued up and over the opposite bank.

A few miles later he topped a low rise and spied the ranch headquarters ahead. The main building was a large, masonry structure, also in need of paint. It followed the same U-shaped floor plan of Alcazar's town house, with plenty of parking in the center. But there was no sign of Jason's Suburban, only a Ford Explorer.

Artemas checked his pistol, it was cocked with the safety on. He patted his pocket, took a deep breath and slowly got out of the mud-spattered Jeep.

Wearing his trademark beret, Alcazar's body filled the ranch portico.

"*¡Bienvenido Capitán. Pasele!*"   The writer stood aside, gesturing for Artemas to precede him.

The room Artemas entered was spacious and not at all what he'd expected. Hand-hewn beams supported a low ceiling fashioned from crudely stripped tree branches. Flooring made from locally quarried flagstone, irregularly worn smooth by generations of footsteps, added to the rustic appearance. Near a large fireplace on the far wall stood Ricardo Chavana.

"I don't believe you've had the pleasure of meeting my lifelong friend, Ricardo Chavana," said Alcazar. "One of our country's finest artists."

Artemas shook hands with the slender, handsome man, and was immediately struck by two things: the weak grip of his baby-smooth hand and the fresh scratches on his right cheek, liberally covered with makeup.

"It's my pleasure. I regret that my inattention has kept us from meeting before," said the policeman.

"That's very kind, *señor*, but I'm reclusive by nature, and you've been rather busy," replied the artist.

Artemas was again surprised, this time at the powerful baritone that bore no resemblance to the flaccid handshake.

"*Señores*, please be seated," said Alcazar, gesturing to several chairs and a wooden bench with cowhide pillows in front of the fireplace. He said to Artemas, "Would you care for some coffee?"

"No thank you. Where are *Señorita* Rendón and *Señor* Peterson? You said they were here."

"Yes, yes," said Alcazar, his eyes twinkling through tiny, gold-framed glasses as he lowered his bulk into a massive chair near the fireplace. "They'll be along directly. Let's pass the time with a little conversation...an explanation, if you will."

Deciding to bide his time, Artemas seated himself in a chair opposite the writer with careful deliberation, keeping the pistol on his hip accessible. Chavana folded his lanky body onto the couch, knees primly together, as if wearing a dress.

"Thank you for coming," began Alcazar. "And please allow me to speak plainly. I realized after our last meeting that you suspected me of some involvement in what's been happening in Bustamante. You said as much. I'm not used to being assaulted — or accused — and was not thinking clearly when we spoke. I asked you to come today to make amends."

He leaned forward and continued, "I've decided to be completely honest with you, and invited Ricardo because what involvement there is, is shared by us. All I ask is that if you decide not to take this matter further—and I hope that will be your decision—that you'll say nothing of what passes between us."

Artemas remained silent.

"Oddly," began Alcazar, sitting a little straighter in his chair, "the background to what happened recently in Bustamante began in the Middle Ages, many years before the forebears of the present day Zamarripas and Alcazars even knew of the existence of Mexico. The family's roots were in the Balkans of Eastern Europe. It was considered noble, at least in terms of its wealth and power."

For a moment, white teeth flashed amidst the mustache and beard. "Just as today, the two were usually synonymous. The family's only problem, and the basis of the current situation, was the method by which their money and ultimately their power were accumulated."

Seeing he had Artemas's full atention, Alcazar leaned back, a more natural position for a man of his girth. "In those days, most success came through brute strength, sometimes exercised callously. Even after wealth and power had been achieved, the power that had created it had to be used again and again to prevent it being taken away by others. But, just as today, there was always someone stronger."

Realizing he was hanging on every word like a wide-eyed schoolboy, Artemas leaned back and frowned, to convey his skepticism.

Alcazar ignored this and continued. "Various means were used to supplement military might, including fear and superstition. You must remember that in those days virtually every disease was fatal, and both science and religion were in their infancy. When people looked to their belief systems for explanations of misfortune and death, they often reached incorrect conclusions. The masses assumed their adversities were caused either by their transgressions against God's teachings or, more often, by the evil power of the devil, a force many believed to be nearly invincible, one that could only be thwarted by avoiding it—or embracing it. The enormous powers ascribed to those invested with evil were believed to come straight from the devil. Do you follow me so far?" he asked.

"In theory," said Artemas. What Alcazar was imparting was similar to Jason's conjectures regarding vampires.

"Hah!" said the writer. "It's more than a theory, as you'll soon see." He paused once again, and Artemas wondered if it was to ensure attention or to consider how best to proceed.

"Are you sure you wouldn't like some coffee? Maybe a pastry?" Alcazar suddenly asked, cocking an eyebrow.

"No."

"Then I'll get to the point. It was all about blood and evil." Then changing tack, he said, "But first I think I'll accept my own hospitality," He looked at his friend. "Could you, Ricardo? Perhaps if you bring the pot and some *pan dulce*, we can yet tempt our guest."

"Of course," replied Chavana, uncoiling himself and rising. "I'll be right back."

When he had left the room, Alcazar said to Artemas, "Don't think I'm playing games. What I'm about to tell you will leave both Ricardo and me quite vulnerable. You must believe that I don't take that step lightly."

Alcazar Ranch

The artist returned with a chrome thermos, coffee mugs, and a plate of sweet breads decorated with green and red sugar. Alcazar poured himself a cup, bit off a piece of bread, and chewed contentedly. Then, brushing vividly tinted crumbs from his salt-and-pepper beard, he continued. "I don't know how it began. Perhaps at a victory celebration in a castle perched on a mountain top; a barbarous toast, silver goblets overflowing with the blood of a vanquished foe amidst cheers and victory songs." He sipped his coffee. "Or perhaps it was a well-thought-out ritual, where the elders renewed their vows to the family, taking their blood communion, while the young boys looked on in awe, yearning for their majority, their own initiation to the sacred rites. Maybe the way today's boys wish to be old enough to drive."

"In any case, the rite of taking and drinking blood was born, and not just in my family. Blood was thought to be the very essence of life. It was taken both to cure and to kill. So why shouldn't this powerful substance be used to transfer power from one human being to another? It seemed only natural. It was the same here in Mexico. To curry favor with the gods the Indians gave them blood by the bucket-full, the most valuable substance they could conceive. There is, *Capitán*, nothing more powerful than such a rite, especially when learned at a very early age."

Artemas caught himself falling under the writer's spell. He could now understand the man's literary accomplishments. But everything else about his host remained undefined, a blank slate colored only by suspicion.

"And," resumed Alcazar, "the taking of blood and its attendant strategies — rape, kidnapping, and torture delivered in the guise of divine judgment and retribution—were carefully passed down from father to son through the generations. Of course, like anything else, not without problems. In the case of Zarco and my forebears, things went too far too many times, and the Zamarripas were forced to leave their ancestral home and emigrate to Spain.

"There, the process began all over again, passing through the same phases until the family was marked by the Inquisition. Once again they had to flee, this time to Mexico. They discovered that Mexico City was not nearly far enough from the Church and royal authorities, so they traveled north, finally settling here in Bustamante."

His voice had grown low and its cadence quickened. He spread his massive arms in illustration. "The area met all their needs: it was far from the seat of power and had a large population of superstitious Indians. They used the same methods but with a difference: they vowed to be circumspect in the use of violence, employing it only as needed.

"Unfortunately, it was like an alcoholic attempting to drink in moderation, and once again things got out of hand. Youngsters don't always heed the counsel of their elders. The atrocities became more widespread, and things again began to slip away, partly because the Indians were far different from European peasants. Although they'd been defeated, they still had violence in their own blood, and things became highly unpleasant. It was at that time, around the end of the nineteenth century, that my branch of the family severed itself from the tradition of fear and bloodshed."

Artemas again caught himself leaning forward attentively.

"My ancestor, Gregorio Zamarripa," the writer continued, "a co-leader among the family elders, changed his name to Alcazar and moved from Hacienda Zamarripa to this ranch, vowing never to resort to the old ways. He was as good as his word and still prospered. But so did the Zamarripas, and to a greater extent."

Alcazar shrugged. "The Zamarripa branch got through the crisis by curtailing their cruelty and continued for some time with moderation. They felt betrayed, and that sense of betrayal quickly became hatred. For their part, the Alcazars regarded the Zamarripas with the disdain a reformed smoker reserves for those still using tobacco. The families never reconciled and although the tensions between them ebbed and flowed, their relationship remained one of loathing."

Alcazar took a deep breath and slumped back in his chair, as if he'd just completed a physically demanding task. "And that's the background," he said with a sigh. "Thank you for your attention *Capitán* Salcido. I will now get to the present circumstances."

Artemas smiled thinly, indicating it was about time.

The writer poured more coffee. "As paradoxical as it may seem, as their wealth increased during this century, both families began to wither away. After Mexico's revolution ended in the early thirties, the glue that held our respective clans together began to dry and crack. There was sufficient money and no longer any reason for family members not to relocate to the more stimulating environment of Mexico City, or even Monterrey. Zarco Zamarripa moved there to pursue his growing financial empire, leaving the once lively hacienda empty. He eventually married, but his wife died after the birth of their second son, and Zarco never paid much attention to his children. Perhaps he realized they weren't—how should I say it—of the blood.

"My own branch of the family drifted away. For many years I've been the only Alcazar left in Bustamante, although Ricardo might as well be a brother. He was born on Hacienda Zamarripa, where his parents lived and worked for the family. Being just a bit younger than Zarco, the boys played together, as boys will. I believe it was when Ricardo was thirteen, and Zarco...oh, probably fifteen, that the relationship changed from one that was normal to something unhealthy.

"While Zarco had probably not been formally initiated into the family secrets and traditions, he was smart. I'm sure he already suspected or knew a great deal and was anxious to take part. Little by little he began to practice on Ricardo a combination of what he'd learned and what his own sadistic mind conceived. Against all family discipline he created his own initiation rites and experimented on my friend. The results were something few of us could have survived with any degree of sanity.

"Zarco presided over the torture of animals, making Ricardo participate in the flaying and burning, then forced him to drink their blood. He himself drank Ricardo's blood in made-up ceremonies and, in turn, made him swallow the blood of younger children of other hacienda employees. But only after Zarco sexually molested the youngsters. Then he would leave Ricardo tied up for hours in some dank, awful place." Alcazar stopped and ran his hand over his forehead. "*Capitán*, there's more, but I can't... I think you understand."

Artemas shifted his glance briefly to the artist. He sat stone-faced in his oddly upright position, knees pressed even more tightly together, as if to protect himself.

Regaining his composure, Alcazar continued. "How long Ricardo's parents suspected what was going on is anyone's guess, but it was more than a year before they found the courage to find out what was happening and do something about it.

"Ricardo remembers spilling the secrets of the dark things he'd been involved with during one long night, like vomiting in an exorcism. Later he overheard his parents vowing to go to Zarco's father. Not a week later they were dead, killed in a suspicious automobile accident. They were in the back of a truck that slid off the road heading to the *grutas,* which in those days was even more dangerous than it is now. There was never an explanation of why they were up there. Of course, the driver, who was the Zamarripa's foreman, managed to escape before the truck went over.

"As soon as my father heard about it he went immediately to the school and took Ricardo home with him. He's been part of the family ever since. It's a wonder his paintings are no stranger than they are," he added. Chavana didn't move a muscle, his features and body frozen.

Sensing that Artemas was about to ask a question, Alcazar held up his hand. "I'll be finished very shortly, and will welcome any questions, *señor*. But this is quite difficult. Please allow me to continue." Artemas said nothing.

"As you can imagine, after my father rescued Ricardo the relations between the families became even worse. But then, as I've said, the aunts, uncles and cousins had already begun to disperse.

Soon, Ricardo and I were the only members of either clan left in the village. The bitterness seemed but a memory. That's until a few months ago when the Zamarripa whelps returned.

"From the first day, they were arrogant and rude, particularly to Ricardo, about whom they had obviously heard something. Perhaps not the whole story, but enough. At one point the skinny one told Ricardo they were going to 'Finish the job' with him and the Alcazars, and purify Bustamante in the process. That was bad, but when the drifter was murdered in such a horrible fashion we believed the threat to be real and were certain that a new generation of Zamarripas had returned to continue the reign of terror.

"Ricardo and I endlessly discussed what to do. We realized that the brothers were suspects in the murder but that there wasn't enough evidence to have the sons of Zarco Zamarripa arrested. At first we contented ourselves with the notion they would kill again, and since they're both quite stupid, would eventually leave incriminating evidence. But as time went on we were less sure that would happen. In fact, most of their crimes weren't even reported.

"As their bad behavior continued, we became convinced that the nightmare was truly back. In fact, Ricardo was unable to sleep without screaming himself awake. That's the only reason I can ascribe to the foolish action we decided on. That was about when you arrived in Bustamante, *Capitán*. Obviously we should have come to you first, but we didn't." Now this is where I literally put our lives in your hands." Alcazar's eyes looked upward, as if imploring some higher authority. Then they bored into Artemas with ferocious intensity.

"We decided to wait just a little longer for the boys to incriminate themselves. If that didn't happen, we vowed that when an opportunity arose we would kill someone and leave sufficient evidence to incriminate the Zamarripas and remove them from Bustamante forever.

Alcazar paused. "*Capitán*, you're thinking I am about to confess to the murder of the American girl. That's not so. Neither of us, thank the merciful Lord, committed murder. But as you'll soon see, it's only through His mercy and grace that we didn't. We thought about it, we decided to do it, but we didn't.

"The day the two American girls walked into the hotel we had just decided that we could wait no longer. You probably never heard about it, but the brothers recently raped a twelve-year old girl from a very poor family in Villa Aldama. They threatened her parents with death if anyone breathed a word. It was all happening just as we had feared.

"You may already know I was the one who helped the girls translate. When they left the restaurant, Ricardo and I looked at each other, got up and left without saying a word. We both knew what had to be done. We would kill them and plant evidence we had already collected to blame the Zamarripa brothers.

"I directed the girls to the tourist parking area, knowing it's at least an hour's hike up to the *grutas*. We calculated we could easily reach the top by the narrow road, which is officially closed, then head down the path and meet the girls on their way up. We estimated it would be relatively close to where the drifter was killed, so the crimes would be easy to connect. Ricardo implored me to let him do it by himself, I finally agreed, believing it would be safer for both of us in the long run.

"His motor bike was already in the back of my Explorer, as was the incriminating evidence we'd accumulated. He kept down low as we drove out of the village. That I was sighted both coming and going by the young scorpion collector, you probably already know. If questioned, I was to say that I became concerned about the girls and drove to the *grutas*. Since I saw nothing that might cause them harm, I left long before they had a chance to reach the entry. In any case, I left Ricardo and his motorbike at the parking area. I will allow him to finish the tale. Coffee, *señor*?"

"You are persistent," said Artemas, "and, for that reason, sometimes successful. Yes, thank you, I'll take a cup."

Zargoza Ranch

As he watched Alcazar pour coffee, Jason and Laffi flashed through Artemas's mind. "I hope we're nearing the question and answer session," he said. Looking at his watch, he added, "I didn't think this would take quite so long."

Alcazar gave his guest a sharp look, then gestured to Chavana. "Ricardo's account will take but a few moments more."

The artist began in his surprising baritone. "When Humberto dropped me off I left my motorbike in the parking area and started down the trail on foot. Ever since we left the hotel I could think of nothing but my mother and father, what happened to them, the fear and pain they must have suffered at the hands of the Zamarripas and of what was beginning again. By the time I began the descent I was so overwhelmed with hatred and vengeance that I was almost looking forward to the act. It never occurred to me that I was about to become what I hated. I was prepared to kill both girls after gaining their confidence by telling them I'd come to guide them. They were so small and unsuspecting; I thought it would be easy.

"I had descended several hundred meters down the path when I happened upon the most bizarre thing I've ever seen." He stopped and looked at Alcazar, who nodded for him to resume. "I came around a corner to find old Father Buendía standing over the body of the girl. He was in his black pants and shirt, his hair was wild and he was shaking a bloody finger at the body, cursing softly the entire time. He was ranting and raving to the extent that I couldn't understand everything he said, but did catch some words, like 'whore, bitch, despoiler of all that is good,' that sort of thing, using old fashioned terminology. All I could think of was that he'd lost his mind and killed her. I was stunned.

"I approached him carefully. I knew him well. He'd been the priest when my parents were killed—but I wasn't sure what to expect. At the same time I saw that the girl's shirt had been torn nearly off and her shorts unzipped. She was obviously dead, her throat ripped open. It was at that moment I realized that I couldn't have done what I'd come to do. I nearly became sick at the horror of it, as well as the memories it brought back." He stopped and stared at Artemas, who remained still.

"The priest looked up, saw me, and said in a calm voice, 'It was inevitable. It had to happen.'

"I realized through the fog of emotion that I'd been presented with an opportunity and only needed to figure out how to take advantage of it. 'What did happen?' I asked the old man, noticing that his hands were covered with blood.

"'I found this...this…here on the pathway, struck down by the hand of the Lord,' he said.

"Are you sure it wasn't you carrying out the Lord's work? I asked him. I know it sounds flippant, but I could think of nothing else to say.

"Then it came to me. I said, 'I'll bet it was the Zamarripas,' and continued talking to him in a similar manner for several minutes. I told him of my fear that the evil family had returned to renew its influence in the village, and that I was certain the brothers had killed and mutilated the drifter and now this girl. He finally agreed, saying it was probable. By this time I guess he'd forgotten it was the Lord." The artist smiled for the first time, and his delicate features seemed to grow younger.

"Of course, he already knew much of the Zamarripa's history. In fact, years ago he told me he was certain they'd murdered my parents. But so powerful was the family that for years he was forced to maintain the illusion they were as virtuous as the donations they sent to the Bishop each year. It took very little effort for me to persuade him to say nothing of the killing, to allow me to direct the investigation toward the Zamarripa brothers. By that time it was nearly dark. He left me and climbed up the mountain to go God knows where. I couldn't believe our luck. Someone else had done what I never could have, and the results would be the same—the end of the filthy Zamarripas.

"I picked up the girl's camera, carefully wiped off any fingerprints and put it in my pocket. I also left the butt of a marijuana cigarette—dropped a few days before by one of the brothers—near the body, and a silver bracelet exactly like the one Armando always wears. Humberto had collected them for just that purpose. I then went back to my motorbike and coasted most of the way back to the village.

"The next day I waited until I saw the brothers in town and drove to the hacienda. It was the first time I'd been there since the death of my parents. It wasn't easy. The old servants were dragging garbage to the fire pit. I told them I wanted to leave a surprise for my friends, Armando and Ignacio, and asked them not to spoil it by telling them I'd been there.

"I could tell that the servants disliked their new masters. They simply waved me into the house and went about their business. I put a small box of candy I'd brought in the middle of the dining room table and stuck the camera well back in a chest of drawers containing silverware. I doubted the boys would notice it. But it would be easily found by anyone making a serious search. In the meantime, Humberto had been carefully spreading rumors that linked the Zamarripas to the girl's death and that of the drifter."

"The stage was set. As you know, the production came off exactly as planned," concluded Alcazar, inclining his head toward Artemas. "Now, we've told you quite truthfully what happened. We realize we're probably guilty of something, perhaps conspiracy and failure to immediately report the murder, but of no really serious crime. Your reaction?"

Artemas regarded him warily. "Giving an opinion at this time is difficult, other than to say it was quite a story. But I have a few questions."

"Please, *Capitán*," said Alcazar. "We have told you the truth and will continue to do so."

"*Señor* Chavana, *Señor* Alcazar; you've made it clear that you did not kill the girl, but you also said you were prepared to do so. How could you even think such a thing, much less decide to do it? Surely there were other ways. Why didn't you come to me for help, particularly regarding the rape of the young girl from Villa Aldama? I knew nothing about it."

Alcazar cleared his throat. "I know it sounds bizarre, *Capitán*," he said. "But you must remember our history with the Zamarripas. We know they have fixed even more serious things with the authorities, and killed those seeking to thwart them. And as much as I abhor the racist connotations, the girls were *gringas*, and the way they were dressed..." "*Señor* Chavana, when you took the camera, did you remove the film that the girl's friend said was in it?"

Chavana looked toward Alcazar, but the writer did not return his glance, keeping his gaze fixed firmly on Artemas. "No, I just took the camera and put it in my pocket, after wiping it on my shirt."

"You said the body of the girl was at least partially clothed when you arrived. When we found it in the morning she was naked, and her clothes had been tossed into the canyon. How could that have happened after you left?"

"I don't know. I left without touching the body. As I said, Father Buendía had already gone. Unless...he or someone else returned."

"You said the girl's throat was torn, but did you see a great deal of blood on the trail?"

"No, I didn't."

"The reason I ask," continued Artemas, "is that when we found the body in the morning nearly all the blood was gone. Any idea how that could have happened?"

"Again, I must say no."

The artist was becoming increasingly agitated under the questioning, and Alcazar broke in. "This has been very stressful, for both of us, but most especially Ricardo. It has brought back memories that were best forgotten...I'm sure you understand. Might I suggest that we all meet again, with the addition of Father Buendía, and go through the account once more to completely clear the air. That would also give you sufficient time to prepare whatever questions you wish to ask."

"That would be a fine idea," said Artemas. "Except for one small detail: Father Buendía was murdered early this morning. In fact, I discovered his body just before you invited me to this meeting."

"Oh my God," exclaimed Alcazar and Chavana, almost in unison. "Where? How?" demanded the writer. "What's happening to us? This can't be. The Zamarripas are gone!"

"It's nevertheless a fact," replied Artemas, "And, after what you just told me, an unpleasant coincidence—the priest being the only living person who could have verified your story."

He was unable to detect anything but surprise, outrage, and fear in the men's reactions.

"*Señor* Alcazar," said Artemas, "a moment ago you said, 'The Zamarripas are gone.' What did you mean by that?"

"I meant that since the Zamarripa brothers were arrested, their threat to the village is gone."

"But, your real enemy, Zarco Zamarripa, actually came to your house night before last. In spite of what you told me, I think it was him who assaulted you and took your beret. Is he also gone?"

"Zarco's no longer a threat. He lives in Monterrey, and Bustamante isn't a part of his life. That visit was only because of his sons. He may never come again."

"Of one thing I can assure you," said Artemas, "Zarco Zamarripa will *never* come again. He and an employee were murdered early yesterday evening at his hacienda. Now, you said you arrived here yesterday evening. Have both of you been here the entire time? And tell me right now where are *Señor* Peterson and *Señorita* Rendón!"

Alcazar looked at Artemas with an expression of pure astonishment. "I had no idea—Zarco dead? It's hard to believe. No wonder you're suspicious. I apologize for the other night." Then he cocked his head toward the front door. "But I believe you are about to receive definitive answers to both your questions. Unless my hearing deceives me our mutual friends have returned."

Alcazar Ranch

With astonishing speed for a man of his size, Alcazar crossed the room to open the door. Artemas could see Laffi beyond the writer's girth, and behind her, Jason. He used the distraction to slip the FBI's tiny listening device under his chair, securing it with a super-glued thumbtack.

"Welcome back," boomed Alcazar. "I hope the morning was successful. I have a surprise for you." He gestured toward Artemas. "Apparently there has been some question as to your whereabouts... and possibly ours as well." His wave included Chavana. "You may wish to enlighten *Capitán* Salcido, who has been kind enough to visit on another matter."

It took a moment for the Americans' eyes to adjust to the dim light, but they soon recognized Artemas and greeted him warmly.

Jason said, "I hope we didn't cause any problems?"

"No," replied Artemas. "It's as *Señor* Alcazar says, I was here regarding another matter."

Laffi spoke up. "We were just coming down from the caverns late yesterday when these two gentlemen met us. *Señor* Alcazar explained that he had just discovered that a bat expert—Jason—was in town, and that he very much wanted him to see an active cave on his property. He estimated there would be just enough time to reach it before dark.

"On the spur of the moment we decided to follow them. Unfortunately, the storm broke just as we arrived, and we couldn't get to the cave. Because of possible flash floods, it would have been dangerous to try and return to the village, so they suggested we spend the night and get an early start to the cave. We agreed and were given an excellent meal, not to mention fine company. We're certainly grateful for the hospitality. Most importantly, Jason has made a discovery that I'll let him describe." Almost as an afterthought she added, "We tried to call you to cancel our dinner date, but something was wrong with the telephone and there's no cell phone service here."

"Well," broke in Alcazar, "you've discovered something in my cave? That's wonderful. Please explain; we could use some good news."

Laffi aimed sharp looks at the writer and Artemas, but said nothing, defering to her companion.

"Yes," said Jason. "What you appear to have is a much larger colony of Mexican freetail bats than I would have thought possible. I'm guessing that it's in excess of forty thousand individuals. What's so surprising is that in all my trips to Bustamante I've never found much bat activity. With your permission I'd love to spend some time, probably in a few months, doing further research."

"That's wonderful news," said Alcazar. "It'll be my pleasure," he added. But as his voice trailed off, it was obvious his attention was more focused on Artemas, than bats.

Recognizing that Artemas was on official police business, Laffi was ready to ask him questions, but Artemas flashed her a disapproving look and cocked his head toward the door. Jason and Laffi took the hint and the three began to leave. As they walked out the door, Artemas cleared his throat.

"This has been extremely interesting. I appreciate your being forthright, but my investigation is far from over. I'll probably have questions for both of you regarding your involvement. No plans to leave, I trust?"

"No *Capitán*, you can find us here," said Alcazar.

Artemas pulled his Jeep alongside Jason's Suburban and asked them to follow him back to his office. He was still digesting what he had heard, but also thought a conversation with the Americans could prove equally important. Overall, this had been a fruitful visit, and Alcazar's account of his family history and bad blood certainly explained Chavana's disturbing painting. The visit, though, failed in one respect. Artemas never found the opportunity to hide the recording device necessary to capture conversations sent from the tiny transmitter he planted, so he was missing whatever Ricardo and Alcazar were saying at that very moment. He'd have to sneak into the hacienda later to finish the job.

It was well after noon when the threesome arrived at the police station. Marta immediately informed Artemas that Moreno had radioed in and was still waiting for the Sabinas officials to complete their crime scene investigation. He had followed the killer's tracks for several hundred yards in the same direction, but they had disappeared into a rocky scree.

Jason and Laffi pulled up chairs in front of Artemas's desk. He extracted a cigar from the top drawer, carefully clipped it with a small pair of scissors, and lit it with a sturdy kitchen match. After one slow draw, he quickly outlined the murder of Zamarripa, his companion and the priest, omitting his trip to Monterrey. He then asked them to repeat, in detail, how they'd met Alcazar and Chavana and what happened thereafter.

When they'd finished, Artemas relit his cigar and asked, "Were both of them with you at all times after you arrived at the ranch?"

"No," said Jason, without hesitation. "When we got there Chavana said he was tired and went to the other wing of the house to take a nap. We didn't see him until supper, I'd guess about two and half hours later."

"That's right," agreed Laffi. "We spent most of the time talking with Alcazar, listening to village history and stories about Mexico's literary politics. About forty-five minutes before dinner he showed us to separate bedrooms, made sure there were linens and towels and left us."

"And the rooms were...?"

"On the other side of the compound from where Chavana was staying," answered Laffi. "Do you think Chavana slipped out and killed Zamarripa, and later the priest?" she asked.

"Bearing in mind your occupation and how good you are at it, you'll understand why I can't answer that question," said Artemas. "There's a lot at stake here, particularly for me. I must ask you, much more urgently this time to say nothing of this conversation."

"I understand," nodded Laffi.

"By the way," added Artemas, "What, if anything, did you discover on your visit to the *grutas*?"

"We didn't have much time," said Jason, "but I took two different samples from the pile of sticks we told you about and left a motion-rigged camera. The samples could be scales and fur. We'll just have to wait and see."

"Tell me again how you get to the entrance?" said Artemas. After Jason complied, Artemas thought for a moment then said, "That may be the only entrance to the caverns, at least until the rubble from the explosions is cleared. And you're probably the only people who know about it. Please don't mention it to anyone else. And don't ask me why."

Although Jason looked puzzled and Laffi seemed worried, both nodded assent.

Artemas paused to make sure that Marta was out of earshot, even though he knew she spoke little or no English. "Look," he said, his voice becoming grave. "I don't want to leave on a melodramatic note, but I must ask you both a favor, and believe me it's a matter of life and death."

"Of course," said Jason.

"I'm going to give you an envelope. Please open it only in the event you hear that something permanently unpleasant has happened to me, then do whatever your conscience dictates."

He tore a piece of paper from the yellow legal tablet in front of him, dashed off a couple of sentences, sealed it in an envelope and handed it to Jason. "Thanks," he said."

"What the hell does that mean?" demanded Laffi.

"Just what I said, and that's all I can say, responded Artemas, his voice almost a whisper.

"Dammit, that's not good enough," exclaimed Laffi. "What the hell's going on? Are you in danger?"

Artemas motioned for her to lower her voice, then said, "I'm sorry Laffi, but at this point that's all I can say, and please keep this confidential."

"That won't be difficult," snapped Laffi. "For some time I've been less than happy with my job. Earler today when I told

Jason, he asked if I would consider working with him in Bat Watch. I told him I'd consider it, and later this afternoon I'll be going with him to Austin to check things out."

Artemas masked his surprise with a puff on his cigar. After a long pause he finally said, "That's wonderful. And please understand that under the circumstances I have no other choice."

Bustamante

Artemas felt a momentary heaviness upon his heart at the thought of losing Laffi. But he had no time for self indulgence. Deliberately, he lit another cigar and considered his next move. The attorney general had been pleased with the arrest of Zamarripa's sons for Julie Conners' murder. It tidied up a messy international incident, documented the efficiency of the PGR, and earned him some points with the president.

Then disaster: the murder of Zamarripa put access to the A.G.'s share of Grupo Vampiro—the payoff for what was undoubtedly many years of corruption—in jeopardy. The similar murder of the priest—after the Zamarripa brothers were behind bars—was the last straw. It would blow the previous case resolution into even smaller particles.

Artemas was certain that Zamarripa was responsible for Jugo Gandara's murder and that Alcazar and Chavana had killed Zamarripa, Father Buendía, and probably Julie Conners. He believed the writer's story was a clever attempt to recast the truth in a way that would clear him and Chavana. The death of the priest made it difficult to confirm his story, and perhaps impossible to disprove, considering the carefully constructed alibi provided by Jason and Laffi's presence at the ranch during the time the last two killings took place. That must have been the "insurance" Alcazar had mentioned in his call to Chavana. The only possibility was there might be some skin under Zamarripa's or Joaquin's fingernails that could be traced to the scratches he'd noticed on Chavana's cheek. The bug he'd placed on the telephone pole was illegal so any evidence he got from it could only be used internally.

He doubted the attorney general would have the stomach for opening that investigation. No, he would want something much simpler and more tidy—something that would confirm the earlier conclusions and explain subsequent events. Artemas had an idea how to affect such a solution but realized that it wouldn't necessarily ensure a favorable outcome for himself, much less justice. If it worked, the mystery would remain, in true Mexican fashion, a more complicated enigma, except possibly to a few whose silence would either be undoubted or made permanent.

He decided he should call the A.G. again to propose his solution. At least that might buy him some time, and he wouldn't be accused of lack of communication. He made the call, was on hold for some time, then was told the A.G. was not in, that he should leave a message. Something about the tone of the messenger's voice, as well as the message itself, made him feel uneasy. He decided to check on the progress of the priest's murder investigation.

On the way to the *Ojo de Agua*, Artemas double-checked the Grupo Vampiro papers stashed under his seat. They were his only insurance. When he arrived at the scene, the investigators were finishing up, and he weathered sarcastic barbs from the Sabinas Hidalgo men. "Maybe you should just keep an apartment, a chemistry set, and some sharp knives for us in Bustamante. Ha, ha, ha!"

But it did give him an opportunity to ask the Medical Examiner if he'd found any skin under Zamarripa or Joaquin's fingernails. "Zamarripa, yes," the M.E. replied. Artemas requested it be preserved for possible DNA testing.

He drove back south toward the village, as if returning to the scene where the drifter and Jugo Gandara's body had been found, but instead, quickly turned right after passing through the gate. He headed up the narrow road to the *grutas*, parked and began writing a detailed explanation of the Grupo Vampiro files and how they fit into recent events. He taped the yellow sheet in front of the first file, and hoisted the bag unobtrusively to his side. Following Jason's directions, he climbed up to the top of the mountain then over and down the other side to the opening.

Jason's rope was still tied to the massive boulder, and Artemas easily lowered himself inside the cave. He was amazed at the immensity of the hitherto undiscovered cavern; it was just as the Americans had described. The beam from his flashlight revealed smooth walls and stalactites strewn across the floor. The large pile of sticks Jason had mentioned caught his attention.

As he approached, a blinding light exploded in his eyes, and he instinctively hit the ground. Clever, he thought, as his vision recovered, remembering Jason's description of the motion-activated camera. He spotted the tripod several yards away. He detected an odd odor that made his spine tingle, something vaguely familiar but just beyond his recollection. He wasn't sure, but it seemed to emanate from the irregular pile of sticks. He'd have to leave this mystery to Jason; he had no time to waste.

Artemas placed his satchel of Grupo Vampiro files in a far corner next to the bags of supplies left by Jason. A final survey pleased him. The papers would not be easily seen by a casual observer, but would be hard for Jason and Laffi to miss. In the note he'd given them, he'd instructed them to look for "evidence" in the cave if anything happened to him.

Famished, Artemas went straight from the cave to the hotel for a late lunch. Eduardo said that Jason and Laffi had just left. On their way to Austin, Artemas concluded, glumly. He ate alone and left the restaurant, determined to dispose of the mountain of paperwork he'd left undone. As he crossed a sidestreet that led into the plaza, a familiar voice sounded behind him. "What's the hurry; the case is closed, isn't it?"

Artemas turned to find Laffi close behind him — alone. "I thought you'd gone to Austin?"

"I changed my mind and told Jason to go ahead. I said that my boss emailed me to do a follow-up peace, and I'd try to get there in a few days."

Perplexed, Artemas said, "But why?"

"Because I'm distressed over what you said. You know, the part about something permanently unpleasant happening to you! It doesn't take a genius to figure out you're in deep shit, and that whatever's causing it is related to corruption. And the only way I know to deal with corruption is to shine a big bright light on it. That's what I'm good at, now what the hell's going on?"

Artemas was both stunned and pleased at the depth of Laffi's concern. But he needed time to decide how to deal with the situation. "Laffi, you're a treasure, and I can't thank you enough. I may even take you up on your offer to help, and you certainly deserve an explanation. Right now there's something I have to resolve. It will only take an hour or two. May I call you when I finish?"

"O.K., but no more fooling around! I'll be in my room."

When Artemas got to the police station, Marta and Moreno

were both there, waiting to see him, with anxious smiles on their faces.

In answer to his questions Marta hurriedly told him the attorney general had not returned his call. Moreno reported, as if in a trance, that the priest's murder investigation had been concluded without a problem. Artemas knew something was off—they both seemed preoccupied, reticent, maybe even a bit embarrassed. *Could they be having an affair? Perhaps… though Marta's married with two children. Have they made some mistake and are afraid to admit it?* Whatever it was it would have to wait, there was too much going on and he needed to tackle the stack on his desk.

Hours later, as he locked the station door behind him, he replayed in his mind the awkward interactions with Marta and Moreno. Something had been wrong, and that something had to do with him. He was certain of it. All afternoon and into the evening the two of them had been unusually somber and refused to look him in the eye. What had triggered their strange behavior? A call from the A.G. questioning his activities? No, that couldn't be it; the A.G. would never involve them. Artemas wished he'd been less preoccupied and had confronted them on the spot. They'd left with barely a goodbye.

Plagued by nagging doubts, Artemas cautiously made his way back to his house. It was a moonless ink-black night, and from the street not even the hint of light behind the living room curtains.

Just as it should be.

Nevertheless, he quietly circled around to the unkempt backyard, choked with lush foliage from the rains and surrounded by a low wall. No light was visible in his bedroom or study, either. Slipping over the wall, he crept to the back door, which opened onto a hallway. His precautions felt a bit foolish in such a sleepy little town, but he was compelled to take no chances. Artemas turned the knob as slowly and quietly as he could. The wooden door, swollen with moisture, grated loudly against the jam as he forcefully jerked it open.

He groped for the light switch. Something powerful gripped him by wrist and hair, flinging him so violently he skidded several feet along the floor. The hall light flashed on and Artemas looked up to see Raymundo Valenzuela staring down at him, lips twisted in a sneer below his well-trimmed mustache.

"Don't try anything stupid until you look behind you," said the PGR man, crossing his arms on his chest.

Artemas rolled to his side. Pointing his chrome .45 automatic at him was the hatchet-faced goon who had spent the night outside the Zamarripa brothers' cell.

"Get up, slowly," said Raymundo, stepping back a pace.

Artemas gathered his legs under him and carefully rose, never taking his eyes off Raymundo. "I thought we were friends?" he said, trying to conceal his fear.

"I have no friends, especially with traitors like you," hissed Raymundo. "Now into the living room, slowly."

Artemas followed the man with the gun as he backed down the short hallway into the living room. "Sit over there." Raymundo waved toward the couch.

Resting on the couch Artemas saw an open briefcase containing what he knew to be an electronic torture device. The rest of the furniture was overturned and slashed. Raymundo pulled up a straight-back chair opposite him and sat, crossing his legs, and once again folded his arms over his chest.

"This can be very easy or very difficult. To me it doesn't matter except that time's important." Raymundo's voice and manner were matter-of-fact, verging on ambivilance. "I'll give you the courtesy of explaining how and why I'm here. I expect your total cooperation in return. Think very carefully; this is your one chance.

"Early this morning when the attorney general learned that the industrialist Zamarripa had been murdered, he sent us to Monterrey in a private jet with a special warrant to find papers vital to the nation's security. He was convinced they were either at Zamarripa's home or office. We didn't find them."

Valenzuela bared his teeth. "But we did find your fingerprints in Zamarripa's home! We came here by helicopter and discovered that you disappeared immediately after finding the body. You took Zamarripa's belongings, including his keys with you. You could easily have gone to his house in Monterrey. It also appears that about sixty copies were made on your office copier without being logged around that time.

"A second matter of concern is your handling of the case since we left, including the additional murders that jeopardize our work. That's the end of the background, and of my courtesy. Now tell me where the papers are, and this can all be over with a minimum of unpleasantness."

His last three words held more menace for the young policeman than anything he had ever heard before. Artemas tried to compose himself. His instincts about Marta and Moreno had been correct. More important, he was in terrible danger. He cursed himself for not remembering that Marta meticulously logged the number of copies made on the machine.

"I appreciate your courtesy," he said, "and will respond with the truth. I only ask that you listen to me with an open mind. I believe I can explain to your satisfaction why your conclusions are incorrect. I fully cooperated with your previous investigation and will continue to do so."

Artemas took a deep breath. "First, regarding the fingerprints, let me say I commend you on your thoroughness. The truth is that I was previously in the house for a brief conversation with Zarco Zamarripa. When I went to visit my father on personal business, I gave him the facts of the investigation that had already appeared in the press. Shortly afterward I received a message that Zamarripa wanted to speak with me. He invited me to his home directly after I landed in Monterrey. Although I had some misgivings, which now appear to have been well founded, I decided to see him as a courtesy. The American scientist who picked me up at the airport and drove me there can substantiate the fact that I met with Zamarripa for no more than ten minutes at his home and took nothing away. Although there were no witnesses, I can assure you that I gave Zamarripa no information that could be considered improper."

Artemas thought about producing the recording he had made of the conversation, but decided it would not help and might create other problems by revealing the trap he had set. "I hope that will explain the fingerprints, which I assume were found in his den, probably on the glass coffee table. I can also assure you they would not have been there had I been in the house to steal whatever papers you're talking about." Artemas knew he had been at least partially truthful as he had worn gloves on his second visit to Zamarripa's house.

Valenzuela's expression betrayed nothing of his thoughts. "Why didn't you tell the A.G. you met with Zamarripa; didn't you think it was important?"

"As I spoke to the A.G., I realized that meeting Zamarripa was an even worse idea than I'd feared. In hindsight, I should have told him."

Artemas paused to see if his words were having any effect, but Raymundo's slitted eyes remained impassive.

"About where I was after discovering Zamarripa's body,"Artemas continued, " I told the A.G. that I had reason to believe that Humberto Alcazar was involved in that crime. I went to see if he was home. He wasn't, so I decided to watch his house to find out when he returned. I spent several hours there but without result, something I also discussed with the attorney general. I later discovered Alcazar was at his ranch outside of town. Before today I didn't even know that ranch existed."

Behind Raymundo, near the hall entrance, Artemas spied a long, narrow cockroach climbing up the wall. In spite of the seriousness of his predicament, he nearly smiled as he thought how much the shiny insect resembled Raymundo's mustache. Suppressing the urge he continued, "I believe your last point was the copy machine tally. I did make some copies that night, of some information the American scientist found on the Internet. It was only a few pages, but at first the machine didn't work properly, so some were wasted, but the total wouldn't be anywhere near sixty. I'll be happy to show it to you. I don't know how to account for the extra pages, but if I were lying to you I guarantee I'd think of something. All I can say is that Marta has made mistakes in the past."

He knew he was taking a risk by not explaining the extra pages, but had already stretched the truth to the breaking point. He hoped this approach might add to his credibility.

"So, you're saying you know absolutely nothing about the papers we're looking for?"

"As I said, the only time I was in Zamarripa's house was for a brief conversation the day I returned from Sonora. I have no idea what they are or where they might be."

Raymund smiled, as if pleased at the answer.

"I should add," said Artemas, sensing that things were going badly, "that in regard to recent events, I've had no control over them, nor could I be expected to have had any. However, I do have a solution that should please the A.G. As I said, it was to that end that I made the copies."

"And just what is your solution."

"Thinking quickly, Artemas said, "The information the American found seems to pertain to a drug related cult. Members commit crimes similar to those that have been taking place here. We already determined that the Zamarripa brothers killed the drifter as part of an initiation. It's extremely likely that the murdered drug lord, Hugo Gandara, was the cult's leader, and just as likely that Zamarripa killed Gandara in retaliation and to throw suspicion on his sons' guilt." Remembering that Father Buendía's heart had been left intact, he added. "The murder of the priest doesn't really fit but can be made to. A solution that can't be disproved. One that's just bizarre enough to be believable to the conspiracy buffs in the press."

Raymundo considered this for some moments; his expression betraying nothing. Finally, he said, "Let's see those papers."

"They're in my study," said Artemas, trying not to visibly expel the breath he had unconsciously been holding.

"Take me, and no tricks," said Raymundo, drawing his pistol. The metallic click of the cocked hammer echoed in the room.

Artemas went to his home office and retrieved the Internet tract from the mess they'd made of his desk. After they returned to the living room, he handed it to Raymundo, careful not to make any sudden moves. Stepping back two paces and keeping his pistol aimed at Artemas's heart, the agent carefully read the document.

After brief consideration, Raymundo pursed his thin lips

and said, "This may have possibilities. "But it doesn't solve the problem of the missing papers. I'm afraid your word — I should say your untested word — isn't enough. Put your hands behind your back."

Raymundo eyed Artemas like a hungry crocodile. The muscles in his taut cheeks, near long, artfully trimmed sideburns, twitched as he motioned to his assistant, who promptly holstered his automatic and produced a set of handcuffs.

Artemas thought of nothing but the wires and electrodes in the briefcase behind him and what they did to a man's body and sanity. His death was probably a forgone conclusion as far as Raymundo was concerned. His body would probably be found tomorrow in similar condition to the others, his drug-ritual-gone-crazy theory a plausible explanation.

Bustamante

Artemas learned what passed for street fighting in the backcountry Yaqui *rancherías* and later studied *Tai Kwon Do* in Mexico City. Whatever edge those experiences gave him would have to do. Anything was preferable to the torture and execution he knew awaited. He pretended to swoon, and carefully placed his right foot in front of the left as a feigned attempt to avoid falling to the floor. Raymundo relaxed with a gloat of satisfaction at this display of weakness.

Once the handcuffs brushed his shirtsleeve, Artemas slid forward with the lighting speed he'd practiced hundreds of times in the *dojo*. A front snap kick connected with Raymundo's pistol, sending it spinning toward the ceiling. Right foot midair, Artemas repeated the kick, driving his foot into the PGR man's crotch with a satisfying *thwack*. As Raymundo gasped and bent over clutching himself, a third snap kick to his face lifted him off his feet and dumped him onto his back.

Artemas caught sight of the other man closing in from behind. He uncoiled his body and delivered a powerful reverse side kick to the man's solar plexus, doubling him over. He followed up with a snap kick to the face. Like his colleague, the man landed on his back, choking and groaning with pain.

Artemas swiftly scooped up both men's pistols, engaged the safety on one and stuffed it into his belt. He pointed the other pistol at the men on the floor. He grabbed the handcuffs and clipped one cuff around the PGR deputy's right wrist and dragged him across the tile floor close enough to snap the other cuff over Raymond's right wrist. Based on how they held their guns, Artemas figured they were both right-handed, so this would put them at a disadvantage.

Plus they'd be facing opposite directions making resistance even more difficult.

Blood poured from Raymundo's nose, and his lips were a pulpy mess. He'd probably lost some teeth. Nevertheless he recovered enough to threaten Artemas. *"Tu hijo de puta,* you're a dead man," he hissed, spitting blood onto his shirt.

The insult, which meant *son of a whore*, was personal, especially coming from Raymondo. Artemas felt both shame and fury. He raised his foot, intending to smash Raymundo's ribs. But some inner voice stopped him before finishing the blow, just as he would have done in practice. His self-discipline was rewarded by Raymond's look of unbridled fear.

"You told me you'd exhausted your courtesy with me," Artemas hissed. "Well, I can assure you that's the last courtesy you'll get from me! Now give me the A.G.'s private number, which I know you have."

"Wh—what for?" he stammered.

"I gave you perfectly acceptable explanations for the questions you raised. You should at least have discussed them with him. I'm sure you would have if you didn't have different orders. I intend to find out exactly what's going on, and perhaps give some orders of my own. The fact that he'll find out what a useless piece of shit you are will be satisfying in itself. Now the number while you can still talk!" Artemas jabbed his toe into the man's ribs

Reluctantly, Valenzuela recited the number. Artemas found his phone and answering machine beneath an upended chair and plucked the phone from the receiver, never taking his eyes off the men on the floor.

"The number, again." Artemas wedged the receiver between his ear and shoulder and dialed with his left hand as the PGR man repeated the number.

After two rings an impatient male voice answered, *"Bueno."* Artemas recognized the attorney general's clipped tone.

"This is Artemas Salcido speaking." There was a long pause, and Artemas continued. "I can understand your surprise, and also why you didn't take my earlier call. I would like to give you a quick explanation, then hear your reaction."

"*Ándele*, go ahead," said the A.G.

"Good. First you should know that the men you sent are handcuffed on the floor in front of me. They accused me of going to Zamarripa's home in Monterrey after discovering his body here in Bustamante and stealing papers of some sort. I told them the truth, that I know nothing of any papers, and explained the presence of my fingerprints."

Artemas repeated the explanation and solution to the problem he had just given Valenzuela. Then he added, "I told them these things after they interrogated my subordinates without informing me. Instead of questioning me in a civilized manner, they attacked me. After I gave them truthful answers, they were going to torture and probably kill me. That's why they're lying on the floor, and why we're having this conversation."

The A.G. listened to Artemas without comment, then responded in calm, measured words. "There's been a terrible mistake. I never intended for that to happen. Put Valenzuela on!"

Artemas put the phone on the floor about three feet from Raymundo, who lay glaring up at him. He handed him the receiver and pushed the record button on his answering machine, waving the pistol at him in warning. Raymundo hardly said one word during his brief conversation, snippets of the A.G.'s ranting loud enough for even Artemas to hear.

Finally, Raymundo said, "*Sí. señor. Claro que sí,*" and looked up at Artemas, barely concealing his intense hatred. Artemas walked over to him and carefully retrieved the phone.

To Artemas the A.G. said "I told him what a disgraceful mess he made and ordered him to apologize to you. I realize how unpleasant this has been for you, that you've been doing a good job under difficult circumstances. I hope this will be the end of it."

"I hope so," Artemas retorted. He'd never heard the man sound so contrite. "But you'll understand if I have reservations—and take some precautions to protect myself. First, before I release these fine examples of Mexican justice, I intend to send a close friend in the U.S. a fax and an email describing everything that's happened. I'll give him instructions to release the information to the media if anything happens to me.

"What you suggest could have grave consequences," said the A.G. I've given you my word that you'll have no further problems. I strongly suggest you reconsider."

"All right," said Artemas after a moment's thought. "I'll send my statement sealed, and in a way that will ensure nobody ever sees the contents as long as nothing happens to me. I understand your concerns, but you must understand mine."

Artemas knew he had started down a dangerous path from which he could not return, but the alternative was a bullet in the back within twenty-four hours. This was Mexico and, based on what had already happened, the A.G. had made his decision. Complying would get him nothing. At least this gambit might buy him some time.

Artemas's calculations were born out by the attorney general's next words. "You're making a big mistake. Now, tell me your solution again."

Artemas repeated his supposition that all the killings fit into the theory that a drug gang headed by Jugo Gandara had committed the ritualized killings as part of their initiation and a general campaign of terror and destabilization. That the only murder not committed by them was that of Gandara himself who was killed by Zarco Zamarripa for both revenge and to create evidence favorable to his sons' case. Even the killing of the old priest could be made to fit, in that he would have been the perfect target for some drugged out satanic cult on a mindless rampage, and the details of his autopsy could be kept secret.

The A.G. paused a moment, then said, "And there are probably other killings, say in Monterrey, that can be made to fit as well, and no end of people involved in drugs that can be blamed. I think it'll work; fax the whole thing to me in the morning. Perhaps, Salcido, if you reconsider your threats, we can start over?"

"I'd like that," said Artemas, not believing a word of it.

Artemas spent the next half hour drafting his account of recent events, even though he did not actually intend to send it. If anything happened to him, the papers and hand written explanation he had placed in the cave would be enough. But he needed Raymundo to believe he had carried out his threat.

When he finished, he lashed the PGR agents' hands and feet together so they couldn't move and left the house for an hour and a half, time enough for him to have taken his letter to Sabinas Hidalgo. He parked his Jeep under a forlorn pecan tree in the outskirts of town and calmly smoked a cigar and counted the stars. When he returned he freed the men but retained their weapons. They left without uttering a word.

Before going to bed, Artemas listened to the taped conversation between Raymundo and the A.G. and understood why no further threats had been directed toward him. The A.G. had told Raymundo that if anything else went wrong he would be the one killed. Then, exhausted, he went to bed. For the first time since he'd arrived in Bustamante he had carefully locked every door and window in the house.

Bustamante

He tossed and turned most of the night, his mind unable to turn off, going over and over every lurid detail of the evening before. About 6:00 A.M. he finally slipped into a dreamless sleep. A couple hours later he woke, groggy and disoriented. He got up slowly and hobbled over to the living room. The first things he noticed were smears of Raymundo's blood on the floor and the mess from their fruitless search.

He showered, brewed coffee and flopped down in his mangled easy chair. He had been right, he decided, to threaten the A.G. The man would never have ordered him tortured if he planned to let him live. He had obviously decided that even if Artemas did not have the stolen files he could not be trusted, and was therefore a liability to be removed.

He was not sure how long the threat and his ad hoc story to explain the recent killings would keep him safe. At first he thought it would depend on the Grupo Vampiro members' success in retrieving their funds. Then he realized it really didn't matter. If all went well he might be O.K. until they had safely squirreled their money away. But by then he would surely become a loose end to be dealt with. On the other hand, if they could not retrieve their money, they would undoubtedly decide to make his silence permanent. Either way the long term forecast was not good.

When he opened the door to leave for the police station, Laffi was stepping onto the porch.

"What the hell happened?" she said, obviously angry. You promised to call me."

"I'm sorry; something came up. Come in for a minute and I'll try to explain." He stepped aside to let her pass.

Taking in the overturned and slashed furniture, Laffi said, "What on earth…? Or are you always this messy?"

"Just my normal disorder. I even leave blood on the floor!" He waved at the stains.

"Good lord, Artemas, what happened?" Her anger turned to concern.

"It's part of what your instinct warned you was happening, but I simply don't have time to explain now. Bear with me, and I promise I'll see you later this morning."

"You damn well better," said Laffi and turned on her heel.

When Artemas reached the station he found Moreno and Marta, heads down, pretending to be immersed in their work. "How could you?" he asked, betraying the hurt in his voice. "Surely you could have found a way to warn me?"

Marta spoke first. "Those men from Mexico City came in and yelled questions about you. They threatened us—and our families—if we said anything to you." She put her head in her hands as tears flowed down her sunken cheeks.

"That's right," affirmed Moreno. "I'm ashamed. I was afraid and did what they ordered. I speak for Marta when I say that nothing like that will ever happen again." He raised his eyes to Artemas. "I pray you will forgive us?"

Artemas looked them both in the eye, and quietly replied, "I understand."

Walking through the village he sensed a change in atmosphere, in the natural rhythms. It felt like the aftermath of some defining, all consuming event, a release from accustomed pressure that left him ill at ease, disoriented. *To hell with all of them!* he thought. After stopping at the station to fax the drug tract and outline of his scheme to the attorney general, he returned to his house. Then and there he decided what to do. He realized there was no way he could avoid Laffi. And wasn't sure he wanted to.

He found Laffi in her room. She invited him in, waved him to the only chair, and sat on the single bed. "Things may be about to sort themselves out," began Artemas. "And I've decided to go away for a few days to get my head together, but I owe you an explanation."

Silently, Laffi mouthed, "No shit!"

Ignoring that, Artemas continued. "The short but accurate version is that during the investigation I discovered a business relationship between the Attorney General and Zarco Zamarripa and removed evidence of it from his house. The men the A.G. sent didn't find what they were looking for, mostly because they didn't know where to look. But they did find my fingerprints, from an earlier visit. Their attempt to interrogate me was what caused the mess in my house. I think I convinced the A.G. of my innocence, but he's thoroughly pissed, so who knows? Now, as I said, I'm desperate for a few days alone—no argument, and I suggest you take off, too. If all goes well, then all will be well. If not, this will be a very unhealthy place for anyone connected to me."

"Where's the evidence?"

Artemas said nothing.

Laffi's face lit. "It's in the cave, you sly bastard! I'll bet that's what you said in the note you gave to me and Jason."

Artemas remained expressionless, just stood and said, "Now I have to go."

Laffi flew from the bed into his arms. They kissed for a long time. Then Artemas gently withdrew and walked out the door.

THE DESERT

Evening found Artemas several miles west of the *Ojo de Agua*. Moreno had dropped him at the end of the road where he'd discovered Father Buendía's body, and he hiked with a small backpack through the mountains into the desert west of Bustamante.

In his hand were several long arrows. Two with barbed hunting tips, the others of the blunt target variety. A wooden *atlatl* was strapped to his pack. At Harvard he'd gone to see a demonstration of the ancient Indian throwing stick and had been amazed by what a group of largely middle-aged Americans had learned to do with that weapon. Those *atlatls* were far more sophisticated than the crude specimens he and has playmates had fashioned. Carefully carved from exotic hardwoods, they were as perfectly balanced as his sleek aluminum arrows. On a lark he'd bought a set and joined the *World Atlatl Society*.

At the University's archery range he'd quickly become proficient at throwing the *atlatl* and even entered competitions, where he excelled. Perhaps most rewarding was how his long black hair and striking copper features had given him an air of authenticity not lost on the sport's female aficionados. During his years in Mexico City he'd lacked the time and place to practice, but he brought the *atlatl* with him to Bustamante, hoping to keep himself busy, not dwell on his diminished career and prospects. He had fallen, though, into a numbing routine of eat, sleep and work, and hadn't found the opportunity until now.

As the sun dipped low in the west it gilded the distant mountaintops, casting a golden purple twilight across the landscape. Artemas threw his arrows, one after the other, into the ubiquitous, meaty nopal cacti, each hitting their target with a satisfying *whoosh* and *thwunk*. He was amazed how quickly he regained his accuracy. Although he lacked his former strength, the arrows passed easily through the tender plants.

After filling his canvas water bags in the creek, he made his camp on the side of the narrow fissure that cut through the escarpment from the *Ojo de Agua*. He calculated that he was about four miles north of the *grutas*. Before him stretched a wide valley that ran to another arid range. He had not seen another human being since Moreno dropped him off and he was beginning to attune himself to his surroundings. He listened to the defiant calls of birds of prey, the fearful chatter of tiny rodents, and the frantic scurrying of lizards. The breeze whistled as it passed through the narrow valley and became a sigh as it emptied into the larger one beyond, like a stream leaving its banks for the vastness of the sea. He conjured up the lines of William Cowper he learned in college,

"Oh for a lodge in some vast wilderness,
Some boundless contiguity of shade,
Where rumor of oppression and deceit,
Of unsuccessful or successful war,
Might never reach me more."

The sun flashed behind far-off peaks, and a rabbit scampered toward him, stopping short in nervous fright. He considered flinging one of his *atlatl's* hunting points and roasting the rabbit for dinner, but changed his mind. He had brought enough of the region's famous *machaca*, finely shredded beef jerky, flour tortillas, and fiery chile sauce to last him for several days. If it became necessary later, he could add variety to his meals.

Late on that first afternoon Artemas found himself in the valley below the *grutas*. He spent some time tracing a route up the sheer cliff towering above him. Although it must have been over a thousand feet to the cave's opening, there were numerous ledges, cracks, and small outcrops that could be used for hand and footholds. This was especially true for the bottom half, which rose in a more gradual slope.

Fancying the idea of an evening meal on the mountaintop,

he tied his well-used arrows to his pack and was about to begin his climb when nature called. He relieved himself behind a large boulder and was surprised to discover a peyote plant poking out of the sand. In shape and size it looked like a peeled, greenish-white orange, studded with round buttons.

Artemas had tried peyote once as a teenager with a group of boys. His memory of the experience was ambiguous: physical discomfort followed by brightly colored hallucinations which left him with a feeling of well being and a vague impression of pathways opening to something important within himself. Afterward he had confessed his experiment to Father Luis. The priest pulled out a volume from his leather bound collection of Bernardino de Sahagún's *Historia general de las cosas de Nueva España*, in which the Franciscan friar recorded the Indian traditions shortly after the Conquest. He read a passage to Artemas:

"There is another herb, like 'tunas' of the earth that is called péyotl; it is white and grows in the northern part. Those who eat or drink it see frightening or laughable visions; this intoxication lasts two or three days and then disappears. It is like a food to the *chichimecas*, which supports them and gives them courage to fight and they have neither fear nor thirst, nor hunger, and they say that it protects them from every danger."

"And that is what it is," he remembered the Jesuit saying, "just another intoxicant, a drug that some pretend is part of their religion so they'll be allowed to continue using it. If God wanted you to see visions you wouldn't have to eat or drink something special in order to do so. Certainly they might come only after a great deal of work, study, and prayer, but they would not be revealed to just anyone with a few extra pesos in his pocket. No, Artemas, the important things don't come that easily."

Artemas took the lesson to heart and avoided further experimentation with drugs. He later learned his mentor had been correct. Peyote contained a complex group of alkaloids, including mescaline, whose interaction in the human body was not totally understood. But there remained within him a lingering doubt, perhaps curiosity was more accurate, and the thought that if he'd just taken that next step... He happened to stumble upon it now, so why not give it a try? After all, he reasoned, there's never been a death attributed to the use of peyote itself.

He had never seen the plant in its natural state. In Sonora, well outside its normal range, only the dried buttons were eaten. He unshouldered his pack, withdrew his knife, and dug around the bottom of the tiny plant, releasing it from its root. He pulled off the white, hair-like filaments that grew along the indentations, brushed it on the side of his pants and cut it into small pieces, each with a button.

He put a piece in his mouth and chewed it gingerly. It tasted somewhat bitter, but not unpleasantly so. He ate another piece, then another, and waited five minutes. Nothing happened so he ate two more pieces. He was beginning to think he'd misidentified the plant when suddenly he began to feel strange and anxious. He started to sweat and get dizzy, then a queasiness making his stomach heave.

Sometime later—he had no idea exactly when—the nausea disappeared, replaced by euphoric bliss, a general feeling of invulnerability and exhilaration. Then the visions began. At first mere shapes, forming and disappearing in a Technicolor more vivid and saturated than anything Hollywood ever produced. Then a lightning storm, but without thunder, just a strange voice quoting over and over a phrase from Joaquin Miller:
"I saw the lightning's gleaming rod
Reach forth and write upon the sky
The awful autograph of God."
The visions soon took on forms of animals and people. His mother was morphing out of one her murals painted on the hacienda wall. Her body grew many times its normal height and was joined by his father. Artemas reached out to them. The further he stretched to meet them the taller and more unreachable they became. His parents finally disappeared into a bank of clouds that quickly descended, then lifted, revealing a deep river of indigo.

Artemas woke sometime during the night, a shaft of moonlight penetrating his eyes. A slight breeze washed over him as he returned to his visions and dreams. In the morning the sun woke him and he reached for his pack but realized he was thirsty, not hungry, so he drank deeply from his remaining water. He again dozed until late afternoon.

A full day had passed since his last meal. He built a small fire of twigs, just enough to bring a splash of water to a boil in his small aluminum saucepan. He added a handful of *machaca,* then a dollop of hot sauce. As soon as they were steaming he dumped the contents into a large flour tortilla he had warmed over the dying fire. He ate, rested, and again woke to the light of the moon. Without conscious awareness, he put away his pan and canteen, shouldered his pack, and set off across the moonlit desert.

As he walked, the moonlight brightened to almost day. Twice he crossed paths with other solitary men. They walked by without so much as a nod or hello, casting brightly colored shadows. He came across dead animals: several rabbits, a fox, a coyote and almost tripped over a goat butchered like the ones he'd seen at Jesús Vargas's farm.

In the hours before dawn he saw lights in the distance and decided to rest. He found shelter amid huge boulders on a small hillock and slept. He woke to the sound of a vehicle approaching, and saw an old pickup bouncing along a rutted dirt track toward a couple of crude adobe buildings. He gazed east through the dusty glare of the sun and could just make out the mountains separating him from Bustamante. How had he come so far? It took him the rest of the day and into evening to return to his former campsite at the base of the mountains. After repeating his cooking ritual he went to sleep.

Artemas woke at dawn with a sense of vitality and wellbeing greater than anything he'd ever known. The vast horizon of earth and sky was his own special kingdom, he was washed clean of life's weight and worry. He fixed himself another burrito and once again contemplated climbing the sheer cliff. His water, however, was nearly gone and the inviting pool in the cavern above was a thousand feet away.

As he stared at the massif before him, the niches, overhangs and other irregularities slowly resolved themselves into a pathway so obvious and predictable as to suggest it had been made by man. Of course, he thought, the Indians would have needed a way to get to the cavern, with its water, shelter and cool temperatures. Still, it was a treacherous route. Burdened by his unwieldy arrows and pack, Artemas calculated the climb would be too dangerous and decided instead to retrace his journey back through the narrow canyon to the *Ojo de Agua*. Even as rough as parts of the trail were, he could easily make it by early afternoon.

For the first time since he stepped into the desert, Artemas's thoughts wandered back to the capricious case he'd left behind in Bustamante. With renewed clarity he laid out the tangled web. The writer and artist claimed they planned to kill Julie Conners and blame it on the Zamarripa brothers, but they had found her, already dead, with Father Buendía beside her. Then the elderly priest was killed before he could be questioned. Too convenient by far. But where was the proof? And how to deal with the alibi provided by Jason and Laffi's presence at Alcazar's ranch, so conveniently arranged to coincide with the priest and Zamarripa's murders? And even if he found proof, surely the attorney general would refuse to reopen the case.

Artemas entered the little valley that would take him back to the village and carefully made his way along the uneven terrain leading to the *Ojo de Agua*, eager to drink from the spring. Looking up he saw several vultures circling the sky. Could it be possible he was hallucinating again? In the distance he could see a lump on the ground and it certainly seemed very real. His heart sank—this was surely a nightmare. As he drew near, he sighed loudly, relieved to see that it was merely a coyote, torn to pieces and left in the sand, much like the animals he vaguely remembered from his dreamlike walk in the moonlight. This was still very odd. Coyotes were mostly nocturnal and though villagers would shoot them if they threatened livestock, this was miles away from any homestead. A mountain lion would have dragged away and eaten the corpse. Surely other coyotes wouldn't have done this, he wondered. Other than humans, coyotes had few other natural predators.

Bustamante

After showering away the grit, grime and sweat, Artemas meticulously shaved off his heavy stubble. He was shocked at the change in his appearance. How could he look both younger and older at the same time? His skin glowed from fresh air and sunshine, his eyes were clear and bright, the dark circles gone. He had lost weight and his muscles were firmer, even his face, where the softness of youth was beginning to fade.

At the police station, Artemas asked Marta what happened in his absence.

"It's been quiet," she said. "I told everyone that you were away on police business, including that blond American reporter. She came every day to ask about you." Artemas sensed a hint of disapproval as she handed him a stack of newspaper clippings and a memo from the attorney general. *On the other hand, maybe Marta is only worried about me.*

The A.G's memo said, "You and your staff are directed to say nothing regarding the recent murders in Bustamante, especially to the press. Your only acceptable response to questions is to quote this memo." The clippings from various newspapers essentially told the same story: "Murder Epidemic Blamed on Drug Cult." The article closely followed Artemas's fabrication, describing how the murders were related either to a drug gang initiation or Zamarripa's attempt to both clear and avenge his sons. Later it recounted a deadly shootout in which three suspects in Monterrey, all known drug dealers, had been killed while resisting arrest. The stories seemed to be favorable toward the government's handling of the case, praising the attorney general for not accepting the earlier, obvious conclusions and for tenaciously continuing the investigation until the real solution had been uncovered.

It worked, thought Artemas. Maybe this will make the A.G. happy. No. That would only happen if he got his hands on his Grupo Vampiro money. *No phone messages from him all week, just a curt memo?* Something treacherous was afoot.

Artemas dialed Humberto Alcazar's number in town, and he picked up after the first ring. Artemas wanted to meet him and Chavana to go over their stories in more detail. Alcazar said they would be at his ranch for several days. Artemas agreed to meet them there at 10:00 A.M. the next day.

Then his thoughts turned to Laffi, his mind darting every which way. He was both excited and anxious that she'd stayed in Bustamante while he was off in the desert. Before he had time to think straight, Artemas phoned and invited her to share his first full meal in a week.

When Laffi saw him at the hotel restaurant for early dinner she marveled at his altered appearance, "Where did you go, a spa? You look more…more, I don't know… *Absolutely delicious* is what she really wanted to say.

Looking across the table at her, all radiant and luminous, Artemas felt swallowed by an emotion he could not contain. He quickly changed the subject, "Laffi, aren't you jeopardizing your job by staying here?"

"Certainly not! My Bustamante coverage and injury in the line of duty made me golden—at least for this month. And as I already told you, I'm seriously considering transitioning to environmental journalism on behalf of Jason's organization. I never realized how important bats are to the ecosystem." She paused, hoping for a hint of jealousy. When Artemas was not forthcoming, she added, "But if you want me to leave, I will."

Laffi was even more perturbed when Artemas evaded the matter and abruptly told her he couldn't stay for their dessert of *pastel tres leches*. She settled for a firm dinner date the next night.

It was almost dark when Artemas reached the turnoff to Alcazar's ranch, but he kept his headlights off as he continued along the crude dirt track toward the compound just over the hill. Given how poorly it was maintained, he doubted there were any servants on the property and he didn't even encounter the usual barking ranch dogs. He spotted an old tool shed within range of the ranch house and hid the recording device in a dark corner behind a stack of moldering boxes.

Back home, Artemas connected to the Internet and spent the next hour reading every bit of news he could find related to Zamarripa and Grupo Vampiro. He searched for anything that might give him a clue as to what was happening to its holdings and any claims thereto. To no great surprise he found nothing of interest and went to bed.

Alcazar Ranch

The following morning, a beaming Humberto Alcazar opened the ranch house's door and greeted Artemas, who was dressed in old Jeans and a polo shirt. Inside, he found Chavana sitting in his oddly prim manner in the same chair as before. Noting that the two men seemed surprised by his attire, Artemas said, "I hope you'll forgive my lack of formality. I'm still on vacation. I assume you've seen the news reports regarding the resolution of our little crime wave?"

"Yes indeed," replied the writer. "We live in a scary world. I've always assumed that killings within the drug fraternity were for business reasons and that the rest of us were reasonably safe. But this..."

"You're right," Artemas said. "This recent development means that what you told me the other day is now irrelevant. There is no need to pursue it any further." He paused then added, drawing out the words, "Unless, of course, something totally unexpected occurs."

"I can't imagine what that might be. You have all the facts," said Alcazar. "I cannot thank you enough for your respect and consideration, especially in light of what Ricardo has already suffered.

Bustamante AND SABINAS HIDALGO

In response to the recent explosions, the village had stationed an attendant at the *grutas'* ramshackle reception center to discourage trespassers. Artemas gave the man a cheerful wave as he headed toward the crude pathway winding up the mountain, where Julie Conners had waved a final goodbye to her friend. The day was clear, dry, and hot, yet he was hardly winded by the climb. Reaching the spot where Julie's body was found, he surveyed the parched ground. To the right of the narrow path, the hillside rose steeply, punctuated by jagged rocks, sagebrush and cactus. To the left, the path plunged deeply into a narrow canyon.

There never was a satisfactory explanation for the film missing from Julie's camera. Artemas was certain the Zamarripa brothers hadn't taken the film. Chavana said he planted the camera in their hacienda, so they probably weren't even aware of its existence, which now made sense given their confused responses during interrogation. So that meant the artist or Alcazar had disposed of the film either at the murder site or somewhere else. But why get rid of the film in the first place? Could Julie have taken an incriminating photo before she was killed?

Artemas thought there might be a chance the film had been hastily thrown into the canyon below. Something as small as a roll of film would be the proverbial needle in a haystack. The chasm snaked hundreds of feet below and was pocked with deep channels and animal burrows. The killer could have safely assumed the film would be impossible to find.

During questioning, Julie's friend Susan said it was an old camera of her father's. She'd kept it in her purse when she left for college and adamantly recalled that it was loaded with Fuji film.

Artemas and his volunteers had searched the general area of the murder scene for nearly a day. But even if they had been lucky and spotted the distinctive green casing, odds were against recovering anything useful, especially if the film had been yanked out of the camera and exposed. On a hunch Artemas did some online research and discovered that Susan's particular model included a safety feature that automatically rewound the film if the camera were opened prematurely. Developing those last exposures could become key to breaking the case.

Artemas tossed several small stones into the canyon, studying their various trajectories. He then began his search, working his way up from the bottom, trying to keep to his imaginary grids. It was slow work. He examined every rock, nook and cranny. He used a small machete to shove bushes aside and probe around the base of rocks. The work was painstakingly tedious and the sun beat down mercilessly as he scrambled over dangerously steep terrain.

It was now late afternoon, and the light was fading into shadow. Just before deciding to call it quits, Artemas came upon a large rock jutting out of the canyon wall and detected a thick layer of earth and twigs at its base. Curious, he poked around with his machete, and found, nestled in dirt, the green roll of film. Plucking it it gingerly from its resting place, Artemas couldn't have been more pleased if he'd discovered an emerald. *¡Hijole!* he exclaimed. He guessed the film must have landed on the rock, perhaps first bouncing off something higher above, then rolled down into an abandoned mouse hole. It had then been covered with dirt and debris by storm winds. He placed the film roll carefully in a plastic bag and began his climb back to the path.

At the police station he lightly dusted the film roll to check for fingerprints but couldn't even find partials to lift. He then photographed and documented his findings, preserving the used lifting tapes as evidence.

Nobody in Bustamante could process film, so Artemas jumped in his Jeep and quickly drove to a photoshop in Sabinas, and ran in just before closing. Once he explained the situation, the young technician agreed to stay late and develop his prints.

While he waited at the counter, he phoned the Medical Examiner. "Yes," he had checked the skin found under Zamarripa's fingernails against the bloody bandage from Zaaragoza's house that Artemas had left him. "No," the two did not match. Of course, he would save everything and would await another sample. Artemas had not expected the skin fragments to be Alcazar's, but wasn't quite sure how to secure a sample from Chavana.

The photo technician poked her head out of the backroom. "It will be just a few more minutes. The prints are drying, *Capitán*." Artemas was almost beside himself when she reappeared ten minutes later and handed him a large envelope.

"Please wait a moment," said Artemas as he ripped open the envelope and withdrew the stack of prints. The first two photos were of road signs to the *grutas*. Then a series of shots documenting the trail and canyon near the cave. Then a photo of a man standing on the trail, facing the camera with a startled expression. It was unmistakably Ricardo Chavana. On closer inspection Artemas saw he was wearing gloves. The last photo—clearly in reverse sequence—was a shot of Susan looking forlorn, taken by Julie before she left for the caves.

"I know it's late, but this can't wait," said Artemas excitedly. Please make two more prints of the entire set, then one extra of this one?" He handed her the shot of Chavana.

"Of course *señor*. It will take about thirty minutes."

"Thank you." Artemas then called a *notario* he had used before, and the man agreed to come over immediately.

Well, that's it, thought Artemas as he waited. The artist claimed Julie was already dead when he found her with the priest. Had that been true she could not have taken his picture. This meant he had justifiable cause for collecting a DNA sample.

Artemas knew the attorney general would not be happy about this new development. But somehow it could be made to dovetail with the *narco* cult explanation already accepted by the press and public. It would be easy to infer that the eccentric artist was involved with drugs and by association, the cult. Artemas decided to say nothing until he had devised a credible story and actually made the arrests. After what Chavana had told Artemas, it was plain that Alcazar was also guilty, at least as an accomplice.

The notary arrived soon after the additional prints were finished. As instructed, the technician signed three copies of a *Declaración* attesting that the photographs had all come from the same roll of Fuji Film and placed the prints in sealed envelopes, kept one set, and gave another to the notary. Besides the film roll, Artemas took the remaining set of prints, plus the extra print of Chavana.

Bustamante

A large-scale topographical map, unrolled on the police station counter, showed a narrow valley running from Alcazar's ranch in a northerly direction. It wound around a small mountain—really a foothill—to the west, then proceeded due south where it joined the road to the *Ojo de Agua* before it ended, not far from where Moreno said the killer's tracks disappeared. Tracing the shadings and elevations, Artemas snapped his fingers, *aha!* He wagered there was a path that followed the valley and that he would find the artist's motorbike tracks there. It probably took less than ten minutes to reach the spring and maybe another ten or fifteen to return to Hacienda Zamarripa. Chavana could easily have been there and back while Jason and Laffi chatted with Alcazar. He also could have made the short trip to the *Ojo de Agua* early the next morning and killed the priest, after somehow luring him there. That certainly fit with the direction of the killer's footprints.

Artemas called Alcazar at his ranch and made an appointment to see him and Chavana at ten-thirty the next morning. He said he had one last item to discuss, recalling one of the few bits of advice his father had offered: "The best lies are the ones with the most truth in them."

His mood quickly changed as a voice inside urged him to leave well enough alone. Once again he was following his heart rather than his head. He was swimming in deep and dangerous waters. Why was he always so determined to make things worse? Then he brightened at the prospect of dinner with Laffi.

Alcazar Ranch

Morning sunlight shot through his bedroom window as Artemas dressed in his best uniform and holstered his pistol. Dread and anticipation made him jittery. In retrospect—though he still thought himself a fool--it was a good thing he'd refused Laffi's invitation to her room last night. Instead, she had grudgingly accepted his confidential disclosure of the incriminating photograph, certain she'd eventually have an incredible scoop.

He forced down a cup of coffee and sweet roll from the *panadería,* hoping the jolt of caffeine and sugar would calm him down, like a Ritalin substitute. Once at the station he fumbled around with the safe and finally managed to lock up a set of the photos from Julie's camera. The other set, stashed behind some books in his home office, he intended to add to the Grupo Vampiro files hidden in the cave.

He called the FBI and was put through to Agent Grunwald. "The case is breaking in an unexpected direction. I need to know where a certain canister of Fuji film was sold in the U.S." He read the serial code from the label. "Can do?"

"That should be easy," drawled the agent, "but tell me what's happening."

"Not yet. Soon!"

"Alright," grumbled Grunwald.

Forty-five minutes later Grunwald phoned back. "The film was shipped to a Walgreens store in Austin, Texas."

"You're a pal, and I'll fill you in within a day or two. I gotta go."

"Don't be in such a damn hurry! You might want to know that the lab results just came back, and the marijuana butts from both murders contained DNA that matched the ones you picked up at the Zamarripa hacienda."

"Okay, thanks." Artemas was not at all surprised by the good news, though by now it took a back seat to everything coming down on him.

"Talk to you later, Agent Grunwald," he said and quickly hung up.

Moreno dropped by the station to get his assignments for the day. Artemas told him to meet him at the entrance to Alcazar's ranch a little before ten and be sure to bring plaster-casting material. "I'll explain what's happening later," concluded Artemas, reaching for the phone. He called the Medical Examiner in Sabinas and arranged for him to come to the station at noon.

It was still too early to put his plan into operation, but Artemas was stir-crazy, picking at piles of papers on his desk and assigning Marta busy-work to keep her occupied. He had to get out of the office, kill some time. He drove slowly toward the ranch, humming the tune to his favorite spirit song. There was not a cloud in the sky, and another passage from Joaquin Miller's *The Ship in the Desert* floated back into his consciousness:

"The very clouds have wept and died
And only God is in the sky."

Just shy of the rise in the dirt road that hid Alcazar's ranch house from view, he turned right, followed faint wheel tracks for a quarter mile and parked in a dry streambed. On foot he cautiously approached the tool shed at the edge of the ranch compound and retrieved the surveillance tape recorder he'd hidden there. He returned to his jeep, drove back to the ranch road entry, and parked to wait for Moreno. In the meanwhile, he was anxious to discover what, if anything, his audio trap had snared.

Elated to find that the device actually worked, he listened to considerable small talk before Chavana's clear baritone asked, "Do you think you can really get it?"

"You mean dear cousin Zarco's property?" said the deeper voiced writer. "I see no reason why not. After all, his sons will soon be out of the game, and with our recent good fortune the rest of the field will also be cleared. I am, in fact, his relative. Never, Ricardo, underestimate the power of greed, especially in yourself."

Artemas whistled. *Of course, the sly sonofabitch is going to try and claim Zamarripa's money.* It made sense; he was related to the dead tycoon. But weren't there immediate next of kin? And what did "With our recent good fortune…" mean?

"Well, *amigo*," he said aloud, "you'll soon be in prison with Ignacio and Armando. Equally out of the game."

Later in their conversation, Artemas heard Alcazar's side of the conversation with him the night before. "*Sí, señor.* Ten thirty will be fine."

The artist asked his friend, "What do you think he wants?"

"I have no idea, maybe he wants me to autograph one of my books. But don't worry, Rici, at this point there's absolutely nothing he can do. Absolutely nothing."

"Want to bet?" whispered Artemas. Nevertheless, there was something disturbing about the assurance in Alcazar's voice.

Right on time, Moreno pulled into the entry a few minutes before ten. Artemas shared what he had discovered in the past 24-hours, careful not to allude to information he could only know from his illegal wiretap. Moreno congratulated him, but also expressed sadness that Artemas's impressive investigative work would mean he'd be promoted back to Mexico City. Artemas knew there wasn't much chance of that happening. *No good deed goes unpunished.* But all he said was, "Let's go see if we can find some bike tracks."

They returned to the place where Moreno had previously lost the killer's footprints. Two hundred yards further in the same direction, they found faint tread marks, the width of a small motorcycle tire. Most fortunate, the tracks were made in clay rather than sandy soil, and the rains had not yet washed away the impressions. Artemas photographed the immediate area and instructed Moreno to make a casting. Moreno quickly mixed the fast-drying powder in a blue plastic bucket, poured the mixture into the tracks, let it set for 10 minutes, and pried up a hardened chunk of molded plaster.

Artemas checked his watch. They had to hustle to make it to his 10:30 appointment and arrived a few minutes late. Alcazar waited for them at the ranch house door, his beret perched at a jaunty angle. He gave Artemas a hard look as he spotted the pistol on his belt, but waved them in with a cheerful smile. Chavana was leaning elegantly against the fireplace mantle at the other end of the room, smoking a long, thin cigarette with a gold filter.

After introducing Moreno, Artemas strode purposefully across the room and shook hands with the artist. Alcazar followed closely behind and stood near the fireplace.

"I appreciate your seeing me on such short notice," said Artemas.

The artist and writer looked at him enquiringly, affecting the attitude of men without a care in the world. Nevertheless, Artemas felt the tension in the room.

"Certainly, please be seated," replied the writer.

Artemas and Moreno took chairs, and the writer and artist sat together on the couch.

"I know you're busy, so I'll come to the point," said Artemas. He looked at Chavana. "I believe you previously told me that the girl, Julie Conners, was dead when you found her with Father Buendía. Is that correct?"

Chavana glanced at his companion. "Yes, of course," he said.

"Then," said Artemas, pulling a photograph from his shirt pocket and handing it over to the artist, "how do you account for this photograph? It was on the roll of film from the victim's camera, found in the canyon below the crime scene."

Chavana blanched and his fingers began to shake as he stared at the picture of himself. He had obviously been surprised by the girl taking his picture. That same expression now spread across his face. Alcazar gave no hint of his thoughts as he viewed the photo over his companion's shoulder.

Before the artist could reply, Alcazar said, "*Capitán* Salcido, how do *you* explain it? What does it matter, anyway? And too, how can you be certain it came from the girl's camera?"

"The film was purchased in the victim's home town, where her friend bought it, and it included other pictures only she could have taken on that day." Artemas drew a long breath, before proceeding.

"And what does it *matter*? It has to do with the law, which I've sworn to uphold. How do *I* explain it? The only thing I can think of is that it proves *Señor* Chavana was lying when he said the girl was dead before he saw her, indicating he had something to do with her death. I came here to see if either of you could convince me otherwise."

The room was silent. Alcazar peered at Chavana out of the corner of his eye then said to Artemas, "Listen, my friend, this matter has already been resolved to everyone's satisfaction. This," he waved dismissively at the photo, "could never be considered sufficient evidence to convict anyone of murder. There are so many explanations that would be credible to a judge. But...what do you intend to do?"

"Unless you can offer one of those explanations, one that's credible to *me*, I intend to arrest *Señor* Chavana for murder, and you as an accessory. I will then proceed to develop additional evidence that will be more than sufficient to convince a judge of your guilt. For example, *Señor* Chavana, I will be surprised if we cannot prove that Zarco Zamarripa's fingernails made those scratches on your face. What happened? Did he and his companion make a last desperate charge?"

Artemas stood up, and Chavana remained silent and tense, conscious of the impulse to touch the fading marks on his cheek.

"This is absurd," said the writer, looking up at the tall, slender policeman, his face flushing around his beard. "You don't know what's involved, the trouble you'll be in. Surely we can work this out in a reasonable manner before it goes further?"

"From what you've said, I don't think so," replied Artemas, his right hand moving suggestively toward his pistol. "I must ask you to hold out your hands while Officer Moreno cuffs you."

"Once more, I implore you to listen to reason," growled the writer, as he rose ponderously to his feet and towered over Artemas, "You simply must understand that this is the wrong course of action. You don't know what's involved. Things have gone too far."

"Please do as you're told," ordered Artemas, his hand edging yet closer to his pistol.

"Don't say another word to this fool," Alcazar spat out. Then he held out his arms, giant fists clenched.

Artemas took great pains to covertly transfer his prisoners into the police station. Everyone in the village knew "The Council of Arts and Letters" as the innkeeper called them. If spotted in handcuffs the rumors would fly, hindering the final leg of his plan—rough as it might be. Inside he found Marta, wide-eyed and the Medical Examiner absorbed in a magazine. After locking the sullen prisoners in their separate cells, Artemas told Moreno, "I'm sending in the Examiner to take a DNA sample from *Señor* Chavana."

Marta handed him a stack of phone messages. At his desk, Artemas shuffled through them. *Nothing here that can't wait.* In a small town where everyone knew everyone's business, day-to-day crime was mercifully low.

The lingering scent of Marta's egg and *chorizo* breakfast taco wafted through the office and reminded his grumbling stomach of the hours passed since he'd eaten anything. As he gathered his things to leave for a late lunch, Moreno came out of the cellblock. "*Señor* Alcazar is demanding to use the telephone," he said.

"Let him. I'll be back later this afternoon. Thanks and good job!"

When he got home, Artemas found Laffi sitting on the stone wall surrounding his porch. She stood to greet him and all he could think of was how beautiful she looked in her jeans and crisp yellow blouse. "How did it go?" she asked.

"So far so good, but something's not right; they're way too confident. Maybe I've missed something relating to Alcazar trying to grab Zamarripa's estate. I'm going to check the internet."

Once the dial up service finally connected, his search yielded instant results. Splashed on his homepage was the headline: "Zamarripa Brothers Killed in Prison Riot."

"*Mierda*," swore Artemas as he clicked to the full text of the article and read it out loud.

"The sons of the late industrialist, Zarco Zamarripa, were killed during a disturbance at La Palma prison this morning. Recently arrested in Bustamante, Nuevo León, for the murder of Julie Conners, daughter of a United States senator, the brothers, aged 26 and 28, were in the maximum security facility awaiting trial. Authorities refused to describe the disturbance or to provide further information. However, it is believed there were no other fatalities."

Artemas's stomach lurched as if he'd just jumped off a cliff. Reading his expression, Laffi said, "What's it mean?

"I left a bug in the ranch house and in the recording Alcazar said, 'After all, his sons will soon be out of the game.' I assumed that meant they would be in prison for life. That was obviously not he case! Then just before his arrest, Alcazar said, 'You don't know what's involved. Things have gone too far.' That was an f-ing understatement! I would bet my life, if it wasn't probably already forfeit, that the phone call I allowed Alcazar to make was to the attorney general."

In frustration, Artemas smacked his fist into his hand. "There's no question that Alcazar and Chavana are guilty. But it's just as plain that they've joined forces with the A.G., and in Mexico, where politics, money, and power always trump right and wrong, that's all that matters. To have a chance at even a small part of the estate, Alcazar needed the Zamarripa brothers dead, as well as any other relatives closer than himself to Zarco. The attorney general wants his Grupo Vampiro money, and a deal with Alcazar to help him grab the inheritance might be the only way he can get it, without being exposed. The proof? Other than the president, only the A.G. could so quickly arrange the murder of the Zamarripa brothers in Mexico's most secure prison. It was a marriage made in hell, and the devil must have enjoyed officiating the ceremony."

"Could it work?" asked Laffi, her voice uncharacteristically meek.

Artemas tried to still the emotional tornado that was brewing in his gut and think logically. "*Yes*, it could work! The attorney general of Mexico could easily arrange for a phony last testament from Zamarripa, one that could be ramrodded through a compliant court. Not that it matters now, I wonder if Alcazar somehow knew of the A.G.'s plight and approached him, or if the A.G. initiated the scheme. What really matters is that it is what it is!"

For once Laffi was at a loss for words. During the silence, Artemas breathed slowly and deeply, trying to clear his mind. He realized he had no control over the future, that he could only affect what he did at the moment. He concluded there was only one course of action he could take.

"Laffi, as the expression goes, 'the shit's in the fan.' I'm going to have to do some pretty extreme things. I don't have time for any more explanations, and I can't deal with worrying about you. And make no mistake, your known association with me puts your life in serious danger. You've got to get in your car and go to the airport in Monterrey, get the hell out of Mexico. No arguments!"

Recognizing the truth of Artemas's words, Laffi said, "I understand. But if I don't hear from you within a reasonable time, or if something tragic happens, I'll find a way to get the evidence out of the cave and expose the whole goddamned mess!"

Artemas kissed her hard, turned her around, slapped her on the butt and said. "*Vaya con díos* — quickly and safely!"

Bustamante
& The Caverns

Artemas quickly typed a summary of recent events on his computer, printed a copy, saved it on a CD, and placed both in a plastic evidence bag. Then he added the notorized photos taken by Julie Conners and the audiotapes of Chavana and Alcazar's conversation. Finally, he removed the computer's hard drive and added it to the bag. Realizing he'd forgotten something, he quickly penned a description of where the remaining Grupo Vampiro files were hidden in Zamarippa's home.

He snatched up some rope, jumped into his Jeep, and headed toward the mountains. On the way through the village, he noticed that the incumbent party's "fix-up-the-village" program was progressing at a furious pace. Although he paid little attention to politics, Artemas heard that pundits were now giving the challenger—the tall, handsome rancher from Guanajuato—a chance to win. After seventy years of nearly uncontested rule, the sitting party was beginning to panic.

Some forty-five minutes later, he lowered himself into the cave on the west side of the mountain. Looking out over the valley behind and below him, he thought he could just make out the little settlement he had reached on foot during his peyote-induced trek.

Once inside, he scanned the cave with his flashlight and found his way to the hidden cache. He was surprised to find that something had disturbed the pile he had so neatly stowed away. It was askew, with bits of mud on the plastic wrapping. Yet something about the way it appeared seemed the handiwork of animals rather than humans. Bats? Artemas wondered. He had no idea what kind of creatures lived in caves; that was Jason's area of expertise. Nothing seemed to be missing, and he didn't have time to worry about all the possible scenarios, so he added his plastic evidence bag to the stack of files and carefully rewrapped the pile.

Bustamante

It was just before 6:00 P.M. when Artemas returned home and headed to the kitchen for a beer. As he popped the top from a frosty Bohemia, the phone rang. He rarely received calls at home, and was surpised to find his hand shaking as he picked up the receiver. *"Bueno?"* he said, in a voice he hoped was casual and confident.

"Salcido?" It was the A.G.

"Sí, señor."

"I just heard that you made additional arrests in our case: respected members of the community. Is that correct?" His voice was calm. *A good sign?* wondered Artemas.

"That is correct. I discovered the girl's missing film, and a photograph on it proves beyond a doubt that they were lying to me when they said the girl was already dead when *Señor* Chavana discovered her body."

"And exactly when did they tell you this, and why was I not informed?"

"Sir, it was a little over a week ago, after we thought the case had been finalized. The artist admitted he had found the priest standing next to the already dead girl. At that time I said nothing because I didn't believe it would have a material bearing on the case, that it would only make matters more difficult, something you didn't want. Then, when I found the picture of Chavana, I realized they'd been lying."

"And what proof do you have that this conversation actually took place?"

Artemas remained silent.

"And what proof do you have that the picture was not taken well before the girl's death, that the man did not come forward earlier because he did not want to become involved? And what evidence do you have that *Señor* Alcazar was involved in any way, much less as an accessory to murder?" As he spoke, the A.G.'s voice rose until his final question was nearly a scream. "And why did you not consult with me before taking this action?"

"Sir, there is no question in my mind that they were both involved, and I'm positive that sufficient evidence can be developed during the next few days to prove it."

Artemas almost mentioned his recording and the skin under Zamarripa's fingernails, but stopped himself at the last moment.

"If so, you'll not be the one developing it. As of this moment you're relieved of your duties." The voice dropped to an outraged whisper. "I am directing you to turn in your uniforms and weapon and remain in your home pending *my* investigation."

Now that the cards were on the table Artemas was suddenly calm. "I respectfully suggest that would be a mistake. I..."

"Salcido," the A.G. hissed. "It was a mistake to give you a second chance when you screwed up in Mexico City. It was a mistake to allow you to work on this case. What I'm doing now is correcting those errors. And whether your outrageous attempt to blackmail me in our last conversation goes on your permanent record will be determined by your actions during the next twenty-four hours. You're to confine yourself to your home. I've already ordered your second in command to pick up your uniforms and weapon. If you don't cooperate he'll arrest you. You are then to remain where you are until the investigation is completed."

The last instruction was punctuated by a click as the attorney general hung up the phone. Artemas knew his worst nightmare was about to begin.

A few minutes later there was a knock on the door. Artemas opened it to find Moreno, shoulders slumped, staring at his shoes.

"I understand," said Artemas. "I'll bring you the stuff in a minute."

He quickly shoved his uniforms into a laundry bag, added his pistol and belt, then handed the bag and Jeep keys to Moreno, who finally looked up to meet his eyes.

"I'm sorry," he said. "I don't know what's happening. But..."

"Don't worry," said Artemas. "Perhaps it's for the best. One question: did you save the cast of those tire tracks?"

"*Sí, señor.*" Then seeming to read another question in Artemas's eyes, he added, "I said nothing about it to anyone."

"Thank you, *compadre,*" said Artemas. "If you can keep it that way...?"

"That goes without saying," said Moreno, offering his hand. They shook solemnly then Artemas gave his former assistant an *abrazo* and clapped him confidently on the back.

"*Vaya con diós,*" Moreno said mournfully, while walking slowly out to the street with his bundle.

Once the door closed, Artemas felt depleted, not just alone but desolate. The only person he knew he could count on right now was Father Luis, but there was really nothing he could do to help. He was virtually under house arrest, with no means of transportation, or escape.

Or was there?

What, in fact, were his options? He listed them mentally, an exercise designed to halt the despair that was engulfing him.

What if he grabbed the evidence and fled to the United States? He calculated he might create a two or three-day sensation before a request to extradite him on trumped up evidence was delivered to the authorities.

He could stay where he was and follow orders. That would be suicide!

Suddenly he knew what he must do.

He packed his most important belongings — driver's license, address book, checkbook, hunting knife, a change of clothes, plastic bottle of water, and a tiny black and white snapshot of his mother — in his backpack. Then he lay down to rest.

Ojo de Agua
and
The Caverns of Bustamante

Sticking to the shadows, Artemas cautiously made his way toward the plaza, to the phone stall near the deserted bus station. It was past midnight and even the stray village dogs were slumbering. To his great luck, he had plenty of credit left on his phone card to dial Father Luis's number in Sonora. He gave silent thanks for the man's aversion to answering machines after he finally picked up on the fourteenth ring. Their conversation lasted over twenty minutes.

On his way home he took one last look at the dimly lit police station. The past months were bittersweet, and he'd grown fond of this sleepy little town. While gathering a few snacks—roasted peanuts from the cupboard, a couple ripe bananas—he secured the *atlatl* and two hunting arrows to his pack and slung it over his shoulder. This time he didn't bother to lock the back door when he left.

Artemas walked beneath the dark canopy of pecan trees, and headed north in the direction of the *Ojo de Agua.* Passing one of the last houses at the edge of the village, he stopped short and locked eyes with a very old woman rocking in her chair in the doorway. Rythmic creaks punctuated the dead silence and after a few moments Artemas resumed his journey, rattled by this strange encounter.

His hasty plan called for him to retrieve evidence from the cave and go to the small settlement he'd noticed on his peyote-infused walkabout at the western end of the valley. To save time, he would approach the cave following the steep, faint path up the cliff he'd detected during his week in the wilderness. He'd soon find out if this more direct—yet potentially dangerous—

route was actually feasible. Then he would make his way to the rendezvous point and have Jason pick up the evidence at a later date.

The eastern sky was tinged with pink and blue by the time Artemas reached the spot where Father Buendía had been slain. Exhausted, he decided to rest an hour, build his strength to safely climb the nearby mountain to the cavern above. He lay down behind one of the huge boulders strewn on the valley's sandy floor, put his lumpy pack beneath his head and stared up into a sea of vastness, sprinkled with stars.

He was startled from a heavy, dreamless sleep, and shielded his eyes from the sun that had climbed over the horizon. A glance at his watch confirmed it was just after eight-thirty. Well, he thought, it should be all right, there was still plenty of time. Yet he felt unsettled. He rubbed his bleary eyes, stood up, brushed sand from his jeans and peered carefully around the boulder toward the village. Finally satisfied that nothing seemed amiss, he stepped away from the giant rock, and headed toward the spring for an invigorating splash of icy water. A glint of light caught his eye, but his groggy mind didn't quite register the significance. After a split-second hesistation, though, he threw himself down toward the shelter of the boulder. Searing pain in his left arm, and the loud crack of a high power rifle, hit his senses simultaneously.

Adrenaline surged into his nervous system, blocking the pain and jacking his energy. He wriggled snake-like toward his pack, tracing the sand with a trail of blood. Grabbing the pack with his right hand he sprinted in a zig-zag to the next boulder behind him, and paused to examine his profusely bleeding wound. Just above his left bicep, shredded skin and muscle exposed partially shattered bone. He awkwardly ripped off his shirt and using his right hand and teeth, tightened the twisted ends around his arm to slow the bleeding. He snatched the *atlatl* and hunting arrows from his pack and fell to his belly. Then he wriggled to the next boulder, about twenty feet from the base of the mountain.

His arm began throbbing with white-hot pain, radiating through his body. To survive Artemas knew he had to draw from every ounce of willpower and stay alert. Whoever shot him — and he had a good idea who it might be—would be able to follow his blood trail and eventually track him to where he stood, pressed against an immense rock. Artemas needed to move quickly.

Ahead of him at the mountain's base was an outcropping of boulders and sagebrush, a good place to hide and a possible means of survival. Artemas recalled a childhood trick that had always fooled the other Indian boys in the wilds of Sonora. He hoped this particular hunter was either an amateur tracker or in a hurry.

Artemas sprinted for the outcropping, careful to keep his steps close together. As soon as he reached his destination he moved backwards slowly, stepping in his previous footprints as best he could. When he returned to the boulder, he carefully positioned himself away from the path of his initial approach. Hugging the giant rock at its base, with his good hand he pushed the barbed tip of the *atlatl* into the sand to steady it. Then he slipped its feathered back end into the base of the throwing stick. He brought his right arm into the cocked position, arrow parallel to the ground.

He didn't have long to wait. The soft crunch of sand told Artemas his pursuer was following his original trail. His muscles tensed, afraid even to breath as footsteps paused on the opposite side of the boulder. Slowly the boots moved on ahead. Artemas waited four or five more steps, then peeked around the rock. A man stood not more than twelve feet away, khaki-clad, wearing a black PGR baseball cap and carrying a hunting rifle at port arms. The well-muscled, intense silhoutte was unmistakable—it was Raymundo Valenzuela.

Artemas held the *atlatl* at the ready, and darted from the security of the boulder to clear his shot. As he did so Raymondo spun around to face him with the long barrel of his rifle following. Artemas released his fingers holding the four-foot arrow, sending it hurtling with incredible speed and power into his adversary. A rifle shot exploded into the sky as Artemas watched Raymundo collapse. The arrow hit him squarely in the heart.

Artemas began to shake uncontrollably. At such close range, if Raymundo had switched to his more maneouverable pistol, Artemas would likely be the one lying dead in the sand. He slumped down and bent his head between his knees to keep from fainting.

It seemed hours since he'd been shot, time stretching with surreal intensity, yet the watch hanging on his mangled arm showed only a mere 15 minutes had gone by. Quite possibly only the two of them had heard the shots, swallowed up by the narrow mountain valley. His head finally cleared, Artemas looked back toward Bustamante and saw nothing to contradict his assumption that Raymondo was acting alone.

He hiked up to the rise that separated him from the parking lot at the end of the road and spotted one lone vehicle, a military Jeep with rolled up camouflage top. Noticing the key in the ignition and a large first aid kit resting in a cubbie, he smiled through the pain. *How could I be so lucky?* He managed, with one hand maneuvering the stick shift, and knee guiding the steering wheel, to drive back to Raymondo's body. He quickly swallowed a handful of Paracetemol painkillers he found in the kit and cleaned his wound, flushing it thoroughly with a disinfectant. The pain was excrutiating. He bit down on his rubber-handled flashlight to keep from screaming. Sweat poured down his back as he applied antibiotic cream, and dressed and taped his wound. He figured he had most of a day before infection set in; he'd have to find a doctor soon. With his knife, Artemas cut a length of gauze, tied it together and looped it over his shoulder and fashioned a crude sling.

He quickly devised a new plan to meet his circumstances. Parking the Jeep close to Raymundo's body, he removed his PGR cap and sunglasses and put them on. He dragged the body into the passenger seat and tried pushing it below the dashboard. He left the *atlatl* bolt in the chest, since removing the barbed tip would produce a gush of fresh blood. In the end he broke the long, aluminum arrow in several places to maneuver the body within the tight space. Artemas threw his pack, spare arrow, and Raymundo's rifle into the back seat.

He drove the Jeep toward Bustamante, pulling the cap down over his face. Steering and working the stiff manual transmission was nearly impossible, so he stayed in second gear. He took the road that passed the village cemetery and continued onto the dirt track used by Julio Martinez and his oxen, a painfully bumpy shortcut to the *grutas* entry gate. He headed up the steep, narrow road, grinding away in second, thankful for the surefooted vehicle.

Artemas pulled around the cavern's small parking area to face the Jeep in the direction he had come. He turned off the engine and secured the emergency brake. Then he laboriously shifted Raymundo's body to the driver's seat and replaced his cap and sunglassess, pausing several times to wait out the waves of pain that engulfed him.

He wiped away all traces of blood he could find in the passenger area and removed his pack, atlatl, and the rifle. He ejected the spent shell from Raymundo's last shot, placed it in his pocket and replenished the magazine with two bullets from an open box he had spotted on the back seat. As he replaced the rifle in the back, he realized his mistake. The rifle barrel would show evidence of recent use, and he forgot to retrieve the shell Raymundo ejected after his first shot. He decided to take the rifle with him.

Bracing himself against the driver's door, Artemas easily pushed the arrow all the way through Raymondo's chest and removed the barbed tip. Wiping off the blood, he put the arrow in his backpack. He then cleaned every surface in the Jeep he might have touched. Feeling dizzy, he drank some water and slowly ate one of the bruised bananas in his pack.

Almost there. Using the rag to prevent fingerprints, he drew Raymundo's pistol from his belt and wrapped his hand around the handle. Raymundo's fingers were still pliable, but it was clumsy work for a one-armed man in pain. Taking deep breaths to steady himself, Artemas aligned the barrel so that the muzzle followed the trajectory of the arrow to the heart. He then held Raymundo's hand tightly on the grip and squeezed the trigger. As the weapon recoiled, Artemas let it fall where it may.

Amazed at his dispassion, he reviewed the damage. The .45 caliber bullet significantly enlarged the hole made by the bolt, mangling the driver's seat in the process. It may fool them for a while, Artemas thought, but the A.G. would know better. He was reminded of one of his first crime scenes. The victim, a high government official, had been shot five times in the back. The seasoned investigator with him had said, "Artemas, as you will soon learn, this is a perfect example of a Mexican suicide." And that was the way it was eventually reported.

By now Artemas's arm was throbbing fiercely, blood soaking through the bandage and oozing down his elbow. He figured, though, that the longer he stayed out in the parking lot the likelier someone might see him. He'd have to wait until safely inside the cavern before redressing the wound. Slinging the pack over his right shoulder, he picked up the rifle and metal arrow with his right hand, and hurried toward the mountain. The main entrance to the cave was collapsed, thanks to the dynamite-happy Zamarripa brothers, so he'd have to go all the way to the top, following a steep and narrow path. After a few hundred feet of tortured climbing, his mouth was parched and he felt nauseous. He crouched for a moment, took a sip of water, and willed himself to push forward. As he crested the mountain he rested again, then slowly headed toward the entrance Jason and Laffi had discovered.

The Caverns of Bustamante

Although the pain was escalating Artemas decided against more pain pills, afraid they would make him sluggish and numb his reasoning. After cleaning and redressing his wound, he laid out the first-aid kit on the cavern floor and was relieved to find a packet of antibiotics, which he took after eating a handful of peanuts. He could stave off infection for a while, but knew if he didn't get medical treatment soon, he'd most likely lose his arm, if not his life. But first he had to reach the tiny outpost several hours walk across the valley. And to do that, he'd have to somehow get down the steep cliff this side of the cavern, a five hundred foot drop to the desert floor.

He wanted to scream. There was no way he could make it down the cliff one-handed, especially with the added weight of the evidence he'd be carrying in his pack. As it was, he could barely function with the pain and fatigue. It galled him that he couldn't use Raymundo's Jeep, but his only chance was to keep out of sight. Feeling hopeless, he lay down to rest.

It was late afternoon when he awoke, light-headed from hunger and bone stiff with the damp of the cavern. The pain in his arm had subsided slightly and the bleeding had stopped. So far he'd escaped the worst of fever and infection. Yet, Artemas was beginning to panic. The march of time was narrowing his options. By now the A.G. was sure to be wondering why he hadn't heard from Raymundo. At this very moment his thugs could have found his body, and worse, figured out it was foul play.

He paced around the cavern several times, careful to skirt Jason's motion-activated camera, and eventually noticed the stash Jason had hidden in a corner. He dragged the duffel bag into the sunlight near the opening. He pulled out several water bottles at the mouth of the bag, and put them aside to replenish his supply. The rest of the bag was stuffed with several coils of orange braided-nylon rope, still in their original packaging. Knowing Jason's proclivity for pro-grade equipment, more than likely it was climbing rope used by spelunkers. He was certain it would support his weight, but would it be long enough to get down the cliff?

He began stringing the rope around the perimeter of the huge room, roughly pacing off the cavern's circumferance, and carefully knotting each length of rope together. As he worked, his mind wrestled with how he'd be able to rappel down the cliff with just one good arm.

He rushed back to the duffel bag and felt around for anything resting at the bottom. His heart lept when he touched cold metal, and he allowed himself a quick smile. Among the objects he found was a carabineer, an oval-shaped device used by climbers to clip ropes to harnesses. Also, two linked metal circles, one larger than the other, in the shape of a figure eight.

Thank God he'd signed up for a one-semester course in rock climbing at Harvard and learned the basics. The instructor spent several weeks demonstrating the intracies of controlling the rope and using a carabineer and the figure eight links to slow a rappel. "Not so fast, Indiana Jones," he said to himself outloud. *That was over eight years ago, and you only practiced on an indoor climbing wall — with a harness and safety mat.* What awaited him outside was real, with only sharp rocks to break his fall. But, Artemas concluded with a shrug, it was better than nothing and at least he had some rough idea of what he was doing.

It took him awhile to unravel all the lengths of rope. Multiplying the number of laps they made around the cavern, he estimated he had *about* five hundred feet of rope. Adding that uncertainty to the fact that the actual drop to the valley floor was also a guess, the question remained: would the rope be long enough? *There was only one way to be sure.*

Artemas shook Jason's duffel bag, confirmed it was empty, and tied it to the end of rope nearest the entrance. He retrieved the opposite end of Jason's rope and carefully knotted it to the short cord Jason had attached to the cavern ledge.

As he lowered the pack over the edge, he heard a loud whumping noice coming from the other side of the mountain and looked up to see long blades slicing the sky. Bright orange rope was like a sign saying "Here!" Artemas quickly pulled up the duffel bag and tucked the rope into cracks around the overhang, then dove inside the cavern, careful to land on his right side. The air above him roared as the heliocopter hovered like a monster-sized metallic dragonfly. It then disappeared over the mountain toward Bustamante.

Had they seen him? Did they spot the cavern opening? How long would it be before they tossed him off the cliff and destroyed evidence in the cave? No one would ever be the wiser. He would be remembered as just another corrupt cop that had met a tragic end.

Artemas was stunned that such resources were being devoted to his demise. Only the Mexican Army had regular access to a helicopter within 100 square miles of Bustamante. Ridding the world of Artemas Salcido had apparently become a personal priority for the attorney general. But, he reasoned, with only two hours of daylight left, it was doubtful his men could reach the cave before dark. Artemas knew he better take full advantage of this brief window, if he did not find his way to the settlement by morning it was unlikely he would see another day.

Artemas dislodged the rope from the crevices, lowered the empty duffel bag over the ledge, and let it slowly fall. When all the line had been exhausted he steeled himself and looked down. The overhang blocked a clear view. Grasping the line in his good hand he leaned outward, balancing his feet on the rock, and caught a glimpse of Jason's duffel bag far below. Rather than swinging to and fro mid-air, as he had feared, it was resting comfortably on a manageable incline, well below the sheer cliff.

Artemas loaded the Grupo Vampiro files, photos and other evidence into his pack, added a couple water bottles from Jason's stash as well as a few critical first-aid items, and then tightly fastened the pack to his belt, so it would hang down, out of his way during his descent. He then set about to fashion a crude harness to cradle his backside and legs, which he attached to the metal links, counting on them to provide enough friction to avoid plunging down the cliff.

Although desperate to be on his way, Artemas paused to visualize his descent, breaking down the interplay of body and rope as he rapelled down the cliff. He discovered a potentially critical problem. The nylon rope would abrade where it rubbed against the sharp ledge, over-stressing its weight bearing capacity. He wrapped the vulnerable spot with the plastic that had packaged Jason's rope, hoping the extra cushion would suffice.

With his back to the sheer drop Artemas jerked the rope. It felt solid. He dropped to his knees and shuffled backward until his body was partially over the edge. Grasping the rope behind him with all the strength of his good hand, he took a deep breath and slowly lowered his body into space.

THE DESERT

As gravity took over, Artemas's knees absorbed his full weight, shredding his pants and ripping skin against rough rock. After taking several deep breaths to calm his racing heart, he played out the rope with his right hand—the makeshift brake held—and he slowly descended. Once he got to the underside of the steep ledge he leaned back, gingerly lifting his left knee to gain a foothold. At the same time he shifted his weight to the right side, hoping to protect his injured arm from banging against the cliff.

Suddenly the rope twisted and he lost control, dropping into space. Frantically he jerked on the rope. It held. But now Artemas and his pack were hanging hundreds of feet mid-air, winding and rewinding like a yo-yo on a string. Finally he was able to push both feet into the cliff wall, finding a tiny ledge to brace himself. He paused to catch his breath and survey his situation. Below him he spotted the network of small cracks and crevices that he believed to be an ancient, rudimentary pathway.

Carefully placing one toe in front of the other and gradually playing out the rope, he began his rappel in earnest. After about ten minutes, he reached the first knot. He found a small ledge to hold his weight while he concentrated on easing the knot through the metal figure eight.

Pain and exhaustion dogged him as he began tugging with his right hand and teeth to force the uncooperative knot through the link. His sweat-drenched body shivered; chill air gusting up from the valley as the sun fell toward the horizon. Thankfully the subtle pathway seemed to improve. As the ledges and cracks became more prominent, he increased his speed and was able to descend with less reliance on the rope. Artemas was elated when he saw the next rope knot come into view, resting off a wide ledge. And less than six feet below the mountain tapered into a walkable slope. Soon Artemas was able to abandon the rope altogether.

Deepening darkness posed a new problem. Slowly he picked his way down the mountain, feeling for each step. Weak and dizzy, he frequently lost balance and soon his right hand was torn and bleeding from his falls. Once his head collided with a rock and he blacked out but soon regained consciousness. At the bottom, he sat down, drank a few sips of water, and gazed toward the deserted valley. He still had a long way to go, and he'd only save himself if all his arrangements came together. Pushing his body beyond its limit was a critical part of that equation. He secured the pack over his right shoulder, drank deeply, and recapped the plastic bottle. Then he aimed toward the far mountains where the sun had recently set.

He stumbled with fatigue, once again feeling as if walking in a dream, this time inspired by pain, not peyote. He worried if he was going in the right direction and strained to see the lights of the tiny settlement. The night seemed unusually hot and his clothes were soaked with sweat. He reached for his water which only had a few drops left. He trudged on until he fell.

He had no idea how much time had passed before regaining consciousness. Struggling to stand up, he looked around. In the distance he thought he saw a blinking light, but he wasn't so sure. He shifted the pack. His left arm was on fire and his forehead was burning. Artemas slapped himself several times, determined not to give into the fever, and slogged toward the dim light. A half hour later, he clumsily climbed through a barbed wire fence, strung along a dirt track. It tore his shirt and gashed his right shoulder.

He could feel the approach of dawn—a sudden chill and a subtle lightness in the sky. The flickering light was still ahead, seemingly a few hundred yards away. Had he made it? Hope squeezed out his last ounce of energy, and he picked up his speed. He followed the dim light to a car parked in the middle of the road, low farm buildings shimmering in the distance. Artemas stumbled toward the car and tried to cry out, before collapsing.

He came to, lying in the sand with his head propped on something soft. Above him a familiar voice said, "Artemas, what's happened to you?" He looked up into Father Luis's face and whispered, "More water please."

Speaking slowly between gulps of water, he related everything that had happened since their telephone conversation the previous morning.

"Dear God!" said the priest, when Artemas finished. "You need medical care immediately, and you're in no condition to travel. We have to call your father."

Artemas protested as the priest helped him into the car, but the man was firm. "Don't be a fool. It's the only way."

COAHUILA

Father Luis drove furiously over the dirt track toward Monterrey, desperate to gain as much distance from the small settlement as possible. Artemas was so far gone he didn't feel the rough ride. They reached the main road at dawn—just in time. Not more than a mile later, a small convoy of state police moved rapidly in their direction.

As soon as he got a cell signal, the priest telephoned Don Alvarado and caught him at breakfast. After listening carefully to what had happened, Artemas's father thought a moment then gave Father Luis instructions, instructions that shocked him—until he grasped the audacity and shrewdness of what he proposed. Don Alvarado told him to circle around the mountain range and drive back toward Bustamante!

MEXICO CITY

The opposition presidential candidate stretched his six foot, five inch frame in a leather chair and swung his polished cowboy boots onto the stack of papers cluttering the desk in his Mexico City office.

"Any good news?" he asked Elizondo Peña, the short, balding man sitting across from him.

"Well, believe it or not, the press is now reporting that since you have the larger mustache in the race, you have what they call the Pancho Villa advantage. *Muy extraño*, and not something we can overtly use, it will turn off the law and order voters. Early polls, however, show…

They were interrupted by the entrance of an elderly woman with severely coiffed grey hair and sharp eyes like an eagle. "*Señores*, please forgive me for disturbing you." Her tone lacked any hint of apology. She focused on the candidate and said, "You have a phone call." She shot a glance at Peña, then back to her boss. "I was told not to mention his name in front of anyone else and have written it down."

She fluttered a small note.

The candidate swept his feet off the desk and held out his hand. The note said, "*Alvarado Salcido, ex-gobernador de Sonora.*"

He and Salcido had been state governors at the same time and worked well together. Even though Don Alvarado represented a more powerful, competing political party, he'd always been a straight shooter. Over the years they had developed a strong, mutual respect.

"I'll take the call." He ignored his campaign manager's raised eyebrows and picked up the receiver. Peña knew his boss's expressions well. As the conversation unfolded he recognized wariness, enthusiasm, anger, and approval.

"Of course I'm interested," said the candidate, "but this is risky." Long pause. "*Está bien*, I'll have my Head of Security, Gunter Robles, contact you. Give Graciela the information." He pushed two buttons and hung up.

For a long moment he stared into space, then broke the spell with a grin.

"Trust me, Elizondo," he said. "You don't want to know. Now, I'm pleased to learn that my mustache has vaulted me into the lead, but if there's nothing else of importance...?"

Peña took his cue, shook hands and left, anxiously wondering what dark scheme his boss was considering.

The candidate returned his feet to the desk and considered the situation. This could be either the straw that broke the camel's back, or the one that lifted just enough weight to cross the finish line. His whole career had been based on risk. He would carefully assess this one and act accordingly. He leaned over and punched the intercom.

"*Sí, señor*," responded Graciela.

"Have Gunter call me on the secure line. And thank you for your discretion regarding the phone call from Sonora. I trust your prudence will continue."

Rancho Las Palomas

When Artemas opened his eyes Father Laverdiere was hovering nearby, quietly chanting and tracing a cross from forehead to chest, then shoulder to shoulder. "What happened? Where am I?" Artemas croaked through lips so dry they stuck together. His rescue had been a blur of strange voices, pain and the sharp smell of chemicals.

"'The glory of God gives life,' " said the priest, dabbing Artemas' lips with a damp cloth. "You are doing well. We've been very worried."

Artemas glanced down at the IV taped to his forearm and heart monitor clipped to his finger. "But what…where?" he said, before collapsing back onto his pillow.

Father Laverdiere explained that Don Alvarado had sent them to a secluded ranch he owned just a few miles south of Hacienda Zamarripa, not more than fifteen minutes from Bustamante. The doctor he had flown in from Monterrey had been appalled at Artemas's condition, adament he be taken immediately to the hospital in Sabinas Hidalgo. But a call from Don Alvarado ended that argument. With the promise of a mobile hospital, the doctor had agreed to stay and keep him stabilized. The next morning a surgeon arrived by air, followed shortly by an air-conditioned semi-trailer filled with sophisticated medical equipment and a skilled nurse.

"The surgery was successful. The surgeon and the other doctor agreed your injuries were not as serious as first thought. Your biggest problem was dehydration and the blow to your head. What you need most now is complete rest."

"I can't thank you enough," stammered Artemas, trying to comprehend the situation. "But this close to Bustamante? I didn't know my father had a ranch here. Of course he wouldn't have told me. But he has two ranches in Coahuila, only a couple hundred miles away. Wouldn't that be better?"

"That's what I thought at first. But Don Alvarado told me that by bringing you here he could ensure your safety — only one other person knows he owns this place, the *presta nombre* who bought it for him."

Artemas knew that a *presta nombre*, or "borrowed name," was a common device used by wealthy Mexicans, especially politicians. Someone fully trusted, or otherwise controlled, would be paid a fee to assume ownership of a valuable asset until it was either sold or the real owner decided to claim it in his own name.

"I see, "said Artemas, the cobwebs clearing from his brain. "Coming here is brilliant. Whatever the A.G. may have heard regarding my father and me, he's not stupid. He'd still look for me at one of my father's known ranches. We're hiding in plain sight! I suppose Don Alvarado uses this place for clandestine entertaining?"

"You really *are* doing well!" smiled the priest. "Your father says there's no better whitewing dove hunting in the world. In fact it's called Rancho Las Palomas. Not to put a damper on things, but you should also be aware that you're wanted for the murder of a PGR officer. They're painting you as some corrupt rogue cop."

Rancho Las Palomas

When Artemas awoke the next morning, he felt better, certainly more alert, though a bit light-headed from all the painkillers. He was hungry, a good sign, and hoped Father Laverdiere would bring a breakfast tray soon. Scanning the sparsely furnished whitewashed bedroom he spotted his pack sitting on a wooden chair in one corner. It looked like it arrived all in one piece, but Artemas was eager to pull everything out to make sure. First, though, he'd better get word to Laffi that he was alive and well, lest she trigger her promise to recover the files he stashed in the cave. Was a week still within her concept of a "reasonable" amount of time?

When the priest arrived with a plate of homemade granola, yogurt, and fruit, Artemas told him that he needed to send a friend an urgent message. Only when Artemas promised not to stay online did Father Laverdiere agree to bring the laptop from Don Alvarado's library. He reminded Artemas to be careful about their location being compromised by the *rancho's* satellite internet provider. Artemas opened a decoy email account and tapped out a quick message to Laffi, "Miss you but all is well! Daddy's taking care of everything."

After he finished his meal he asked Father Luis to bring over his backpack. The priest watched silently, sitting in the chair with a book in hand, as Artemas methodically examined the evidence for which he'd risked everything. His stomach turned queasy as he realized it was less damning than he remembered.

Yes, the Grupo Vampiro notations—undoubtedly in Zamarripa's handwriting—documented the attorney general's secret account of three million dollars. But how could he prove that account actually existed and that these files weren't a complete fabrication? Surely the A.G.'s withdrawal of $1 million could be traced and the money's original source identified. But who exactly would, or could, follow the money? Certainly not himself! He was on the Most-Wanted list for the murder of Raymundo Valenzuela.

Also, as the A.G. had already asserted, the photo of Ricardo Chavana — positively linked to Julie's camera — merely proved she had encountered the artist on the *grutas* trail prior to her death. It was, in fact, only Artemas's *word* that Chavana had tried to cover-up his guilt by initially claiming he'd never seen Julie alive, only her body next to the now dead priest. Alcazar was an artful liar and would deny that conversation ever took place, and likely claim, with a disdainful sigh, that Artemas was a wanted felon with a history of incompetence, inventing this story to save his own skin.

His illegal tape recordings of Alcazar's conversations helped connect the dots, but did nothing to tie the A.G. to the sordid affair. To make things worse, although he was certain the A.G. had ordered the deaths of the Zamarripa brothers and might be ordering hits on other potential heirs to Zarco's fortune, Artemas had no proof.

His thoughts took a downward spiral. Though he had plenty to warrant an investigation, it would mean suicide for anyone foolish enough to take it on. There was nothing he could do. The doctor had warned him that his medication could cause mood swings and depression and he felt helplessly in its grip.

An airplane passed low over the house, compounding Artemas's gloomy thoughts. *What now,* he thought, *a paramilitary death squad?* Father Luis was equally startled and rushed out of the room. A few minutes later he returned, agitated and out of breath. "We have an important visitor. There's no time for explanations, but he comes on behalf of one of Don Alvarado's old friends — a man who could be the next president! Listen carefully to what he has to say and be completely truthful."

A fair-haired man in pressed khaki slacks entered the room. Artemas noticed he was lean like a long distance runner, but with tightly muscled forearms, as if he'd spent a lifetime working a jackhammer. His closely cropped hair and erect bearing indicated a military background. The man introduced himself as Gunter Robles and made a vague reference to being involved with security.

In precise Spanish, with the merest hint of a German accent, he explained he'd been sent by his employer—whose name, though it might be familiar, should not be mentioned—to ascertain the facts of Artemas's situation.

"I've heard what you've been through and know how uncomfortable you must be, but if you could perhaps just give me the highlights of your story?

"*Sí, señor*," replied Artemas. "And I have some written material for you." He nodded at the papers covering the bed. "It's what's behind this whole thing."

Artemas shared what he thought to be the salient events of the past few months, ending with his analysis that, while proof was lacking, the basis for a successful investigation had been established.

Robles had no immediate response to Artemas's extraordinary story, and after several moments of silence, finally asked, "I don't suppose you've seen the news, but it alleges you murdered a PGR officer sent to arrest you for some undefined corruption."

Artemas met the man's unflinching gaze. "You and your employer are risking a great deal just being here. You deserve the truth, and I've given it to you. I was close to exposing *real* corruption at the highest level and was hunted down like an animal."

His face noncommittal, Robles said, "With your permission I will review the files and return when I'm finished."

In spite of the ambiguous nature of his conversation with Gunter Robles, Artemas was greatly relieved to share what he knew with someone who appeared to have political capital, and therefore the leverage and means to effectively use the information. Exhausted by the intensity of his thoughts and emotions, he soon fell asleep. An hour later he awoke to a tap on the door and watched the blond man step quietly into the bedroom.

"How do you feel?" asked Robles.

"Like I've been through a rock crusher. Probably the way you feel everyday in politics."

The man pulled a chair to the bed with its back facing Artemas. He placed the manila envelope on the bed and seated himself, resting his huge forearms on the chair back.

"I've reviewed the documents. As you said, the key is the Grupo Vampiro information you claim you found in Zamarripa's house. If it's accurate, and more important, if it can be authenticated, half the battle is won. You said you took only a few records?"

"Yes, just the ones with names I knew."

"So, the rest should still be there?"

"Possibly. But some very rich, very desperate people have been searching for them. Surely they will have been to the house?"

"That's true, but you said the safe is cleverly hidden; you only discovered it by accident, because you had this remote device?" He picked a small Ziploc bag from the envelope and shook the contents. "It was clever of you to bring it with you."

Gunter continued. "Please understand that before we can help you we have to make certain you're telling the truth and that we have at least some evidence."

"*Claro que sí*," replied Artemas. "And the only way to do that is to see if the rest of the material is still there."

"When do you think you'll be well enough?"

Artemas considered, his fingers lightly touching his wounded arm. "The doctor said a week and a half, but a quick trip to Monterrey doesn't sound too strenuous. Three days will do."

Gunter consulted a pocket calendar and rose. "I'll be back early on the ninth. In the meantime, don't shave; the police are looking for a clean-shaven man."

Artemas felt the stubble on his chin. "I'll be ready."

Rancho Las Palomas

The next morning Artemas felt even more clear-headed. Even though his body ached, it was bearable and he was no longer on heavy-duty pain medication. He spent the day dozing on and off between meals and intermittent conversations with Father Luis. Sunlight peeking through wood shutters mellowed into late afternoon when he heard the throaty rumble of another airplane landing. Ten minutes later, Laffi walked into the room.

Stylish in her tight jeans, desert boots and khaki safari shirt, she paused for a moment just inside the door, gazing intently at Artemas. As Artemas's eyes widened in surprise, she rushed to his bedside and held her cheek tenderly against his. Then she brushed his lips with a kiss. "Oh Artemas," she said, "Thank God!"

"Laffi!" stammered Artemas, "How in hell did you find me? How did you get here? I..."

"All in due course," said Laffi, as she pulled a chair beside the bed and sat down. "Excuse me, but it's been a long couple of days."

"Seriously, Laffi, you're a dream come true, but how...?"

"Actually it was pretty simple. After I got your email I tried to call your father, but he either couldn't or wouldn't take the call. Sure as hell didn't return it. Then I called *my* father. Do you remember what I told you about him when we were at Harvard?"

"That he used to be some sort of diplomat at the U.S. embassy in Mexico City?"

"Give the wounded man a gold star!

"What I *neglected* to say was that before he retired earlier this year he was involved primarily in intelligence work. I asked him if he knew your father and, since he did, would he be willing to intercede to get me some background information I urgently needed to finish my Bustamante coverage. At first he was wary — I was never allowed to use him as a source — so I told him it was about your early years, nothing sensitive. I'm shameless...I even dangled the prospect of winning a Pulitzer! But I asked that he avoid specifics and just pass along to your father that I was looking for help. To make a long story short, it worked. "

Artemas shook his head. "I know my father, and there has to be a lot more than you're telling me for you to end up here."

Laffi shot him a scornful look. "There's always more! I honestly don't know the details, but I gathered that while my father was in Mexico City he learned several things that your father — at the time a powerful governor — would have found incredibly embarrassing if they were made public. My father ingratiated himself by keeping them confidential. I don't know what my father actually said in their recent conversation, but whatever it was it sure as hell worked!"

"I understand, and I'm eternally grateful for your concern, but why are you here?"

Laffi glared at him. "To help you, you jackass! How hard did you say you hit your head? And why the hell do you think your father flew me here — because I told him how I planned to get you out of this mess. He approved and didn't want me to have to take the time to organize a flight to Monterrey, rent a car, etc."

"Did he mention the other help he arranged?"

"No...tell me."

After Artemas described his agreement with the presidential candidate Laffi scoffed, "So, if they find the rest of the Grupo Vampiro material in Zamarripa's house, they'll help you? Or will they maybe just use it for their own advantage and leave you up a fucking tree? Do you really trust any Mexican politician?"

"In this case I trust my father's judgement; he's even more cynical than you are."

"Okay, that makes at least some sense. I stand potentially corrected. And God knows we could use some political muscle. Without it, nothing we do may mean anything. But my point is that what I plan to do can only help."

"But what *can* you do? asked Artemas, who added, "Maybe I did hit my head harder than I thought."

Laffi bent and kissed his cheek, and her tone softened. "I used the considerable good will I earned in Bustamante and requested a month's leave of absence to follow up on the story and to finish a mythical book on Mexican politics. That will give me all the cover I need to use my father's contacts and old family friends to gather information to expose the bullshit that's going on and help get your ass out of the crack it's in."

Artemas laughed, "You have the mouth of a mule driver! That sounds like a plan, as long as nobody figures out what you're really doing. You could end up like me — or worse."

"Not to worry! I'll definitely be careful with anyone I don't trust. In that regard, until the candidate commits to helping you, his people shouldn't know about me."

"Agreed. In fact, why don't you go to Mexico City and maybe begin researching something with no connection to me?"

"Good idea. Your head must be in better shape than I thought."

"How will we stay in touch?"

"I though you'd never ask!" Triumphantly, Laffi pulled a zippered bag from her purse, extracted four cellphones and handed two of them to Artemas. "Prepaid untraceable phones: two for you and two for me. My numbers are already programmed into yours. Let's plan on my calling you at nine-thirty every evening. You should only call me in an emergency."

"*Está bien.*"

"But before I fly out tonight," said Laffi, "I'm going to borrow one of your father's cars for a quick trip into Bustamante."

When she returned later that evening, Artemas listened greedily to her news. "I spoke to your assistant, Moreno, who says the A.G. is going batty, thinks you either fled to the U.S. or are hiding in Mexico, possibly Sonora. He's already scoured your father's other ranches looking for you." Artemas smiled. After a lingering kiss, Laffi boarded Don Alvarado's plane for the trip to Monterrey, connecting with a commercial flight to Mexico City.

COAHUILA

The day before he was scheduled to meet Gunter Robles for their trip to Zamarripa's mansion in Monterrey, Artemas took his first walking excursion outside the *rancho's* main house. Fresh air and exercise lifted his spirits and he felt remarkably well for someone who'd been so close to death. He discovered that Rancho Las Palomas was nestled in a stubby valley at the base of the mountains, yet with enough elevation for panoramic views to the east and south. A series of hills obscured the narrow airstrip and *rancho*. The low-slung buildings of natural adobe and sand-colored tile blended into the raw, arid landscape. *No flies on Don Alvarado.*

Two men arrived early the next day with Gunter Robles. One was a notary public, the other an alarm systems expert. They drove the hour and a half to Monterrey and entered Zarco Zamarripa's empty house without incident. The rooms were a mess, but while Zamarripa's office walls had been splintered in muliple locations by an axe, the previous searchers completely missed the panel hiding the walk-in safe. Gunter found the remaining files just as Artemas had described. The notary drafted and signed a document testifying to their discovery.

Over the next week the candidate, through Gunter, was as good as his word. After conferring with Laffi, Artemas told them he had an accomplice already helping him under the guise of a journalist on assignment. For the candidate's security, they agreed there should be no direct contact between Gunter and Laffi, that Artemas should be the go-between.

Artemas worked ceaselessly, communicating daily with Gunter and Laffi to record and correlate the information they uncovered. With the assistance of a handful of former PGR colleagues Artemas knew to be honest, they were able to corroborate much of the evidence from Zamarripa's files. Artemas chafed at being restricted to a clerical role, but with a bounty on his head, he knew no hint of his whereabouts or investigation could reach Alcazar or the A.G.

In the midst of it all Artemas found himself wondering what was happening in Bustamante, such a short distance away.

A few days later Gunter told Artemas that two men on their list of Zamarripa's relatives had been murdered. A former PGR officer was the suspect. He had been detained and interrogated, and agreed to testify if the election results went against the incumbent party.

"That means if your boss wins, he'll cooperate?"

"Yes."

"Anymore details?

"Yes," replied Gunter. "One of the relatives who was killed was Andres Zamarripa, a distant cousin to Zarco. He was killed by a blow to the head in his home in Queretaro, which was then ransacked to make it look like a robbery. The suspect had previously been fired from the PGR for corruption. The day of the crime he rented a car that was seen parked nearby. A neighbor who uses that spot noticed the rental agency sticker on the bumper.

"Interestingly, the murdered man has a son, Marco Zamarripa. Not long ago, he was rescued by the local police from being lynched in a remote village in Chiapas. When the police arrived, the villagers had him tied to a stake and were dousing firewood piled around him with gasoline. They claimed that Marco had killed and mutilated two teenage girls. The young man was taken into custody, but no conclusive evidence linking him to the killings could be found, and he was released. Then he disappeared. That could be a real problem for our adversaries."

"Yeah, and for a lot of young women," said Artemas.

"I also have to tell you," said Gunter, "that the banking information your journalist friend developed confirms the attorney general's corruption. She must have high-level contacts. We're getting damn close!"

Finally, late in the afternoon of June thirtieth, two days before the election, Gunter and Laffi flew to the ranch in separate planes supplied by Artemas's father. Their pilots were given shotguns and told to go shoot some doves, while the three of them spent hours organizing a report that Artemas and Gunter would present to the candidate at his ranch in Guanajuato the next day. Once they finished Gunter spoke, his tone uncharacteristically tentative. "*Señorita* Rendón, you've done an incredible job, helped in ways I could not have done for political reasons. But I think it would be best for all concerned if your role is kept secret..."

"I agree," said Laffi, without hesitation. "I never wanted to be part of the story. Although, of course," she added with a tiny smile, "my adventure in the cave did work out well for me. But seriously, what I did here was only for Artemas. *¡No quiero más!*"

They high-fived each other, broke open a bottle of expensive brandy and got drunk. When the bottle was empty Gunter said his goodnights.

Left alone together on the living room couch, Artemas rested his hand on Laffi's shoulder, looked into her eyes and opened his mouth to speak. "Artemas," she interrupted, pressing her index finger against his lips, "before you say anything I have something important to tell you."

Artemas stared at her through an alcohol fog.

"When we were at Harvard, the only thing that kept me apart from you was that we were at such different stages in our lives. I was preparing to launch a brilliant career; you were a naïve country bumpkin from Mexico. You laugh, but it's true! When we reconnected in Bustamante I was ready to go for it. Dammit, you were even hotter than I remembered! But I've come to realize that you're truly wedded to your work, something I always swore to avoid in a serious relationship. However, I was willing to accept that—until I met Jason. During these last weeks, I've had a lot of time to think. It's been all very confusing. While I love you to death, the bottom line is I'd always be second place to your work—it's like your spiritual quest. And that's okay—it's what makes you who you are. Then too...there's the fact that Jason still wants me to come to Austin."

Artemas tried to speak again and Laffi shushed him with a raised palm. "To be fair," she said, "it's more than just an attraction to Jason. Serious journalism is a dying profession — we're competing with 24/7 info-tainment, and losing. With Jason's organization I'll have an opportunity to use my skills on something that makes a real differerence. It's not just about bats, you know. What all this means, Artemas my love, is that while you're meeting with the candidate tomorrow, I plan on going to Austin to see if I can get my life back on track."

Artemas gazed at her sadly, then lightly kissed her lips. "You sure know how to sober up a guy! While this isn't at all what I expected tonight, I can't honestly disagree with anything you've said. Laffi, your happiness means everything to me, and it's certainly not worth risking to become lovers. Especially now. Perhaps, dare I say, one day the third time will be the charm?"

GUANAJUATO

Laffi and Father Luis left for the airport in Monterrey the next morning. Artemas masked the ache in his heart as he hugged his closest allies in the world and waved them goodbye. Then Gunter loaded the files into a two-engine Cessna and they were soon airborne, heading southeast about 300 miles. They landed at the candidate's ranch well before noon.

Artemas did not think the place was particularly grand, certainly not pretentious. Gunter took him to a guesthouse and left him there. Artemas was thankful for air conditioning and made himself comfortable on the soft pigskin couch.

After a knock on the door, a very tall, handsome man entered, squinting his eyes to adjust to the light. "*Señor* Salcido," said the man who might be the next president of Mexico. "It is a pleasure to meet you."

Artemas thanked him profusely for his help and confidence.

Waving it away, the man said, "I have spoken with Gunter, and he tells me your investigation has born fruit."

Artemas said, "I'm pleased."

"Good. I have an hour before I leave for the Capital to await my fate."

"Sir, may I ask how the election looks to you?"

"Truthfully, I'm optimistic. Only massive fraud can steal it from me. But that happened in the last election, so we shall see. Gunter will be here momentarily, so let us begin." He extracted a gold Mont Blanc fountain pen from his suit pocket.

As they seated themselves on the couch in front of a glass coffee table, Gunter arrived, and for the next hour Artemas reviewed the evidence. When he finished, the candidate looked intently at Artemas and Gunter, threw the report down on the coffee table and sprang to his feet. He rushed to the window, looked out and quickly returned, casting a towering presence over them.

"I think you've done it! Now it's up to God."

He looked again at Artemas, and added, "It would be despicable to leave all these men at large: the people who really killed the senator's daughter, and the attorney general who later assisted them. If all goes well tomorrow, I'll see that you have an opportunity to bring them to justice."

He saluted the two men and hurried out to his waiting plane.

GUANAJUATO

Artemas never paid much attention to presidential elections. Like most Mexicans he assumed the establishment party would win and nothing would change. But this time the very course of his life depended on the outcome of that day's vote.

After meeting the candidate, he was convinced that if he won it could mean the beginning of an epic shift toward real democracy. Unseating the attorney general would eliminate a significant obstacle to fighting corruption and would help create the type of orderly society he had dreamt of all of his adult life.

He sat in the candidate's guest house, glued to a big screen television. Notwithstanding the fact that the ruling party had pulled out all the stops: bribery, extortion, and even murder, Artemas had a palpable feeling that something powerful was afoot. It began as a faint vibration, had grown in intensity to a tremor, and was now like the beat of native drums signaling throughout the land the approach of some propitious event.

As afternoon sunlight slanted through the large living room, Artemas stared at the television, mesmerized by crowds of ordinary people making their way to voting booths. From hip, young adults in jeans and tee-shirts carrying cellular phones, to ancient *campesinos* in rough cotton clothing and battered straw hats, they came in the thousands. Most striking was the lack of the usual fiesta atmosphere. The people's expressions were serious; there was little frivolity. At first the commentators, most of whom were in bed with the ruling party, tried to ignore what was happening before their eyes. But as the exit polls began rolling in, predicting a huge win for the challenger, the talking heads began to capitulate, hoping to salvage whatever influence they might have in the new administration.

The mood of the crowds shifted abruptly. They became raucous, parading through the streets waving their arms and flashing victory signs to the cacophony of car horns, firecrackers, and spontaneous outbursts of music and song. This was no ordinary celebration, realized Artemas, but a lightning bolt of hope exploding from the psyches of a normally fatalistic and cynical populace.

Artemas found himself on his feet raising a clenched fist in victory. Like the rest of the non-elite, for the first time in his life he could taste the possibility of a better life—not to mention, in his case, exoneration and revenge.

Artemas's solitary celebration was punctuated by the telephone ringing on the kitchen counter. It was Graciela, the candidate's secretary, telling him the new president wished to meet with him at the guest house the following afternoon.

MEXICO CITY

Since his inauguration was still some time off, the president-elect held preliminary meetings at his suite of offices, high up in the murky smog of Mexico City. Two days after the election he was in his favorite position — tilted back in his chair, black snakeskin boots propped on his desk, preparing to meet the attorney general. At precisely the agreed upon time his intercom buzzed. "Send him in," he rumbled, and came quickly to his feet, moving to the front of the desk.

The A.G. wore an immaculate gray Italian suit. In spite of an uncharacteristic queasiness, his thin lips stretched into a smile under his pencil mustache as he approached the man he hoped would be his next boss. As far as his Grupo Vampiro dealings being leaked, the A.G. believed he was far too skilled in the art of corruption to worry. His main concern was the new president learning of his covert support for the other candidate. While the A.G. had been careful, he exercised little control over that situation.

For a moment the two men sized each other up, then the A.G. moved in for the obligatory *abrazo*. He knew that at six-one he was tall by Mexican standards, but as they embraced he realized just how much taller the other man was. He stepped back and said, "I'm honored to be able to offer you my congratulations in person!"

"I'm grateful for your support," replied the bigger man. He waved toward a blood-red leather chair in front of the desk. "Please sit down; we have a lot to discuss."

After seating himself and carefully crossing his legs, the A.G. watched the president resume his position behind the desk. His usual confidence returned as he realized the preliminaries had gone well. Being invited to meet so soon after the election was a good sign, and he detected nothing to alter that assumption. In a voice calmly modulated he said, "I hope you understand that my position of neutrality during the campaign was entirely due to the sensitivities of belonging to a different party than the president I served."

"I understand fully," replied the new president through gleaming teeth.

"*Muy bien*," said the attorney general, "I also want to tell you how much I am looking forward to working with you. I've been giving considerable thought as to how to proceed. I..."

"In a moment," said the president, holding up his hand. "All in good time. First I would like to ask you some questions."

"Of course, *señor*." The A.G. searched the poker face behind the desk for any hint of trouble. He found none.

"I have been presented with some information that I would like to review with you." The president-elect flipped open a file on his desk that the A.G. hadn't noticed. "Let's see, your father worked as a mid-level executive for Conasupo, the national food cooperative, and he still lives with your mother in the home you grew up in. You attended college in the United States on a scholarship. Prior to your becoming attorney general, two years ago, you served as the attorney general of the State of Jalisco for two years. For the ten years prior to that you were a professor of law?"

"*Sí, señor*, that is correct." The A.G. relaxed, further reassured by the president's amiable manner.

"*Muy bien*," continued the president. "I appreciate how valuable your time is so let me get to the point." He leaned forward and without warning bared his teeth. "I have information, backed by proof, that you are a member of a secret camarilla called Grupo Vampiro that was controlled by the late Zarco Zamarripa. According to that information, which is recorded in *Señor* Zamarripa's own hand, your share totals over $3 million U.S. dollars, including over $1 million you have withdrawn during the last two years."

"Absolutely untrue!" hissed the A.G. His skin blanched as a wave of dizziness hit him.

"Oh, that's a relief," interrupted the president with a low chuckle. "Then I assume you also deny that you purchased a villa near Nice in France and wired $250,000 to an account in the Caribbean."

Fidgeting incomfortably in his chair, the A.G. flushed as blood rushed back to his head.

The president plucked two documents from the file and waved them in the air. "Good, because with your family's modest financial background and the fact that you haven't earned that much total over the last ten years, eyebrows might be raised. But again, I don't want to waste your time so please allow me to continue."

The A.G. felt like a skydiver who realizes both his parachute and its backup failed to open.

"Now," said the president, pulling a sheet of paper from the file. "I believe you are acquainted with a judge named Enrique Lopez. I have a statement from him saying that you attempted to bribe him to look, shall we say *generously*, upon the claim of one Humberto Alcazar to the Zamarripa estate. By the way, I believe that's the very same Humberto Alcazar you ordered released after his arrest in Bustamante."

"*Señor, presidente!*" said the A.G., springing to his feet. "Those are lies and can be explained."

"I'm sure they can, but not at the moment. Please sit down." He pulled another document from the file and continued, "I also have information that you requested considerable background data on some of Zarco Zamarripa's closest relatives. Two of them were subsequently murdered. They were individuals, it should be noted, who would have been in a position to contest Alcazar's claim to the Zamarripa estate.

"And even more interesting, just yesterday a former PGR officer confessed to one of the killings. He says he was paid to do it and was told that you were behind the contract. The man who actually paid him has been detained and is being questioned."

The president smiled. "Just a few more minutes of your time, my friend. Please note that I also have signed testimony from three of your subordinates that you squelched an investigation into the dealings of Jugo Gandara, the drug lord who was murdered near Bustamante, as well as two other *narcotraficantes*. That, despite the fact that a substantial case with considerable evidence had been built. All three men belonged to Grupo Vampiro."

"Oh, and one final item." The president pulled yet another piece of official looking paper from the file. "This is a statement from the warden at La Palma prison, testifying that you ordered the Zamarripa brothers be put in the most dangerous wing of the prison, even though he warned you of rumors they had been marked for death."

The attorney general remained silent, traumatized as much by the complete surprise as by the words themselves.

"Now," continued the president, "I'm sure you have, or will have, explanations for all those charges. You may be surprised to learn that I don't want to hear them. I've already determined that your tenure as attorney general will be over no later than my inauguration. Let me tell you what I expect to happen between now and then and see if we can save each other considerable time and unpleasantness."

He cleared his throat and fixed the A.G. with cold eyes. "The following are not negotiable. I expect you to resign by the end of the week, and I don't care what reason you give as long as it doesn't involve me. I also expect you to immediately — and that means *today* — see that all charges against Artemas Salcido are dropped and that he receives a formal apology for the errors made in charging him. In addition, you will provide a written statement detailing whatever offers Humberto Alcazar made to induce you to help him in his quest for the Zamarripa estate. You don't have to admit you accepted any of them. After all, it will be his word against that of a former attorney general," he added scornfully.

"In return," the president continued, "I will take no further action. You will be free to salvage whatever you can from Grupo Vampiro, although I doubt you'll have much luck. And you can keep your overseas account and villa. As long as you stay out of trouble, including having no further dealings with Alcazar, this will go no further. But just one hint of *mierda* from you and I'll set the dogs loose and see you hounded from the face of the earth. Now get out before I throw you out!"

As the president started to rise the A.G. lurched unsteadily to his feet. Without a word, he turned and slunk from the room.

Bustamante

As he drove past Bustamante's plaza, empty and serene under the midday sun, Artemas suddenly felt like a stranger. He'd lived here almost a year yet the village now seemed foreign and surreal, as if it had all been a dream. He guessed this feeling of being an outsider, or worse, a *turista*, could be attributed to all that had happened to him since he'd been gone, if only a few miles away.

He looked forward to squaring accounts with Alcazar and Chavana—they'd been released from jail during his absence, under the A.G.'s authority—and informing Moreno of his promotion to station head. He was also elated over his own prospects. The new president had promised him a yet unspecified, senior position under the new attorney general, so he'd soon be heading back to Mexico City. Most of all he was looking forward to seeing Laffi.

He had spoken to her the same day charges against him were dropped; the same day he had received a personal, written apology from the A.G. It was the first time he had contacted her since they parted at Rancho Las Palomas. When she learned Artemas was returning to Bustamante, she suggested that she and Jason meet him there. "Nothing's for sure yet," she had advised him, "but the relationship is going well, and the job at Bat Watch looks like it will be everything I'd hoped for. I just resigned from the paper."

"Congratulations!" said Artemas. "And I mean it—with only one minor regret."

Artemas parked in front of Hotel Ancira and was blasted by the late summer heatwave as he stepped out of the car. It was almost one-thirty and the restaurant was filling up for *la comida*. He spotted Jason and Laffi at a table near the door just as they saw him. When Laffi rose to hug him he couldn't help but notice how beautiful and self-assured she looked, and how relaxed and happy Jason seemed.

Over a meal of the finest *cabrito al horno* — roast kid — Artemas had ever tasted, he described the political end game and the new president's meeting with the now disgraced Attorney General, which had, of course, been leaked to the media.

"Okay," said Laffi, "Now that we're wrapping up I have a couple of questions."

"Of course," said Artemas.

"I understand how Alcazar and Chavana enticed Jason and me into providing alibis for the murders of Zamarripa and the old priest. But why did they volunteer they had planned to kill Julie, and then suggest a meeting with the priest? Was it a last resort or a clever trap?"

Artemas did not hesitate before answering. "I don't know for certain, but I believe Alcazar recognized the depth of my suspicion. He knew the evidence against the Zamarripa brothers in Julie's murder might not hold up. At that time he may not have concluded his negotiations with the attorney general. The story could have been concocted to muddy the waters, to buy time.

"Obviously, he wanted to confuse me and establish grounds for ruining my credibility. I'm sure he never thought I would find Julie's photograph of Chavana. That couldn't have been planned. But it turned into a trap when I later used the photo as evidence to arrest them. All they had to do was claim that Chavana had been concerned about Julie's welfare and had Alcazar drive him to the *grutas* to check on her. That he was startled when she took the photo, but she assured him she was fine, and was very much alive when he left."

"That makes sense," said Laffi. "But did they really kill Father Buendia just so he couldn't dispute the story they planned to tell you?"

"The priest undoubtedly was already a problem for them. Maybe Chavana did meet him on the trail, either before or after he killed the girl. How, or what happened, I have no idea. When they heard I already had an appointment with Father Buendía they must have rescheduled their own meeting, chosing a time and place where Chavana could get to him first."

"But how did they convince Father Buendía to go to the *Ojo de Agua*?" Laffi asked.

"That I don't know. Alcazar is extremely clever. He knew the old man—who was definitely demented—all his life. Same with Chavana. In the end, unless there's a confession...we'll just have to see what happens after they're arrested."

"Just one more question" said Laffi. "It's completely off topic, but this has bugged me for years. I keep asking you about the curious spelling of your first name, and from your evasiness, I know there's a story behind it. Now give it up!"

Artemas's expression shifted from good humor to wistfulness. "The last time you asked I blew you off by saying my mother named me Artemas, and left it at that." He paused and looked for a moment at the ceiling then back at Laffi.

"My childhood memories are not altogether pleasant, and I'm just now appreciating the sacrifices made for me. When I was very little I used to follow my mother around the hacienda as she painted. When people would compliment her frescos, she would point to me and say '¡No, aqui es mi arte...y más! No, here is my art... and more!' Eventually everyone started calling me *Artemas*.

"After I went to live with Father Laverdiere, he saw to it that my name was legally changed...But don't ask me my given name, because I won't tell you. Oh, and by the way, the meal's on me as a very small thanks for the climbing rope, which I need to replace!"

Over dessert, a generous helping of coconut flan accompanied by Bustamante's famous *dulce de leche* and pecan candy, Artemas asked, "And what have you two been up to...other than the obvious?"

"Not too much, at least not yet," grinned Jason, speaking for the first time. "We're going to the cave this afternoon. I'm anxious to see what we caught on film."

"Me too!...besides photos of me, that is," laughed Artemas. "Now, I better leave. Time to arrest Alcazar and Chavana, something I admit I've been savoring for a long time."

Laffi and Jason urged him to be careful. "Don't worry," he said with a wave. "I'll take Moreno and his trusty shotgun…. How about dinner this evening?"

Once they agreed on a time to meet, Artemas wished them good day and headed over to the police station. Although Moreno was already acting as station chief, Artemas was pleased to see he had kept things the same and had not claimed his desk. Moreno was overjoyed at the news of his promotion and invited Artemas to celebrate with a meal the next night. "Of course. I'd like nothing better! But first we need to make those arrests."

They got down to business, first reviewing the evidence, which by now included a sworn statement by the attorney general accusing Alcazar of bribery to influence the Zamarripa estate's court proceedings and to eliminate competing heirs. Moreno had also matched the tires of Chavana's motorbike to the tracks leading to and from the site of Father Buendia's murder.

Moreno had also quietly kept track of the suspects' activities since their release from jail. "I'm certain they're staying at Alcazar's ranch." Donning bulletproof vests, they armed themselves and left.

Alcazar Ranch

It was late afternoon, but the sun still blazed down from a cloudless sky. As they neared the turnoff to Alcazar's ranch on the road to the *Ojo de Agua*, memories of being shot and wounded and killing Raymundo flooded Artemas's mind. So much blood to be shed in one place, like human sacrifices to thirsty earth gods.

Once the ranch house came into view, they saw Alcazar's Explorer parked in front. Moreno and Artemas got out of their Jeep and stood quietly, watching and listening for any signs of life. There was not even a breeze to rustle the leaves. The dead silence felt odd.

Directing Moreno, who carried a short-barrel shotgun, to a spot twenty yards behind him, Artemas approached the house, hand resting on his holstered pistol. *No point in placing both of us within the suspects' crosshairs*, thought Artemas. Their senses tensed as they drew near.

Artemas stood to the left of the doorway and motioned Moreno to remain in place. He banged on the door, calling out, "*¡Policia, ven aca!*" There was no answer. After a long silence, Artemas knocked and called out again. Still nothing. He edged over to the nearest window to look in, but the curtains were drawn.

Motioning for Moreno to stand on the other side of the door he drew his pistol, grasped the latch, and flung the door inward. The stench blowing over him foretold what they would find. Still, moving cautiously, he slid into the living room, pistol outstretched from his stiff right arm. The smell inside was appalling, like sweetened, rotting meat. The room was dark and he heard the sound of a whirling ceiling fan clacking against its loose mooring, and the unmistakable buzz of blowflies near the vicinity of the fireplace.

Once his eyes adjusted to the dim light Artemas saw a large mass on the floor in front of the couch and he crept closer. What he saw shocked him. Two naked, corrupted bodies. The bear-like remains of Humberto Alcazar lay on top of Chavana's tall, slender body, as if in a sexual embrace. Stooping down, he saw their mouths met in a grisly death kiss, both throats brutally gashed. Based on the blunt force, Artemas concluded the murder weapon could be something as crude as a garden hoe. Yet there was surprisingly little blood on the bodies and floor. Clearly they'd been moved here and staged.

He stood up, looked toward Moreno, and said softly, "It's your turn now."

Bustamante

The ranch phone was out of order, and there was no cell phone service, so Moreno decided to stay with the bodies and process the evidence while Artemas drove back to the police station to call in the murders.

When he finished notifying the Medical Examiner in Sabinas — who couldn't resist taunting Artemas about yet another murder in Bustamante — a random question flashed into his mind. "Can you tell me what happened to Zarco Zamarripa's body? Is it in the morgue in Monterrey, or has it been buried?"

"Strange that you ask," answered the examiner, adopting a serious tone. "Day before yesterday I learned the body was missing from the morgue. Nobody seems to have any idea what happened. It was left there awaiting arrangements of next-of-kin and then forgotten. I guess they don't need the space. Then the new chief examiner decided to do a full inspection of the premises. They couldn't find the body or any paperwork, not a hint of where it could be." Laughing, he added, "Maybe Zamarripa belonged to the undead and just got up and left. Maybe he's heading to Bustamante for some revenge."

"Maybe," said Artemas softly, and hung up.

At dinner, Artemas found Jason and Laffi in a state of excitement, glancing at each other repeatedly while saying nothing in particular. Artemas had an inkling of their good news, but didn't want to spoil the surprise. He met their requests for news of his activities with, "No, you first."

Although the heat of the day began to dissipate with nightfall, the temperature within the inn's dining room was rising.

Cooled only by ceiling fans, it felt like a sauna, and from time to time they held icy bottles of beer to their cheeks and foreheads for relief. Finally, after they ordered their meals, Jason pulled out a large envelope and passed it over to Artemas.

Out slid three photos that Jason quickly explained were taken by the camera he'd placed in the cave. The first was a blurry shot of Artemas, caught in the flash like a startled deer. He put it quickly aside and looked at the next shot. It was out of focus but appeared to show a strange bird-like form, eyes blazing from the flash. The third photo was even less sharp, but caught the creature as it moved away from the camera. Artemas's eyes met Jason's as he handed back the photos. "What do you think this means?"

Jason paused a moment then said, "It means to me what you think it means. But by itself it won't mean much to anyone else. In fact, if circulated without additional evidence it would undoubtedly be declared a hoax. Did I tell you I took some samples that looked like fur and scales from what seemed to be a nest?"

"Yes."

"The fur has been positively identified as goat hair, but so far nobody has been able to identify the scales except to say that they appear to be from some sort of reptile. Anyway, that's the best guess so far. What it leads to is further investigation, and avoiding any publicity. This is just the kind of thing that brings out the wackos. Laffi and I plan to return next month under the guise of documenting the cave on Alcazar's ranch, that is, if we can get access to it?" He raised his eyebrows questioningly.

With a straight face, Artemas said, "I don't think that Alcazar will have any objections." Then he described the shocking scene he and Moreno had come upon that afternoon.

"Who in hell did it?" exclaimed Laffi. "Who's left?"

Artemas raised his hands in defeat and slowly shook his head.

After a moment's consideration, Laffi said, "Maybe this will turn out to be another one of those Mexican mysteries that remain a mystery."

"And there may be another one, as well," interjected Artemas. "I just learned that Zarco Zamarripa's body is missing from the morgue."

At that, both Jason and Laffi stared at him, mouths agape. Laffi carefully put down her beer and said, "I'll ask Eduardo to hold our order. We have something to show you. Trust me, it won't wait!"

They scrambled into Jason's Suburban and drove toward the mountain, parking on the street in front of the cemetery. Though the moon had not yet risen, the fence, gate, and tombstones glowed a luminous white.

"We walked by earlier this afternoon. I'm not sure why we went in, except that I wanted to overcome the creepy feeling I got the last time I was here," explained Laffi.

With Laffi leading, guided by Jason's flashlight, the three of them picked their way carefully among the gravestones. Above them the mountain loomed in the darkness, and a light breeze dried their sweat. Laffi slowed as they approached a large mausoleum, and Jason aimed his beam at the entry, illuminatimg the carved words *Familia Zamarripa*.

They entered the narrow passageway in single file and slid along the smooth marble walls. Once inside, Jason shined his light over one of the compartments. There, crisply chiseled in the marble, were the words: *Zarco Zamarripa 15/11/1938 – 18/04/2006.* "How the..?," exclaimed Artemas. That's when he died, but how and when did he get here?"

"I thought you might find it interesting," whispered Laffi.

"You were right," said Artemas. "I needed to see this. A stop at the Municipio tomorrow morning to find the cemetery manager seems to be in order. He better have some answers!"

They exited the mausoleum and saw a light bobbing across the cemetery. After a few steps they recognized Officer Moreno. "I'm glad I found you," he said, breathing hard. "I went to the hotel and they said you'd left. I stopped here when I recognized the professor's car."

"Well?" said Artemas.

"What I wanted to tell you is that... Do you remember you told me about Marco Zamarripa, the son of Zamarripa's murdered relative, probably the closest in line to inherit the estate?

"Yes," said Artemas. "The sicko who raped and killed two girls in Chiapas then disappeared after being released for lack of evidence? Of course I remember; I told you about him just this afternoon, and my memory's not that bad."

"Well, I was just informed by the former caretakers that he's moved into *Hacienda Zamarripa*. He told the old couple he's the heir to the estate and plans to live there. Then he fired them. Gave them a half hour to clear out."

This new piece of information triggered within Artemas a series of mental calculations that began with the grisly spectre of Alcazar and Chavana's bodies. He began muttering the words from a favorite poem by Edith Sitwell:

"Still falls the rain—
Dark as the world of man, black as our loss—
Blind as the nineteen hundred forty nails
Upon the Cross."

Jason, Laffi and Moreno stared and he repeated the first line loudly enough for them to hear: "Still falls the rain." Then he looked directly at Moreno and added a verse from Virgil's *Aeneid* he often used as a mantra: "Yield not to evil but attack all the more boldly."

Artemas looked at each one in turn. "I guess I now have one more stop to make."

To Moreno he said, "I left my pistol at the station, may I borrow yours?"

"Of course," replied Moreno, pulling the .45 semiautomatic from its holster.

"What do you need the gun for?" challenged Laffi.

Artemas winked. "Just think of it as a metaphor for a wooden stake."

As he walked away, he began to whistle his favorite Yaqui spirit song.

The End

ACKNOWLEDGMENTS

There is no way to thank everyone who helped with a novel, but you can certainly express your gratitude to those whose efforts were most significant. In this case, that means those who read the story and took the time to make suggestions. My sincere thanks to Bill Lende, Candace Andrews, Judy and Donald Gordon, Jane Armstrong, Judy Davis, Jerry Winakur, and Mindy Reed, a terrific editor. And an extra special thanks to my wife Andrea, who accompanied me on the many visits to Bustamante and never ceased to encourage me. My agent, Sally Van Haitsma, has my undying gratitude for her help, encouragement and expertise. She put in far more effort than anyone could expect, and it is primarily due to her that the manuscript is as professional as it is.

ABOUT THE AUTHOR

James Peyton has published four acclaimed books on Mexican cooking, history and culture and has written for *Fine Cooking*, *Food & Wine* and *Texas Highways*, as well as chapters for three *Lonely Planet* guidebooks to Mexico. His outdoor kitchen was featured on Bobby Flay's Food Network series. James has a B.A. in political science from Trinity University and an MBA from Southern Methodist University. He lives in San Antonio, Texas and hosts a popular website: www.lomexicano.com. *Vampires of Bustamante* is his first novel.